A WALLFLOWER AT THE HIGHLAND COURT

THE HIGHLAND LADIES BOOK TWO

CELESTE BARCLAY

OLIVER
HEBER
BOOKS
GNARLY WOOL PUBLISHING
EST 2016

To all the wallflowers who struggled to bloom or are waiting to bloom,
your season shall come.
Happy reading, y'all,
Celeste

SUBSCRIBE TO CELESTE'S NEWSLETTER

Subscribe to Celeste's bimonthly newsletter to receive exclusive insider perks.

Have you read *Their Highland Beginning, The Clan Sinclair Prequel?* Learn how the saga begins! This FREE novella is available to all new subscribers to Celeste's monthly newsletter. Subscribe on her website.

Subscribe Now

THE HIGHLAND LADIES

CHAPTER ONE

The din of music and loud conversation–along with the pervasive odor of too many unwashed or over-perfumed bodies crowded into Stirling Castle's Great Hall– gave Maude Sutherland a pounding headache. As she observed the dancers from her position at the side of the chamber, part of her envied the other ladies-in-waiting who twirled with ease and confidence, but mostly she wished for nothing more than the blessed silence of her chamber. While Maude propped up the wall, she spied her younger sister, Blair, who moved through the country reel with what must have been her seventh partner that evening. Though she was only an observer, sweat trickled down Maude's back and between her breasts. A warm snap—unseasonable for spring in the Highlands— had the doors to the terraces wide open. This should have been enough to ease Maude's discomfort, but the breeze did little to offset how her thick brown hair trapped the heat on her head and neck. Unlike most maidens, Maude wore her hair up almost every waking moment. She possessed a massive amount of thick, coarse, mousey brown hair that was unruly even on the best of days. By evening the weight of the hair, regardless of whether it was up or down, pulled on her neck and contributed to her headache. She would have loved nothing more than to cut it all off and wear it short like her father, Laird Hamish Sutherland, or her brother, Lachlan. She envied them the freedom to wear their hair however they wanted.

A crimson gown floated in Maude's periphery, so she turned to watch her closest friend, Arabella Johnstone. She and Arabella were as different as chalk and cheese but had somehow struck up a close friendship. Where Arabella's hair glowed in the candlelight, Maude accepted her hair was dull. Where Arabella's face looked like an artist's masterpiece, Maude was aware she was plain. Where Arabella was petite and lean through her hips and legs, Maude considered herself far too broad across the beam. As she grew into womanhood, her frame filled out, and while she had a bust most women would envy, her hips and legs were proportionate. Whenever Arabella or Blair glided across the dance floor, she recalled the many adjectives her brother and his friends had come up with for her when they were younger. "Sodgy," "bamsey," "bowzy," "jostly," "podg," and "flobbed up" were the ones that always came to mind. Her brother had since repented for the unkind and merciless teasing. Lachlan noticed that the more he and his friends teased Maude, the less she ate. On the day she collapsed and nearly fell down the stairs leading to the family chambers, he was the one to catch her and carry her to her chamber. In her hazy state, she confessed to have only eaten dried fruit and bannocks the previous three days in hopes of slimming. Lachlan never said an unkind word to his sister again and thereafter became fiercely protective of her, fighting more than one friend when they failed to cease teasing her.

Maude's attention snapped back to the dancers as the song concluded and Arabella made her way to Maude's side. "I caught the Gordon twins glancing at you while they danced with Blair and Cairstine Grant," Arabella murmured.

"Aye, glancing at ma bust nae ma face." Maude grimaced as her brogue slipped out. She made a conscious effort not to allow her Highland burr to flavor her accent. At court, where

Lowlanders were dominant, she stuck out like a sore thumb. Despite Stirling straddling the border between the Highlands and Lowlands and King Robert the Bruce's affinity and dependence on the Highland clans, Highlanders were considered an oddity at court. "I mean, they were only interested in what was below my chin. My maid cinched this gown far too tight this eve. I can barely breathe, let alone move."

Arabella gave Maude a measured stare, but chose not to comment. Arabella was aware of how self-conscious Maude was about her appearance. While she, Arabella, frequently reminded Maude of how beautiful she thought her friend was, it did little to counterbalance the snide comments they both heard. Arabella secretly wished she was as endowed as Maude, but she was aware most of the other ladies-in-waiting didn't share that sentiment. On more than one occasion, Arabella overhead people wondering how Maude became Arabella's friend. It broke her heart to hear the disparaging comments. She knew why she was friends with Maude: she was the most kindhearted and generous person Arabella knew. Maude smiled at her friend as she passed a mug of ale to Arabella and took a swig from her own.

"How much longer do you think until the queen retires?" Maude asked behind her mug.

"I have no idea, but it can't be soon enough. I've had my toes trod on at least thrice, and Laird Macintosh's clammy hands have left my gown damp. It wouldn't surprise me if he left greasy marks on the back." Arabella twisted as though she might spy the back of her gown.

"He did seem to be in a bit of a lather."

"You're too kind, Maude. His sweat threatened to drip from his face to my chest. I don't know that I could've hidden my revulsion if that happened."

"Aye, you would've. Your mother drilled manners into you far too deeply. But that doesn't mean you wouldn't want to retch," Maude's sly smile morphed into a full grin until she remembered people could see the small gap between her top teeth and the tiny overlap of her bottom two teeth. For that reason, it was a rare occasion that she smiled with her mouth open.

"Come dance. Don't leave me alone out there," Arabella pleaded.

Maude shrank back against the wall, wishing to melt into it. She was an accomplished dancer, but she'd been embarrassed too many times when men shifted to avoid partnering with her. She didn't consider herself overweight, but she looked it compared to the other young women. Lachlan was the only man who regularly partnered with her, but he was back at Sutherland. She wished for the umpteenth time she could be home, too.

"Don't look at though you're going to the gallows," Arabella quipped.

"I told you, my gown is far too tight."

"Then let's step onto the terrace. I'll loosen it for you."

"Why are you so insistent?" Maude kept her smile in place even though her stamina for the evening withered.

"Because I want you to have fun. I want you to see there are plenty of men looking at you and wishing they were dancing with you."

"So they can peer down my gown, but the moment they touch me, they realize I'm a pudding. Leave off, Bella. Please."

There was a long pause before Arabella nodded. There wasn't a chance to say more before a man requested the next dance with Arabella. She looked over her shoulder as her new partner led her toward the other dancers. Maude nodded her head and continued to smile. Once Arabella was out of sight, Maude slipped onto the terrace. She loved Arabella as much as she did Blair, but there were times when it was difficult not to be jealous.

Even our names tell how different we are. Arabella means "given in prayer," while mine means "powerful battler." Hers even has the word beautiful in it, while mine is as dowdy as I am. We both fit our monikers.

Maude slipped into the shadows as she welcomed the cool

4

air on her face and neck. While she now ate proper meals, this evening had been difficult with her lacings digging into her flesh. She hadn't lied; her maid had pulled the ribbons snug. While the young woman only tried to help, Maude was certain she looked like a sack tied in the middle rather than lithe and shapely. When the air shifted from refreshing to chilly, Maude realized she needed to return to the Great Hall. It was still early spring, and the temperature would continue to fall as the night grew late. She walked back to the open doors but halted when she caught her name being whispered by another lady-in-waiting.

"Have you seen how ridiculous she looks standing next to Arabella? It's like a dove and a sow became friends," Laurel Ross tittered. Maude hung back and listened as her heart sank.

"Arabella claims she has a big heart," Cairstine Grant mused. "She certainly has a big chest."

"Obscene is more like it," Laurel sniped. "She looks little better than a dairy cow with those tits. She's more suited for a tavern than a castle. If I didn't know who her parents were, I'd wonder who let her in off the street."

"Laurel, that's a bit harsh. She's no slattern." Madeline MacLeod's words were censuring, but her tone barely hid her laugh. "Men would have to want her first."

The three women dissolved into giggles as Maude swallowed the tears that threatened to burst free.

CHAPTER TWO

K ieran MacLeod crept onto the terrace, watching as Lady Bevan slipped through a door further down the way. Their tryst had been quick and vigorous, as it was the only way for him not to freeze his cods. Now it was his sister's voice that made him freeze. He hadn't caught what the young woman before her said, only the sound of a voice, but Madeline's words rang clear. He clenched his jaw as his sister and her friends continued disparaging another lady-in-waiting.

"Maude's better suited to be a farmer's wife than a laird's wife. She's a bit brawny to be a lady," Madeline continued. "What laird will want hers to be the face that greets his guests. They'll think he sent a servant. And she can barely say more than five words at once without getting uncomfortable."

If this is who Maude has to talk to, I don't blame her. My sister is horrid. I've told her to mind what she says at court. She never knows who might be listening.

As if to prove his point, something moved in the shadows on the other side of the doors. Kieran peered through the dark, but it was impossible to see who lurked there. He heard whoever it was draw in a ragged breath. It was too loud in the Great Hall for anyone to hear it, but it seemed to echo in the still air outside. Kieran changed course while he was still invisible to the gossiping ladies. He approached on silent feet and attempted to discover who stood eavesdropping. As he approached, the first thing he noticed was that it was a woman. As he drew closer, his breeks tightened at the lush form. He hated wearing the pants but acquiesced to courtly standards of dress. His breacan feile, or great plaid, would be more comfortable as his rod continued to swell. He hadn't had this reaction to Lady Bevan when he met her in the gardens only minutes ago. The woman was attractive and lusty, but her body looked like a twig compared to the woman in front of him. He couldn't see her face, but lust and curiosity drove him forward.

"You shouldn't be eavesdropping. Curiosity killed the cat," Kieran whispered. He didn't miss the hypocrisy of his own statement, but he was too intrigued to ignore the young woman.

The woman gasped and spun around. She seemed about to take a step back but remembered doing so would put her in the doorway's light, where the women would catch her. Kieran realized that she had the most incredible bosom he had even seen, one which heaved because she was sobbing. It took little deduction to realize he must be staring at the unfortunate Maude. Without a clue what possessed him, he pulled Maude into his embrace and sheltered her against his chest. She attempted to pull away just as she should, but she settled as he caressed her head.

"Shh, lass. They'll see or hear us," he murmured against her ear.

Maude nodded and allowed her body to relax against this strange man. She hadn't sensed his approach and nearly screamed when she realized she was no longer alone. When the man pulled her into his arms, she had a moment of terror that he would accost her, but his gentleness reminded her of her father, though nothing about how he made her feel was like her father. His steady heartbeat thudded against her ear, and his fresh scent of sandalwood and pine made her think of home, a place she would much rather have been than at court.

Kieran discovered his error within a heartbeat of embracing Maude. His cockstand was rampant, and he feared she would feel it and go running for the hills screaming bloody murder. He kept his hips away from her and prayed the thick material of her kirtle would serve as a buffer. Yet he couldn't bring himself to release her. Her arms were tentative as they wound around his waist. Her frame was rigid until he whispered to her again, and then she melted against his chest. His heart broke all over again as he realized how what he thought of as a simple embrace comforted her. He likened her to an abandoned kitten brought in from the rain. He wondered what it would take to make her purr.

"Wheest, buttercup. I'm here. Don't cry. They aren't worth the salt in your tears. Don't listen to those harpies," he crooned. She rewarded him with a small nod of her head. One hand continued to stroke her hair as the other ran circles over her back.

"Her father will have to buy her a husband," Laurel's voice floated to them. "What mon would pick her?"

Maude went still, the breath in her lungs stuck. Fresh tears threatened to fall as the conversation continued inside. The stranger's arms tightened around her, and she burrowed her face into his chest as though she might tunnel her way to escape. She noticed his breath catch, and it did little to reassure her.

"They called Elizabeth Fraser a spinster, but at least she was beautiful. The real spinster will be Maude. She'll be on the shelf if her father doesn't bribe someone to take her off his hands," Madeline sneered, and if Kieran hadn't been unwilling to unwrap his arms around the trembling woman, he would have wrapped them around his sister's throat. "Maude on the shelf. That's what we shall call her. Maude on the shelf."

Kieran cringed as the other two heartily agreed. He

9

understood how the ladies-in-waiting could be. His sister had been one for three years, and to his great misfortune, he had to visit court more often than he would like. Kieran was aware the new epithet would spread and be on everyone's lips by morning.

"Maude," a woman's voice hissed. "Maude, where are you?"

The jerk of Maude's head was so unexpected it snapped Kieran's jaw closed. He'd been leaning his head down as he whispered to her and was unprepared for her sudden movement. He stifled a curse as Maude pulled away. Even in the dim light, he could see her eyes widen.

"I'm sorry," she murmured. "I must go. Thank--"

Maude froze when Arabella stepped near them. Maude couldn't see the man's face, but she was certain Arabella had seen them embracing. After all, his arms were around her waist, but as Arabella drew closer, Kieran shifted so his larger frame partially hid her.

He's trying to protect me.

Maude tapped his arm and nodded when he looked down at her.

"It's all right. She's my friend." Maude stepped around him and stumbled as Arabella grasped her hands and dragged her away from the doorway into the light of a wall sconce burning at the end of the terrace. She was certain she looked a fright when Arabella gasped.

"Why're you crying? What happened? What did he do?" Arabella demanded. She glared at the shadowy figure who followed them.

"*He* didn't do aught other than offer me a moment of sympathy."

"Sympathy for what? Why was he embracing you? And you still haven't told me why you're crying."

"I overheard something I wasn't intended to, and it saddened me. He heard, too, and comforted me when he found me upset. Naught more."

Kieran listened to the two women, and his heart slowed when he was confident Maude wouldn't accuse him of any untoward behavior. However, he couldn't agree with her summation that there was nothing more. There had been plenty more for him, and his semi-aroused rod agreed. He'd never enjoyed holding a woman more than he did Maude. He regretted that his sister and her friends upset her, but his arms ached to encircle her again. She felt perfect.

"Maude, what did you overhear?" Arabella's voice softened, and Maude wanted to cry yet again. She hated the pity that colored Arabella's voice.

"I don't want to talk aboot it. At least not right now and not here." The other women humiliated Maude enough without having to repeat everything so her unknown protector could hear her shame again.

Arabella pulled Maude into her arms, and while her friend's embrace comforted her, it wasn't the same as the one she had received in the dark.

"You haven't introduced yourself," Arabella squinted at the hulking figure. She hadn't realized the man was so large until he stepped into the light. His face seemed familiar. Maude turned to face her mystery protector and couldn't believe she could be so unlucky in one night.

"Oh dear God, no." Maude shook her head as she tried to back away. Her humiliation was a *fait accompli*. While she wasn't acquainted with the man, he was easy to recognize.

"What? Do you know him?" Arabella looked between the man and Maude several times.

"No, but how can you not tell he's Madeline's brother? They look too much alike to be otherwise." Maude glanced around, looking for a way out of this untenable conversation, and considered running into the gardens. She was sure Arabella and this still unnamed man would follow her.

"Laird Kieran MacLeod." He bowed as he took Maude's hand and bussed a kiss onto the back of it. She was unaccustomed to such courtly manners directed toward her. She

11

assumed it was perfunctory before his attention would settle on Arabella, as it inevitably always did. He stunned her when Arabella only received a nod and a glance from him. "I must apologize for my sister's cruelty. I'm ashamed on her behalf, and I wish I could take it back. I will have words with her."

"No!" Maude practically shouted. She shook her head with vehemence. "Don't either of you say a word aboot this. Please. It's embarrassing enough without them discovering I overheard them. It'll only make them believe they were successful."

"Maude," Kieran liked how her name sounded as he spoke it for the first time, and from the flair of her nose and the rise of her chest, she seemed to like it too. "Madeline doesn't need to ken you were here too. I'll tell her I was returning from the gardens and couldn't help overhearing them."

Kieran watched color flood Maude's face as she glanced at the garden and then him. He watched her eyes dart to his waist and then away. He realized she understood why he had been in the garden, and for some reason, shame filled him even more. Arabella's hardened expression told him she understood, too. But it was before he even knew Maude existed, he reasoned with himself.

"Please, no. Just leave be. The less said the better," Maude sighed.

"I wish that I could, buttercup." Kieran wanted to bite his tongue as the endearment slipped out. It was one thing to use it when he and Maude were alone, and he attempted to comfort her. It was a different matter to do it in front of her friend. "I won't mention that I met you or that you were anywhere near here, but I can't let Madeline's behavior stand. It's a disgrace to our name. If she speaks this way aboot you, I can only imagine what she is saying aboot other people. Her loose tongue could do more damage than she realizes. Hurt feelings destroy alliances all the time. Besides that, I abhor her willing cruelty. It's disgusting, and hardly ladylike." Kieran forced himself to stop speaking before he became guilty of his sister's sin and spoke too ill of her in front of others.

"Do as you must," Maude sighed again.

The resignation in her tone once more made Kieran wish to protect her. Disregarding her friend, Kieran lifted Maude's chin and leaned next to her ear to whisper.

"They arenae men. They havenae a bluidy clue what they're talking aboot. You can take those words to the grave, lass." He placed a kiss on the corner of her jaw before pulling away.

Maude stared up at Kieran as she processed what he said. A smile made the corner of her mouth twinge as she nodded.

"Thank you."

"I bid you good eve, ladies. I have a little sister to find." Kieran once more bowed to Maude but didn't even look at Arabella. Maude wondered if she'd be insulted by the slight. They watched him walk back to the doorway where he discovered Maude and disappeared into the Great Hall.

CHAPTER THREE

Maude and Arabella didn't speak until they reached their chamber. Once inside, Maude yanked at the laces to her gown, but Arabella swatted her hands away before they became knotted.

"What was that aboot?" Arabella checked her tone as she pulled Maude's laces through the eyelets. She didn't want to sound accusatory, but it had stunned her to see her friend in a man's embrace. Not because she thought Maude didn't deserve a man's attention, but because she was terrified for her friend's reputation. If anyone else found them, Maude would be betrothed as they spoke.

"I stepped outside to get some fresh air." Maude began as she pulled the kirtle from her shoulders. The freedom eased her aching ribs. "I was aboot to come back inside when I heard my name. I stopped and listened. And now I wish I hadn't. Madeline, Laurel, and Cairstine were discussing my many and singular flaws. They described all the ways in which I'm unappealing to a mon and how my da will have to bribe a mon to want me."

Arabella snorted, then giggled before covering her mouth as her friend's distressed expression reminded her that her reaction was inappropriate.

"They didn't see the way Kieran MacLeod was looking at you. He was salivating as though you were the first meal he'd had in a sennight."

"Stop, Bella. You don't have to make me feel better." Maude walked to the jug of lemon verbena-scented water and basin. She scrubbed her face and neck before changing out of her chemise and into her nightgown. She had given up trying to hide from Arabella while she changed, but she still turned her back.

"Gracious! Your maid did tie the gown far too snug. You have lines all across your back." Arabella winced when she realized how much pain Maude must have endured that evening.

"She was only trying to help."

"Everyone is always just 'trying to help.' I wish they'd leave you alone." Arabella walked to her own jug of rosewater and washed her face.

"Anyway." Maude didn't want to discuss how her maid swore she'd make Maude appear thinner if she pulled just a little harder before tying the laces. "He came from the gardens and heard the women's voices. He stopped and listened but noticed me. I guess I moved at some point. He sneaked up behind me and teased me aboot being too curious. When I turned around, he realized who I was. There could be little doubt since I was crying. Before I understood what was happening, he pulled me into his arms and comforted me. Then you came looking for me."

Arabella assessed her before raising an eyebrow. "Just how long was he holding you in his arms before I came out?"

"He wasn't holding me," Maude denied. "He embraced me and told me not to worry aboot what they said."

"He was holding you. I saw him. I also saw how he looked at you when you were looking at me. I can't explain it, but it was a glare, a warning to me and concern for you. Along with a strong dose of lust."

"Bella, don't. I told you, you don't need to make me feel

16

better. I'd rather you stop trying to make me think men are interested when I know they're not. He caught sight of my bust like most men do, but that's it. I'm sure he could feel I'm--" Maude shook her head, unsure how to finish. "It embarrassed him when he discovered his sister's behavior, and he tried to make me feel better. I'm sure he felt guilty."

"He felt a few things, and guilt might have been one of them, but that's not what I saw. He tried to protect you and pushed you behind him when I approached."

"So he had good manners? He must have known what would happen if anyone else caught us."

"And yet he persisted in holding you against him. I'm telling you, the look he shot me was protective. It was almost as if he dared me to speak against you. Once he realized we are friends, the expression was like he wanted to comfort you and devour you all at the same time."

Maude climbed into bed and waited for Arabella to do the same before snuffing out her candle.

"Good night, Bella. And good night to your overactive imagination."

"Humph. Night, love."

Maude lay on her side, staring into the dark. This time there was no mystery man in the shadows. There was just nothingness. It fit how she felt. She replayed his final words in her head, but they made little sense. Or rather, they didn't make sense when said to her. She couldn't fathom how they had anything to do with her, so she assumed he'd merely attempted to make her feel better. But once again, the meaningless words made her heart feel hollow. She wished she could fall asleep at court and wake up in her chamber at home.

Maude rubbed her eyes as she came awake to the sound of Arabella and her maid moving about. She looked over to see

Arabella fully dressed and her hair nearly done. Maude glanced toward her dresser and spotted her own maid brushing out her kirtle. She pushed back the covers and slipped from the bed.

"We should've been quieter," Arabella frowned. "I'm sorry we woke you."

"Sorry? Thank goodness you did. I'll be late as it is. Why'd you let me oversleep?"

"Because you must be exhausted not to wake up before me. Are you poorly?" Arabella stepped away from her maid with her hair falling out of the unfinished braid. She approached Maude and looked over her face as though she searched for an invisible malady.

"Naught is wrong with me. I had a headache last night, but I'm well this morning. I suppose I just needed a little extra sleep." Maude encouraged her maid to hurry to assist her with her gown. "Not so tight, if you please."

While the maid assisted Maude into her stockings and chemise, Maude awkwardly balanced as she twisted her hair into a bun she secured with copious pins. She was certain that was part of what gave her headaches. It wasn't just the weight of her hair, but all the pins that dug into her scalp. If she were at home, she could have gotten away with wearing her hair in a long braid down her back, but she learned soon after her arrival that the other ladies called her a country bumpkin for looking like a milkmaid. She resorted to wrapping her hair into a tight circle instead. It was only for feasts that she would sit while her maid braided her hair into more intricate styles.

Once Maude and Arabella were ready, they made their way to the queen's dining hall, where the other ladies-in-waiting were gathering to break their fast. Arabella led Maude to a spot where several of Arabella's friends sat. Maude believed she had a vicarious friendship with most of the women only because Arabella befriended her, and that was why they welcomed Maude at the table. She spotted Madeline and Laurel sitting a few spots down and across the table from her. The glare Madeline sent her told her Kieran must have spoken to her already. Maude lowered her head in prayer before beginning her porridge. Arabella was busy speaking with Cairren Kennedy and Blair. Maude and Blair had argued with the Mistress of the Bedchamber when she assigned them separate rooms upon their arrival. The woman had refused to entertain their complaints and insisted she separate them. It had been fine for Blair, who was far more sociable than Maude and who made friends with ease. Maude had been fortunate to move into Arabella's chamber after her former roommate returned home. The separation allowed Blair and Maude to become more independent, but it was times like the night before when she missed Blair climbing into bed next to her. She smiled at her sister and gave her a speaking glance, to which Blair nodded. They would find each other after the meal to talk.

"Should we ask a stable hand to find you a shovel? You'd be able to inhale that porridge faster." Madeline taunted. When Maude refused to answer, remaining focused on her meal, Madeline slid closer on the bench. Arabella, Cairstine, and Blair stopped talking, and Maude saw her sister lean forward. She placed a fist on the table, and her sister saw their sign to stop. "Thanks to you, the queen overheard my brother harping on aboot me being unkind to you. Now I have an afternoon of prayer to look forward to."

"Thanks to Maude?" Cairren asked in confusion.

"Aye. My brother overheard part of a conversation last night that wasn't intended for him, and he took pity on the poor wretch and chewed my ear off this morning. Of course, he doesn't know how to whisper, so the queen overheard since he waylaid me outside the hall just as she was entering."

"If she weren't so pathetic," Laurel chimed in. "He wouldn't have pitied her enough to say aught. He doesn't even know you and he thinks you're pathetic."

Maude looked up, the stubbornness that got her in trouble as a child rearing its head. She looked at Madeline and Laurel but said nothing. Her gaze dared them to say more. She was aware her expression could intimidate, so she enjoyed seeing the discomfort her adversaries experienced as she continued to stare. Madeline looked at the pitcher of cream near her right hand, and a cruel gleam entered her eyes. Maude sensed what was coming, but with other women on the bench, she couldn't push back far enough to escape the liquid splashing down the front of her as the jug rolled across the table.

"My pardon, Maude. I'm usually not so clumsy," Madeline purred.

"Bitch," Blair growled as she stood and looked ready to reach across the table. "You did that on purpose, and we all ken it."

"Blair," Maude warned. She eased from her seat and notched up her chin. She forced her hands not to reach for her unfinished bowl of porridge. Chucking it in Madeline's face wouldn't endear her to the queen, and her parents would be livid if they learned of it. "It's not her fault that those mitts of hers are so ham-handed."

Madeline screeched as the other ladies giggled. Maude stepped away from the table, certain Madeline wouldn't have her restraint. She didn't want to wear any more of the morning meal than she already did. She turned on her heel and walked to the exit. Arabella and Blair would have more to say to Madeline, and she had no remorse.

Kieran's gaze followed the velvet-clad woman as she hurried down the passageway. He recognized Maude at once, even though her back was to him. He didn't understand how he could be so certain, but he was.

"Excuse me," he muttered to the other men he milled about with as they waited to make their way to the lists. His long strides made it easy to catch up with Maude, but he waited until they turned a corner and were out of sight before he reached for her arm. She tugged it away, and a fist came flying toward his jaw. It was close to his shoulder before Maude realized at whom she aimed.

"Apologies. You startled me. You're very silent." Maude felt thick-tongued as she took in Kieran's appearance in the full light of day. She had suspected he was handsome, but she was unprepared for his rugged good looks. His tawny hair had touches of carrot to it, but rather than looking garish, it gave the tone richness. His eyes were gray with a touch of green. It made for an unusual combination. She remembered how his broad frame encompassed her the night before as his large but gentle hands slid over her hair and back. In the dark, it had been impossible to tell just how large Kieran was. In the daylight, it was clear that he was a veritable mountain. It was clear he was a Highlander by his size and his bearing. He was similar in build to her father and brother, she realized; that was why his hug seemed familiar. However, the men in her family didn't draw her like Kieran did. Women ogled her four braw cousins--Callum, Alex, Tavish, and Magnus—but never had the Sinclair brothers made her breath catch in the back of her throat.

Heat rushed through Kieran as she offered him her half-smile. He perceived she didn't wear it often. It was genuine; not a courtly smile that he was sure she employed throughout the day. His eyes gorged on the ample bust hidden under her kirtle. The top of her cleavage showed, and he wished for nothing more than the chance to run his tongue along the deep crevice. He appreciated the trim waist that had been firm and curvy in his hands the night before, and he forced himself not to gaze at hips he wanted to thrust against. Randy thoughts were stirring his rod, and his breeks would again display his interest if he didn't calm himself. Instead, his brow furrowed as he noticed the kirtle had a long stain running from the middle of her chest to where the material would have pooled while she sat. There was a faint scent of dairy as he sniffed. He smelled lemon verbena, but he also caught the odor of milk.

"A little mishap?" He kept his voice low. As soon as she heard his words, her smile vanished and a stubborn set to her jaw took its place. He understood two things in that moment: she had more mettle than the other women gave her credit for, and his sister was responsible for the mess. "What did she do?"

"I think it's rather obvious. Excuse me, but I must hurry." Maude turned to continue down the passageway, but Kieran matched her stride. When they rounded the corner that led to the ladies'-in-waiting chambers, she halted and turned to him. Before she realized what she was doing, she placed her hand on his chest and nudged him back. "You can't follow me."

"Then stop and talk to me."

"I told you, I can't. I must hurry and change if I'm to join the queen on her walk. If I arrive late, it will be obvious, and then I'll need to either lie or explain. Neither of which are appealing." Maude turned away, but paused and looked back. "You may whisper to me, but apparently your voice carries when you speak to your sister. It carries straight to the queen."

Kieran's eyes flashed wide before regret filled them and his shoulders slumped. He looked like a guilty child being remonstrated by an adult.

"I'm sorry, Maude. You warned me not to say aught, and I insisted I knew better when you're the one who survives her at court while I just visit. How much worse have I made it?"

"Significantly."

Kieran was unprepared for the flat and succinct response. He looked at his feet as he tried to come up with something else to say. Maude took it to signal the end of their conversation.

"But how will you get out of your gown?" Maude spun around with such haste that her skirts twirled out before settling against her legs. "Bluidy hell. I didn't mean it as it sounded. I mean, I wasn't offering. Unless--- No. I meant should I fetch your maid?"

"I can manage on my own." Maude turned away once again. "But thank you."

Kieran had little choice but to watch her walk away. Unless he wanted to jeopardize her reputation, there was no way for him to follow her any further. And unless he wanted to jeopardize the little self-restraint he possessed at the moment, he had to let her go. He hadn't intended to imply that he would help her undress until the image took shape in his mind. By the time he finished stumbling over his words, that was precisely what he wanted.

CHAPTER FOUR

M aude spent the rest of the morning avoiding both friend and foe. She arrived in the gardens as the women set off, easing her way into the center of the group with her sister and best friend. Several women strolled on each side, and her new nemesis trailed after the queen at the front of the pack. She kept her cowl over her head, the wind brisker than it had been the day before. After their constitutional, she accompanied the others to the queen's solar, where she found the book on medicinals she'd been reading for several days. Blair and Arabella accepted that she wanted to be left alone, so they found other friends to sit with. She situated herself where no one else might sit near her, but if anyone approached, the queen would notice.

The queen and her ladies remained in the solar until the noon meal. Maude slipped away to her chamber until she was certain the meal concluded. She lay on her bed, staring at the ceiling for most of the time. Though tired, she didn't dare fall asleep, lest she nap the afternoon away. The morning and the night before had drained her.

Upon leaving her chamber, Maude traversed the passageways until she reached the Great Hall, where she peeked through the open doorway and spied the queen rising. Her timing had been perfect. She slipped along the wall until she reached the group of ladies who congregated around the queen. Certain she went unnoticed, she failed to prepare for the queen to look at her with an assessing gaze.

"Lady Maude, I believe you planned to spend the afternoon at Cambuskenneth Abbey to collect more herbs and medicinals for the castle's spense. They informed me this morning that it looks a wee sparse. We aren't yet past the ill season, so I appreciate your assistance. Be sure to take guards."

"Yes, Your Grace." Maude dipped into a deep curtsy and would have liked to hug the woman if it wouldn't have resulted in a furor. She recognized that the queen had taken pity on her. Maude had been to the monastery only a fortnight ago, but between what she overheard of Kieran and Madeline's conversation and what she'd most likely been informed of the morning meal, the queen had offered Maude a reprieve.

Maude wove through the castle until she came to the undercroft where the spense was located. A large storage room of sorts, it was where they kept herbs and medicinals that needed hanging and drying. An aging monk from Cambuskenneth Abbey served as spenser. He was patient and gracious with Maude, who had shown a natural talent for healing since she was a young girl. She found the sick rarely cared what she looked like if she made them feel better. The monk had taught her a great deal since her arrival a few months prior, and she enjoyed her time with him. Going blind, he relied on her for help. The monk also took no interest in her appearance since he barely saw in the dark storeroom, and he was a man of the cloth. When she pushed the door open, she found the chamber empty, so she gathered two large baskets and made her way to the garrison. Since neither of her parents were in residence, only two Sutherland guards remained at Stirling. She breathed a sigh of relief when she recognized one of her father's men walking toward the barracks' door.

"Donald," she called out to him. She would send him to search for Tomas instead of having to find another man to assist her. She became uncomfortable around too many guardsmen when there was no one else with her.

"Aye, ma lady."

"I'm riding out to the abbey. Could you and Tomas please escort me?"

"Aye, ma lady." While neither man was old enough to be her father, they'd known her since she was a wean, and they were two of the few men her father entrusted with his daughters' safety.

"I'll be in the stables readying Trioblaid." Her horse's name, Trouble, still made Donald laugh. She'd named the gelding Trouble because within hours of being born, he wandered out of the birthing stall and tried to enter a pasture where his father, an enormous stallion, was exercising. The colt toddled over to his father on gangly legs and tried to whinny. It sounded like a smothered trumpet. The stallion's eyes rolled before he charged at the newborn. Lachlan had only moments to restrain his mount before the horse charged at his own son. A fortnight later, the colt proved to be an escape artist once more. He ambled out of his stall and away from his mother and discovered a barrel of apples. Maude found him with his head down to his withers as he chomped on the fruit. It was one of her early healing experiences, since the horse gave himself colic. His temper rivaled his father's when he was a few years old, and Maude's father insisted they geld him before he broke down any more walls to the stable. His powerful legs were his favorite tool to display his anger. Maude was one of the few people who had the ability to control him before his gelding. While no one would describe him as docile now, he was manageable. She guided him out of his stall once she'd saddled him and stood in the bright sunlight of the bailey while she awaited her guards. The sun was warmer than it had been that morning.

"Good afternoon, my lady."

Maude knew who possessed the warm baritone coming from over her shoulder. She continued to stroke Trioblaid's neck but glanced at Kieran.

"Good afternoon, Laird."

Kieran frowned. He was unsure why at first, but he realized he didn't care for Maude using his title. He would have rather it had been his name, and before he could stop himself, he said as much.

"It's Kieran to you, lass." Just as he had that morning, he kept his tone low. Maude rewarded him with a pretty blush that spread across her cheeks.

"I can't call you that. Laird."

Kieran grinned as Maude tacked his title on as an afterthought.

"You can if you want."

Maude seemed to size him up, and Kieran had a moment of panic that he would be found lacking.

"What I want isn't of consequence, Laird MacLeod."

"Nay, lass. You're going in the wrong direction. I don't want my full title from you, Maude."

"Are ye ready, ma lady?" Maude was relieved to hear the burr of Donald's voice. It excused her from the awkward conversation spiraling beyond her control. She suspected Kieran flirted with her, and she was ill equipped for such banter.

"Aye."

"Where are you going?" Kieran's brow furrowed as he assessed the two men who would accompany Maude to wherever she ventured.

"Cambuskenneth Abbey for the afternoon. I need to collect some herbs and medicinals for the castle."

"Really?"

"Really." Maude gathered her reins, prepared to mount when a large hand covered hers.

"You're only taking two guards?" Kieran's breath feathered across her ear, and when she turned to peer at him, she was certain he was close enough to kiss her.

"That's how many I always travel with in Stirling." She was proud that her voice didn't sound as breathy as it felt. "I've been to the abbey many times since moving to court. It's not a long ride. I could be halfway there by now."

"Cheeky, buttercup." Both froze as Kieran used the endearment for a second time in less than a day.

"Why do you call me that?" Maude whispered.

"I'm not sure. I've called no one else that, but it seems to fit you. You appear fragile, but you're stronger than most give you credit for. And there's a wildness to you, as though you wish to be free of all these trappings," he waved his hand toward the castle. "And simply allowed to roam free."

"What Highlander wouldn't want to be free of this?" Maude didn't glance away as her brown eyes bored into his. "I'm not wild. I'm just not cut out to be a courtier."

Kieran leaned closer, just as he had the night before. "I suspect you can be wild if given the opportunity. Would that I could be there for it."

Maude blinked several times and started when the clatter of another set of hooves approached. A stable boy brought out an enormous bay horse. Its chestnut coat gleamed in the sun as it knickered at the sight of Kieran.

"Where are you going?" Maude hoped to change the topic of conversation.

"With you."

"What?" Maude looked around and shook her head. "Where were you planning to go? I doubt it's to Cambuskenneth."

"It wasn't. I planned to retire to my chamber, but I'm not letting you leave with only two guards." Before Maude protested, large warm hands grasped her waist and hoisted her with ease into her saddle. She arranged herself, embarrassed at how her stockings showed while she rode astride. It hadn't mattered to her when she planned to travel with her family's guardsmen, but now she felt exposed. Kieran didn't help matters when his palm brushed against her calf. The gleam in his eye told her it wasn't an accident. She watched as he vaulted into the saddle of a horse she never saw or heard him summon.

She nudged Trioblaid, and the four riders set off. Her guards attempted to flank her, but Kieran refused to relinquish his spot on her right. Donald rode in front while Tomas rode in the rear.

"See." Kieran gestured to the left. "Not enough guards. You have a vulnerable side. There is no one to your left. Where are your other guards?"

"I don't have any others, and I don't appreciate you insinuating that Donald and Tomas can't protect me. They have been guardsmen my entire life. They've kept me safe on more than one occasion. You aren't the only Highlander who can wield a sword."

"I ken that." Maude liked how Kieran's brogue sometimes appeared, even when he tried to hide his accent. "I saw them in the lists this morning. It's the only reason I didn't insist on bringing some of my own men."

"I should ask my brother if high-handedness is bred into every laird or if it's something that's taught to heirs."

Kieran's chuckle was deep and made her toes curl in her boots. He steered his horse a little closer to hers, but Trioblaid shied away before baring his teeth.

"That's why I don't need more guards. I don't think Trioblaid cares for you getting too close."

"Apt name apparently. In truth, you think your horse is more sufficient than one of my warriors?"

Maude smirked at him before whistling. Donald moved aside, and Trioblaid shot forward. She leaned low over his neck and squeezed her thighs against his flanks. She let

Trioblaid gallop for a few minutes, giving him his head, before she reined in and swung him around.

"Do keep up! I'd like to be home before the sun sets!" She called out to Kieran. Her guards already knew what she and her horse were capable of. It was one reason her father remained comfortable with only two guards to accompany his daughters. Blair's horse had the same lineage and was just as fast as Trioblaid, even though he was two years younger. Both horses were faster than any except for their father who belonged to Maude's brother. She pulled the rein and turned Trioblaid to face the direction in which they traveled. She waited until Kieran was almost abreast before she spurred her horse again. By the time they arrived at the gates of the monastery, both horses and riders were winded.

Kieran wasn't sure if he wanted to haul Maude off her horse and kiss her senseless or haul her off her horse and throttle her. All he knew was he wanted to hold her again. She had terrified him as she took off on her horse. She angered him when she stopped to taunt him before spurring her horse on again. It wasn't because he doubted her riding skills; it was because he didn't trust the roads to be free of highwaymen. He leapt from his horse just as Maude swept her leg over her mount. He reached up and lifted her free, his body brushing against hers as he settled her on her feet. They stood that way for a moment before Maude turned to unfasten the baskets and hand her reins to the stable master who came to greet them. It forced Kieran to step back and remind himself that he was crowding her in the courtyard of a monastery. Women were rare guests, let alone one who was on the verge of being pawed as lust thrummed through his veins.

"Do you always take such risks? And before you tell me you've been riding your entire life, I mean do you always risk riding apart from your escort? You have guards assigned to you for a reason."

Maude looked into eyes the color of the North Sea as a storm approached. She saw hints of anger, but what she saw the most was concern. Genuine worry and perhaps fear.

"I wouldn't have let us get too far ahead of you. Couldn't you tell I held back so your horse could keep up once I stopped the first time?"

"Could keep up?" Kieran clenched his jaw to keep from snapping at her. His steed was a battle-tested warhorse, not a plow animal. His horse was among the best he'd ever seen, but Maude's put him to shame. Loyalty to his ride kept him from accepting that hers was superior horseflesh. "Do you outpace your guards every time you ride here?"

"No. I thought it would be fun to race. I do with my guards all the time, but I never push Trioblaid to get too far ahead. Those horses are from Sutherland, too. They keep up as well as yours did. I'm never out of sight and never more than a furlong ahead, if that." Maude placed her hand on Kieran's arm before she realized what she was doing. When she attempted to snatch it away, Kieran pressed it against the bunched muscles. "I was enjoying the ride, and I thought you might like to race me. Lachlan can't help but accept the challenge whenever we ride together. You remind me of him."

Maude watched the darkest scowl take root across Kieran's face, but she didn't understand what she'd said to make matters worse.

"I won't race you on the way back if it bothers you that much," she tried for a conciliatory tone.

"I remind you of your brother."

"What?" Maude was confused about why Kieran latched onto that part of her explanation.

"You said I remind you of your brother. That is not a comparison I care for."

Maude's lips drew into a fine line as she tried to keep from snarling at him. She glared at him as she tried to push past him. She swung the basket on purpose so it would hit Kieran's stomach.

"My brother happens to be one of the finest men I ken. You should be so lucky to be considered in his company."

Kieran grasped her arm and almost jerked her back into place before crossing his arms. He was aware it made him appear imposing, but it was the only way to keep from wrapping them around her. The stubborn set of Maude's jaw told him he didn't intimidate her. He leaned forward as he had the night before to whisper in her ear.

"But your brother doesn't want to do the things to you, and with you, that I do."

Maude's eyes narrowed before she used her shoulder to push past him.

"You have a cruel sense of humor. I don't find you funny."

When Kieran came abreast of her, he reached for her again, but he realized she was livid.

"Remember where we are," she hissed. As she crossed the courtyard, Kieran watched her face relax and settle into the mask of serenity he was certain she wore every day at court. She flashed a warm smile as a monk came out to greet them. The man was tonsured, and he wore a flowing black chasuble over his white cassock and a large cross swinging against his chest with each step. His hands were tucked within his opposite sleeves. Kieran was shocked to realize how young and handsome the man was. "Father Michael, the queen sent me to request if I might impose upon your generosity and gather more herbs and medicinals. The ague swept through the castle a few sennights ago, and it depleted many of the supplies."

"Aye, lass. Well I know, since Brother Christian said as much when he returned. You ken you're always welcome in our gardens, Lady Maude."

Maude shifted so to glance between Kieran and Father Michael, who she sensed were sizing up one another up. Kieran's face hadn't relaxed, while Father Michael wore a knowing expression. What he knew, Maude hadn't a clue.

"Father Michael, I'd introduce you to Laird Kieran MacLeod. Laird MacLeod offered to accompany me to ensure I was well protected on the road." Maude once more smiled at the priest, and Maude thought Kieran growled, but it was too quiet to be certain. "Laird MacLeod, please meet Father Michael, the priest in charge of the herb gardens. He graciously allows me to pilfer from his garden and stored herbs whenever I need to."

"I'm pleased to make your acquaintance, Laird MacLeod. Perhaps you'd care to join Lady Maude's guards in the refectory."

"I do not."

Kieran begrudgingly stuck out his hand and was surprised when the monk gripped his forearm in a firm warrior's handshake. The men stared at one another as their grips tightened on each other's arms. Maude watched and wanted to roll her eyes. She understood there was some sort of silent standoff; she'd seen her brother engaged in such plenty of times, but she still didn't understand what this one was about.

"If we might make our way there. I'd like to be back on the road well before dusk," Maude attempted to ease the tension.

"Lady Maude's correct. She won't be on the roads in the dark," Kieran decreed, which earned him another scowl from Maude. He followed the priest and Maude toward the back of the monastery, where a large garden spread before them. Kieran noticed that it was a multipurpose patch of land. He spied vegetables, herbs, and flowers, each in their separate plots. He tripped over Maude when she came to an abrupt stop.

"Father Michael, to make this quicker, could you please show the laird the spense and assist him with collecting the dry medicinals while I cut fresh shoots?" Maude handed Kieran a basket. As his fingers wrapped around the handle, they grazed Maude's. A charge of electricity surged up his arm, and from the way Maude held her breath, he sensed she experienced it, too. Father Michael turned toward a building that ran parallel to the garden and began walking, expecting Kieran would follow him. Maude whispered, "Please. I'm sorry for earlier. I would appreciate the help. It will make this go faster. I promise I'm safe here."

Kieran nodded. He recognized that she had added the last bit to reassure him once she watched him scan the area, his hand involuntarily on the hilt of his sword. Kieran kept Father Michael in his periphery, but he didn't turn to follow the man until he saw Maude settled in a patch of chamomile. He joined the priest in a cool storage room with poor lighting, where the holy man already gathered bunches of dried herbs and flowers.

"How long have you known Lady Maude?" Father Michael asked, adopting a tone meant to sound conversational. Kieran didn't believe the priest meant to chat.

"I met her last eve."

His response made the priest pause, and the expression of shock might have been comical if Kieran's temper wasn't already on the brink of getting the better of him. Father Michael turned away and reached overhead to lift a basket from a top shelf. As his arms extended, his sleeves slid down his arms, and Kieran was surprised to see the corded muscles in his forearms. He'd felt them when they shook hands but seeing them confirmed his suspicions. This man was familiar with physical labor that went beyond anything that a priest would know, even those who served as farmers.

"I wasn't born a priest, ye ken," Father Michael let his burr surface and smiled at Kieran's obvious surprise. "I'm a Sutherland. I've kenned Lady Maude since we were weans."

"You're a long way from home."

"Aye, but I was able to secure a place at this monastery, which is what I wanted. I heard God's calling and wanted to join the Augustinians. Aye, I trained as a warrior before I trained as a novice. I was fortunate that my father allowed me to follow my calling."

"Very lucky indeed." Kieran found he couldn't muster more than a few brusque words at a time. He recognized the emotion that had a stranglehold on him. It was jealousy. He recognized it as one he experienced often as a child when his mother paid more attention to his sisters and overlooked him except to chastise him. Except this time, his jealousy wasn't over not receiving a sweetmeat or attention. It was about a woman. The emotion choked him, but he couldn't seem to push it aside. He realized it was illogical to feel this way after meeting the woman less than a day ago, but he did. And it was even more irrational to be jealous of a priest, but he was.

"Lady Maude is a kind soul. She's always had a talent for healing. I ken she's missed back at Sutherland, but Queen Elizabeth requested Maude serve her. Fortunately, her sister, Blair, is there. Blair often overshadows Maude, but I think Maude prefers that. She can hide that way." Father Michael added the bunches to the basket Kieran set on the table, but he stopped to look Kieran squarely in the eye. "The other boys and I weren't very kind to her when we were younger. It hurt her deeply. She made herself ill trying to fix what we said were her flaws. Her brother and I fought more than one of other the boys our age once we learned how she'd taken our taunts to heart. Lachlan and I made certain the other boys kenned we'd erred and made certain they stopped. While her health improved, I think the damage was already done. She's not shy by nature; she's painfully insecure."

Father Michael handed the full basket to Kieran and came around the table before walking to the door. He stepped through into the bright sun and waited for Kieran. When both sets of eyes adjusted to the light, Father Michael turned back to Kieran.

"I don't ken what you intend, but if it's aught less than honorable, be assured I will find you. I may be a priest, but I'm also a warrior. Don't let the robe and tonsure fool you. I haven't forgotten the skills drilled into me for years. Play her for a fool, and I will be sure it's more than just God's wrath that rains down on you."

Before Kieran had the opportunity to respond, Maude walked toward them with an overflowing basket that she struggled to carry. Kieran aided Maude rather than argue with the priest.

"Thank you once more. Until next time, cousin." Maude grinned as she shook out her arm before wrapping her arms around the priest, who pinched her cheek before she gave him a peck on his own.

"Take care, lass. Send for me if you need aught." Father Michael proffered a chaste kiss on her cheek before smirking at Kieran. Maude looked back and forth between the two men. Her cousin had grown into one of her closest companions. They had a rough patch during their adolescence, but they'd become close again just before Michael left for the abbey. When she arrived at court, it relieved her to discover the monastery's proximity to the castle. She was able to visit every few weeks. Between Blair and Michael, the early days of being at court were tolerable. With Arabella's friendship, she was able to survive the rigors of her service and navigate the treachery of the other ladies-in-waiting. As her gaze settled on Kieran, she had a shocking realization that she already accepted that Kieran would be an important person in her life. She wasn't sure how she was so confident about her intuition, but she was.

When they reached the horses, Father Michael stepped forward with his arms outstretched to assist Maude onto her horse, but Kieran stepped in front of him, using his larger frame to prevent the priest from reaching Maude. His fingers tingled as they gripped Maude's trim waist. He forced himself to release her as soon as she was in the saddle. He tied the baskets back onto her saddle and mounted his own steed. They rode out of the gate, and Kieran watched as Maude turned back once to wave to her cousin. He felt foolish that he'd wanted to plow his fist into the priest's gut, but how was he to know the man was her kin? Neither said anything until the end of the visit. Maude glanced at Kieran, but the scowl that remained in place convinced her to remain silent. He realized his surliness made her retreat, but he wasn't prepared to converse with her guards in earshot.

CHAPTER FIVE

Maude breathed a silent sigh of relief half an hour later when they rode into the bailey. Her head hurt, and she wanted nothing more than to slip into a hot bath, request a tray for the evening meal, and spend time alone until she fell asleep. Kieran helped her down once more, but he didn't allow his body anywhere near hers. He unfastened the baskets and shook his head when Maude tried to take them.

"No, Maude. They're cumbersome. I'll take them wherever you need. Point me in the right direction." Kieran accepted that his foul mood had ruined the outing that started out with Maude smiling and laughing and ended with her trying to rub her temple inconspicuously.

"Thank you, but I must put everything away in their place to make sure they keep."

"Let me help you." Kieran looked into her smoky brown eyes. The hue closest to her pupils was like young whisky that had only been in the barrel a few months, but the outer iris was the deep amber of the barrel-aged spirit, and he wanted to drown in both colors of her open and questioning gaze. "Please let me help you. I'll explain when there aren't so many ears to overhear us."

Maude nodded and led the way to the castle's spense.

When they arrived, Kieran wanted to groan because the monk who oversaw the storage room was there. He wanted to speak to Maude alone. If he was to humble himself, he didn't want an audience.

"Lady Maude, I am relieved you brought more supplies from the abbey. We sorely need skullcap and lungwort. I hope you brought bunches of each."

"Good afternoon, Master Spenser. I have both in abundance. I will put everything away. You needn't linger on my account. It must be getting close to the evening meal, and the other priests will expect you."

"That they will, my lady." He glanced at Kieran and furrowed his brow, unsure if he should leave the unwed couple together.

"Laird MacLeod will assist with the items that belong beyond my reach. It'll only take us a few minutes, and then we will be on our way, too. I must ready for the evening."

"Very well, my lady. Then I shall bid you a good eve."

"Thank you," Maude nodded.

Kieran had taken a place by the door after placing the baskets on the floor. He stood across the room from Maude, ostensibly to appear as though he wouldn't act untoward to her, but he wanted to close the door behind the man and ensure no one would walk in on them. Maude heard the key click in the lock and crossed her arms.

"Explain."

"Which part? Why I locked the door or why I was an utter arse all afternoon?"

"Both," Maude's clipped tone warned Kieran that he had better not dawdle in his apology and explanation.

"I locked the door because I don't want anyone to interrupt me eating crow." When Maude's eyes darted between the lock and Kieran, he put his hands up. "I won't keep you trapped here. You can leave at any time. I won't force you to remain. I'll never force you. Ever."

Maude uncrossed her arms and sighed. Her shoulders

drooped as though the effort was too great to maintain her perfect posture. She didn't disguise rubbing her forehead. Kieran eased his way across the room, and when she didn't retreat or push him away, he tucked a lock of hair behind her ear before cupping her cheek.

"What did you want to tell me?" Maude whispered.

"I'm sorry. I'm sorry for being an arse, a jealous arse. I'm sorry for ruining your day and the little time you had with your cousin. I'm sorry for causing you discomfort, especially the headache I obviously gave you."

"I didn't understand you earlier, and I still don't. What were you jealous of? What did you want?"

Kieran eased closer and wrapped an arm around her. He settled her against his chest as he had the night before. It was easier to make his confession when her penetrating gaze wasn't boring into him.

"My jealousy was directed at the priest. You greeted him with such warmth, and it's obvious you're well acquainted. I didn't like that such a handsome mon was so familiar with you. I wanted that smile directed at me. I wanted that excitement to be for my arrival, my welcome, not for another mon. I realize he's a priest, and trust that he'd never take advantage of you, but I feared you held a different affection for him than what you would for a cousin."

Maude leaned back enough to glance up at his face, but all she saw was the underside of his chin. She gave up trying to meet his eyes, so she returned to leaning her head against his chest. Her deep inhale and sigh pressed her body against his before her body released the tension.

"Maude, I was unaware he was your cousin until we were aboot to leave. By then, I'd already ruined the outing. I didn't want to push you further, so I tried to give you peace on the ride back. I feel like such an eejit. Worse than that. I feel guilty for my unkind thoughts toward your kin and jumping to conclusions and for being self-centered. I joined you because I feared your guards wouldn't protect you to my standards when, instead, you really needed protecting from my foul temper."

"Kieran, I understand what you're saying, but I still don't understand why it mattered to you who I smiled at."

"Because I want you."

"Want me to what?"

Maude's innocent question flooded his mind with lurid images of all the things he wanted with Maude, but when he pushed those aside, he glimpsed very different scenes. He imagined them walking together on his land holding hands. He saw them sharing a chalice of wine as they laughed together on the dais in his great hall, her sitting in his lap before a fire in his–no, their–chamber. The last image was of them once again walking, but this time, they were elderly. He had a stick, and she leaned against him, their hair white. It was his turn to lean back as he felt himself getting lost in the warm pools of chocolate that were her eyes. He wanted to taste her lips, but he forced himself not to rush. Just as Father Michael warned, he wanted Maude to believe his intentions were sincere. He hadn't known her long enough to kiss her without her assuming he only wanted one thing. He tilted her chin up but placed a chaste kiss at her temple.

"I want you for many things, many of which are too inappropriate for me to share aloud, but I also want you to consider allowing me to court you."

"Why would you want to do that?"

Kieran realized Father Michael hadn't exaggerated Maude's lack of confidence. She couldn't fathom why he wanted her.

"Because I've never been drawn to a woman more than I am you. Because I've never been so curious to get to know another person. Because I struggle to keep my hands from roaming everywhere on you as I taste your lips. Because I *want you*."

Maude's mouth formed a perfect circle, and Kieran's cock stood at full attention. He'd tried to keep their hips apart, so she wouldn't brush against his semi-aroused shaft, but now there was no hiding it. Her eyes widened to match her mouth as her mound rubbed against his cock because her hips moved forward as she leaned back to gaze at him. Kieran blushed. He hadn't blushed since he was a child. His ears burned.

"Do you understand now?"

"Yes. Well, not really, but sort of."

Kieran laughed, his deep baritone filling the room. He kissed her temple once more. He glanced around the small room and spotted two chairs. He led Maude to them, and once they sat, he took her hands in his. He couldn't keep holding her and hope to overcome temptation. He'd be riding back to the abbey to confess if he wasn't careful. But he also couldn't bring himself to let go of her. Her earnest expression made him realize she was too innocent for him to speak in euphemisms, and he suspected she would prefer the candor.

"When I approached from the gardens and caught a glimpse of you on the terrace last night, I only saw the back of you, but my reaction was instant. It surprised me for more than one reason, but I wanted to touch you, press your body against mine. Even when I was consoling you, my body wanted yours. I didn't question Father Michael's vow of celibacy or your respect for such, but seeing another mon with you, any mon, made me want to bay at the moon. The thought of another mon touching you suffocates me."

"So, you want to couple with me? Like you'd been doing just before we met." The second part was a statement, and his ears were going up in flames.

"Yes and no." Kieran wanted to sink through the floor. "Yes, I'd like to do those same things. But no, it's not the same. I want it to mean something with you. I want it to be more than just the act. I can't describe it, Maude, because I've never felt this way before. I want to be the mon who introduces you to passion, but I also want to be the only mon who ever sees that side of you."

"I still don't understand why."

Kieran released one of her hands to run his through his hair. After tugging his hair until it stood on end, which garnered one of Maude's half-smiles, he returned his hand to hers.

"I told you. I desire you. I found you on the terrace and then I held you in my arms. I told you last night that those lasses didn't know what they were talking aboot. You are all that a mon desires. You are what I desire."

"So, Laurel was right. I'm better suited as a tavern wench since you want to tup me." Maude tugged her hands away and stood. Tears threatened, but she refused to allow Kieran to witness her cry twice in as many days.

"That bitch is awfully haughty for a chit with little dowry and no mon sniffing at her skirts," Kieran grumbled. He looked up at Maude, shocked at what he'd just uttered.

"Men are always asking her to dance."

"Aye, because she's the daughter of Laird Ross, but she's the fourth daughter. Her father has neither coin nor land left to give away. The men who ask her to dance are hoping for introductions and to rub elbows, but no mon wants to be saddled with that shrew, not without land to go along with her."

"But men never ask me to dance. They may stare at my bosom, but they aren't interested in me."

"Good," Kieran huffed until he realized how that would sound to a woman with insecurities. "That didn't come out right at all. That was jealousy once again. I'd rather not share you. But the reason the men don't ask is that you hide away. I asked around this morning under the guise of looking for a potential husband for Madeline. God bless the mon who ends up with her. I feel guilty aboot that alliance already. But I asked aboot which women might be more desirable candidates for marriage. Your name came up over and over, and before you say it was for your dowry, it wasn't. I wanted to smash my fist into more than one face after hearing some of the more lascivious reasons you're considered a catch."

"Wonderful. The men who don't want my father's coin or land only want me because they suspect I'll be a good swive. Laurel is still right. I appear little better than a tavern whore. I don't resemble a lady."

Kieran was on his feet in an instant, pacing as his hands fisted and opened. He looked at Maude thrice before he stopped in front of her. He wanted to reach for her, but he didn't dare when she thought men only wanted her for coupling.

"Perhaps that's the case with some men, but that's not the case with me. I don't need your dowry, and if I wanted a tavern wench, I would find one. Instead, I am with you. Driving myself crazy. It's clear I'm a glutton for punishment. I desire you, Maude. I do want to couple with you. Badly. But that's not the reason I want to court you. Passion fades over time and is replaced with familiarity and hopefully companionship. That's not to say that I won't continue to desire you, but I want more than that. I want someone whose company I enjoy. A woman who is intelligent, kind, selfless, funny, daring, stubborn, honest. I can keep going, and I've only known you a day. I want the chance to discover if we suit. If you find you don't want my attention, then I will go my own way. But not without a fight."

"I'm a wee overwhelmed, Kieran. I'm unsure what to say other than I'd like to get to know you better. But you don't have to spin falsehoods, ever, to make me feel better."

"What falsehoods have I told?" Kieran demanded. "I don't lie to you."

"Those men do want my dowry. They hear there are two Sutherland daughters here, and they seek us out. They stare at my bust, and they smile at my breasts rather than my face. Then they take in the rest of me, and it's inevitable: their smiles drop until they spot Blair. They're aware I'm the elder, so they pray someone else will marry me, so they can hope to wed Blair." Maude looked away before Kieran glimpsed the pain in her eyes, but he didn't have to try hard to imagine it.

He'd seen it the previous night. "Besides, there are far more desirable women available for marriage. Arabella is the most beautiful of the ladies-in-waiting. Two men will approach us, and one will speak to me until the other leads Bella out to dance, then the one left behind walks away."

Kieran put a damper on his lust and pulled Maude into her embrace. She needed respect and patience at that moment, not a sword searching for her sheath. He tucked her against his chest and stroked her hair.

"I learned of some of what happened when you were younger. Michael told me," he murmured against her hair as he kissed her crown between words. "I wish I had the power to go back in time and keep that from happening to you. But alas, I can't. All I can do is try to prove to you in the present that you're so much more than you think. Lass, will you let me court you?"

Maude's arms tightened a fraction around his waist, and she nodded her head against his chest.

"Do you not sense how perfectly we fit together?" Kieran whispered. They stood in silence for a long time, both comforted by holding one another. When the shadows shifted through the window, Kieran accepted they had to leave. They'd already been tucked away together far too long. More than one person noticed they had returned from the monastery, but if neither of them could be found, people would speculate that they were together. Kieran might want Maude, but he wouldn't force her to marry him because he destroyed her reputation. "Buttercup, we need to go. It's getting close to the evening meal. We'll be late. I don't want people to gossip aboot why we're both missing."

Maude tensed before nodding her head once. She pulled away but wouldn't glance at him. He understood she interpreted his words to mean he didn't want people linking them together. Kieran wrapped an arm around her again and tipped her chin up. He longed to lower his lips to hers and discover if they were as soft as they looked.

"I only meant that I don't want people to speak ill of you. If you decide to marry me, it'll be because you want to, not because I ruined your reputation, and they forced you to. It's too soon to enter the Great Hall together, but I will ask you to dance tonight."

Maude gave a noncommittal nod before moving toward the door. Kieran opened it and stepped outside, keeping Maude tucked behind him. He counted to fifty in his head, and when no one appeared, he led Maude out. They parted ways, entering the castle through separate entrances. Maude would have Arabella make her excuses if Kieran looked for her. She still intended to take that bath and tray in her chamber rather than go to the Great Hall. She'd had as much time with other people as she could manage that day.

CHAPTER SIX

The servants hadn't yet served the second course before Kieran realized Maude wasn't coming to the hall for the evening meal. He worried that her absence was his fault and hoped she'd ordered a tray brought to her room rather than go hungry on his account. When the servants cleared and pushed aside the tables while the musicians warmed up, he wove his way through the crowded Great Hall until he found Arabella. To his misfortune, she was standing with his sister and her friends. He approached with care, but Madeline spotted him. She pushed Laurel toward him with all the subtlety of a fishwife. He looked past them and raised an eyebrow at Arabella, who shook her head. Madeline watched her brother, then looked over her shoulder at Arabella. Her eyes narrowed before glaring at her brother.

"You're in time to claim the first dance," Madeline said by way of greeting as she pushed Laurel a couple more steps forward.

"Thank you, but nay. I came to tell you I've received a missive from Adam, and I need to return home for a short time." He glanced at Arabella and hoped she was listening and would relay the story to Maude. "There was a raid, and they razed a village. I need to return to see the damages and

49

determine our next steps. I'll be gone a few sennights, but I will return. There are matters I haven't settled here." He wasn't about to admit that his matters with the king had concluded and his unfinished business was with Maude.

Madeline, for all her vanity and smarminess, was loyal to their clan and protective of their people. She stepped around Laurel until she linked her arm through Kieran's. They stepped aside to speak in private. When he was ready to leave, he glanced again at Arabella. She nodded once, and it relieved him that she understood what he needed from her. However, Madeline was watching him again. Her eyes narrowed once more as she looked between Arabella and Kieran. He understood what she assumed, and he was not about to disabuse her if it meant it protected Maude from being locked in her sights. He would be away long enough for any suspicion that he was interested in Arabella to fizzle. He just hoped that Maude's interest in him wouldn't fizzle, too.

Kieran slogged through the rain and mud in the bailey the next morning, the extra material from his plaid pulled over his head. He entered the stable and pushed his wet hair from his face as he moved along the stalls until he came to Trioblaid's. He offered the horse an apple.

"Take care of her, lad." He moved down to his own horse's stall, but feared he'd jump out of his skin when a soft voice reached him.

"You never told me his name." Maude stepped out of the shadow and walked to the stall door. She raised her hand for his horse to sniff her before she attempted to stroke between his wide-set eyes. The horse nickered and swished his tail as he nudged her with his head.

"I believe Peat would like you to give him an apple."

"Pete? As in Peter the apostle? You gave him a person's name?"

"No, Peat as in mòine."

"Ah. He is the same color as fresh peat, but I'm not sure he smells as good as a warm fire."

"Wheest. You'll hurt his feelings by calling him a smelly beast." Kieran grinned, relieved to see Maude in good spirits. He'd worried that his behavior from the day before might have ended their courtship before it even started.

"I'm nae the one who called him names. There is only one wee beastie here, and it's nae yer steed." Maude allowed her brogue to flow as she returned Kieran's teasing. She flashed one of her rare open-mouthed smiles, and Kieran didn't stop himself from brushing his thumb over her plump lower lip.

"Why don't you smile like this more?" He whispered, but wanted to kick himself when the smile dropped.

"I'd rather not make all my defects obvious," she muttered.

"Defects?"

"My teeth."

"Are you missing some?" Kieran pressed on her chin as though he might examine a horse's gums. He was aware she wasn't; he would have seen the gap by now if she was. She swatted at his hand.

"Nay. I don't care for how they look."

"How they look? I haven't noticed aught aboot them."

"That's because I rarely smile with my mouth open." Maude huffed as she recognized he wouldn't let the matter rest until she explained. "I have a gap between my top two teeth and my bottom two are a little crooked and overlap at the top."

"Let me see." Kieran's request was in earnest. Maude looked at him as though he sprouted a second head and shook hers. "Let me see, buttercup. I will eventually."

Maude rolled her eyes but pulled her lips back in a parody of a smile. The imperfections were so slight, Kieran wouldn't have noticed them if she hadn't drawn his attention to them. It was his turn to shake his head. He stepped closer to Maude and twirled a few loose strands of her hair around his finger. His other arm snaked around her waist as he drew her against him. If he would be away for several weeks, possibly a moon or longer, he would be sure she remembered him.

"The only thing you succeeded in doing is making me want to taste your mouth." He lowered his head toward Maude but paused before their lips met. "Has a mon ever kissed you?"

Maude shook her head. A voice in the back of her head wanted to snap "of course nae. What other mon has ever wanted to?" But the sight and smell of Kieran pressed against her filled her senses, and a moment later, she tasted him. His minty breath wafted to her as his lips pressed against hers. For several heartbeats, the kiss consisted of only their lips touching, but he swiped his tongue along the seam of her mouth and pushed it forward with a gentleness that made her give in.

His words about wanting to taste her floated back to her, and she was curious to discover how that would work. Maude already tasted the mint on his breath. She was certain it was from him, even though she had chewed on a sprig on her way to the stables. She opened her mouth, and his tongue dove into her mouth. The sensation was strange, but pleasurable. She moaned in surprise at how much she liked it. The sound encouraged Kieran to pull her fully against his body. The fingers that captured her hair released the strands to cup her jaw. The arm around her waist was like a steel band holding her against him, but he didn't need to grip her. She had no intention of pulling away. Instead, her hands flattened against his chest but were soon roaming over the broad expanse as his muscles shifted and bunched under her touch.

Kieran pulled her onto her toes as the kiss continued. His hand slid from her jaw, along her neck and over her shoulder, grazing her breast before gliding down to her waist and eventually her backside. The sensation of kneading the ample flesh released the beast within. He backed her against the stable wall, pulling her hands free from his chest. He grasped her wrists in one of his much larger hands and trapped them against the wall over her head. His other hand went back to her bottom. He stretched his fingers wide and feared he would spill his seed as he squeezed. He pulled his mouth away long enough to murmur a confession.

"If you were my wife, I'd have my way with you, right here. Do you feel what you do to me?" He pressed his rod against her mons, and when she shifted with restlessness, he once again pulled her onto her toes, slipping his thigh between hers. Maude moaned once again, and Kieran's conscience screamed to let her go before he tossed her skirts. But the small noises she made only chipped away at his control. She twisted her wrists, and he released them in favor of kneading her breast. He was certain he leaked as her breast and bottom spilled out of his hands. Her hands once again roamed over his chest before snaking around his neck.

"What are you doing to me?" She panted when she ripped her lips away, trying to catch her breath before diving back in for more. She was a quick study. Her tongue dueled with his, and even pressed into his mouth. He taught her how to stroke her tongue along his and to tangle them together, but when she tentatively sucked, he accepted he lacked the fortitude to hold back. His cock throbbed as his seed jetted within his breeks. He palmed her backside in both of his hands and rocked her against his thigh. He refused to take his pleasure without ensuring she found hers. She picked up the rhythm and altered it to meet her own body's need. When her nails scored along his scalp and her other hand fisted his leine as her body tensed, he realized she was experiencing her release.

"I'm introducing you to passion, and helping you find your release." Kieran answered her question at last.

"That was---that was---was---I don't even know how to explain it other than I can see that it can be addictive." Maude's grin was back in place and Kieran's heart skipped, knowing he was a rare recipient of her toothy smile.

"I'm happy to feed that addiction, buttercup." He ran the

back of his fingers over her cheek. "I hope you can wait until I return."

Maude peered into the stormy gray eyes and saw doubt for the first time.

"Do you fear that now I know what passion feels like, I'll seek someone else?"

"Yes."

She tugged on his leine until he lowered his head enough for her to initiate their kiss. She was ravenous and aggressive. Kieran hardened again as he pressed her against the wall once more. She nipped at his lip and swept her tongue through his mouth, tilting her head to find a better angle to explore the depths of his satiny cavern. He pressed his thigh between her legs once more but gripped a thigh and lifted it to rest on his hip. He rocked against her. His groan vibrated through her chest. They pulled apart only when they both couldn't last another moment. Maude wasn't sure if the lightheaded sensation was from going too long without a deep breath or from the power of Kieran's kisses. She suspected it was as much the latter as it was the former.

"I don't want anyone else. You're the only teacher I want." She frowned as a concern registered. "What aboot you? You didn't get your turn."

Kieran chuckled before giving her a peck on her lips. He lowered her foot to the ground and stepped back. He used his hand to point to the front of his breeks. While his grin remained in place, his face heated. He hadn't spilled his seed like that since he was an adolescent, but he hadn't been that overcome with lust since he first began coupling.

"You needn't worry aboot that, buttercup. I found mine before I even brought you to yours."

Maude covered her nose and mouth with her hands, so all he saw were eyes wide as saucers. She dragged her hands over her mouth to her chin.

"Ye canna go aboot like that," Maude didn't realize she

had slipped back into her burr. "It'll leave a stain. Everyone will ken when ye get off Peat."

Kieran grinned at how horrified Maude appeared. He stepped back but leaned forward to whisper in her ear. He dropped a kiss at the corner of her jaw as he had the night they met. "Dinna peek, lass. Ye dinna want to see more than ye can handle."

He turned away and reached to unclasp his plaid from his shoulder but missed a step when a quick swat landed on his backside. He swung around, but Maude's hands were tucked behind her back as she rocked on her toes, a questioning expression on her face that would have been convincing if she wasn't trying to swallow her lips to keep from laughing.

"Do that again, and no one will see us til dawn, and I won't be leaving until tomorrow."

Maude's laugh followed Kieran as he ducked into a nearby empty stall. He hated laying his plaid on the floor in the hay, but he had no choice. Maude was right that he couldn't wear his breeks. He wasn't sure which would be worse: people knowing he'd shot his seed in his clothes or people assuming he'd wet himself. Maude was still laughing when he stepped out of the stall, but it died on her lips as she took in the sight of Kieran as a true Highlander. He took her breath away. Her gaze began at the tips of his boots and traveled up to his bare calves and knees to the tiny patch of visible thigh, lingering below his waist before skimming over his broad chest and thick arms before settling on his handsome face. Her body heated all over again. A niggling doubt about why such a braw and handsome man might want her tried to take root, but she pushed it aside as he once more wrapped her in his arms. Rather than kiss her again, Kieran searched for something in her eyes. She feared he wouldn't find what he sought.

"Will you wait for me, Maude?"

"Where would I be going? I live here now."

"That's not what I meant, and I think you know that.

Even if it takes me a moon or two, will you wait until I return for you? You won't replace me?"

"Replace you? I don't want anyone else. I'm not going to turn loose just because you taught me to kiss."

"I'd never assume you'd be loose, but you might find someone else who's here, who can be with you when I can't."

"I hadn't met anyone before you. I doubt there will be anyone else. I don't want anyone else, Kieran."

"I need you to believe me when I say there won't be anyone else for me. We might not have met under the most auspicious circumstances, but I won't touch another woman. Maude, I know you'll worry, and I know you'll try to rationalize it. You'll try to tell yourself men have needs, that I'm neither a virgin nor a monk, and you can't expect me to act like one. You'll wonder if I'll forget aboot you or change my mind, if I'll pass my time with someone from my past." Maude's expression, first startled, then guilty, told him his suspicions were correct. He'd considered her likely fears at length the night before, after palming himself twice as he envisioned her. "I swear to you, Maude. There won't be anyone else because I don't want anyone but you. You're too special to settle for anyone else. There's no substitute for you. I wish I were taking you home with me, and I hope to do just that one day."

Maude wasn't sure what to say, so she nodded. She rested her head against his chest, returning to a comforting place. However, now she wondered how she ever compared him to how her father or brother felt when they embraced her.

"Buttercup, look at me." Kieran waited until her whisky-tinted eyes met his slate-hued ones. "I know we don't know each other well enough for you to completely believe me. I've tried to anticipate your doubts, but I'm sure you'll come up with more. Maude, I've never committed to a woman before, but I'm not the philandering type by nature. I've never courted another woman, but I've known since I was a young mon that I wouldn't consider marriage to any woman I couldn't be faithful to. I want to be faithful out of desire rather than out of duty. No matter who I marry, I will never stray from my wife. I know we're not married, not even handfasted, but I want my intentions to be clear. I intend to marry you, Maude Sutherland. There will never be another."

"How can you be so certain? So adamant?"

"Perhaps it is experience. I know what I feel for you is naught like any experience I've had in the past. I've been in lust. I've been infatuated. But this is different. I don't know how to put it in words, but I can only swear that I know it is. That it's more real, more significant than aught from my past."

Maude listened to Kieran's declarations and, despite her suspicious nature, something about his demeanor and the earnestness of his words and expression made her believe him. She put her finger against his lips then brushed them with her own.

"If I'm your buttercup, are you my turtledove?" Maude murmured.

"I don't know that I'm as delicate as a turtledove, but aye, when I find my mate, it's for life. I'm your turtledove." He buried his nose in her hair, inhaling her fresh lemon verbena scent as though he would imprint it in his mind and heart.

"I'll miss you, buttercup. It's as though you've been a part of my life for ages rather than a few days."

"Do you believe in fate?"

"I didn't before two days ago. Now I do."

"Come back to me, turtledove. I'll be here waiting." Maude graced him with one of her half-smiles, and he thought he found those even more alluring than her grins. "And dinna fash, I willna go aboot caterwauling that name when ye return."

Her smile transformed into that broad, open-mouth grin, and he questioned his thought from only a moment ago. Her smile transformed her face from ordinary to a picture of beauty.

"I must go now, or I'll never be able to leave you, buttercup."

"I know."

They kept their kiss short, lest they lose control again. Maude walked out of the stables with Kieran and Peat. The sun still hadn't risen, and a little mist hung low. Kieran looked around before wrapping his arm around her waist and kissing her cheek.

"Promise me you'll be careful and not take any unneeded risks. I'll worry anyway without you coming to trouble." He kissed her once more before hoisting himself into his saddle. He clenched the reins to keep from pulling Maude into the saddle before him and riding away with her somewhere no one recognized them. They would go to neither MacLeod territory nor Sutherland; rather, somewhere they'd just be buttercup and turtledove, not laird or laird's daughter. "If you need me, you need only send a missive, Maude."

"I'll be fine. I'm used to it here."

"Aye, mayhap, but I also know that you'll fret that you're taking me away from my people when I'm leaving to handle an emergency. You're just as important to me. Write me, and I will come."

Maude nodded and squeezed the hand he offered her. She watched him clatter out of the bailey. He looked back twice before they could no longer spy one another through the light fog. Maude returned to her chamber and climbed back into bed, squeezing her eyes shut to keep her tears from falling. Kieran forced himself to keep his eyes on the road and his surroundings, rather than picturing Maude as she came apart in his arms. He felt as though something had been torn from him, and now he was incomplete.

CHAPTER SEVEN

One week bled into another until nearly a moon had passed. It had shocked Maude to receive a missive from Kieran only a sennight after he left. He must have dispatched his messenger within hours of returning to Stornoway. It was a brief message, but one that reassured her that he arrived in one piece. He would travel two days after his arrival to Assynt, where the raid took place. Her heart sank when she read his destination. While any loss to Kieran's clan saddened her, she had hoped that the raid had taken place on Lewis or even Glenelg which was further south. Assynt bordered both Mackay and Sutherland territories. Both clans were her family. She was born a Sutherland, but her aunt had married the Sinclair laird, and her cousin Mairghread Sinclair had married the Mackay laird, Tristan. Her cousin now lived at Castle Varrich with her husband and bairns. The messenger awaited a response from her, but she wasn't sure if she should dare ask the man what he knew of the events. She opted not to involve the courier and asked Kieran instead.

It was close to a fortnight before she received his response, but she had already heard from her father. She was already aware the blame lay with the Sutherlands living near the border of Mackay and MacLeod territories. She avoided going into detail when she wrote to her father, but informed him that she had learned of the attack and their clan's involvement concerned her. Kieran's second missive was brusque and short. He outlined what he'd learned of the events and what his people told him. He admitted he would have to parlay with her father to resolve the matter. It was the final five lines that reassured Maude that the conflict hadn't ruined their chances.

This would be so much easier to deal with if you were by my side. I feel as though you would know what to tell my people during this time of sorrow, and I believe you would offer me sound council. I miss you, buttercup. I hope to return before the moon is up.

Maude wasn't convinced any words she offered would be a welcomed comfort, since they would come from the daughter of the laird whose people killed his. However, the thought that he trusted her opinion warmed her. Maude replied honestly and told him that she had already learned of the events from her father, and that his intentions were to meet with Kieran. She asked if they'd agreed to where the meeting would occur. She hadn't wanted to appear curious by asking too much of her father. At the fortnight mark, Kieran had hoped to return within the next fourteen days, but Maude lost hope that there was time for her father and Kieran to meet and have him return before the new month began.

His third missive came six days before a moon would have passed. She realized Kieran must have dispatched the missive four days earlier. He wrote that he and her father agreed to meet at court as they both had matters to attend to that couldn't wait.

I don't know what brings your father to court, but I would return to you as soon as I can. I want to see your smile, hear the burr you try to hide, and feel you in my arms. I've said naught of us to your father. I wanted to ask how you would like to proceed. I intend to leave in five days. I shall dispatch a messenger the day before to confirm my departure, and it's my fervent hope to meet my messenger on the road and perhaps deliver my final missive in person. I miss you, buttercup.

Maude cherished the pet name; neither she nor Kieran used their real names to address or sign the missives in case someone should intercept them. Her response was simple and took but a moment for her to write before she shooed the exhausted rider back to his mount.

Turtledove,

I eagerly await your return to the nest. While your messengers have been most polite, I would rather receive your next missive from your own hands. I cannot offer the messengers a token of thanks, but I can offer one to you. What boon would you request?

Maude's heart was heavy as she pushed the food around on her tray. She had slept poorly the previous three nights as she grew excited for Kieran and her father to arrive. She and Blair both missed their father. All three Sutherland children were close to their parents, who still doted on them. Her father's father had been a cruel man who mistreated his children, in particular his only daughter, her Aunt Kyla. She had faded memories of her father's sister, who allowed her to climb into her lap while she told stories to her own five children along with Maude, Blair, and Lachlan. Her father swore to be nothing like his father when it came to parenting and leading their clan.

She'd received a notice that her father would arrive late that night, but she'd heard nothing from Kieran, and the day was almost done. It was the last day of the month, and it disappointed her to not see Kieran. She understood anything from a new clan matter to the weather might have slowed his progress. However, she had received no missive informing her of his departure. She had no sign that he was making his way to Stirling.

Maude stood from her seat and pulled her robe tighter as she poked at the peat in her fireplace, making her think of Kieran's horse for the hundredth time. She had kept her spirits up throughout Kieran's time away, but she'd grown melancholy over the past two days. She'd had another run in with Laurel and Madeline that left her shaken and humiliated. Maude had no desire to tell Kieran what happened, but she wished she could lean her head against his chest, his steady heartbeat against her cheek. She wandered to her bed and pulled back the covers further before pulling the sash at her waist. Before she had the opportunity to shrug out of her robe, someone pounded on her door. The only person she knew who knocked like that was her father. She tied her robe, and her face relaxed into a smile. If she wasn't to be in Kieran's arms, then an embrace from her father wasn't a poor substitute.

Maude pulled the door open and squeaked. Kieran's arm shot out to wrap around her waist as he lifted her off her feet. He pressed the door open wider and stepped inside her chamber before kicking the door shut behind them. Maude clung to him as their mouths sought one another. His hands slid down to her backside as he pulled her against him with such force, he feared he might hurt her. Her hands fisted in his leine, and she continued to pull him closer even when there was no space between them.

Another round of knocking interrupted their reunion. Kieran eased her to the ground and placed his finger over his mouth. He stepped beside the door, knowing it would shield him once it was open. Maude opened the door and squeaked once again.

"Da!"

"Aye, lass." He gave his daughter a quick squeeze and bussed a kiss on her cheek before pushing into her chamber. "Where the bluidy hell is he?"

"Da?"

"Dinna look innocent, lass. I saw MacLeod enter yer chamber." Maude noticed her father was out of breath, and realized he must have run to reach her chamber when he was already on his way. Kieran had arrived sooner. "He's been kissing ye, Maude. I can tell. Where is the bluidy lecher?"

Laird Hamish Sutherland grasped the door, suspecting where the man would be hiding. He slammed it shut and rounded on Kieran, who held his hands away from his sides, making it clear he held no weapon.

"Explain. Now." Hamish barked. He looked between Maude and Kieran before growling when neither answered fast enough.

"Da, please, come sit down." Maude took her father's hand and led him to one of the two chairs in the chamber. Kieran stepped near her despite Hamish's warning glare. He moved the other chair closer to the one she offered her father. Hamish didn't sit until Maude did, but he fixed his gaze on Kieran, who stood behind Maude with his hands on the back of her chair. It was both possessive and protective.

"Leave off, MacLeod. I'm nae going to lash out at ma lass. I may strike ye, but I'd never harm ma daughter."

"Da--"

"Laird Sutherland--"

Maude looked back at Kieran, who nodded to her.

"Da, I met Laird MacLeod—Kieran— just before he had to return to Lewis. I was upset one eve after overhearing a conversation I wasn't intended to, and Kieran was kind to me. He stayed with me until Arabella found me on the terrace." She looked back at Kieran and offered him the chance to speak.

"Laird Sutherland, this happened before I had the chance

63

to learn of the attack in Assynt. It's for your daughter's sake that I didn't lead a hot-trod to regain my cattle or to seek revenge. I asked Lady Maude for permission to court her before I received the missive calling me home."

"Did ye now? And how do ye ken I dinna already have plans to wed Maude to someone else?"

Hamish watched as the knuckles on both of Kieran's hands turned ghostly white as his fingers clutched the wood. A vein pulsed in his neck as the cords strained.

"I would request you reconsider. I've formed an attachment to Maude that is genuine and special. I ask that you give us time to see if it develops into more."

"Och aye, I'm sure ye do," Hamish scoffed. "I believe it already has looking at ma daughter's red chin. I'd say it looks an awful lot like a beard rubbed against it."

"Da, if you've someone else in mind, please don't move forward with it. Give us more time."

Hamish looked at the young couple and remembered a situation similar to this one, except it involved himself and his wife when he fell in love with her at first sight.

"For starters, I dinna care for ye sounding like a bluidy Lowlander. I hope this manner of speaking dinna stick. Second, yer cousin says the young laird is quite attached to ye. Apparently, he was ready to come to blows with a priest over ye. That must be an awfully powerful connection to risk yer soul within a sennight of meeting one another."

Maude shot out of her chair but sank back into it just as abruptly. Kieran didn't care for how she looked, as though she might cry. Despite the discomfort of being found together, he recognized it delighted Maude to see her father, at least until she realized he was already aware of the secret she kept from him. Kieran shifted toward Hamish and watched him as the back of his fingers skimmed Maude's shoulder blades.

"Enough, damn it! I told ye I dinna harm ma bairns!" Hamish glared at Kieran. "Ye dinna need to be ready to spring at me as though I might attack her. I might go after ye, but never Maude."

Maude's brow furrowed at her father's unexpected outburst. She leaned her head forward as though she might study her father better if she were closer. The dim light from the fireplace made it more difficult for her to see.

"Yer mon is positioning himself between ye and me in case I should try to strike ye."

"He is?" Maude asked her father before turning toward Kieran. "You are?"

"Your father didn't gain his reputation by sitting at home and going to fat."

Hamish chuckled and eased back in his chair before crossing his arms over his chest and his ankles as he stretched out his legs. "As long as ye ken that, lad, we may get along."

"Are you saying you might consider Kieran's suit?"

"Aye. Between seeing ye together, which I amnae pleased aboot mind ye, and Michael's missive, I feel better than I did when I was ready to run Kieran through a few minutes ago. Just because I agree that ye may court ma daughter dinna mean ye're allowed back here. I shall post Donald or Tomas at yer door, lass, if I canna trust yer mon.

"Laird Sutherland, I returned only this evening. You might be able to tell I came here directly from leaving my horse at the stables. I've not visited Lady Maude here before, and I will not return. But I promised her I would be back before the new moon began, and I refuse to break my word. I feared I'd wake her, or she would sleep through my knocking if I waited any longer."

"Ye look surprisingly clean for a mon fresh off a sennight of travel."

Kieran grinned at Hamish as the older man gave him a pointed look.

"I may have pulled a clean leine from my satchel and used a freshwater trough in the stables to clean up a mite before seeking Lady Maude's company."

"Aye well," Hamish's lips pulled tight before he grinned at Maude and stood. "Come 'ere, lass. I didna get a proper hug."

Maude sank into her father's arms. It was like having an enormous bear wrap her in a cocoon. She closed her eyes as the heat seeped from his larger frame into hers, and it reminded her of being a child. She had never felt as safe as she did with her father until she met Kieran.

"Thank ye, Da," she murmured as she squeezed him. Hamish dropped a kiss on the crown of her head before easing his arms away. His heart expanded when she didn't pull away. His little girl still appreciated his affection.

"I suppose we can do away with the formalities." Hamish stuck his arm out to Kieran, who grasped it around the forearm. "I'm Hamish to ye now. And ye dinna need to keep up the pretense of calling ma lass 'Lady' when we are together. I ken ye dinna use titles between the two of ye."

"Thank you. Hamish. And I'm Kieran."

"I ken, lad. I met ye for the first time when ye were in raggies. Handsome even then. All the ladies cooed over him." Kieran recognized the test for what it was.

"There's only one lady I'll let coo over me, and it isn't my ma. Hamish, I speak the truth when I say Maude is the only woman I want." Kieran placed his hands on Maude's shoulders as he stepped behind her. Hamish watched his self-conscious daughter blossom at the mere touch of the man claiming to care for her. He prayed Kieran didn't disappoint Maude or there would be a clan war after he killed Kieran.

"It grows late. I shall await ye in the passageway, Kieran. Dinna dillydally." Hamish walked to the door and looked back. Maude was already in Kieran's arms, his head resting on top of hers as they held one another. Neither noticed as Hamish slipped out of the chamber.

Maude inhaled the fresh pine and sandalwood scent once again. She'd wondered how he smelled so clean when he arrived. He cupped her face in his large hands and kissed the tip of her nose before drawing her into a searing kiss that left them both groaning as they pulled apart.

"Will you allow me to escort you on a walk tomorrow morn?"

Maude bit her bottom lip, and Kieran pounced. His tongue pressed her lips apart before he nipped at the bottom lip she'd sunk her own teeth into. Their tongues dueled once again before a singular knock came at the door, warning them that her father's patience was dwindling.

"I'd very much like that, but if we go in the morning, the queen and ladies will be there."

"Do you fear I won't want people to realize I came to join you? Or would you rather people not see you're linked to me?"

"I'm not worried for myself."

"Buttercup, don't look for trouble where there is none. I'd very much like for people to see us together. I'm proud to have garnered your consent to court you."

"But that's not what they'll say. They wouldn't have said that before, and now that news of the clash has made it to court, people will say my father sold me to you as repayment for what happened to your clan."

"Let someone say as much, and they won't be long for this world."

"But they will. Perhaps not to *your* face, but they will."

"You worry aboot Madeline."

"Among others," Maude sighed.

"What happened?"

Before there was time for Maude to explain, the door burst open with Hamish glaring at Kieran. "I warned ye nae to dillydally."

"Hamish, I would ask you to give us a moment. Something's happened between Maude and my sister. She's been unkind to Maude before, and I would find out what Madeline's done now."

"You sound as though you'd defend Maude." Hamish's skepticism was clear.

"Of course I will. Even if I wasn't aware of my sister's mean streak, I would still defend Maude before any others. I intend for her to be my wife. She comes first." Kieran sensed Hamish was testing him, but he couldn't keep himself from being provoked when it came to protecting Maude. Whether it was from potential highwaymen or his sister's viperous tongue, he refused to back down if there was any chance Maude might be hurt.

"Vera well. I shall send Donald to stand guard outside yer door, lass. He will tell me how long the lad stays."

"Da, can we come to the Sutherland suite instead? Wouldn't it be easier if we use the solar? That way you can be certain how long Kieran stays?"

"It would, but I dinna want ye wandering the passageways alone when ye return here, and it seems to defeat the point if Kieran escorts ye right back here."

"I can stay in my old chamber."

"Vera well. Come along."

CHAPTER EIGHT

Maude compromised with her father and agreed to leave the connecting door between the family solar and her parents' dressing chamber open. Her father retired to his chamber, leaving his door ajar. While she negotiated with her father, Kieran built up the fire in the solar and in the chamber where Maude would sleep. When she returned to the solar, she peered over her shoulder but didn't see her father moving about. Kieran took her hand and led her to a loveseat, but rather than sit side-by-side, he pulled her into his lap and arranged her so she had room to stretch her legs on the open cushion. She leaned her head against his chest and closed her eyes. Kieran didn't rush her to tell the story; he enjoyed the peaceful embrace as much as she did. It was only when he feared one of them would drift off that he asked what happened.

"When you informed your sister aboot your departure, you must have looked one too many times at Arabella. Madeline began demanding Bella explain why you were looking at her and how long you'd been lovers. Bella insisted that you only looked at her because she was restless and couldn't stand still. Bella had already told me aboot how Madeline tried to push Laurel toward you, but you weren't interested. She told

Bella that your parents had practically promised you and Laurel to one another since the cradle. I figured she was trying to get a rise out of Bella, but it was my face that must have reacted. I didn't even feel it, but the next thing I know, Madeline is standing in front of me, in the Great Hall just as the evening meal is aboot to start, laughing and pointing. She demanded I explain why I would care who you were intended for. She mocked me, saying you would only look my way if you needed a sow to roast or if you wished to lure a wildcat since I have plenty of meat to spare." Maude had stood in silence as Madeline humiliated her, refusing to add to the scene by caterwauling like his sister.

"When she finished, I leaned forward and said either way it meant you wanted me, which was more than she could say aboot any mon at court. I should have left well enough alone and continued to ignore her, but she got the better of my temper. Once I insulted her, she began accusing the Sutherlands of massacring your people. That we intended to overrun the MacLeods of Assynt and steal their land from honest, God-fearing people. Madeline called my father and brother butchers. She swung back around to her earlier comments, adding you'd only want me if you could toss me in a dungeon to rot as punishment to my father. She said even the rats in Stornoway wouldn't want me."

Kieran sat stunned. He believed every word Maude said. He knew his sister all too well. His only disbelief was that his sister was that naïve or that narrow sighted to not recognize the damage her ranting might do to their clan. The Sinclairs and Mackays were the Sutherlands' allies, which meant they greatly outnumbered the MacLeods of Assynt. It was that reason that the rogue band of Sutherland cattle rustlers attacked. If Madeline didn't still her tongue, she would cause a feud between the MacLeods and the Sutherlands along with their neighbors. The sept in Assynt was far too small to defend itself, which would mean he'd need to send men from Lewis to protect them. If he did that, he'd weaken his own defenses at

Stornoway. Beyond that, Madeline once again humiliated the clan by showing her mean-spiritedness in public. He'd received inquiries from the Matheson laird looking for a wife for his fourth son. What he needed more than a woman was the bride's dowry that accompanied her. But Kieran was familiar with the man, and his sons were all close to his own age. Of all Matheson's sons, the fourth one was the best suited to deal with a hoyden like his sister. Kieran didn't fear the man would ever raise a hand against Madeline, but he wouldn't tolerate her behavior either. He would respond to the missive he'd received while at home. He would make arrangements to send Madeline to a new home and new husband.

"You've gone awfully quiet." Kieran hated hearing the timidity in Maude's voice. She might have been shy and self-conscious, but she wasn't timid.

"I'll arrange a marriage for Madeline to the Matheson's fourth son."

"Not because of me." Maude tried to scramble off Kieran's lap, but he kept her in place and kissed her temple.

"Not entirely. Madeline's lack of diplomacy at court makes her a danger to our clan's standing, not only here, but at home. If she's willing to insult the Sutherlands without fear of repercussions, then she has no clue how clan matters work. She would risk a feud with your father, which would rally the Sinclairs and Mackays against us when Assynt is unprotected. To make sure they'd have a fighting chance, I'd have to send men from Lewis, which would only weaken us against the MacDonalds and the Mackenzies. Beyond that, her behavior reflects badly on our people. I don't want my clan, my family in particular, to be known for being spiteful and hateful. That won't strengthen any of our alliances. Who wants to be seen supporting a clan in disgrace?"

"Once she knows you're courting me, she'll put two and two together and find me at fault for her being sent into exile."

"I don't want to hide that I'm courting you. I'm proud to be asking for your hand, but I also don't want to put you at risk for more of my sister's vitriol while she's still here. Nor do I want to ruin any chance of a peaceful keep when she visits us. I'm certain she'll hold a grudge." Kieran stroked Maude's back until she leaned against him once more.

"Then I think, for now, you pursue the betrothal with the Mathesons if you believe it would be a good match for her, not a hurried one to distance her from court. Once that's secure, you can take her to her new home. After that, we can make it known that you are courting me."

"Buttercup, that might take months. I don't want to be forced to skulk aboot trying to steal a few minutes with you here and there. How're we supposed to get to ken one another if we can never see each other?"

Maude nodded against his chest. "Especially since I suspect we wouldn't spend those few stolen moments in conversation." She giggled when Kieran pinched her bottom.

"Cheeky lass." He palmed her backside and squeezed, ensuring she understood his double entendre.

"Only for you," Maude purred. The sultriness of her own voice surprised her. Kieran growled low in his throat and tilted her chin back to kiss her. His hand trailed down her neck to her breast. She still wore her nightgown and robe, so her nipple pebbled beneath his ministrations.

"You tempt me far too much. Your father will find us with my hand up your nightgown and your breast bared if you continue with that voice. It goes straight to my cock."

"And does what?" Maude shifted to make her hip graze along his rod. She noticed it harden when she sat on his lap, and it had grown the longer she remained pressed against him.

"What have I unleashed?" Kieran's hand kneaded her breast.

"Only time shall tell."

"And it's time for him to retire," came a voice from the other side of the door.

Maude and Kieran looked at each other and struggled to

smother their laughter. Kieran eased Maude from his lap and walked with her to the door of her chamber. He looked back at the solar, reassured that the angle of the doorways would keep Hamish from seeing him enter Maude's chamber.

"Be quick, buttercup, and I shall tuck you in."

Maude's eyes grew wide, but she nodded. She hurried across the room to the bed. She kicked off her slippers and tossed the robe on the foot of the bed before diving under the covers. She pulled them up to her chin and kept darting nervous glances at the door.

"Even if he follows us in here, all he will see is me giving you a chaste kiss goodnight. It's all I can manage when we're so close to a bed." Kieran brushed the loose hair from her cheek. He had noticed the thick braid that hung down her back, but he hadn't commented on it. He wondered what she would look like with her hair unbound, it spread over her pillow and his chest. He groaned before dropping a kiss on her forehead.

"Are you all right?" Maude whispered.

"Aye, just picturing you in a manner I shouldn't until you're my wife, yet my mind keeps returning to."

"Is it any consolation that my mind does the same thing?"

Kieran choked as he looked at Maude, who looked virginal in her white nightgown against white sheets pulled to her chin. Yet her words proved she had a wildness that reminded him of why he'd started calling her buttercup.

"Nay. It doesn't help a whit. It only makes me want to climb in beside you, but if we're to marry and have a family, I'll need your father not to geld me. Goodnight, my bonnie lass. Sleep well."

"Sleep well, my braw protector." Kieran pulled away before their kiss grew more heated. Showing restraint was one of the greatest feats of his life when his mind and his body screamed for him to stay. He crossed the room and paused at the door. Maude had rolled to her side and watched him.

When he returned her smile, her eyes drifted closed, and he shut the door behind him.

Kieran's head jerked up as his heart sank when Hamish's voice greeted him.

"Ye may have spoken quietly, but with nay other noise in the suite, yer voices carry. Did ye ken that I kenned that?"

Kieran followed Hamish, who waved him over to the whisky decanter. Hamish poured them both a dram and gestured toward the table with several chairs around it. Kieran realized it was where their family would dine when they were in residence and chose not to go to the Great Hall.

"Ye're good for her. She's like a spring bloom that's had too much heavy rain dropped on it. She will blossom, but she needs a reprieve from what weighs her down. Michael wrote that he shared a bit aboot Maude's childhood, or rather the time when she became a young woman. She'd played along-side her brother since she could chase after him. Blair did too, but she hasnae loved being outside like ma Maude. She ran, swam, climbed trees, and rode along with her brother. While some women turn lean from so much activity, Maude did the opposite. I would still wager on her to win any horse race even if she wasna riding Trioblaid. She can still best most of ma archers, and I caught her climbing an apple tree the last time she was home since they'd already picked all the low hanging fruit. She learned to do all these things to keep up with Lachlan. Blair preferred to be inside, but Maude has a wild streak to her, but ye'd nae guess it from how shy she's grown. Without Blair to play with, it was difficult for the laird's daughter to play with other children her age. That's why she worked hard to keep up with Lachlan. Lachlan grew tired of being teased aboot his wee sister always trailing behind her. Rather than speaking to her, he did what a lad of four-and-ten is wont to do. He passed along the teasing because it embarrassed him. He and Michael began the taunting, but the other lads grew far meaner. Michael's ma mother's sister's grandson. He grew up in a croft within the walls, and until he left to become a monk, he was Lachlan's closest friend."

"He seems very close to Maude now. I didn't realize they were related until the end of our visit, after I made an arse of myself in front of Michael and my jealousy nearly drove Maude away.

"Ye remind me a great deal of maself when I met ma wife, but that is a story for another day. It wasna until after the fact that Lady Sutherland and I learned of what the lads were saying to Maude. They told her she looked more like a mon than a woman because of her strength. They teased her aboot being built differently than the lanky lasses her age. They kenned she was strong, but they didna ken that that's why she wasna light as a feather. When she developed, the boys began making crude comments aboot how they wished the wenches at the tavern had her attributes. All the while, they teased her aboot being the plain one. They would ask why Blair got all the looks, and she got all the girth."

Hamish paused to collect himself, and Kieran realized retelling this story pained Hamish. The older man blinked several times before he continued. Kieran sat in silence, refusing to risk Hamish ending the conversation.

"She began starving herself and refused to go outside. Her mother and I thought she was taking more of an interest in learning to be chatelaine because she understood she was approaching a marriageable age. We didna realize she was hiding, retreating into herself. Blair tried to tell us, but Lachlan laughed it away, and since she'd spent more time with him than with Blair, their mother and I listened to Lachlan. It wasna until Lachlan sought Lady Sutherland and me to say he noticed Maude was acting strangely that we truly paid attention. The four of us noticed Maude arrived after meals began, offered to get aught or do aught that would take her away from the table, took the smallest servings, even slipping food under the table to the dogs, and excusing herself as soon as she could."

Hamish looked at the door to Maude's chamber and wished the same thing he had wished for years: that he had the power to go back and rescue his little girl before insecurity and self-doubt took hold. He'd understood that trying to get slimmer was only a partial reason for Maude's disinterest in eating. He recognized that she believed she possessed little control over her life and her appearance other than what she ate. He'd seen his brothers do the same, except they'd used an excess of alcohol where Maude fasted. His brothers felt powerless in the face of their belittling and belligerent father, and Maude felt powerless to the unrelenting teasing.

"One afternoon, Lachlan tried to coax Maude to go for a ride with him or to go down to the loch, but she declined, saying she needed to finish her sewing. She was retreating to her chamber as she did most days, but Lachlan refused to give up. Thank the blessed angels and saints that he didna. She collapsed on the stairs and pitched backwards. Lachlan grabbed her and stopped her from rolling more than two or three steps. He bellowed for me and their ma while he carried Maude to her chamber. He was as white as a sheet when ma wife and I arrived. Lachlan shook as he told us how one moment she was refusing to go outside, and the next he looked back to see her tumble backwards. It took the healer all of five minutes to determine what was wrong with Maude. She'd passed out from hunger. When Lady Sutherland stepped out to speak to me in the passageway, she was inconsolable. Maude's kirtles hid the wrong things. While she looked to have a wide-set build, her ribs were practically poking through her skin and her hip bones stuck out so far from her stomach being so flat, that the healer pinched them."

"Is she—is she still that way?" It embarrassed Kieran to ask her father such a question, but he feared for Maude's health. He wanted to bundle her up in his plaid and run far away from anyone who might hurt her.

"Nay, lad. She isnae. But even after months of coaxing and encouragement to eat again, she never came out of her shell. It devastated Lachlan when he learned what was wrong. He shouldered the entire guilt even though we were all to blame for nae noticing and speaking up sooner. He developed a reputation for being a hothead, but it was only when it came to comments aboot Maude. A few of the lads realized that they had the power to goad him in the lists by continuing to make fun of Maude. He and Michael ended up in a brawl against the other young warriors who had once been my son's and cousin's friends. I'd been aboot to step in and cease the crude taunting, but before anyone realized I'd entered the lists, Lachlan and Michael launched themselves at the ringleaders. I hated seeing my son take so many fists to the face and ribs, but I recognized he believed he needed to prove and redeem himself. The fight didna last long, as he and Michael partnered throughout the years and complimented each other's fighting style."

"Did the taunting cease?" Kieran held his breath, fearful that Hamish would say no. He didn't want to keep Maude from her clan, but he couldn't imagine ever taking her somewhere where people would mistreat her. It was bad enough that she had to remain at court.

"Aye. Mind ye, this was aboot four years ago. Some lads grew up and matured past their nastiness. The others discovered that I'm even less forgiving of those who treat ma family poorly. One of the many sad parts to this whole story is that everyone loves Maude. She's got a generous soul and compassion that's helped heal many patients. She has a quick wit and an agile mind, but she doesnae see these things in herself. Even though she rides and hunts and swims again, she lives in Blair's shadow and now even more so with her friend Arabella. She sees naught but how plain she believes is when she compares herself to her sister and friend. Blair's written to us aboot some of the incidents here, and it's tempted me to demand the king order his wife to release ma lasses from her service. I'm sorry to say, but I've heard aboot how yer sister treats Maude. It made it into more than one of Blair's missives. It seems Madeline stepped into Mary Kerr's role of being the ringleader of the ladies-in-waiting and is as sharp tongued as her predecessor."

"Mary Kerr? She's the one who was Archibald Hay's mistress. Something to do with your nephew Magnus."

"Aye. That is a story that requires several more drams of whisky before I can tell it. Too many lives came close to ending in ma family, and a few didna end soon enough in the Hay and Kerr clans." Hamish refilled his mug and Kieran's before settling back into his seat. "I tell ye all this so ye can understand Maude because she can seem to have many contradictory traits. She's brave and wild, even reckless at times, but she'll retreat into herself if she perceives she's inferior to the women around her. It's as though other women smell her insecurity, and the more she shies away, the more they dog her steps. She willna engage unless pushed too far, but she keeps from lashing out because her mind is agile and fast. But that only leads to cutting comebacks that can go deeper than even the worst taunts thrown at her. She understands the power words have and how she canna take them back. She's cautious nae to commit the same sins she would be avenging. She's picked up on tiny flaws that nay one notices but her, but she's certain they're the first thing anyone sees when they meet her. Her weight and body are the most obvious, but she doesnae like her teeth. Something aboot them nae being spaced right. She doesnae care for her hair. She believes it's the color of mud and matches her muddy colored eyes. She doesnae admit this to many, but she has trouble seeing distances that most people can see with ease. She says she can see the same things, but they're blurry."

"She doesn't like her hair, her eyes, her teeth, her body. What's left that she does like?" Kieran looked back at her door and wished once more to take her away from court, and even her clan, if they caused her painful memories.

"She kens she's bright and has a keen mind for herbals and medicinals. She enjoys treating animals as much as, if nae more than, people. She finds it rewarding since rarely do the sickly care what their healer looks like as long as they improve. She kens people trust her because she cares for each person she tends. She's loyal to her last breath and enjoys kenning her friends and family trust her. She just can never believe why anyone cares aboot her. She doesnae see what we all do."

"Hamish, what is it like for her when she returns to Sutherland?"

"It's her home. It always will be nay matter where she settles with a husband and family of her own. She kens she's loved and appreciated there, and she kens she'll always be wanted and welcomed. But it holds painful memories. We all have memories from our past that haunt us, that linger long after the event fades in others' minds. I imagine ye have ones of yer own from yer childhood, but that doesnae make Stornoway any less yer home. I wish I could undo what a handful of eejits wrecked, but the vast majority of our clan kens how special ma lassie is. They adore her, and perhaps even more so because she doesnae realize it."

Kieran sat back in his chair as he stared into his whisky. He let everything Hamish shared settle as he reviewed what he learned. He swirled the liquid before taking a quaff. He looked back into the mug before finishing its contents.

"Her eyes remind me of the different ages of whisky. Close to the center is whisky that has only been in the barrel a few months, but the outside rim is like the finest uisge beatha aged for years. It has a smoky hue and warms you from the inside out, just as Maude's eyes do when they crinkle at the sides the rare times she smiles. I mean, really smiles. I know she dislikes her teeth; she told me as much, and that's why she doesn't like to smile wide because she fears people will notice the imperfection. So those rare smiles are as priceless as the finest aged whisky." Kieran looked up to catch Hamish watching him. "I shall disabuse her of the idea that her hair and eyes resemble mud."

"Be patient with her. She has a great deal to offer if she

didna let herself live in other people's shadows. Dinna let her hide from herself or others."

"You are entrusting me with something precious and rare. I won't break that trust. I want you to have faith that I will protect Maude and do my best to make her happy."

"That's what I hope for in ma future son-by-marriage."

"Does that mean you'll consider my suit? That is if Maude wishes to marry me, you'll agree?"

"I do. If ye can nae punish her for the sins of a few members of her clan, then I consent."

Kieran glowered at Hamish. "I'm insulted you even feel the need to ask. What happened has naught to do with Maude. It had little to do with either you or me, but we are the ones with the responsibility for fixing it. It's bad enough that she's convinced people will think the only reason I'll marry her is for restitution. I don't need you whittling aboot whether I'll abuse her. Haven't you already seen how I react when I think there may be a threat to her? I'm hardly aboot to be one myself."

"Vera well. Then we shall see how things unfold. Ye and I can meet again tomorrow as lairds rather than as a father and a swain." Both men stood and once again shook forearms. Kieran returned his mug to the table and moved toward the door to Maude's chamber. Hamish was already walking in that direction. "Where do ye think ye're going?"

Kieran held up his hands in surrender. "I only wanted to check on her."

Hamish jutted his chin out as his lips flattened into a thin line. "So did I."

Both men crept to Maude's door. Hamish eased it open, and they peered in. Maude's shoulder rose and fell while she lay on her side, turned away from the door. Hamish prepared to shut the door when her groggy voice carried to them. "Night, Da. Night, turtledove."

"Turtledove?" Hamish chortled once the door was closed.

"Aye," Kieran's tone brooked no further comment, yet it almost challenged Hamish to say more.

"Goodnight, lad." Hamish clapped his hand on Kieran's shoulder as Kieran stepped into the passageway.

"Thank you, Hamish. For everything. Goodnight."

CHAPTER NINE

The next morning, Kieran followed Maude's suggestion for discretion. Rather than join her for a constitutional in the gardens with the queen and other ladies-in-waiting, he returned to his chamber after breaking his fast. He sorted through his recent correspondence and found the one from Laird Matheson. It didn't take long to draft a response outlining Madeline's dowry and his conditions for her safe-keeping should she be left a widow, especially one with daughters. He dispatched the missive and hoped Laird Matheson didn't propose having the couple meet beforehand. Madeline had the tendency to belittle and look down upon others even as a child, but she hadn't unleashed her worst cruelty until she arrived at court. It fed an ugly part of her that Kieran prayed would go back into hibernation once she was away from the intrigue and competition of the other ladies-in-waiting. He worried Madeline would ruin this opportunity, and in fact any opportunity, to marry if she met the potential groom too soon before the nuptials. He had a moment of guilt as he wondered how she would fit in with three older sisters-by-marriage. He hoped her husband and new family reined her in, or he might open his keep's door to find her there.

Once he dispatched the letter with his best rider, he

returned to other correspondence that had gone untended during the crisis at home. He found more than one that contained the same message he'd just sent, except these inquired whether he was interested in a bride. He kept his responses brief. He thanked the laird for his interest but politely declined, explaining he wasn't looking for a bride. He didn't include that he wasn't looking because he hoped he'd already found one.

He ventured to the lists and was in time to spy the ladies returning from their morning walk. It took only a moment for his eyes to seek Maude. She huddled into her cloak, her cowl up against the brisk morning air, as she walked with Arabella and Blair. She glanced at him and offered her half-smile, but nothing more. Her gaze snapped back to in front of her as she listened to the conversation flow around her. Kieran was determined to meet with Maude everyday even while they waited for him to arrange Madeline's marriage. He wouldn't accept a long betrothal for his sister. If the Mathesons were unprepared to marry off their son within the next few moons, he would search elsewhere. He entered the lists, and while his mind failed to put Maude aside, he spent the rest of the morning and into the afternoon swinging his sword. It was cathartic.

⚜

Maude was miserable. She awoke with a headache just as she'd gone to bed with one. The noise from the other ladies' chatter grated on her nerves, but she plastered on her serene expression and joined in the walk. Seeing her father the night before had been both exciting and exhausting. She'd laid in bed listening to her father recount her endless streams of humiliation, and while she wanted to sink into a hole never to return, it relieved her to not be the one to tell Kieran about her past. She was embarrassed and found it hard to meet Kieran's eye when she passed him on the return to the castle. She spent the morning in the queen's solar sewing, but she retired to her chamber in the afternoon for a lie down. She drifted in and out of sleep until Arabella returned and informed her it was time to dress for dinner. She'd shared an abridged version of what happened when Maude visited Kieran in the stables before he departed. She retold the previous night's incidents in detail, including what her father told Kieran. Arabella sat while Maude spoke, then wrapped her friend in her arms while Maude fought unsuccessfully to hold back tears.

"We are more alike than we realized," Arabella spoke when they drew apart at last. "I had much the same issue with food when I was becoming a woman. Except mine came from the pressure to always be pretty. I couldn't control how God made me any more than anyone else, but I could control what I ate. If I had to live up to everyone's expectations of beauty, then I would do so on my terms. Turns out I decided those terms were not eating enough. I was lucky not to collapse on the stairs. Instead, I did it during Mass. The priest screamed the devil possessed me. My poor mother was quick-witted enough to say it wasn't the devil but the Holy Spirit. Apparently, the joy of God's presence overcame so much that I collapsed. A couple days in bed with my mother supervising my meals helped me improve. But Maude, know that even I struggle to eat when people are around. I fear they're watching me and judging me for how much I eat. It's also why you're the only person I let call me Bella. It's too much pressure otherwise. I'm certain you'd love me as a sister no matter what I look like."

"How sad is it that *this*," Maude waved a hand about. "Is another thing that binds our friendship?"

"It just proves we're kindred spirits."

"Not possessed of the Holy One?"

Arabella giggled. "Most certainly not. At least not after what you've been up to with Laird MacLeod." She wiggled her eyebrows. "Was it wonderful? I mean is kissing him as mesmerizing as it's made to sound in poetry?"

"It is. But I don't think it would be with someone else. It's because it's Kieran."

Arabella nodded but remained quiet. It made Maude uneasy as she wondered what her friend thought about that made her withdraw.

"What is it?"

"Naught," Arabella forced a smile, but she was sure Maude would remain unconvinced until she explained. "I wondered if it's the same for men. After all, they engage in the pleasures of the flesh long before they wed. By the time they get to their wives, do simple things such as kisses still mean aught to them, or are they just that well practiced?"

"I don't know," Maude answered truthfully. "Kieran makes it seem as though it's different, better, since he cares aboot me, but I don't ken aboot other men. I think it is. I've seen my cousins with their wives. Callum and Tavish were both rakes before marriage, but meeting their wives changed them, tamed them. Now none of my cousins pay attention to the women around them. They have eyes for only their wives, and they can barely keep their hands off them. They don't keep them off them. That's why all of them are expecting bairns."

"It doesn't bother you that Kieran was coupling with Lady Bevan just before meeting you and within a day he was professing his feelings? It seems rushed." Arabella clapped a hand over her mouth when she realized what she's said.

"Lady Bevan?" Maude choked. The woman was a beautiful widow. A beautiful young widow. She was said to have been the most attractive lady-in-waiting for years, and Maude could believe it.

"Maude, I shouldn't have said that. I spoke without thinking."

"It's naught. I can't underdo the past." While Maude reassured Arabella, she felt anything but calm.

Why would he trade Lady Bevan for someone like me? What does he want in truth? Is he fooling me and planning to keep a leman like her once he's married me?

"You don't appear well. I'm so sorry aboot what I said. I suppose I assumed you were aware who he'd been with that night. It was careless of me to throw that at you with little consideration to what we'd just been discussing."

"Really. It's fine, Bella. I can't change the past. Not mine, not his." Maude went to stand at the window and looked out at the stars. The lights of Stirling made them hard to see. She longed to be back on her clan's land, where the Highland sky appeared to be an infinite collection of twinkling lights. The moon was behind a shadow, as though it hid from the people below, and Maude wished to do the same. Her headache hadn't eased as the day went on. "My head still hurts from everything last night and then too much noise all day today. I'll take a tray in here and try to retire early. I need to catch up on my sleep."

"Maude, don't. Please join us. I don't want you to hide in here."

Maude shook her head before saying, "Make my excuses, please. If you run into my father, let him know I retired early and will seek him out in the morning. I'll call for a bath, too. A good long soak in hot water will set me to rights."

Arabella looked doubtful as she dressed for the evening meal but agreed to convey Maude's regrets.

⚓

Kieran observed the ladies-in-waiting as they entered the Great Hall. They resembled a flock of exotic birds with their gowns of various colors, but they reminded him of a pack of wolves. As he searched, he couldn't find his lamb. He waited until all the ladies settled at their tables before he started to worry that Maude wasn't there. He caught sight of Arabella and Blair sitting together, so he wandered close to their table.

Both ladies looked at him with regret and shook their heads. Kieran's shoulders slumped, but he took a deep breath and looked for his sister to be sure she wasn't watching. She had her back to him and was engaged in an animated conversation with Laurel, who batted her lashes at him before he turned away.

"She's nae feeling too perky this eve. Last night gave her a headache and spending the day with those she-wolves didna improve it," Hamish said by way of a greeting. "She's taking a tray in her chamber."

Kieran nodded and swept his gaze over the crowded gathering hall. He had no reason to stay now that Maude wasn't there. His eyes landed on Lady Bevan, whose gaze followed him. She offered him a coy smile and raised an eyebrow. He understood her silent invitation. Just as he'd done moments ago with Laurel, he turned away without reacting. He kept the lusty widow in the corner of his eye to be sure she wouldn't be in a huff. The last thing he needed was an angry former lover, but she'd returned to her conversation as though she'd never seen him. Kieran was relieved that their one-time encounter was as insignificant to her as it turned out to be for him.

"Would ye join me and sup alongside the Sutherlands?" Hamish asked, but Kieran understood Hamish wanted everyone to witness there was no bad blood between the clans despite recent events. He longed to escape and seek Maude. He wouldn't fall asleep that night unless he saw for himself that she was well. But with Maude's fear that people would assume her father gave her to him in exchange for the damages the raid caused, he accepted the invitation. "Smart lad. I will protect ma daughter, nay matter what. Sowing the seeds that we are allies nae enemies before anyone kens yer intentions will keep Maude's reputation intact."

"I agree. I appreciate your forethought," Kieran nodded as he took a spot on the bench beside Hamish. The sight of the two of the most powerful Highland lairds breaking bread together created a buzz at the nearby tables. Kieran clinked mugs with Hamish and his clansmen. He relaxed when he realized Hamish's good cheer was genuine; however, that didn't change the fact that he pondered how to excuse himself before the meal ended.

"While I believe family is everything," Hamish lowered his voice. "It reassures me that ye would put ma Maude before even yer sister. I believe yer feelings for her are as genuine as mine were for her mother, even though they began just as quickly. I have a good life with a wonderful woman who makes me a better mon. She's given me three children who are the apple of ma eye. I hope ye find the same happiness with Maude." Hamish twirled his eating knife carelessly as though he gave it little consideration. "But deceive ma wee lassie and break her heart, I will kill ye."

Hamish slammed the tip of his knife into the tabletop, leaving it there to vibrate. The unexpected sound snagged the other Sutherlands' attention, but they turned away when they caught sight of their laird staring at Kieran. Kieran opened his mouth to defend his feelings for Maude, but a page interrupted them when he arrived with a missive for Kieran. He looked at the seal and realized he had the perfect excuse to leave the meal early.

"This is from Matheson. I would read it and respond before his messenger leaves. It'll be aboot Madeline's betrothal. We should pray he's accepted. Please excuse me."

Kieran wound his way through the tables before leaving the Great Hall. More than one woman flashed him a welcoming smile, but they didn't register with him. He was determined to visit Maude before the night grew too late. If she was already asleep, he would leave her in peace. He tucked the unopened missive into a pocket on the inside of the doublet he wore to the evening meal when at court. As he approached the ladies' chambers, he caught sight of a maid leaving Maude's chamber. He hoped it meant she was still awake. When he reached her door, he knocked once but feared lingering in the passageway. He pushed the door open, stepped inside, and froze. Maude stood in the tub with water streaming down her trim torso and toned legs. Her hair was parted and covered her nipples like Lady Godiva, but he could see them poking through. Kieran gulped before he realized he shouldn't be looking. He spun on his heel and stared at the door as his cock throbbed painfully. He needed to adjust it, but he didn't want to draw attention to the bulge that continued to thicken.

Maude assumed her maid returned for something when she heard the door open after a brief knock. She was unprepared for Kieran to pass through the doorway, nor was she prepared for the look of astonishment, then hunger, that flashed across his face before he regained his senses and turned away.

"Forgive me, Maude. I had nae idea ye were bathing. I wouldnae bother ye if I had." Kieran's refined speech slipped as he stumbled over his words. "I'll leave."

"No. I mean I'm covered now." She'd grabbed a towel and rubbed quickly to get most of the water off. She'd slipped into her robe and ensured it covered her.

Kieran swallowed and closed his eyes. When he turned, there would be no way she wouldn't spot his arousal. He believed he'd been hard when they kissed in the stables, but that was nothing compared to the discomfort he was in now. His breeks had never been so tight. He couldn't bring himself to look her in the eye when he faced her again. He looked to the window instead. So even though he had her in his peripheral vision as she approached, he was unprepared for her to run her hands over his chest. He clamped his hands around her wrists to keep them from exploring. He didn't trust his self-restraint or what remained of it. He shook his head with his eyes closed once more, but when she tried to pull away, he shook it again and pressed her hands against his scorching chest. He radiated heat even through the doublet, and Maude's hands grew warm.

"If you touch me any more than this, I'll lose control. I should step away, but I can't."

"Should I?"

"Nay," Kieran croaked. "Just give me a moment to compose myself. You gave me a shock."

"*I* gave *you* a shock? You're not the one caught in the buff."

Kieran's groan sounded painful. "Don't remind me, buttercup. I already can't get the image from my mind."

Maude snatched her hands away and pulled the material tighter across her chest and held it in a fist. Kieran recognized she did it in defense and hopes to feel more covered, but all she succeeded in doing was form a second skin over her breasts that were still wet in places, making the material thinner.

"If I'm that unappealing, you can go." Maude snarled.

Kieran's eyes jumped from the breasts his mouth watered for to her eyes.

"Unappealing?"

"Aye. If the sight of me troubles you so much." Maude turned away, leaving a view of her lush backside for Kieran to feast upon.

"You assume I mean that in a bad way? Like you've scarred me?" Kieran was upon her in three strides. He spun her around and lifted her off her feet. He wrapped her legs around his waist and backed her against one of the bedposts. This time his growl was feral as his mouth attacked hers. He gave her no mercy as his tongue plunged into her mouth. There was no finesse to this kiss, just consuming need. He held her so his sword pressed against her bare sheath. Her robe came apart around her legs when he lifted her. Now he pressed his hips into her mons and held her, trapped against the wooden post. "If you were my wife, I'd be inside you spilling my seed already. If you were my wife, I'd make you scream my name as you came apart with me buried to the hilt. What I glimpsed has me harder than I've ever been in my life. I've never wanted to couple with a woman as much as I want you right now. It's only the memory that you're a virgin and not *yet* my wife that keeps me from surging into your cunny. I fear I would be rough with you, anyway. I wouldn't be able to hold back once I started."

Kieran's lips sought the corner of her jaw. He'd kissed her there the first time on the terrace because her lemon verbena scent was too inviting in that very spot. Now he enjoyed kissing her there because it seemed even more intimate than her mouth. It was a spot few would consider, and it was all his. His mouth trailed along her jaw, and down her neck until he reached her collarbone. He flicked his tongue into the hollow before laving her. He pulled her robe wider open, allowing his mouth to continue its path. He smattered kisses over the supple flesh of her breast before his hand slid beneath the fabric and cupped her breast.

"I wish to take your breast in my mouth and suckle. But I assure you, you willna doubt I'm all mon and nae a babe." He pulled on her nipple until it pebbled as it had when she stood in the tub. He pinched, and when Maude moaned, her eyes squeezed shut, he bared the object of his attention. Her breast was full and perky, making it easy to reach despite being a tall man. He circled his tongue over the raised flesh as Maude's moans transformed into needy mewls. Unwilling to make either of them wait, he took as much of her breast into his mouth as he could, his teeth grazing her until he reached her nipple as he drew back before once more consuming most of it. He shifted her in his arms so he could press his thigh between her legs as he had in the stables. As she settled into a rocking motion, he grasped her wrist and guided it toward his cock. Maude's sudden intake of breath coupled with the sensation of her hand tightening and loosening its grip on his cock had him throwing back his head with his Adam's apple bobbing with each groan.

Maude watched in awe as Kieran explored her breast, and then as he trembled in her hand. She couldn't see his face, but his reaction as his fingers bit into her backside encouraged her

92

to thrust harder against this thigh. The same tightening in her sheath and then her core that she had before she climaxed in the stables began to grip her.

"Keir, it's happening again. Like before," she whispered. Kieran looked down at her, and it was her turn for her eyes to shut.

"Look at me, Maude. Let me see you when you shatter because of me. Watch me as I come apart in your hand. I'm going to spill my seed." Kieran covered the hand that held his rod and pressed her to squeeze him before his hips jerked forward. The sudden pressure against her pearl brought on the spasms.

As their climaxes receded, their mouths found one another. The kiss was tender and languid as Maude ran her fingers through his hair and adjusted herself to rest higher upon his waist. He kissed her neck, but rather than inflame her, they made her feel cherished. He returned to his favorite spot over and over as his hand cradled her nape.

"You devastate any restraint I try to have around you. I'm like a child who can't withstand the temptation of sweets. I want you and will risk being caught for the delight having you brings me." Kieran sat on the foot of the bed as he ran a soothing his hand over her back. She rested her head on his shoulder, occasionally pressing a kiss to his neck. He reveled in the peaceful aftermath of their frenzied lovemaking. He realized that even though he didn't penetrate her, it still struck him as making love. Or at least he assumed that was what making love felt like. He'd never experienced anything like that in the past. He'd been eager and randy enough times, but he'd never been so consumed with the need to show a woman the depth of his feelings. He'd considered the notion of fate to be ridiculous until he met Maude.

"Kieran?"

"Aye, leannan." *Sweetheart.*

"What just happened? I mean, I *know* what happened. It's the same as in the stables. But why was it so intense?"

Kieran chided himself for his disregard for her inexperience. While the emotions were new to him, the motions were not. He understood physical want, but this had been a consuming need. If he wasn't sure how to process all that transpired, he realized Maude would be adrift. He opened his mouth to speak, but Maude's next question had him swallowing his tongue.

"Is it that way with Lady Bevan? With your others?"

Kieran gripped Maude's shoulders and pushed her away. She was embarrassed to be so naïve and curious. He tilted her chin up as his jaw set.

"Look at me, Maude." They were the same words as before, but his tone was harder. "Let me be abundantly clear aboot this, so I leave no doubt in your mind. Ever." His eyes bore into hers as he waited for her to turn her full attention to him. "What just happened is unlike aught in my past. No, it wasn't like that with Lady Bevan or any other woman from my past. And my past is exactly where it shall stay. I admit I have lusted after other women and enjoyed coupling. I'd say I'm a skilled lover, but those skills now belong to you and you alone. When I glimpsed you naked, my cock swelled faster than I ever thought it could. It strained against my breeks much harder than it ever has when aroused by any other woman. If you hadn't touched me when you did, I'm certain I would've taken your maidenhead. I wanted to be inside you, thrusting, more than with anyone else. Your touch was enough to tame me. But it wasn't just a physical need for you. I wanted to pour every last drop of my feelings into you, to share how much I care aboot you, to bring you the pleasure you bring me. To answer your first question, at least from how I see it, it was so intense because fate is pushing me down the path to falling in love with you."

"It was that different for you? As in better?" Maude's tone showed she was unconvinced. Tears pricked behind his lids and made his eyes sting for the first time since his father passed away when he was only seven-and-ten. He'd locked

94

himself in his chamber the day it happened and the day of the funeral. He'd sobbed until he had no more tears to produce. It was much the same now. He swallowed several times before he trusted his voice enough to speak.

"I would give aught to go back in time and keep you from suffering those taunts and cruelty. I'd throttle my sister if I could for her part in your insecurity. Maude, you are a desirable woman with your clothes on, but what I saw tonight is a secret I would kill to keep. I will kill to keep. You have breasts men dream aboot. Your stomach is flat, and your waist narrow and trim. I'd felt as much when I lifted you on and off your horse and when I've held you against me. But the way it connects your breasts to your hips, the contrast is—is—I don't know how to describe it, but talking aboot it is making me hard again. I might say something practical and unsentimental aboot your hips, that they're broad enough to keep me from worrying when you bear our children. But what I'm picturing, in truth, is having your arse in my hands again. The lushness makes my palms tingle. I want to bend you over that chair and take your from behind, so not only can I watch my cock enter you, I can hold your arse while doing it." To reinforce his words, his hands squeezed her bottom as he drew her higher on his lap. His arousal once more brushed against her mons. "I saw your thighs and wanted them wrapped around me. I want to settle between them this very moment and have them cradle me as I drive into you over and over. I can't imagine a single mon who would choose another woman over you if they based their choice on a woman's body alone. Do my words shock you? Are you shocked at how much I want you?"

Maude nodded. They were the antithesis of everything she'd convinced herself of for so many years. She'd wanted to hide in her clothing, using them as a shield because she considered herself so dowdy and heavy compared to the other women her age. While Kieran's words brought her immeasurable relief, they didn't allay all of her doubts. As if he read her mind, Kieran ran his forefinger over her eyebrows, then down her nose. He swept the pad of his thumb over her cheeks before brushing it over her lips.

"You now fear I may lust for your body, but you still believe you're not pretty. Am I right?" Maude's noticeable swallow was his answer. "I'm seeing you as I'm sure no mon ever has. Your hair is unbound, as it should be for a maiden, and I saw it rest against your breasts. Wearing it up doesn't diminish your attractiveness, but having it down softens your face. I'm drawn to your eyes; their color fascinates me. They're amber, yet they blend into cinnamon with a walnut band at the outer ring. They still remind me of whisky." He grinned, relieved when she joined him. "The small gap between your teeth and the ever so slight crookedness are endearing. Some women are so beautiful they seem untouchable. Others are so beautiful that a mon seeks her as a conquest, as a chance to prove to himself that he possesses the ability to catch the woman's attention. Your beauty comes from your guilelessness, your unassuming manner. You not knowing how attractive you are only adds to the effect. I wish it didn't matter what anyone else thought, or at least anyone but me, but I know it does. You are judged for your beauty every day here. I can't imagine how it would feel for my looks to be all that people judge me upon."

"That would be easy for you. You're very handsome."

"There are plenty of good-looking men who are horrible people. I'd rather people judge me—I'd rather you judge me—by how I lead my people and how I can defend them with my sword and my mind."

"Your ability to defend them with your sword has led to a devastatingly attractive body," Maude pointed out.

Kieran shrugged. "Is that your opinion?"

"Aye and every other woman who's ever seen you."

"I don't care what those women think. I only care aboot what you think. Buttercup, I would whisk you away from here and return you to the Highlands where you belong. You need to be somewhere where you can be yourself, where you can let your guard down. And maybe even your hair." Kieran grinned again.

"It's too thick and suffocating in the Great Hall. It's not so bad at home, but here, I wish I could chop it all off." Maude ran her fingers through her drying hair, but Kieran caught her wrist.

"Never," he growled. "I'd be happy if I was the last mon to ever see you with your hair down."

"It would ease my headaches. While my hair makes me too hot, the weight makes my head ache and having it pulled so tight constantly tugs. I must reconsider wearing it down."

"Fine," Kieran grumbled. "Then I shall stick one of those hideous kertches on your head once we're wed. You could keep your hair down but covered. It would be my privilege to see you with your hair unbound."

Maude guessed Kieran was only half kidding. She suspected he would do such a thing.

"Only if you didn't wear your breacan feile again. I don't like other women seeing your knees. It gives them ideas."

Kieran's laugh was deep and vibrated against her when he pulled her close.

"For you, I would do aught." Kieran grew serious when he shifted again, and the missive pressed against him within the inside pocket. "Matheson's response came this eve, but I haven't opened it yet."

Kieran withdrew it and ran his finger under the wax seal. He unfolded the parchment and scanned its contents before going back and studying it, a smile spreading across his chiseled face. He saw Maude shifting behind the vellum, trying to glimpse his reaction.

"Here. Read it. He'd like her there within a fortnight."

"That soon?"

"Aye. It's all there. See?"

"I do. She'll be livid. She won't want to leave court."

"She's known all along that part of being sent to court was

to find a husband. That the mon wasn't found here doesn't change her being of a marriageable age. For all her faults, she's loyal to the last breath when it comes to our clan. I didn't agree to the marriage or alliance just because it would be expeditious. Their proximity to Skye will strengthen the MacLeods of both Lewis and Harris, the Harris in particular since they're surrounded by MacDonalds. Madeline loves Lewis, but she fell in love with Skye when we visited as children. I've granted her dower lands there. While the Mathesons won't own that land, they may use it if they wish, or they may simply be a reminder to the MacDonalds that we don't stand alone. We may be far larger than the Mathesons, but an alliance in that region will strengthen us."

"When will you tell her?"

"In the morning. It's too late now."

"Speaking of which. I'm surprised Arabella hasn't caught us yet. You must go before she returns. She wouldn't say aught, but if she's retiring for the night, then so will the other ladies. We can't risk your discovery here."

"I know, leannan. But it doesn't mean I have to like it."

"If we find we suit in more than the bedchamber, then you shall have me in yours arms whenever you wish once we're married."

"Whenever I wish? That will be every night. Lass, there will be no separate laird's and lady's chambers. There will only be our chamber."

Maude's mouth formed an "o" that made Kieran's cock twitch. He was already struggling with saying goodnight without being reminded that no part of him wanted to leave. He kissed Maude once more, taking advantage of her open mouth to sweep his tongue around hers. He accepted her attention, but they both pulled apart before things advanced. Maude opened the door and peered both ways down the passageway. She counted to twenty before she stepped aside. Kieran stood in the doorway for another count of twenty before bussing her cheek and slipping away.

CHAPTER TEN

M aude watched the tempest that was Madeline MacLeod storm into the Great Hall. Maude knew Kieran must have spoken to her because Madeline hadn't been in such a state when they gathered in the chapel for morning Mass. No. This thunderstorm had developed far more recently. Maude attempted to stay out of Madeline's line of sight, hoping to avoid acting as the woman's outlet. She wasn't to be so fortunate. Madeline's sight narrowed onto Maude, who sat between Arabella and Blair. Maude had sought her sister's company that morning. She'd confessed to everything that happened between her and Kieran. She didn't hide, or rather downplay, anything as she had with Arabella. She felt guilty sharing more with Blair than Arabella when they considered themselves sisters of the heart. But some things should only be discussed with someone who shared the same blood. Blair had been supportive, if not a little smug, when Maude described everything Kieran said about her body. Maude feared Blair would judge her for wantonness, but her sister's only response was "I told you so."

"Good morn, Lady Madeline," Cairren Kennedy made the fatal error.

"What's good aboot a morning when your brother has sold you like a slave?" Madeline bemoaned.

Neither Blair nor Arabella showed any response, Maude having forewarned them. Maude kept her eyes down as she poured honey into her porridge, using it as an excuse not to look at Madeline.

"I beg your pardon," Cairren responded.

"My profligate brother has betrothed me to the fourth son of Laird Matheson. Can you believe that? The *fourth* son!"

Maude kept her eyes averted, but her mouth twitched. It would seem Madeline wasn't upset about the betrothal or even that it was to a Matheson. It was that it was to the youngest son. She believed she should marry a laird or at least an heir.

"Shouldn't he retire to a monastery somewhere? Couldn't he have the decency to disappear? Then I couldn't marry him." She pouted when she finished.

Despite her rant, Madeline spied the small upturn of Maude's mouth and turned her temper toward Maude. She leaned across the table, making it impossible for Maude to ignore her. Madeline pulled Maude's bowl away from her, removing Maude's excuse to not engage.

"What're you smiling aboot, you fat dowd? At least someone has agreed to marry me. You shall rot as a spinster until your bones grow brittle. I may not like who my brother chose, but at least my brother's seen to my future. Your father couldn't be bothered. He's happy to be rid of you here. I'll have a mon while you'll have naught but your fingers," she hissed. Several of the ladies drew back at Madeline's crude reference.

"Madeline Eloise MacLeod!" The bellow was followed by the pounding of a fist on the table. Kieran marched over to their table, glanced at Maude, then hauled his sister away with an arm around her waist. Maude never imagined anything could enrage Kieran so much, and it frightened her. She wanted to follow them to reassure Kieran that Madeline's words had done no real harm and to be sure Madeline survived, but she knew she couldn't. It would only make the scene worse, and she was certain Madeline would spew more foul things even if Maude came to her defense.

They conducted the remainder of the meal in stunned silence with only the occasional whisper of questions about whether Kieran would whip her, exile her home, or throttle her. Maude prayed it was none of those. She didn't want to come between brother and sister. Kieran may swear now that he would choose Maude, but she didn't want to test the bonds of family. Or worse, be what severed them.

The ringing in Kieran's ears didn't end even when they reached his sister's chambers. She'd flailed and ranted until he dropped her on the stairs, letting her believe he would allow her to fall. He'd given her the option of coming quietly or going over his shoulder where he could swat her arse until his hand stung. He'd never threatened to raise his hand to a woman before, and much like he would never let her fall down the stairs, he wouldn't follow through with his pledge. When they arrived at Madeline's chamber, he swung the door open so hard that it smashed against the wall and some of the plaster crumbled. He flung her into the room and slammed the door shut, making the wall rattle.

"I have never been so ashamed of anyone in my life. You are a disgrace to the laird's family and to our clan. You were naught short of a vulgar bitch in front of half the court. Do you realize every table surrounding you witnessed your tantrum? Do you realize that turning your viperous tongue on an innocent woman only shamed you more? Do you realize, little sister, that you shall never, ever show your face in that Great Hall again? I may forbid it while you're still unmarried, but you can be certain the queen will forbid it once you are wed. What will you say to your husband if he can't present you at court?"

"That this is your fault!" Madeline stalked away before picking up the pitcher and hurling it across the chamber.

"Oh, no, you don't, princess." Kieran's fingers bit into her wrists so deeply that he was sure there would be marks, but he kept her from lobbing the basin too. "Your theatrics have never worked on me. Your performance, for that's what it was, was for the sake of your so-called friends and your hangers-on. But you went way too far. Rather than sympathy, you shall receive naught but scorn. You were angry when we left here and may have worked yourself into a lather before reaching the Great Hall, but that display was because of your narcissism, and it shall come home to rue. Pack your belongings. We leave within the hour. What doesn't fit within a satchel I might send to you later."

Madeline sneered at him and crossed her arms, tapping her foot. Kieran took a deep breath, expanding his chest to its full breadth before leaning over her.

"You will do as I say this minute, or it won't be marriage you're heading to. It'll be Inchcailleoch Priory for you, where you can take not only a vow of poverty but one of silence." Madeline took a step back, at last realizing she'd pushed her brother too far. It was rare that he lost his temper, but it fizzled if Madeline waited in silence for long enough. She wasn't so confident that he would forgive her this time.

"I'm sorry for my behavior in front of everyone and for my uncouth words." If only Madeline had stopped there. "But it was just Maude Sutherland. She means naught."

Kieran's hand shot out, but he stopped himself before it went around Madeline's throat. She knew what he intended, and her eyes widened in shock.

"You're involved with her. Is she your mistress?" Once again, if only Madeline knew when to stop. Instead she muttered, "That little slut."

"The wedding is off." Kieran grasped his sister's chin but was careful not to be rough. "See me and hear me well. You will go to the convent. I will make your excuses to the Mathesons and say you have a calling of faith. You've insulted the woman I will marry for the last time. I heard you on the terrace a few days before I returned home. I've heard aboot the other things you've said since then. It was only for Maude's sake that I didn't say aught. I didn't trust you not to be vindictive, but you have proven you can't be trusted to show your face in good company. I can't risk you unleashing this behavior on any of the Matheson women, especially not the wives of the laird's sons. Forget packing. You need not bring aught."

"You can't be serious, Kieran. I didn't know. I would have kept such things to myself if I had."

"And that's why you still can't be trusted. You don't see the sin in having those thoughts. You just don't want to be caught. You've far exceeded Mother's and Abigail's pettiness. You have a cruel streak that I won't make others suffer. You are a laird's daughter and a laird's sister. You have had the best in life, yet for all your supposed loyalty to our clan, you can't see how your actions harm our people. Do you understand what would happen to Assynt if the Sutherlands, Sinclairs, and Mackays rally together to avenge the slight you've given Maude? What if the Mackenzies join with the Sutherlands? That would decimate Assynt. Not to mention the Mackenzies are allied with the Mathesons. If you married into that clan, where would that put them if they're allied to both us and the Mackenzies? The Isle of Lewis might be safe, but we have clan members on the mainland for whom I'm responsible. You think of no one but yourself. And I'm through. You're too great a liability."

Tears streamed down Madeline's face as she listened to Kieran's accusations. She knew they were all true. She'd arrived at court and gained attention from the male courtiers while her sense of style and confidence enabled her to rise in the social hierarchy of the ladies-in-waiting. The taste of power brought out the worst in her, but she hadn't cared so long as she remained on top. She saw all that crumbling before her. She had one last plea.

"You'd choose her over me, your own sister?" Her voice trembled as she wiped her nose with the back of her hand.

"This isn't aboot Maude. You could have just as easily unleashed on one of the other ladies today, or you might target any one of them once Maude leaves. You are no longer the lass I knew. The woman you have become is not one I wish to have in our clan. Even now, you're attempting to manipulate me."

"Fine." Madeline's tears stopped with the abruptness with which they started. "Send me to the convent and see how well that goes. They'll force you to retrieve me within a fortnight."

"You underestimate the nuns' experience with unwilling novices. It's not called the "Isle of Old Women" for naught. Once there, no one leaves, and no old woman will tolerate your tantrums." Kieran ran a hand through his hair and stepped back. "Madeline, you're my sister, and naught can change that. That's why it pains me so much to see who you've become. You're unrecognizable to me. I wish I could say I'll send you to the convent and give you the chance to repent and change your ways before returning home, but the way you're trying to manipulate me now makes me fear that I can never trust you again. I will marry Maude, and I will take her home to Stornoway. I will *not* take her some place where she must suffer your wrath any time you're displeased or merely for the sake of you feeling superior."

"So, you are choosing her!" The tears began anew, but it was in truth this time. The brother she had once adored and idolized now couldn't stand her. What was worse, he not only had no affection for her, but he bore great affection for a woman who couldn't be more her opposite. She swallowed and could only force out a whisper. "I suppose this is how I must make Maude feel. Wretched and unlovable. It's rather miserable and painful. God, how this hurts."

Madeline sank to the floor on her knees as her shoulders

shook between her sobs. Kieran squatted on his haunches and once more tilted her chin up. He caught a glimpse in her eyes of the young girl she had once been before their mother's influence took hold. Their mother was snide and condescending, but she lacked the meanness that Madeline possessed. He'd worried more than once if he was selfish to want to bring Maude home to a family who might be little different from what she'd always experienced, but he believed his influence as laird and a fresh start would be enough to make Maude welcome. From there, her kindness and warm heart would win his clan over.

"It most likely is, lass. Now I'll give you a moment to change your kirtle, put on your riding boots, and gather your cloak." Kieran took a piece of vellum and the quill with the inkstand that sat on the table beside the window. He stepped into the passageway and scrawled a note for Maude.

Buttercup,

I must leave again, this time to take Madeline to Inchcailleoch Priory. I'm calling off the wedding. She's demonstrated that not only can't I trust her here, but I should worry about how she will behave with a new clan. I fear her behavior won't improve and she will cause strife with Matheson's other sons' wives. She's tried to manipulate me into forgiving her, but while I might eventually, I must also think about the clan. She need only say the wrong thing to the wrong person once, and she could cause a feud. She has much growing up to do. Perhaps a life dedicated to prayer will assist her. At the very least, some time spent in austerity might make her appreciate what she never has before.

I shall miss you until I return and have you in my arms again. The memory of the taste of your lips on mine will be my succor. Even if it is only a couple days. It shall take me two days, most likely, to settle her there and to ensure her dowry is transferred to the convent while restitution is paid to the Mathesons for breaking the betrothal before I even formalized it.

When I return, I shall make my intentions clear to all and sundry. There will be no hiding that I'm courting you. That I will marry you.

Yours always,
    Turtledove.

PS I didn't have the chance to say it, but your hair looks lovely today. I believe I'll need to have several kertches made to keep such a treasure all to myself.

He folded and sealed the parchment before knocking on Madeline's door. When she called to him, he entered her chamber. He scanned the chamber and saw that nothing besides the shattered pottery was out of place. He returned the ink and quill to the table then warmed a square of wax with the candle. He pressed his signet ring and was careful to ensure the markings were clear.

"Let's be on our way. It isn't far."

"It could be all the way on the moon for how close I will feel to the life I've known."

Kieran didn't disagree with her. They left the chamber, but paused when he summoned a page, giving him explicit instructions that the missive was to go to no one's hands but Maude's. Not her friend, her sister, or her father. It was for her alone.

CHAPTER ELEVEN

aude was in the queen's solar when the page delivered
Kieran's missive. She was certain she blushed as she
read and reread the note thrice. She felt sorry for Madeline,
but she also understood Kieran's decision. Her parents had
drilled it into her, as well as her brother and sister, that their
behavior would always reflect upon the clan. They, as the
laird's children, would always be held to a higher standard and
that they should remember their duty to the clan in all their
decisions and actions. She didn't envy Kieran or Madeline,
but the woman had brought this upon herself. Maude feared
the reaction that would come with Kieran's outburst, but
while her table remained quiet, she caught the comments
floating from others. It seemed Madeline wasn't as well liked
as she and her friends would have everyone believe. But
Maude also understood it was easy for others to stand in
judgement after the fact. Even as she sat embroidering, she
worried that Laurel would be her next antagonist, but the
woman had been remarkably demure since Madeline's abrupt
exit.

Maude was about to ask the queen if she might excuse her
to find her father. She wanted to keep him abreast of why
Kieran disappeared, but Laurel approached first.

"May I sit?" she asked.

Maude nodded and gestured toward the other half of the window seat.

"I owe you an apology many times over. I said hurtful things to you and aboot you and knew it was wrong even as the words spewed from my mouth." Laurel looked around to see who watched them. When she was convinced no one was paying too much attention, she lowered her voice further. "Madeline discovered something aboot my brother I wish to remain secret. She promised she wouldn't say aught if I supported her among the ladies. It became all too easy to cut you to the quick when Madeline made it, or rather you, seem so insignificant. When the others joined in or at least latched on, the power of being popular became addictive. You know I'm the youngest of five sisters. I loved having people pay attention to me after always being the bairn of the family. The one my mother was too tired to remember, and the one my father begrudged having to pay yet another dowry for. I made myself feel better at your expense, and I was so deep into following Madeline's lead in fear of what she might say aboot my brother, that I sinned without remorse. I offer you my heartfelt contrition, Maude. I know these are but words, but they are true."

Maude watched Laurel as she spoke. The woman endeavored to maintain eye contact, but at times she struggled and looked down at her hands which she clenched in her lap. Maude was wasn't prepared to trust Laurel's sincerity yet, but she wouldn't throw the woman's apology back in her face. Time would tell whether Laurel had reformed, but for now, Maude could be gracious. It cost her nothing.

"I appreciate your honesty and your apology." She also didn't have to gild the lily by being effusive with her thanks. Laurel nodded once when she realized nothing more would be forthcoming from Maude. She returned to her own sewing, and Maude approached the queen.

"Your Grace, a missive arrived that will concern my father. May I be excused to look for him?"

"I hope naught is wrong. He will be in the lists at this hour."

"Aye, Your Grace." Maude was already aware her father would be training. If he wasn't in meetings with the king in the morning, then he was outside swinging his sword. He might be well into his fourth decade, but he was just as strong and hardy as a man half his age. He reminded his own guardsmen of that frequently. She wound her way through the castle until she stepped outside. It was an unusually warm day, and the sun was brilliant. It was a day that would have been nice spent strolling through the gardens with Kieran. Shading her eyes with her hand, Maude picked her way to the lists, but stopped well before stepping foot into the training ground. She looked for anyone she might recognize near the boundary or anyone she could ask to find her father. There was no one. Maude knew better than to walk onto the field while men were swinging swords and axes, no matter how dull those weapons might be. She also knew she needed to speak to her father sooner rather than later. Maude did the only thing she could think of. She whistled the signal her father used when he wanted to summon the men from the lists. The shrill sound traveled across the field bringing most of the men to an abrupt halt. They looked around until she whistled again, this time not as loudly. She recognized her father, who jogged toward her with the Sutherland contingent behind him.

"What's wrong?" Hamish's eyes swept over his daughter. It was rare for Maude or Blair to interrupt training at home, and it would be even more significant when men from so many clans practiced.

"Naught, Da. I need to speak to you aboot something though. I didna mean to interrupt everyone's training, but I wasna sure how else to find you." She peered around Hamish's shoulder and offered an apologetic smile to the Sutherlands who'd rushed over with their laird. She allowed her brogue to overtake her courtly speech as she relaxed into the conversation with her father.

"Vera well." He turned back to his men and nodded before escorting Maude to a bench at the entrance to the garden. "What's happened, lass?"

"I dinna ken if ye heard what happened this morning before ye arrived at the Great Hall."

"Ye mean yer mon carrying his caterwauling sister from the morning meal? Aye, I heard."

"Kieran's plans changed because of Madeline's behavior. Rather than moving forward with the marriage to the Matheson's son, he's set off to take her to Inchcailleoch Priory."

Hamish's face blanched as he looked at his daughter. "The Isle of Auld Women?"

"That would be the place."

"I canna imagine much worse than that abbey. They dinna allow anyone to speak except for when they're in prayer. They make the women wear hair shirts under their robes. He must truly want to do away with her."

"Da, he's nae trying to kill her. He needs her to distance herself from the MacLeods before she says the wrong thing to the wrong person. If ye arrived here and didna learn that Kieran and I had developed a fondness for one another, and if ye didna realize how different he is from his sister, what would have happened when ye learned of Madeline's treatment of me?"

Hamish ran his hand over his beard. He let it grow out when he was away from her mother. Lady Sutherland didn't gainsay her husband about much, but she despised Hamish's beard. She declared many times over the years that she didn't want to look at a mountain man but rather the handsome and braw man she married. He tried to argue that the beard made for easier grooming, to which his wife responded by offering to shave him. Lachlan, Blair, and Maude had learned better than to interrupt their parents' morning ablutions. They'd learned at a young age that far more than washing their faces went on.

"I admit ma temper might get the better of me. I believe I've grown wiser and more judicious with age, but I'm an angry bear if I believe someone is harming ma bairns. While I wouldnae have picked a fight, it might have come to that if Kieran defended his sister."

"Aye, and what would Uncle Liam do if he learned of it?"

"He'd take our side. Our fight is his fight."

"And his fight is who else's fight?"

"Aye, lass. I ken. The Mackays."

"Kieran understands that such a disagreement might never come to swords. He also knows he doesnae need more hostility and animosity directed toward the MacLeods. I'm sure he feared the Mackenzies would side with us, which would leave Assynt vulnerable. If the Mackenzies joined and Madeline married into the Mathesons, that would put her new clan squarely in the middle, since they'd be allied with both the Mackenzies and the MacLeods. Part of me feels a little bad for Madeline, but I also understand feuds have started over less."

"True enough." Hamish watched his daughter for a moment before rubbing his hand over his beard again. "What else did he say?"

"Kieran didna have the chance to say any of this," Maude admitted. "He sent me a note. He's declared he willna wait to court me in the open any longer."

"He's convinced the two of ye are well matched. I want to ken if ye see beyond just his good looks. Looks fade with age," Hamish grinned. "Nae yer mother but every other woman I ken her age. What will ye have once the physical attraction wanes?"

"I hope we grow to love each other like you and Mama, but I canna know for sure. I respect him and am at ease, safe, with him. Kieran can be high-handed, but it's only when he worries aboot me. He's compassionate and he's astute. I admire his loyalty to his clan even in matters that set him against his family. I suspect we'll find we have much in common once we spend more than a few minutes together at a time." Maude gifted her father with one of her brightest smiles. "And nay, he isnae hard on the eyes."

"Lass," Hamish playfully warned, but grew serious as he took Maude's hand. "I would have ye find someone who can cherish ye and bring that same smile to yer bonnie face every day for the rest of yer lives."

Maude looked toward the garden as she considered whether to share her next thought. She returned her gaze to the weathered and familiar face. "He makes me feel confident aboot myself, like I'm good enough. I ken you and Mama, and Blair and Lachlan, even Arabella now, try to make me feel that way, but it's different with Kieran. And before you scowl, it's nae aboot the kissing. Da, dinna fash." Maude rested her hand on her father's arm as he pretended to reach for his sword. "I ken you ken he's kissed me. You've said as much. But it's not aboot that. Kieran makes me feel that way even when we're nae touching. He doesnae look down on me for ma insecurities, nor does he offer hollow platitudes. He knows they're very real to me, but he accepts me nonetheless."

"Lass, I'd say ye have the foundation for a good friendship. It will take time to ken if it will develop into more, and to ken if that more is enough to build a life upon together. Being the laird's wife isnae easy. Ye'll be tested often. It helps when ye have a partner that ye can rely upon, lean upon. I have that with yer mama. She is ma greatest ally, and I trust her always. I wish the same for ye and Kieran because I ken in ma heart that it's possible."

"Thank ye, Da. I love ye." Maude didn't hide her burr as she hugged her father. She remained in his embrace as she absorbed the comfort she still found there, and she realized her father missed being able to do it more often.

"I love ye, lass. Nae matter what."

Kieran was dirty, tired, and annoyed, but at least he could see the gates of Stirling Castle as he galloped closer. While arrangements for Madeline didn't take as long as he expected, the abbess was a master negotiator, making it clear within minutes that she had experience haggling over dowries for the brides of Christ. It cost him more coin than he planned, but the settlement was on its way from Lewis. It would come to him at Stirling, where he would sign the deeds to the dower lands over to the Priory on the condition that the nuns on Iona could use them if they so chose, but they reverted to the MacLeods upon Madeline's death or her release from servitude. It would take five years for Madeline to move from being a novice to a postulate to a nun. During those five years before taking her final vows, Kieran was willing to reconsider his decision to commit her to the nunnery, but only if she proved true remorse and a real desire to make amends. If the abbess doubted her sincerity, she would remain, spending her life in prayer with the hopes of redemption upon her death. He'd also arranged for two of his guards to deliver his regrets, along with a small chest of coins, to the Mathesons with an explanation that Madeline had been called to a life of service. He didn't mention that it wasn't God who'd called, but Kieran himself. He hoped that the money would be enough to smooth things over. It wasn't as substantial as her dowry, but it was a generous settlement nonetheless.

Kieran reined in Peat alongside the stables. As he unfastened his satchel, he considered using the trough again to refresh himself as he did the last time he reunited with Maude. Despite the journey being shorter and faster than returning from Lewis, he somehow felt grimier this time. He pushed aside the idea of going to his chamber and summoning a bath and followed his guards to the barracks where he could wash and change clothes. He was ready within a quarter of an hour. It was early afternoon, so Kieran was aware that the ladies were probably in the queen's solar. Short of pounding on the door and being skewered by the queen's guards, he needed to find another way to reach Maude. He wound his way to the spense and found it unlocked but empty. Kieran looked around outside to see if anyone was working nearby, but there was no one. He lit a candle and looked for a scrap of parchment or even bark upon which he could write. He found a piece of discarded parchment, surprised that anyone would waste so much, and a charcoal pencil. Kieran prayed she understood his note's meaning and trusted that she would. Kieran crossed the bailey to the castle and found a page before returning to the spense where he had already extinguished the candle. He waited in the dark.

Maude looked up when a young page came to stand beside her in the queen's solar. She'd been reading and was unprepared for the boy to appear at her shoulder. She noticed the missive was unsealed and the parchment seemed to have crossed out writing. Maude glanced at the page, but he shrugged before leaving. She held her breath, hoping it might be from Kieran.

The spense.

Td

It was from Kieran. She recognized the handwriting, but more than that, she understood Td stood for turtledove. She looked around, thankful that the queen had stepped out to use the garderobe and that the Mistress of the Bedchamber went with her. Maude seized upon the lack of supervision to slip out of the solar. She didn't care who might have noticed. She still had her cloak with her, since she hadn't returned to her chamber since her morning walk. Maude pulled the hood over her hair and held it in place, hiding her face as she hurried through the passageways. She entered the courtyard through a side entrance near the storerooms that included where they stored the herbs and medicinals. She crept to the door from the side that was least visible to the rest of the bailey. She pressed the door open and waited, but when no one moved, she pulled her dirk from her waist and stepped inside.

"Keir-"

"Put that away before you spear me, buttercup."

Maude dropped the knife, not caring that it clattered to the ground. A figure emerged from the dark, and when Kieran reached for her, she kicked the door shut. Kieran lifted her, and she wrapped her legs around his waist as he pressed her back to the door.

"I recognized you since the light was behind you." That was the only explanation he offered before their lips met. It was a hungry kiss, but it lacked the recklessness of the last two times they met in secret. There was tenderness where there had been pure lust in the past. "I've missed you, buttercup. It's been a day, but I was so worried aboot you and didn't see you before I hauled my sister away."

"I worried aboot you, too. I wanted to follow you but knew it would only make things worse. I felt horribly for you and, honestly, scared for Madeline."

"I frightened you, little one?" Kieran experienced more remorse than he did when he terrified Madeline. He'd wanted his sister to fear him so that she wouldn't attempt to defy him any further. But it had never been his intention to intimidate Maude. "I'm sorry you saw that part of my temper. I can't remember the last time I was that livid. It got the better of me. But I need you to know I never laid a hand on my sister in anger. I don't hit women."

"And I never thought you did. It never crossed my mind that you'd hit her. I imagine she tempted you to throttle her, but I feared the amount of anger you held. I'd hate to come across you on the battlefield." Maude stroked Kieran's bristled cheeks even though she couldn't see them. "I missed you, too."

They sank into another kiss, Maude's arms wrapped around his neck, her fingers running through his hair as he squeezed her backside. She could feel his cock as it once again strained to find her. However, with her skirt's many folds of material, she wasn't spurred on as she had been when there was only the thin layer of his breeks separating them. Kieran moved them to the table in the center of the room, taking tentative steps to avoid slamming Maude into it. When he found it, he seated her on its surface and found the ends of her skirts. His thumbs caressed the sensitive spot on the inside of her ankles before sliding along her calves. He hooked his hands under her thighs and pulled her closer to him.

"Would I shock you if I told you all the things I want to do to you?"

"Not as shocked as you'd be if I told you what I've dreamed of."

Kieran growled as he nuzzled her neck and kissed along it before returning to nibble on her earlobe. His hands remained on her thighs, away from the temptation of sliding to her sheath. Her skin was smoother than anything he had ever touched, but the muscles beneath the skin were toned and strong.

"I want to bury myself inside you, but not before I taste you."

"And how would you do that?" The purr in Maude's voice made Kieran recognize it wasn't an innocent question. Maude knew the answer but wanted to hear it from you.

"I would lick your quim like I was lapping up the finest honey. After I made you writhe and beg for release, I would thrust into you. You'd have to hold onto the other edge of the table to keep from sliding across. I'd hold your hips up, so I reach the deepest edges of your core. I'd ride you until you scream my name then lay insensate as I lean across you, having spilled my seed in you."

"And if I told you I'd like to lick you like a honey cake, what would you do?"

"Maude," he warned.

"Only you're allowed to tease?"

"Aye, but you have far more self-control than I do. Plant such images in my mind, and I will come undone."

"And you think it's any easier for me to resist? I want to taste you just as you would me. I would try what I've overhead the older women discuss. My mouth aches to feel your cock inside it."

"Dear God above, Maude. That is the singularly most arousing thing I have ever heard." Kieran stepped back from the table not trusting himself. "If I keep touching you, you won't leave here a virgin, my wild buttercup."

Maude straightened and pushed her skirts down. She wriggled further back onto the table, restless and unsatisfied. She sensed more than saw Kieran pacing in front of her and could tell he was in the same predicament.

"I shouldn't meet you in secret anymore, Maude. The temptation to take things too far will be my undoing. I don't want you to fear my interest in you is only to bed you." Kieran came to stand before her again, and Maude could make out the outline of his broad shoulders from the small amount of light that shone through the crack between the door and its frame. He reached for her hand and held it between his two. "I don't want your interest to only be aboot bedding me."

"You fear my feelings are that superficial?" Maude was incredulous.

"This thing between us has moved quickly, and it's clear we're physically compatible, but I want more than that with you, Maude. I want something of substance that will last until we are old and gray." He lifted her hand to his lips and brushed his lips over her knuckles. "I would make my intentions known and be able to court you in the open rather than sneaking around."

"I'd like that. I spoke with my father yesterday, and he knows that this is what we want."

"Will you allow me to escort you on your walk tomorrow?"

"Aye. You dined with my father when you returned from Lewis. Would you do it again? With me there this eve?"

"Are you allowed to do that? I mean dine apart from the other ladies."

"Do you imagine even the king or queen would deny my father? He may rarely use the title, but he's not just a laird. He's the Earl of Sutherland. He's a powerful ally to the king, and my father's niece and nephews are all godchildren of the king and queen." Maude shifted uncomfortably for a moment before sharing something that she never discussed with anyone outside her immediate family though her clan knew. "They're my godparents, too."

"What? King Robert the Bruce and Queen Elizabeth de Bourgh are your godparents?"

"Aye. I don't make a fuss of it, since I don't want anyone to claim the queen plays favorites."

"She allowed my sister to kick you around like a lost kitten?"

"She didn't allow aught," Maude retorted. "She may be aware of all that goes on, but she isn't our mother. We're grown women. I didn't need her to come to my rescue as though I can't handle being taunted. Should I have run crying to tittle-tattle every time something was said that hurt my feelings?"

"That's not what I meant. I know you're capable of taking care of yourself. You've been doing it for far too long, but that doesn't mean she should turn a blind eye to something so wrong. I've known you for two moons, and I wanted to throttle my sister and her friends the night I met you. It's not that you needed rescuing so much as it's she shouldn't allow such behavior among her ladies."

"Do you think they make it obvious? Do you think we snipe at each other in front of her? Of course not. It's done behind hands and fans. It's done when she isn't near. It's done while gossiping between dances. No one will confess to hurt feelings, so they leave her none the wiser. Going to her would be the same as cutting my hand open in front of a pack of wolves. One sniff of blood, and they would have been on me because she wouldn't spare the few innocent ladies. Then they'd all have some bone to pick with me. No. I keep my head down and carry on until I leave."

"That's so wrong. It's dishonorable. It's--"

"Kieran," she snapped. "Not everyone here is a Highlander. They don't hold themselves by the same values we do. Consider those who've served the queen most recently. A Kerr, a Dunbar, a Johnstone, an Elliott, a Maxwell, a Kennedy. They're all Lowlanders. There's me, Blair, and Cairstine Grant who was cozy at times with your sister. Laurel Ross was as thick as thieves with Madeline, though she apologized to me just before I left the solar. Elizabeth and Deirdre Fraser are both married now. Your sister—well we ken aboot that. I'm outnumbered here. It's Blair and me. I can't expect the others to understand our way of life and adopt Highland values. Not when life as a courtier is aboot gossip, intrigue, backbiting, and politics. The other three Highland ladies banded together against me because they understood life at court. It was best to leave well enough alone, and that's how I'd like to keep it."

Kieran wanted to argue with her and convince her he was correct, but he wasn't a lady-in-waiting, nor had anyone made him live here for the past seven months. His sister had been here for years. When he examined it in those terms, he realized Madeline's changes shouldn't have shocked him. The influences here were not ones to make her a paragon of virtue.

"If that's what you want, then I will stand beside you. But I say that with the full disclosure that I won't turn a blind eye or a deaf ear to anyone who speaks ill of you."

"I know, turtledove." Maude slid her hand up his chest until she found his nape and guided him toward her for a long, last kiss. "I must prepare for the evening meal."

"Where I shall sit beside you."

"We'll see what Da has to say aboot that."

They slipped back to their own chambers to prepare for the evening meal.

CHAPTER TWELVE

The evening was going perfectly. Maude didn't remember the last time she enjoyed supping at court. She and Blair joined her father moments before Kieran arrived. His presence garnered attention since it had been days since the last time he sat at the Sutherlands' table, and this time, he sat far too close to Maude for anyone to doubt his interest. Their arms brushed together throughout the meal, and Kieran pressed his thigh against hers under the table. Hamish's glare warned him to keep both hands where the old warrior could see them.

Kieran leaned toward Maude and reached past her for the jug of ale, using it as an excuse for his chest to touch her shoulder as he whispered. "I touched your hair when it was down this afternoon, but it was too dark for me to see it. I didn't have a chance to say aught yesterday. But I shall not be remiss any longer. Your hair looks beautiful. You look beautiful."

Maude blushed but offered him her half-smile. Kieran decided he found it enigmatic. He also noticed more men looking at her as the meal progressed, and he feared they would think the same way. It would act as a siren to them to figure her out, discover what mystery lurked behind it. He forced himself to keep his jealousy at bay and not make an arse of himself as he did the day at the priory. Maude gave no indication that she noticed anyone else, though Kieran knew that would change when the dancing begun. Maude would have more dance partners than she'd had the entire time at court. He knew she would draw some men with honest intentions, but her physique would draw the lechers as well. Her clothing was no different than before, but her hair down gave her a youthful look that was appealing. She smiled more that evening, laughing at both her sister and her father while sharing that enigmatic smile with him. Men would circle like birds of prey despite Maude having been at court for months and never garnering such interest.

When the meal finished, servants swept in and pushed the tables and benches aside. While they cleared the floor, Maude stood beside Kieran as she spoke to Blair, who stood on her other side. The back of Kieran's hand rubbed against the back of her own, causing bolts of electricity to surge up her arm to her breasts, making them feel heavy and full before settling in a pulsing tingle between her thighs. It was a brief and light touch, but she experienced it all the way to her core.

Hamish stepped next to Kieran and clapped a hand on the younger laird's shoulder. He had missed none of their heated glances, nor how Kieran positioned himself to reach for the jug so he might touch her and whisper to her. Hamish hadn't heard what Kieran said, but it made Maude blush, then smile. He'd almost forgotten how lovely his little girl's smile was, but he reminded himself that she was a woman now. No longer a wee lass bouncing on his knee, she had a suitor who would soon twirl her around the dance floor.

"This is yer chance to stake yer claim. Make it clear. The vultures are circling now that Maude has come into her own. I'd thank ye if I didna want to thrash ye for bringing the attention to her. Dance at least thrice with her and be sure to dance the first two. People willna doubt yer intentions."

"I thought to dance every one with her," Kieran grinned

before looking down to find Maude's smiling face looking up at him. He took her hand in his and led her to the dance floor. Their approach, hand-in-hand, sent a ripple through the crowd. Instead of her hand on his arm as was customary, they showed an intimacy that most married couples and lovers lacked.

"People are staring," Maude hissed.

"I know," Kieran smiled. "The men are jealous."

"I doubt that, but the women will call me a wanton."

"As long as that wanton side is only for me." Kieran pulled her into his arms for the first dance. He'd expected it to be a country reel, but it was one that would keep them together through the entire set. "If I can't feast on you in private, then I shall enjoy every minute you're in my arms in public."

"Don't you think this is a wee over the top? You not only sat with my family for the meal, you sat practically on top of me. No one looking at our backs missed how close we sat. Now you're holding me indecently close."

"I'm making up for lost time."

"And if my father weren't here, people would whisper that I was your mistress, not your possible intended."

"There's no possible, Maude. You are."

Maude relented and enjoyed the dance. As one set ended, and the dancers lined up for the next, she thought she might sit it out or pair with someone else, but Kieran stood across from her in the line. The music began, and they came together before turning to their neighbors. They moved through the dance, always returning to one another. When that set ended, Kieran guided her through the crowd toward her family, avoiding the men converging upon where they stood. Once back at the Sutherland table, Kieran filled her chalice with ale before quaffing his. He refilled it for her again before returning the jug to the table. He reached up to brush away hair that stuck to her temple but caught himself and pushed his hair from his face instead. That would have been too great a breach of propriety, and he doubted Hamish would forgive such a blunder.

"Lady Maude," a young Lowlander dared to approach. "Would you share the next dance with me?"

Maude glanced at Kieran, who looked pained but attempted to smile at her as his jaw twitched. Maude accepted the man's offer and left Kieran to watch. The courtier's smile was polite, but his eyes were riveted to Maude's bust, making her uncomfortable. Kieran recognized that the man stumbled on purpose, so Maude's bosom would press against his chest. Maude jerked away and looked over at Kieran, seeing the heat rise in his neck. Kieran waited for Maude to signal that she needed him; he wouldn't intervene unless she asked. The song drew to a close without further incident, but before Maude returned to his side, another man asked her to dance. Once more, she glanced at Kieran, this time with an apologetic shrug. He forced himself to smile. He wanted Maude to enjoy the evening and to enjoy the attention after being starved for it. But, as he feared, the men who approached Maude were ones that only wanted to bed her. A third man pulled Maude too close despite her drawing away and attempting to put more space between them. His hand spread across the small of her back as he pressed her closer. Kieran observed Maude shake her head to something the man said. He maneuvered them further from the center of the dancers as though he would lead her outside. Kieran caught the moment Maude panicked and began a frantic search for him. He plowed through couples and those mingling about until his hand encircled the man's bicep. Kieran's fingers and thumb almost met as he yanked it from Maude's back. He twisted it behind the man's back and leaned to his ear.

"You aren't taking the lass anywhere. She's spoken for." Kieran squeezed. "By me."

"I—I wasn't," the man spluttered. "Barbarian. Uncouth lout."

The man still had hold of Maude's hand, which she

squeezed until the man winced and leaned back as his knees buckled. She bared her teeth as she prepared to defend Kieran.

"I dinna ken who ye think ye're speaking to, but I do ken *Laird* MacLeod is a far better mon than ye are, ye swine. The only barbarian here is ye. Ye're lucky it's Laird MacLeod who stopped ye because ye were aboot to get ma knee to yer bollocks. How's that for uncouth, ye arse?"

She released the man's hand, and Kieran shoved him away. Maude's former dance partner stumbled away as he glanced over his shoulder several times. Kieran pulled Maude into his arms and guided her back into the dance.

"Are you well?" Kieran murmured.

"Aye. Thank you. I panicked when I couldn't see you anymore. I would have kneed him if I had to, but I--" She shook her head. "I didn't like knowing if I couldn't see you, then you couldn't see me. It frightened me."

"We shall dance through this song, and then we'll return to the table. We drew too much attention, and I would diffuse it by appearing as if all is normal."

"This is our third dance together when I have danced that many in the seven moons I've been here. That is hardly what anyone will consider normal."

"Mayhap, but they will understand that you're under my protection, and it will be clear in the morning that I'm courting you. And by the by, little one, you might not have been able to see me, but I can reassure you I had my eyes on you the entire time. I'm a touch taller than you, buttercup. I can see over everyone's head here who isn't a Highlander, too. These Lowlanders don't eat enough as weans. They're puny." Maude grinned, and Kieran's heart stuttered. "Keep smiling at me like that, my bonnie buttercup. You make me feel ten feet tall."

"You are the brawest mon here." Maude's eyes twinkled as a crease formed at the outside of each one. Kieran glimpsed the tips of her bottom teeth where they overlapped. He yearned to run his thumb over them before doing the same with his tongue.

"Compliments will get you everywhere, mo leannan." *My sweetheart.* The one tiny extra word, the ownership of the sentiment, made Maude's hands tighten around Kieran's.

"I shall hold you to that, mo ghràidh." *My darling.* Kieran's eyes widened, and his nostrils flared. It was the first time she'd used an endearment other than turtledove, and she'd only used that a handful of times. "Will you sit with my father, Blair, and me during the morning meal? We can go for our walk after."

"I'd enjoy naught more. I will meet you at the end of Mass by the chapel doors."

Maude canted her head to the side as she ruminated on plans for the next day.

"Do you mind missing time in the lists, or will you go in the afternoon?"

"One day of missed training won't harm me. I'd rather spend the time with you."

"Then I intend to ask my godfather for a favor." Kieran raised his eyebrow at her statement. "I'll ask him to join the queen in her solar tomorrow afternoon and have you accompany him."

"You'd ask the king to rearrange his schedule and share our courtship with him?"

"And the queen. She will know before any of us arrive in her solar. I've asked them for naught since I was a child and begged the queen for candied apples."

"Where did your desire for subtlety go?"

"After tonight? There's no point. People have already taken notice. I'd rather make the most of our time than waste it."

"Do you think he'd indulge you?"

"Aye. Unless he already has a meeting or something urgent takes him away, he will. If not for me, then because he enjoys the time with the queen. Despite the flowery poetry and tittering, he enjoys the reprieve from his advisors badgering him."

"When will you ask?" Kieran led Maude back to the table as the song ended.

"Now." Maude flashed a smile before stepping around Kieran and walking to the dais. She curtseyed and waited for permission to approach. Two sets of eyebrows rose as she walked to the stairs and climbed onto the dais rather than stepping forward and remaining below the king and queen.

"Lady Maude," the king intoned. "This is a pleasant surprise."

Maude looked around to determine who watched or, more importantly, who listened. The other people on the dais appeared disinterested. She knew her father had a place at the table if he wished to take it, but he preferred to sit among his clansmen. Maude leaned forward so she was close enough to whisper as she stood between her godfather and godmother.

"I would ask a boon of you, not as my king and queen but as my godparents." Maude paused and waited for their reaction.

"You've asked naught of us before, Maude," the queen mused. "You might have asked for a boon many months ago."

Maude understood the queen meant Maude should have asked for help with Madeline and the others. She appreciated the offer, but she didn't regret her choice. She prayed she wouldn't regret this one either.

"Uncle Robert," she began. She used the title the Sutherland and Sinclair children grew up calling the king, one that felt familiar and comfortable. "My request is that you would join Aunt Elizabeth in her solar tomorrow afternoon."

"That isn't much of a boon, lass," the king mused.

"That isn't the boon, or at least it isn't all of it. I'd ask that you have Laird MacLeod accompany you."

"Kieran MacLeod?" The king wondered aloud.

"She's grown fond of him since he arrived. They've developed a tendre for each other, and it wouldn't surprise me if the lad doesn't ask your permission to marry our Maude," the queen attempted to hide her smile, making the corners of her lips twitch. "I suspect Hamish has already given his blessing. At least he will soon if he hasn't. The lad was practically sitting on the lass's lap this eve. And I feared for a moment that Allan Maxwell's life would end on the floor of our Great Hall."

It shouldn't have surprised Maude that the queen had seen so much and deduced most of the situation.

"Maxwell?" The king looked between the two women.

"Lord Maxwell attempted to force me off the dance floor and onto the terrace."

"What?" The king's hand slammed down on the table and made the platters and chalices rattle. People looked toward them, seeing the king's ruddy complexion flush even brighter. He scanned the crowd, searching for the culprit.

"Kieran, that is, Laird MacLeod, resolved the issue. Lord Maxwell won't approach me again."

"That's a polite way, Maude, to explain how your young mon nearly ripped Allan Maxwell's arm from his body. And you looked to have crushed his fingers."

"I'd hoped that went unnoticed, Aunt Elizabeth," Maude murmured.

"It did, lass," the queen reassured her. "The better view of those before us is why the dais is raised. We would observe those present to better prepare and protect ourselves."

The king reached out and patted Maude's hand. "I'm happy to fulfill your request. You, your brother and sister, and cousins never ask aught of us despite being family. The few times one of you is in need or wishes for something, your queen and I do our best to oblige. None of you have ever tried to take advantage of or exploit your position as our godchildren. I miss hearing the pack of you call me uncle. It seems too long ago."

"Ye wouldnae have a piece of treacle for me in yer pocket would ye, Uncle Wobber?" Maude grinned and the king's chuckle morphed into a hearty laugh that once more drew attention. The queen's laughter was more circumspect and daintier, but just as merry.

"As it would happen, lass," The king reached to a platter further down the table. "I don't have it in my pocket, but I have it here." He passed her the sweets from which she nabbed a piece. She was about to reach for another but pulled her hand away.

"Take one for your lad. And one for your sister, too. She has a sweet tooth the same as yours." The queen nodded. "And you may as well take one for Hamish, since that's who you inherited it from."

"Thank you." Maude paused and her smile faltered. It was one of many times when she wished she could return to her childhood. She would have kissed her godparents on the cheek and received one in turn. The king tapped his cheek just above his beard. She pressed a quick kiss and beamed when he offered her one.

"You won't be skipping me, lassie." The queen proffered her cheek, on which Maude dropped a kiss. The queen returned it and squeezed her hand. "I hope you'll be happy with him, Maude. You deserve the very best, and I suspect Kieran MacLeod is a mon who will spend his life making you know how special you are."

Maude's eagerness was infectious, and Blair embraced her sister when Maude presented the treacle to her. Kieran kissed her hand, stroking his thumb over her palm when she offered him the sweet. Hamish grinned and kissed the crown of her head. It had been many years since Maude felt so loved and happy.

CHAPTER THIRTEEN

K ieran waited at the doors of the royal chapel as the members of the royal court socialized while they left morning Mass. He was impatient to speak with Maude, and didn't understand why people about to sit together to break their fast needed to linger in the narthex. Seated by rank and clan significance, the MacLeods and Sutherlands sat further forward, with the Sutherlands sitting directly behind the royal couple. This trapped Kieran and Maude and forced them to wait until the congregation filtered out. He looked over his shoulder several times, offering Maude a secret smile. She returned it, but kept her eyes down. The other ladies-in-waiting surrounded her, jostling one another as they squeezed up the aisle. When he reached the door, he greeted the priest and received his blessing before pressing his way through the crowd to stand near the wall. It wasn't long before Maude exited with Blair and Arabella chattering alongside her. She caught sight of Kieran, and her cheeks flushed. The evening meal had been exhausting for her, but she relived the moments when she sat with and danced with Kieran. Images of them dancing at their wedding feast had swirled around her mind and through each of her dreams that night. Maude looked forward to breaking her fast, then going for a stroll with Kieran at her side. Her father invited Kieran to sit with their family for the morning meal, and Maude was eager to make her way to their table. As she walked past Kieran, Lairds Gordan and Grant, who were once more at court, stopped to speak with him. She watched as he shook his head and glanced at her, but his face tightened as he looked at Laird Grant and nodded. Maude saw regret in his expression, and she realized he would not be joining them for the meal. She prayed that he'd still join her in the gardens.

Maude felt more comfortable sitting with her clan members during meals, and ate until she was full rather than leaving the table still hungry. She gathered her cloak and said goodbye to her father as he prepared to head to the lists. She spotted Kieran still engrossed in conversation with the two lairds who waylaid him after Mass. She sighed, but straightened her spin and lifted her chin. She wouldn't allow her disappointment to show. As she glided past Kieran's table with the other ladies, Maude watched Kieran stand while Laird Gordan talked to him. He shook his head at something the Grant said and stepped over the bench. Both men called after him, but he stalked across the gathering hall with a singular purpose.

Kieran wasn't interested in listening to the two lairds ramble on about crops and herds. He agreed that they were important topics, but they weren't in line with his plans for the day. He stepped next to Maude and slid her arm around his and placed her hand on his forearm.

"Good morning, lass."

"Good morning, Kier." Maude cast her gaze over her shoulder and saw the two lairds watching Kieran depart. "Should you have left that conversation so abruptly?"

"Mayhap not, but they shouldn't have demanded a conversation so abruptly. A conversation aboot coos and crop rotation."

"Was that what they wanted to talk aboot?"

"More aboot trade in spring when the weather is reliable once again."

"When is the weather ever reliable in Scotland?" Maude chortled.

"Nearly never, but when the roads are clear, they'll want more of our Highland coos, and they know my clan would benefit from their grain. I'll speak to them at another time."

"Kier, I don't want to come between you and clan business. If this is something that you need to attend to, the garden will be there tomorrow."

"Unless you tell me you don't want to walk with me, naught is keeping me from accompanying you."

Maude searched Kieran's steely eyes before nodding. She didn't push the issue, and allowed Kieran to escort her outside. There'd been a dusting of snow during the night, and the steps were slippery. She was glad to have his sturdy frame to lean upon while the other ladies gripped one another, and windmilled their arms to keep themselves upright. The slick ground didn't faze Kieran, who walked surefooted toward the garden's entrance. He stopped Maude where it was possible for him to stand and block the wind from her.

"I like the pink in your cheeks and the tip of your nose. It's a shade that reminds me of your raspberry nipples," Kieran whispered as his hands rested at her elbows while she rubbed her gloved hands together.

"Wheesht. Someone will hear you." Maude attempted to make her words stern, but the giggle that bubbled forth reassured Kieran that she enjoyed his randy comments. She made a sound of disappointment when Kieran stepped away when the other ladies and the queen approached.

"Maude!" Arabella called out to her, holding up Maude's scarf. Maude shuffled to retrieve it from her friend. "I rushed back to our chamber to nab mine when I realized the poor weather and guessed you might want---"

Maude turned to see what was happening behind her that made her friend trail off. A group of matrons and widows had joined the ladies-in-waiting. Several stared at Kieran, but when Lady Bevan stepped in front of Kieran, her heart felt pinched like a vice grabbing hold. Kieran watched her and barely glanced down at Lady Bevan's upturned face. Maude saw Kieran's lip moved in what looked like the words "pardon me" before he stepped around his former lover. He walked toward her and Arabella.

"Thank you, Lady Arabella," Kieran said as a greeting. "It's a wee brisk this morning. Lady Maude will benefit from an extra layer." He took the scarf dangling from Arabella's hand. They had quickly forgotten it as the two women watched with bated breath to see what would pass between Kieran and Lady Bevan. Arabella nodded before muttering "you're welcome." Kieran stepped before Maude and wrapped the scarf around her neck, leaving enough slack for her to pull it up over her mouth and nose. The act of intimacy seemed even more forward than when they walked out to their first dance holding hands.

"Kieran, you're drawing attention to us."

"Didn't we assume my presence would?"

"Aye, but I didn't imagine you'd be so bold. You might as well run through the streets announcing it to all and sundry."

Kieran adjusted her hood to better cover Maude's ears, but dropped his hands when he realized that he'd done it without thinking about it. It seemed natural to take care of Maude as though she were already his wife. He turned them to join the others, and she wrapped her arm through his once more.

"It makes you uncomfortable?" He asked.

"I've spent my time here attempting to blend in and go unnoticed. I've gone from enduring an angry tirade to being the prey of the worst lechers at court to now openly receiving attention from one of the most eligible bachelors in the country. All in the space of two days. So much for being inconspicuous."

"I'm sorry, buttercup. I didn't think before I acted. I saw

the scarf and didn't want you to grow too chilled. It seemed natural to wrap it around you, but even I remember a betrothed wouldn't take such liberties. I tried to be thoughtful and rather ended up being thoughtless."

"I appreciate it. I like your concern and feeling important to you, but it makes me anxious having so many people looking at us. Lady Bevan wanted to speak to you, and you ignored her. I don't want people to think ill of your manners."

"There is only one reason for her to speak to me. Two, actually. One to see if I'll bed her again, and the other to prove she can take my attention from you. Neither will happen. There was little point in engaging in mindless chatter when I couldn't be bothered. I came to be with you, not anyone else."

Maude nodded but fell silent. They walked through the gardens as the queen led the way with the matrons who accompanied her. The ladies-in-waiting paired off or gathered in small groups as they followed the queen's leisurely pace. The cold never seemed to bother the woman, and her morning walks, unless it rained or sleeted, lasted at least an hour. She insisted upon her morning constitutional, even when it snowed. The Lowlanders complained when out of earshot, but the Highland ladies pulled their hoods up, tucked their chins, and grinned and bore it. The weather remained milder than most were accustomed to on their clan's land. Maude's home, Dunrobin, sat on the North Sea's coast. It remained one of the most northern keeps, with her Sinclair cousins' home of Dunbeath being a day's ride further up the coast. While she didn't enjoy the cold, even in the dead of winter the weather in Stirling seemed balmy compared to her home. She picked her way along the path, shuffling her feet when she sensed a patch of ice would appear underfoot. She clenched Kieran's sleeve more than once when she feared slipping. His sturdy presence kept her anchored even when her heart dropped, then raced with the gut clenching moment of fear that she would fall.

"How was the weather while you returned home?" Maude realized Kieran sacrificed his morning in the lists to walk with her so they might become better acquainted with one another. Sulking in silence wouldn't further her cause if she wanted to learn whether they suited.

"Rather mild considering the season. It snowed thrice and rained every other day, but the wind didn't chill me to the bone like it often does."

Maude had never been to the Outer Hebrides, but was familiar with their geography and clan territories. She remembered an interesting connection that hadn't come to mind even when the incident in Assynt increased tensions in the north.

"We're distantly related, but not by blood," Maude blurted out.

"I don't know aboot that. I've never learned of such a connection to the Sutherlands. At least not within the past several generations."

"It's in a rather roundabout way. My cousin, Callum, who's the son of my late aunt who was my father's sister, married a woman who was a Mackenzie, but her mother was a MacLeod of Assynt. So, we're related of a sort but indirectly through marriage."

"Aye, the chieftain there is a distant cousin. His grandson is near my age."

"He's Siùsan's cousin. Her mother was the chieftain's daughter. She's a wonderful woman, but her childhood was atrocious." Maude peered up at Kieran, unsure if he wanted to listen to her story.

"Tell me, buttercup. I would learn aboot your family."

"Siùsan's father handfasted with her mother against his father's wishes. They were traveling to be wed by a priest when approaching riders spooked her horse. The riders were from the Gunns and included the woman Siùsan's father was supposed to marry, the one Siùsan's grandfather arranged. Siùsan's mother was thrown, and she went into labor, delivering Siùsan before dying. Her father took her mother's body home on his own horse but refused to look at his newborn daughter. He even suggested they leave her in the woods. One of the guardsmen brought Siùsan back to Mackenzie land, and they placed her in the care of a village woman where she spent the first ten years of her life living with this other family. She was aware of her position as the laird's daughter but didn't understand what that meant until he summoned her to live in the keep. Her father still refused to have aught to do with her, and her stepmother—for her father married his Gunn bride—used Siùsan as a servant. She made Siùsan clean and serve in the keep and gave her a servant's chamber rather than one that befitted the laird's daughter. Her stepmother gave her the responsibility of being governess to her two younger brothers."

"That's reprehensible. I suppose Siùsan's grandfather wasn't any better if he allowed his son to abandon Siùsan to a villager."

Kieran's shocked expression was a replica of her own when she learned of Siùsan's past. She was a gentle woman who was too forgiving in Maude's opinion. But she had a backbone of steel and made Callum come to heel. He was a better man and better tánaiste for it. They loved each other beyond measure. That was the way of all her Sinclair cousins and their spouses.

"It turns out that Siùsan's mother was best friends with my aunt Kyla. My father's sister didn't have much of a better upbringing that Siùsan. From what I've been told, my grandfather was a tyrant who abused all his children. Kyla would visit Siùsan's mother, Rose, whenever possible. When my Uncle Liam discovered how Siùsan lived, his conscience wouldn't allow the daughter of his wife's best friend to continue suffering. The Mackenzie laird led him and Aunt Kyla to believe Siùsan died at birth alongside her mother. Uncle Liam investigated and learned what he could with members of his own clan going to live amongst the Mackenzies to report back to him. When he decided the timing was right, he arranged a betrothal between Siùsan and Callum. A much longer story short, after a rocky start, Siùsan and Callum are in love with their own growing family. Siùsan is the model of a perfect mother, and Callum dotes on his bairn. There's another on the way already. I suspect all of my cousins shall follow their parents lead and have large broods. Uncle Liam and Aunt Kyla were an arranged marriage but fell in love before they wed. Theirs is a love story well known throughout the northern Highlands."

"Aye. The story's made its way to even the Hebrides. What of your parents?"

Maude's smile softened and reflected her deep affection for her parents. She pictured her mother, who she hadn't seen in months. She'd last breathed in her mother's familiar lavender scent and experienced the embrace of her soft body pressed against her several moons earlier when her parents brought her to court to begin her service. Maude's eyes threatened to water as she pictured her and her own parents' love story.

"My parents were a love match from the start. My father was never meant to be laird. He was the third son, but Rosses killed his father and two older brothers during a hot-trot. They'd regained their rustled cattle and even won a skirmish against the Rosses, but they counted their victory too soon. The Rosses ambushed them within sight of Dunrobin. By the time my father and our warriors joined the fight, my uncles and grandfather had already fallen. Da and his own uncle beat back the Rosses and kept the keep from being attacked. Both of my uncles married but had no bairns. Their wives returned to their own clans after they buried their husbands. My father rode into the Sinclair keep asking for help on the day of Uncle Liam and Aunt Kyla's wedding. He and my aunt had been close, but their relationship became strained because of their father's abuse and their brothers' animosity. My father struggled, out of his depths and all of a sudden responsible for the clan. Aunt Kyla and Uncle Liam returned with Da and stayed a moon while they assisted with getting the clan back on their feet now that they had a caring and wise laird. Shortly after my aunt and uncle left, the king summoned Da to court to recount what happened with the Rosses. The story the Rosses spun differed from the one he'd detailed in his missive to the king."

"It was a powerful enmity; the Earl of Sutherland and the Earl of Ross edging toward a blood feud," Kieran ruminated aloud. He'd been told of the battle and how Hamish came to be laird, but it interested him to listen to it from the Sutherland's daughter rather than a rehashed story from his father. "What happened when your father arrived at court? From what I remember, the dispute ended before a feud took root."

"It did. At the time, politics were too fraught with the threat of the English invasion. Balliol had just ascended to the throne and was in the midst of submitting Scotland to English rule. Arguing over cattle seemed petty with our county's independence at stake. My clan and the Rosses didn't reconcile or even agree to a truce. They put the disagreement aside because, while they disliked one another, they disliked Balliol far more. They both supported King Robert and always have. My father met Lady Amelia Ross, the earl's daughter and lady-in-waiting to Isabella de Warrene, while at court. He wasn't aware of who my mother was when he first saw her, just as she didn't know who he was either. He asked her to dance that night, and they struck up a conversation. Somehow their clan names didn't come up despite discussing politics. It was dangerous ground to tread, speaking of supporting Robert the Bruce while dancing in King John's great hall. My mother's intelligence struck my father, and my mother appreciated that he respected her and listened to her opinions. She'd never experienced it before."

"It's hard to conceive that neither revealed their clan name. I can't imagine how the Earl of Sutherland danced with the Earl of Ross's daughter, and neither was aware of its significance. Didn't people stare? Didn't they catch the whispers that must have been buzzing?"

"They did, but my parents are both strikingly good looking. They each assumed people spoke of their partner. It wasn't until the next morning when Da and the Ross accompanied the king on a walk much like this one. Da grew excited to see Mama and offered to walk with her until my grandfather lunged at Da and got his hands around Da's throat. It took six guardsmen to pull them apart. Da didn't understand why Grandfather attacked, and he said he was halfway through the brawl before he realized who he fought. He wasn't prepared to lose to anyone, let alone the mon responsible for the deaths of his father and brothers. That was a matter of honor. But what enraged him most was that whoever attacked him did it while he stood close to Mama. It made him livid that someone would risk injuring her. It wasn't until the guards restrained them that Grandfather accused Da of being too forward with Mama, who was in tears watching her father and the mon she'd hoped would become a suitor fight one another. Da ignored Grandfather and hurried to Mama to make sure they hadn't injured her. When she reassured him that she hadn't been hurt, he unleashed on Grandfather for being so selfish, arrogant, and vengeful that he risked his own daughter's safety. The very daughter he was huffing and puffing aboot protecting. That brought Grandfather to a spluttering stop from what I've heard."

"I'd be livid too if someone attempted to draw me into a fight with you too nearby. I can't imagine coming to blows with your father, even though I worry we might meet on the battlefield. He is a very different mon than your grandfather. He took me to task when he discovered my interest, but rather than beat me senseless, or at least try to, he talked to me. He's given me a chance to prove myself." Kieran realized how fortunate he was as he listened to the story about the couple he wished would soon be his parents-by-marriage. "Obviously something went right. Your father and grandfather lived, and your parents married."

"Aye, my father refused to put Mama in the middle. He escorted Mama back to the keep, then demanded an audience with my grandfather. He made a case for being allowed to court Mama. Grandfather gave Mama one moon to decide whether she wanted to marry Da. They became inseparable the entire time. They walked together, danced every evening, attended chapel together even though they sat apart. Da brought Mama along on a hunt when he learned she enjoyed it and bragged to anyone willing to listen when Mama brought down the largest stag that day. Within the moon, they'd told each other everything they could think of from their past. The good and the bad."

"It sounds like a love match. It's sounds as though they had an idyllic courtship once your grandfather stepped aside."

"If only it had been. While Da had eyes for Mama, Lady Fraser, who's Mama's cousin, also wanted Da. Grandfather latched onto that and tried to navigate his niece into disrupting Mama and Da's courtship. She spread rumors that Da secretly courted her. Lady Fraser tried to make Mama jealous. She even tried to seduce him, but Da never looked in her direction. The rumors never took hold because it was obvious to anyone with eyes that Da devoted himself to Mama. Mama's cousin already interested Laird Fraser and is now his wife. He swooped in and drew her into a courtship while arranging a marriage through her father. Lady Fraser never forgave Mama for what she claimed was stealing Da from her, and she never forgave Da for spurning her. She's held that grudge to this day. The Sinclairs are our neighbors and our friends; after all, my aunt married into the clan. Lady Fraser assumed she got her revenge when she separated her daughter, Deirdre, from my cousin Magnus. She and Laird Fraser hid Deirdre here at court, intercepting every missive for seven years until Magnus discovered her here when Uncle Liam sent him to resolve some conflicts with other clans. While there isn't a rift between us and the Rosses, we aren't warm to one another. Laurel is a cousin, but she has never been a friend."

"That's incredible. Are your parents still happy together?"

"Aye. They say they love each other more than they did when they wed. Their bond is unbreakable. They show affection regardless of whether they are alone or around the clan. They're devoted to one another."

Kieran considered that for a long time. While he hoped for a love match and a happy marriage with Maude, the realization that it might be possible remained foreign to him. His parents' marriage couldn't have been more different.

"I'd like the same for us, buttercup. But if it takes more than a moon for you to be sure you want to wed me, I won't rush you."

"But you can't remain here indefinitely. You have your own clan to lead and responsibilities at home."

"You're right, that I do. I will have to return within the next few sennights, but we can send missives back and forth. It's not ideal, but we communicate well enough that way."

"Your poor messengers will grow weary of shuttling back and forth between Stornoway and Stirling."

"It's a good thing I have several able riders to take turns."

Maude inched closer to Kieran, and he slid his hand down to hold hers among the folds of her skirt. The group returned to the castle before he had the chance share a story about his own family. He would have to save it for the next morning, since he expected little privacy that afternoon in the queen's solar.

CHAPTER FOURTEEN

Maude shared the midday meal with the other ladies, who were unafraid to pepper her with questions about her relationship with Kieran. When she kept her answers succinct and evasive, they turned to Arabella and Blair for details. She'd told everything to Blair and nearly everything to Arabella, but they remained loyal to her. They ate more at that meal than they had in a moon. They kept their mouths full, so no one could expect them to respond.

After the meal, she decided on another walk, but this time with her father and Blair. It was one of the few times they had to catch up in private. She and Blair learned of the bairns who'd joined their clan, a few elders who'd passed away, and that Mama grew lonely without them but had accepted they would both leave home, whether it was in service to the queen or to marry. Hamish readily admitted that he despised being away from his wife, but he was too happy to be with Maude and Blair to let it overcome him. He told them he sent missives to their mother every three days. They each wrote most of their response before the messenger arrived, then added to it if they had anything to say about the contents in the one just received. They'd done it for years, and their system kept them both content and assured of one another's well-being.

Neither Blair nor Hamish broached the topic of Kieran, sensing Maude needed a reprieve from the constant examination of her relationship with him. They appreciated the changes they saw in Maude since meeting Kieran. She appeared more confident and self-assured. She wore her hair down with intricate braids and ribbons woven through them. And she smiled more. Seeing Maude come out of her shell was priceless to her father and sister.

Kieran returned to his chamber after the nooning to respond to correspondence that included reviewing an expense report. He rubbed his eyes and leaned back in his chair as he read the list for at least the fifth time. It astonished him how much his mother and other sister, Abigail, had spent on gowns. They'd ordered bolts of costly material along with the frippery they would argue were necessities. They'd done this before. When he travelled, they ventured on spending sprees. Part of why he rarely left home for extended periods of time was because he didn't trust them not to make paupers of them.

Kieran rubbed his temples, dreading the idea that he may need to return to Lewis sooner than he wanted. He'd been correct that he and Maude might exchange their own correspondence, but it wouldn't be the same as getting to know one another in person. He wondered if he might convince Hamish to come for a visit with Maude. Kieran had grown eager for his mother and sister to meet her. They were more materialistic than Maude, but he was certain Maude would win over every member of his clan with ease. It was impossible for him to fathom anything to dislike. He responded to his steward's distressed message with reassurance that he wouldn't allow them to spend another coin. He wrote explicitly in the missive that he gave his seneschal permission and discretion to deny the two women any unreasonable request. Kieran wrote a similar letter to his mother and sister, admonishing them for their lack of restraint. He warned them of the consequences to their clan if they continued to spend as they had. He prayed they would heed him and not force him to return before he was ready.

As the afternoon progressed, Kieran found the king in the Privy Council chamber and walked with him to the queen's solar. The king inquired about the progress Kieran made in his relationship with the Sunderland's daughter, and threatened him with an extended holiday in the Stirling dungeon if he did anything to break Maude's heart or spirit. While the sovereign glared at Kieran the entire walk to the royal suites, he became all smiles once he entered. The young women giggled and whispered as Kieran entered. Many batted their eyelashes at him and smiled, some coyly and others provocatively. The others darted glances between him and Maude before giggling and whispering. The former were unappealing in their brashness, while the latter were girlish and annoying. Kieran's eyes swept the chamber until he spotted Maude in a window seat reading. She looked up when she noticed the disruption. When Kieran was a few feet away, she stood. He met her with a bow, and she offered a curtsy. She pulled her skirts close and sat pressed against the wall to offer Kieran as much space as possible. He was too large for the embrasure, so crowding a second person onto the seat made it awkward. He angled his body, so Maude's shoulder rested against his, and he stretched one arm behind her to brace himself. Kieran kept his hand close enough to graze her backside when he moved his thumb, which he did repeatedly. When he asked what she read, he used the guise of pointing to something on the page to cover her hand with his. His thumb swept over the back of hers before twisting to caress the inside of her wrist. Maude found it difficult to concentrate as she attempted to explain the book. Kieran's breath tickled her ear, and she smelled the fresh mint on his breath. She'd chewed a spring on her return from her second walk. They passed the afternoon in quiet conversation about the books Maude had read and Kieran's favorite subjects when he was younger and had a tutor. The time came to change for the evening meal before either was prepared to end their quiet chat.

They spent the days that followed in the routine they established during that first day together. They broke their fast together, then Kieran joined Maude on her walk, but some days he left halfway through to go to the lists. On the days he returned in time for the nooning, he sat with her, but other days he took a light meal on the field. He was able to join her in the solar only when the king visited. When it wasn't possible, he tended to clan business that seemed never ending and often returned to the lists for an afternoon session. He would wait for the evening meal to conclude, which the queen expected Maude to share with the ladies-in-waiting rather than her father or Kieran. Then he pulled Maude into his arms to dance together to the first song. He reserved the slower, more intimate dances. He made his intent clear to any man who became overly friendly, and eventually the men gave up their pursuit, which relieved Maude. The men made her uneasy because none had a sincere interest in her beyond wanting to see her bosom and hoping she'd show them more. Kieran and Maude allowed themselves rare moments alone, and while they both grew frustrated and needy, they agreed that focusing on getting to know one another remained more important than deciding based on physical attraction. It didn't take either of them long to realize they were falling in love, but neither dared say it aloud.

When a fortnight passed, Kieran accepted that it was impossible to ignore the need to return home. He wouldn't be an absentee laird. He spoke to Maude and explained the situation. While he saw the news saddened her, she understood his duties and even made suggestions about concerns he shared with her. The weather had turned foul in Stirling, and he worried the Highlands had forgotten it was supposed to be the beginning of spring, not the beginning of winter. He admitted to Maude that he considered asking her father if they might accompany him, but he was unwilling to have her travel such a distance in the poor weather because he wouldn't risk her health or her safety. It was a gut-wrenching goodbye for them both.

CHAPTER FIFTEEN

Kieran spurred his horse as he saw the gates of Stornoway come into view as he descended the last hill. The sense of relief and peace that usually greeted him as he approached his home was absent that day. He'd left it in Stirling along with Maude. The journey took a full week, which was three more days than it should have. Weather slowed him and his guards, then two horses threw shoes along the way, and his own horse went lame, causing them to make camp early and leave late the next morning. He wanted nothing more than a hot bath, a good meal, and Maude. He would take two out of the three, but he gritted his teeth as he accepted that seeing his mother and sister first were unavoidable.

The contingent of riders clattered into the bailey as the bells rang, announcing the return of their laird. Kieran couldn't help but smile at the warm welcome he always received as he rode through the village that sat beyond the bailey wall. His people respected him and proved loyal, so he never took his position of authority for granted. He understood his responsibility for the well-being of each man, woman, and child in his clan. That included the farther-reaching villages comprising MacLeods of Lewis. It had been a hefty burden to shoulder at seven-and-ten, but with ten years of experience, he felt like he was on the path to be a good leader like his father had been. Inevitably, pain settled in his chest whenever he thought of his father. They'd been close, much like Maude and Hamish, but a weak heart struck him down when he was in his early forties. Kieran struggled with debilitating guilt for years because his father collapsed in the lists while sparring with Kieran. He feared he'd caused his father's heart failure despite the reassurances from everyone that his father's death had been unpredictable; he'd been the model of health and strength.

Kieran lingered in the bailey, greeting clan members who came to welcome him. Then he avoided the keep by insisting upon tending to Peat himself, using the animal's recent lameness as an excuse. When he'd had sufficient time to prepare himself and gird his loins, he entered the Great Hall. As he suspected, his mother and sister sat before the fire with their sewing in their laps. From what he saw, they both were working on new kirtles, the expensive fabric shimmering in the light from the flames. He had a moment of temptation to toss it all in the fire, but that would be a waste of costly material that had already cost his clan too much.

"Kieran!" Abigail called, the first of the two women to notice him. She tossed her sewing to the ground and ran to him. His jaw clenched again at his sister's easy disregard for what was a luxury to everyone else in the clan. His mother was more careful and placed her own sewing on her chair but stepped over her daughter's, showing little concern but a great deal of entitlement. He supposed neither knew any better. His mother was the oldest daughter of a laird and wife to one of the most powerful in the Hebrides, and his sister was the youngest child. His father had spoiled his mother, not out of affection but to buy himself peace. Abigail and Madeline were cut from the same cloth. The analogy wasn't lost on him as he approached. He opened his arms as his sister launched herself at him. For all her faults, she was always happy to see Kieran return, though the older she grew, the more he believed the happiness came from anticipation for what more she might order or receive.

His mother moved more gracefully across the floor. As he embraced them both, he looked over their heads at the Great Hall. It disappointed him to see the state in which the keep looked. Their housekeeper, Agatha, was aging and unable to keep up as she had his entire childhood. He'd offered to pension her off, but she whittled that the keep would fall down around their ears if he did. Neither his mother nor his sisters took great interest in the duties of chatelaine. All three had been trained, but his mother preferred to spend her time venturing into the local market, creating her new clothing, or reading poetry. Her pastimes had prepared Madeline well for becoming a lady-in-waiting. Kieran would have to see about finding Agatha's replacement before he brought Maude home. The rushes needed changing, the fireplace needed cleaning, the tapestries needed beating, and the wall sconces needed wax scraping from them. And that was what he observed from a brief scan of the Great Hall. He could only imagine what he'd find when he inspected further. He hadn't noticed such details before this return home because he'd trusted that between Agatha and his mother, the keep was being maintained in proper order. Now he had to swallow his disappointment and make plans for improvements before introducing Maude to his home. He didn't want her to regret coming or resent the amount of work she would have waiting when she stepped in as chatelaine.

"Mother, Abigail, I'm glad to be home."

"As we are glad to have you here, son." His mother's welcomes were never effusive, but he believed they were sincere.

"You've been away so much," Abigail pouted. "I began to think you forgot where your home was." Kieran wrapped his arm around his younger sister's shoulders as they walked toward the fire. He warmed his hands and backside, appreciating the roaring fire after so many nights with a meager campfire.

"I agree with the lass. It's been a long stretch since ye were home for more than a meal and a sleep. We're happy to have ye return, laddie." Kieran's smile was genuine for the first time since he arrived. Agatha hobbled toward him, relying on her walking stick. She'd been the housekeeper before her parents married and had practically raised him. She was like a kindly grandmother who wasn't afraid to give him a good thrashing when he needed it as a child. Kieran embraced Agatha and noticed how frail she'd become. When Kieran bent to embrace her, she whispered, "We need to speak and soon, Kier."

As Kieran straightened, he feared what Agatha would tell him. Her loyalty was to the entire family, but her priority was service to the laird. She gave him honest reports when he was home and through the steward's missives since she was the seneschal's mother. Agatha's astute eyes swept across the Great Hall before an eyebrow twitched. He knew she shared his disillusionment with the keep's condition.

"How long are you home for this time?" his mother asked. Kieran looked at Lady Adeline MacLeod closely for the first time. He took in the beautifully sculpted high brow, the patrician nose, the same gray eyes he possessed, and the mouth that carried small lines around it from being pursed in constant disdain for those around her. She had aged more rapidly over the last few years, and lines now bracketed her mouth. Most would think they were laugh lines, but Kieran realized they were from frowning. His mother was a difficult woman to please when she presumed something, or someone, didn't meet her standards. He'd hoped to avoid the question until at least after he'd eaten.

"That depends, Mother." Kieran deflected.

"On what?" Abigail latched onto her mother's question with an eagerness that made Kieran wonder what she wanted to be sure to ask for before he departed once more.

"The weather and the state of things here."

"Where will you be off to now? It seems as though you're rarely home these days."

"That's an exaggeration, Mother. Before going to court, I hadn't been away even for a night for several months."

"But now you are," his mother quipped.

"I have been at court longer than usual." Kieran decided to just have it out with his mother, hoping that having the ensuing argument on his first evening home would enable him to leave sooner. He already found being home was the last place he wanted to be. It was a new and painful sensation. "I've met a woman who I'm now courting."

"Pardon?" His mother snapped. "I believe I misheard. You traveled to court to resolve tax payments, then a raid, not to find a wife. I've been arranging that."

"And I was fine with that until I met someone. Mother, I would've had final say no matter who you presented to me. I'm laird, not a lad."

"Who is she?" Adeline demanded. "Is she at least from a good family?"

"She is. Maude Sutherland is the earl's older daughter." He waited for the fall out, and it came a heartbeat later.

"The Sutherlands? The treacherous bastards who attacked our people only sennights ago? You'd get into bed with our enemy?" Adeline sneered.

"Mother, I'd already expressed my interest before the incident. I've met with Laird Sutherland many times since he made his way there, too. I have settled both the resolution of the conflict and my courtship. This isn't up for discussion. It's my intention that upon my next return, my bride shall be with me. Arrangements may keep me away for a couple more moons, but then I should be home indefinitely, with only patrols taking me away."

"What's her dowry?"

Kieran studied his mother before responding. "Untouchable by you."

Adeline's eyes widened before her lips pinched together. She knew Kieran was aware of just how much she and Abigail spent in his absence.

"That isn't a response," she snarled.

"But it is, Mother. I will invest the coin she brings into the clan's business, and the land will remain in her name as her dower lands while it secures our border with the Sutherlands in Assynt. In other words, it's not your pin money. You can't spend it as you have the massive amounts of the whisky and wool profits." Kieran looked around as the Great Hall filled with people arriving for the evening meal. "We will speak of this after the meal in my solar. I'm going to my chamber to bathe and prepare for the meal."

"We are not done yet," his mother threw down the gauntlet.

Kieran stepped close to his mother, so only she and Abigail heard.

"We are done when *I* say so. You may be my mother, but I am your laird. Never disagree with me, or command me like that in front of our people again. You will find yourself with none of your luxuries if you test me. You know where Madeline is. Would you care to join her?" Kieran stalked away before he lost his temper and couldn't retract what he said.

The evening meal grew tense with little said among Adeline, Abigail, and Kieran. Kieran focused his attention on his second-in-command, Kyle. They'd grown up together and were second cousins. Kyle was Kieran's most trusted advisor and warrior. When Kieran had to be away, he remained confident that Kyle would ensure the clan's safekeeping. They'd fought at each other's backs since they entered the lists as adolescents. They had an easy comradery that Kieran appreciated as his mother fumed and his sister babbled incessantly to no one in particular. Abigail sensed the tension and tried to ease it; instead, the sound grated on Kieran's frayed nerves.

"How have things been?" Kieran asked around a mouthful of roast duck.

"Quiet. Blessedly quiet. At least outside the keep." Kyle grinned at Kieran as he looked past his commander and cocked an eyebrow at Adeline and Abigail. "The weather hasnae been on our side the last fortnight, but we finished refortifying the northern wall. The repairs you ordered on the mill are underway, and another lot of lambs are aboot to drop. All in all, things have been running smoothly."

Kieran sighed as he sat back and sipped from his chalice. He'd filled his with whisky that night rather than the wine and ale served. He was still chilled despite the hot bath, and he needed the liquid courage to go another round with his mother.

"Remember the woman I told you aboot?" Kieran was careful that his hushed tones didn't float down to his mother who was only a few chairs over to his left.

"Aye. The Sutherland lass."

"I'm leaving again as soon as I can. I'm going back to Stirling and will return with her as my wife."

"You really are going to marry her."

"That's my goal. She's unlike any woman I've ever met. I just worry aboot how Mother and Abigail will treat her. This latest disaster with the accounts, and how Mother responded to my intention to wed someone other than her choosing, now has me concerned that they won't be much better than Madeline was. I'm second guessing whether it would be right to bring her here. I don't know if I should break things off."

"Can she nae manage without a warm welcome?"

Kieran glared at Kyle, who put his hands up.

"She can manage better than anyone I know. She's had to far too often. She's survived my sister and serving at court for almost a year. She has a backbone of steel, but she's reserved. People underestimate her because of it. She's bonnie as the day is long, but she's not what most would consider beautiful, or at least not what most women would. Men, on the other hand, are entirely too appreciative of what they can guess lurks beneath her kirtle."

"And have you sampled that?" Kyle leaned away as he asked.

Kieran's hand made a fist on the table. If anyone else had asked, Kieran would have driven that fist through his face. He forced himself to unfurl his hand and place his palm on the table.

"She's a maiden and will remain such until we wed. But aye, I'm attracted to her. More so than any other woman I've ever seen. It's as though she's in my blood. I crave her like some men do whisky. I trust her council, and I'm certain she'd manage this keep a far sight better than my mother. The clan will like her, but only if Mother and Abigail approve. The others won't go against them, so I fear they'll snub her. Madeline made her life difficult, but she's overlooked my sister's sins and judged me for who I am, not to whom I'm related. Mother's outburst when she learned Maude is a Sutherland leads me to believe she won't be so openminded. Kyle, I love her."

"Love? That's a rather soft thing to say."

"I'll watch you tell that to your father. I can see him from here, and I believe he has his arm wrapped around your mother's waist." Kieran strained to see over the heads at several tables before grinning at Kyle. "And I believe he's feeding her a bite of cheese."

Kyle pretended to grimace but couldn't help but smile. Unlike Kieran's parents' arranged marriage, Kyle's parents had married for love. It showed in everything they did, including how they raised their children. Kyle was courting a woman from the village as they spoke.

"As long as you dinna tell Glynnis, I should survive. How soon will you leave?"

"I'd go tomorrow, if I could just to escape Mother, but I

have too much to do here before I can. It may be close to a fortnight."

"And you dinna worry aboot leaving her behind at court?"

"No." It was an easy answer to give since he trusted Maude implicitly, but he also recognized she was uncomfortable with the attention she'd garnered of late. He suspected with him away, she would wear more practical hairstyles and return to being a wallflower. "Maude can be rather shy. People mistake it for timidity, but she would rather observe and take everyone's measure before joining in."

"So, she's untrusting of others? What caused that? She's still young, isn't she?"

"Aye. Nine-and-ten. She was teased without mercy when she was younger, and my sister opened old wounds."

"What was wrong with her?" Kyle snapped his mouth shut and scooted his chair away, anticipating the fist that would surely fly his way this time. Instead, he looked at Kieran and found his friend and laird was gripping the edge of the table so tightly that his knuckles were white. Kieran's jaw ticked as he turned his head toward Kyle.

"Naught is wrong with her. There never has been. I told you, she's bonny but not in the way most women see it. She's fit and sturdy but lean after years of chasing after her brother. She rides and shoots as well as most men and is strong. She's not a rail like most women. She was teased by boys when she grew into womanhood, and then by my sister and her friends at court." Kieran measured his next words, since he hated saying them to any man, as though he was spilling a secret. "She's well-endowed on top, so men often make comments better suited to a tavern wench. She's self-conscious and with good reason, after what she's had to put up with."

"I suppose it boils down to this: you say you love her, but do you think she will make you a good wife?" Kieran's nod was immediate. "Do you think she'd be a good lady of the clan?"

"Without a doubt."

"Then marry her and bring her home. Abigail will leave to marry soon enough. Madeline won't be returning, at least not for a few years. Your mother can move to her dower lands or retire to a convent if she's that opposed to your marriage. You deserve happiness after what you've sacrificed for this clan, and if that's with Maude, then so be it. If you believe she'll be good for the clan, then all the more reason to bring her here, because we're in need of a woman who can do her share of leading."

Kieran considered Kyle's words and felt better for hearing the affirmation. But his relief was cut short when his mother rose and signaled to Abigail that they would retire. Kieran wasn't about to allow his mother to disobey him again. He nodded to Kyle and rose to step in front of Adeline and Abigail.

"Well timed. I was just aboot to summon you to my solar." Kieran didn't wait for their response before moving to the dais steps. He led them to his solar on the ground floor and experienced a moment of calm as he entered his sanctuary. While he conducted clan business here, it was one of the few places where he could close the door, reassured no one would bother him short of an emergency. His mother's voice shattered the feeling.

"This shall have to wait. It grows late, and I wish to retire. We can discuss whatever it is in the morning," Adeline's expression was cold and off-putting.

"You do not get to decide that, Mother. I decide where and when I conduct clan business." He moved to the seat behind his desk and took it without waiting for either of the women sit. He pulled forward the ledger that Adam, the steward, had left on top. He already anticipated what he would find since Adam copied the columns and included it in one of his missives. "Sit, Mother. Now."

Adeline huffed but took a seat, with Abigail following suit. Her eyes darted between the two, nervous about the standoff taking place. She'd never seen Kieran address their mother with such cold efficiency, even when their mother pushed back against his authority. Abigail feared she and their mother had gone too far this time with their spending, but she didn't understand how it could be of much consequence since they were wealthy.

"I didn't appreciate learning of how depleted our coffers are while I was at court to resolve taxation complaints. Neither of you seem to understand that our funds are not for our personal disposal. They are for the safekeeping and well-being of our clan. I still need to pay the masons who worked on the north wall. I need to pay the drovers who will take our sheep to market. I need to ensure we make repairs to crofts that suffered during the snows. I need funds to buy grain and barley for our food and our livestock. All of that comes from the accounts you raided to buy cloth for your own gowns. It's not as though you did it to acquire material to make clothes for our poorer families. You did it to flaunt wealth you're pissing away. I told you before I left that you were not to spend any more money on items for your own comfort. The only approved expenses are ones for the keep. I return to a home that's not being run by its chatelaine."

"Are you saying I'm inept as lady of the keep?" His mother's tone was frigid.

"I'm saying your entitlement and disinterest in being a respectable lady of the keep will drown us in debt."

"You've always been one for exaggeration, Kieran. There isn't the catastrophe afoot that you're making this out to be. You're selfish and miserly. I didn't raise you that way," Adeline sniffed.

"No, you didn't because Agatha is the one who raised me when I wasn't at Da's side. He indulged you to placate you and buy himself peace. I am not my father, and I will not continue to condone this behavior. You have a choice, the two of you: amend your spending habits and indifference toward your duties here, or I will send you to your dower lands, Mother, and marry you off, Abigail. Make your choice. I will hear from you in the morning. Goodnight." Kieran turned his attention back to the ledgers, dismissing his mother and sister. He couldn't bring himself to look at either of them lest he cave. He loathed threatening either of them, but neither showed any remorse or intention to change on their own.

"Kieran?" Abigail's nervous voice forced him to look up. "Who are you going to marry me off to? Is he old and fat and ugly?"

Kieran's mouth thinned. No apology was forthcoming from his sister, and her greatest worry about her potential husband was his appearance.

"I haven't decided which offer to accept." Kieran lied. There had been few serious offers for Abigail's hand since Madeline was still unwed. He had considered brokering a marriage for Abigail with the Matheson's son, but that bridge had already crumbled. He hadn't intended to marry his younger sister off yet, and he feared she was ill-equipped to marry a laird or heir, but he realized it might be the only way for her to mature and escape their mother's influence. Finding her a suitable husband was one more thing to add to his growing list of tasks. He doubted he would resolve that before he returned to Stirling.

Once he was alone, he pulled a piece of vellum out and wrote his first missive to Maude.

Bc,

I've arrived safely, if not later than I expected. For the sake of your safety and health, I am glad you didn't accompany me. The weather was atrocious, and we suffered several setbacks that drew the journey out an additional three days. Nonetheless, I miss you. I long to see your smile and hear your voice. It's been only a sennight, and I feel adrift without you. How have you come to mean so much to me in such a short time? I believe we agreed it was fate.

I've had the first showdown with my mother. I'm certain it won't be the only one before I leave. I've given her the choice to stop spending and fulfill her duties more effectively, or she can retire to her dower lands. That was after the evening meal, only moments ago. I admit I lost my temper within minutes of seeing her and threatened to send her to Inchcailleoch Priory to join Madeline. Part of me wishes she would choose the dower lands. That's wretched of me, isn't it? What type of son says such a thing? I dislike sharing this with you as I fear it's inevitable that you will form a poor impression of my mother and sister. They aren't all bad. It's their inability to see how their spending affects the clan that bothers me most. They only see the comfort and wealth and not the effort and monies spent to maintain it. I blame my father for spoiling my mother and sisters, but I'm as much to blame for perpetuating it.

What do you think I should do, bc? What would you do in my position? I wish for your council and hope you understand that I ask in earnest. I hope this missive finds you well and enjoying your father's extended visit. What have you and Arabella been doing during my absence? I miss our walks tremendously and have already thought of the route I plan to take when we go for our first walk here.

Please be reassured that my intention to marry you hasn't changed, but if you find that while I am gone, you prefer not to pursue our courtship, you have but to tell me. However, I can't guarantee that I will bow out gracefully. I realize I'm not painting a splendid picture of what you may find upon your arrival here, but I find I can't lie to you whether it be by word or omission.

I look forward to your response, bc.

Yours always,

Td

Kieran sealed the missive and took it with him. His solar was supposed to be private, but he didn't trust his mother that night. Intuition told him she would delight in nothing more than to interfere with Maude. He carried the ledgers with him, not trusting their safekeeping after his confrontation with Adeline.

CHAPTER SIXTEEN

Maude read Kieran's missive for the second time. It arrived that morning, and Maude slipped away to her chamber to read it in private. As she came to the end, she was uncertain of her reaction. Her heart ached for Kieran's dilemma, but part of her feared making a home among his family. She was certain even without meeting Adeline or Abigail that she wouldn't be welcome. She considered whether her feelings for Kieran were strong enough to withstand the inevitable tests the other two women would present. She wondered if she would grow to resent Kieran or if she would put him in the middle. Would he side with her or would blood win out? She closed her eyes as she let the concerns run through her head. She moved the pieces around in her mind until she heard what her heart was trying to say. She was certain she loved Kieran. It hadn't taken long, but she was certain. Her father had commented on it, and so had Blair and Arabella. While she might not have confessed it to Kieran, she was honest with herself. She didn't anticipate moving to Stornoway with eagerness, knowing a cold reception awaited her, but she had dealt with such before and came out the other side. For Kieran's sake and for the chance to have a loving marriage, she would bear the difficulties with as much grace as she could muster. She picked up the quill to put her decision to paper.

Td,

I am much relieved to learn of your safe arrival. The weather here has been little better, so hearing from you eases my worry. I miss you too, td. I wish we were together, wherever that might be. I'm sorry you had such an unpleasant reunion with your family, but it seems rather unavoidable from what you shared. I wish for everyone involved that you can come to an agreement and make amends. It pains me to think of you at odds with more members of your family. You may not wish to hear this, but I think you may have to follow through with your ultimatum. Ask yourself what is best for your clan, not for your family. It's the price paid by all lairds. Sometimes what one wants for their loved ones can't be easily reconciled with one's duties. I'd venture to say King Robert experiences that daily. There is much he would have liked to grant my cousins during their trials and tribulations at court, and certainly what he must have wished to do for his brother and Lady Elizabeth. Leadership comes with quite expensive costs.

I'm not sure if I should say this as I don't want you to take offense, but my parents offer sound council if you should ask for it. I won't say any more than that but be reassured that the offer stands.

Arabella gripes at me because I have reverted to wearing my hair up more often. I'm guessing you suspected I would. While it isn't the "austere matron's knot" that Arabella called my previous style, it's simpler than the intricate braids. It's something I can do myself. While my maid is skilled at creating those styles, she isn't the gentlest of hair dressers. My scalp thanks me for retaking control of my hair.

In less inane news—well, I can't rightly say that there is any news. Naught but the usual has occurred since you left. It's the endless routine of praying, eating, walking, dancing, and sleeping. I could do it in my sleep. I wish I could be doing it in my sleep. I look forward to the weather improving, so I can take Trioblaid out. I've kept the poor lad cooped up in his stall for sennights. I visit him and sneak him extra apples and carrots, but we haven't been able to gallop in ages. Fear not, td, I will take

Donald and Tomas with me and at least two more of Da's guards if I ride out. I need to visit the abbey and Michael since the castle's medicinals are running low once more. I may have to brave the wind and snow. Trioblaid never minds, but I don't enjoy the wind up my---well, never mind where. Suffice it to say, I don't care for it.

Until your next missive, yours fondly,

Bc

PS I have no intention of relinquishing you. Fear not, I'm prepared to give you the answer you seek.

Maude sealed the parchment and sent it with a page to find a Sutherland messenger. She prayed he had safe passage once he arrived on MacLeod land. Tensions had eased in Assynt, but she wasn't sure that the MacLeods on Lewis had forgiven her clan yet. She'd discussed her dowry at length with her father the day before. She recognized it was unusual for him to do so, but he believed his daughters should be aware of their options for their future, so no husband or clan could take advantage of them. Maude hadn't told her father about Kieran's financial concerns. They didn't seem dire, more an ongoing source of frustration. However, it relieved her to discover her dowry included a sizable portion. If Kieran safeguarded it, there would be enough to refill their coffers. Her father selected land near the border with Assynt as her dower lands. She understood and appreciated that he did this on purpose. While the MacLeods wouldn't be allowed to build on the land, and she didn't think Kieran would ever send any MacLeods to live on it, it would make the border less contentious.

When the time came for a wedding, she hoped Kieran would be amenable to traveling to Sutherland, so her mother and brother could be a part of the festivities. She would stress that they invite Adeline and Abigail, too, but she wasn't sure they would accept.

Maude didn't share how much better her experience at

court was now that Madeline left. She was still a wallflower, and at times, it was still difficult not to envy Arabella's beauty and poise, but she felt more confident thanks to Kieran's support. She danced more often but was relieved when few men asked for more intimate dances. She politely refused until they no longer asked. Several assumed Kieran's absence would open the door to seducing her. Her father disabused them of that idea. She'd overhead two men discussing her, and their comments had crushed her until she reminded herself that she wasn't seeking their approval. They'd commented on how her breasts and backside would feel in the dark would made up for her lack of beauty, and what they intended didn't have to involve looking at her face. She'd stumbled away and excused herself from the evening meal. It took a hearty cry before she remembered that the only man's approval she sought was Kieran's, and she accepted that she'd gained that by being herself.

Missives from Kieran arrived every four days, so she'd received three more in the fortnight that passed since Kieran arrived home. He remained away almost as long as the last time he returned to Lewis, except this time, he regretted it was impossible to pledge to return within a moon. Maude looked forward to his missives and found it offered her a different way to become acquainted with Kieran, as they shared many private thoughts on how they viewed their positions as laird and lady of a clan, and they discovered they had similar stances on how to lead. They appreciated one another's ideas and values. She offered council when he requested it, and while she had little need to ask his advice on navigating the world of ladies-in-waiting, his suggestions made her laugh. The only thing missing was the opportunity to be in each other's presence, to touch and to feel. They shared their longing for one another and even hinted at what they wished to do once they wed. Maude's ears often burned as she read and wrote the suggestive comments. It made the separation a little more bearable.

Kieran paced like a caged lion. He was even more incensed than he had been when he arrived to deal with his mother's disregard for their clan's finances. He'd suspected she might be intercepting his correspondence, but he hadn't had proof until that morning. He'd been in the lists and returned to discover a missive had arrived from Maude. He'd wondered if his mother had been opening, then resealing, the letters before they were given to him. After the last missive arrived, he instructed Adam or Agatha to find him when the next one arrived. He allowed Adam to leave it on his desk as he did with all of Kieran's correspondence. He watched his mother skulk toward his solar before entering and locking the door. He waited a couple of minutes before letting himself in. She stood beside his desk, missive in hand, sneering at it. She didn't bat an eyelash at being caught. She tossed the parchment on the desk before telling him that men bedded wantons like Maude but never married them. He fought the urge to wring her neck but ordered her out of his solar. He locked and barred the door before rushing to retrieve the precious letter.

Td,

I miss you. I realize that I shouldn't greet you with that. That I shouldn't bemoan our separation but rather reassure you that all is well in your absence, but I can't. I miss you and find myself in a foul mood today for it. I hear your voice in my head, but it's not the same as when you kiss my neck and whisper to me. The spot at the corner of my jaw tingles with the same need for your attention as the rest of me does. I wish to lay my eyes on you again, for you are the most handsome mon I know. It still mesmerizes me that someone so fine as you should have chosen someone like me. I admit I still worry others will think you've settled. But enough of the doldrums. Suffice it to say, I look forward to your return.

. . .

Kieran paused and considered what his mother accused Maude of. These sentiments

were benign, and even the racier things they shared were innocent. But Adeline couldn't have known or considered Maude's comments questionable based upon this letter. She'd read the others.

I hope things are on the up and up with your family and clan. I dislike thinking of you bearing these burdens alone, but it seems that Kyle lends a good ear. I wish there was more for me to do to assist, but I feel rather hopeless so far from you. And it's not my place. While this might add salt to the wound, Blair convinced me to order a new gown. It's arriving in a sennight. I shall save it for your return. I'd like to look my best when you arrive. I hope you haven't forgotten what I look like. I'm about yay tall— place your hand on your breastbone — with dark hair and dark eyes. I'll be the one waiting for you.

Yours always,

Bc

Kieran folded the letter before retrieving the other ones he stored in a locked drawer. He no longer believed they were safe in his solar. The knowledge that his mother invaded his privacy ruined the notion that this chamber was his sanctuary. He would keep the letters in his sporran if he had to. They were too special to share with anyone else. He pulled a fresh parchment forward and considered what he would say.

Bc,

How could I forget what you look like when you are on my mind constantly? I'm intrigued by this new gown. I would ask you to describe it, but I intend to see it and you before your response can reach me. I've concluded the business that took me from you, and I plan to leave here in two days. I will send a rider ahead when we are an hour outside of Stir-

ling. Meet me in the spense and wear your new gown, if you would. I long to see you in it almost as much as I long to slip you out of it. Bc, I ache to touch you, to taste you. I hope it is the same for you. Promise me a smile for when I return. The one where one corner of your mouth twitches up. I'm always desperately curious about what you're thinking when you gift me with one of them. I shall take you in my arms and hold you for as long as we dare.

Will you say yes if I ask? Consider your answer, for it shall be the first thing I say. I miss you, bc. Not much longer, mo leannan. Not until we're reunited and not till I claim you as my wife.

Devotedly yours,

Td

After sealing the parchment, Kieran summoned his messenger. The man nodded before Kieran had the chance to give his instructions. They were always the same: the messenger is to deliver missive into no one's hands but Lady Maude. He tucked the stack of older missives into his sporran and went in search of Kyle. He acknowledged that he was letting his mother chase him from his home, but he was fed up with being delayed and manipulated. His mother met his announcement of his imminent departure with silence, while his sister shed crocodile tears. When he rode out two days later, anyone watching would have thought the flames of hell were licking at his boots.

CHAPTER SEVENTEEN

Maude sensed someone followed her, but she couldn't hear the sound of any footsteps. She increased her pace, but she failed to shake the intuition that someone was approaching. She prepared to run when she heard her name.

"Lady Maude," a man's voice called. "I bear a missive from the MacLeod."

Maude spun around and recognized the messenger. She placed her hand over her chest, her heart racing. She ran her clammy hands over her gown as the man approached.

"You startled me, John. I didn't realize it was you."

"I didna want to call out and draw attention to ye. Ma laird instructed me to tell ye he sends good news." John handed the parchment over before bowing and leaving her alone with her letter.

Maude rushed to her chamber, uncaring that she was supposed to make her way to the gardens for the ladies' morning walk. She pried the seal off and unfolded the letter. She sat on her bed as she read the distinct handwriting she would now recognize anywhere. She covered her mouth to keep from crying out when she read Kieran was on his way. Receiving the missive meant he would already be halfway to Stirling if all went to plan. She had only two more days to wait. Happy tears trailed down her cheeks as she lay back on her bed with the missive resting over her heart. She wished she might fall asleep and wake up two days later since it would be even harder to pass the next couple of days, remembering he was so close but not yet there.

Kieran dried his face and put on a fresh leine but kept his breacan feile on rather than take the extra few minutes to don breeks. The sun was already setting, and he didn't like picturing Maude wandering the courtyard and storage buildings alone in the dark. He made his way toward the spense and rounded the last corner as a small figure walked toward him. He recognized Maude immediately, and it seemed she recognized him too because she ran toward him. His longer stride brought him to her as she launched herself into his arms. He clasped his arms around her waist and twirled her around.

"You're back!" Maude burbled. She couldn't think of anything else to say, so she grasped his face and kissed him. She poured all her excitement and frustration into that kiss. Kieran groaned and hoisted her higher, encouraging her to wrap her legs around his waist. He pushed the door open to the nearest storeroom before kicking it shut. Maude's back bumped into the wooden portal as his tongue dove into the silky recesses of her mouth. Their hands were everywhere as they explored one another. As Kieran's eyes adjusted to the dim light, he scanned the room and found a table off to the side. He carried Maude to it and eased her to lie back, his body covering hers as his lips trailed fire and ice over her neck and chest.

"I've waited months to taste you, Maude, and I won't wait any longer." Kieran's fingers danced a path from the inside of her ankles to her knees. His hands stopped on her thighs in the same place as the last time they were alone like this; now, he bent and placed kisses there. He pushed her long skirts higher as his mouth nipped and licked until it met the juncture of her leg and hip. He trailed his tongue along the joint's crease before repeating the same rapturous exploration on the other side. His thumbs inched closer to her sheath, drifting with a slow glide to give Maude time to adjust to the new sensations. Her fingers fisted the shoulders of his leine as his mouth returned to her chest. "I anticipate you shall taste like rich honey that I shall want to lick over and over. I've fantasized aboot bringing you to release with my tongue, and I shall live out that fantasy now."

Kieran's thumbs pulled her nether lips apart before the flat breadth of his tongue swept from bottom to top, his lips furling around her nub. He flicked it twice before drawing hard on the cluster of nerves that made her hips lift from the table. He pressed her back down as his tongue made another pass, this time the tip delved into her sheath. She writhed and moaned as one new sensation after another ricocheted from her core outward.

"Kier?"

"Yes, mo ghaol. I'll make it better. Wheest and let me feast upon you, so I can bring you the relief you seek."

Kieran continued to tease the heated flesh until Maude's moans turned to whimpers. He realized he was pushing her to her untried limits. He ran his finger along her seam, following then leading his tongue. He slipped a finger into her and groaned at how smooth and tight she felt. His cock strained to reach her, insisting that it should be within her rather than his finger. He wished to toss his plaid over his shoulder and ease the ache in his bollocks, but he admitted he would be inside Maude before either of them considered the consequences. Instead, he worked her with his tongue and fingers while stroking himself. He was careful not to pierce her maidenhead when he thrust a second finger into her, but when she guided a third finger to her sheath, his essence shot from him, pooling on the floor between his feet. His groan of satisfaction rumbled through Maude's core and set off her own reaction. Her inner muscles clamped around Kieran's fingers as he continued to work the sensitive flesh. Maude cried out her pleasure as the last jets of seed spurted from his cock.

Maude held Kieran's body against hers as she trembled from the aftershock of her release. Each time Kieran brought her to climax, the sensations were more breathtaking and addicting. Her knees shook until she capitulated and allowed them to cave in, bracketing his hips and pressing him against her. She ran lazy circles over his back as her heart slowed enough to draw a deep breath. Kieran stroked her hair and whispered soothing words as her mind drifted back to earth. As her thoughts became ordered once more, she paused and turned her head to look at Kieran, which was difficult with his head tucked against the crook of her neck.

"What aboot you?" she murmured.

Kieran pulled back enough for them to look at one another. "What aboot me?"

"I got to--- but you--- it doesn't seem fair," Maude finished flatly, unsure how to verbalize her thoughts.

"Oh, I did, buttercup." Kieran's grin was all male pride and made her core clench for his attention all over again.

"But I didn't touch you." Maude's brow furrowed in confusion.

Kieran eased back and kissed the creases on her forehead before moving to her temple, and finally the corner of her mouth. His large hand wrapped around her neck, his thumb caressing her jaw.

"If you had, Maude, we'd be standing before a priest this very moment. I wouldn't have been able to stop myself from making you mine. I won't take that choice from you. I---I---" Kieran experienced a sudden wave of shyness, unsure how to admit he'd taken the matter into his own hand. He didn't want Maude ever to experience embarrassment about what they shared, so he swallowed and explained. "I palmed myself. If you touched me, or I moved my plaid aside, I didn't trust myself not to take your maidenhead. I want to feel your hands on me, to thrust inside you, to feel you climax around me, but I don't have the right. My release would have come anyway, so I eased the tightness in my bollocks by stroking my cock."

In the dim light, Kieran saw Maude's face hardened in the mask of someone who looked like he had robbed them. He realized she was angry that he'd stolen her opportunity to offer him what he was far too eager to offer her. Her jaw set and lips thinned before her eyes drifted closed. She continued to play with the hair at his collar, but when her body went lax, he recognized it wasn't the last of the tension leaching from her; it was in frustrated resignation.

"Buttercup?"

"Hmmm? It's naught."

"It is something. Do you regret me touching you?" Kieran feared his heart would shatter if she answered in the affirmative.

"Of course not. I'm sure I would have combusted if you hadn't." Maude tilted her head further back and looked into the darkness, her gaze toward the ceiling. "I haven't been able to touch you any of the three times. And I'd hope this time—I wanted to be the one—I wanted to be the reason for your climax like you're the reason for mine." She choked out her thoughts and stiffened when Kieran chuckled.

"Mo leannan, you have been the reason for my climax every day, at least once if not twice a day, since the night I met you."

Maude pushed at Kieran's chest and tried to scramble out from beneath him. He didn't understand her reaction until he realized that, in her innocence, she had no knowledge of how men and women eased their own lust. He clasped a wrist in each of his hands and drew her arms over her head. Her squirming body arched under his and froze as a new awareness coursed through her. Her breasts strained against his chest, her nipples painful darts beneath the heavy fabric of her kirtle. Kieran shifted both of her hands into one of his before gripping her hip and pulling her down the table. His rod jerked against her entrance as he pressed her against the table. His thumb found her pearl and circled.

"Do you feel that? Feel how my hand makes you come alive?" He continued to draw slow circles as he pressed. Her writhing told him he'd found the correct rhythm. He paused to draw one of her hands down to the juncture of her thighs before guiding it between her legs. He showed her how to work the bundle of nerves as she strained toward him. "You can ease your own ache, mo leannan. You don't need me."

"I do need you," she whimpered.

"Shh. That's not what I meant. You don't need me to feel release if I can't be with you. Just as you can climax on your own, so can a mon. I've been stroking myself every day since I felt you against me on that terrace. It's the only way I survived not being able to make love to you. I close my eyes and picture you. I can see you, smell you, taste you as I work myself. You make me so hard so many times throughout the day, just from the image of you in my mind, that I had to ease my cods, or the only thing people would remember of me is my rampant cockstand. And it would take little for them to figure out the reason. I suspect people have picked up on my interest."

"Why didn't you teach this to me before you left?" Maude accused and harrumphed at the press of Kieran's grin against her cheek. She pushed his hand away from her bud. "I don't find any of this humorous. You knew of a way to ease my discomfort and never told me, rather keeping the secret to yourself and enjoying its benefit. Then when we are together, you steal my chance to show you how much I--"

"How much you what?" Kieran held his breath. Would she admit that she loved him just as he did her? She gazed at him, but it had grown too dark to make out his expression.

"How much I care." Maude was unprepared to admit her feelings when she was unconvinced Kieran shared them, at least not to the same depth.

176

"I didn't realize it would upset you. I wasn't rejecting you. I was protecting you."

"I don't need protecting from everything, turtledove. I want to experience the same pleasures you do."

"And if now that I've taught you how, what if you discover you no longer need me?"

Maude paused, and if Kieran could have seen her aghast expression, he would have laughed.

"Is that why you didn't show me how to pleasure myself? You feared that if I knew how, I'd stop wanting you? You seem to still want me even though you pleasure yourself. You make no sense. I think that now I know, I want you all the more."

"I do want you. In every way, Maude."

Maude pressed against his shoulder until he stood up, and she followed. He helped her slip from the table.

"What do you mean, turtledove?"

Kieran wouldn't propose to Maude in the dark. Nor would he do it only moments after they came so close to coupling. He wouldn't allow her ever to wonder if he'd asked merely out of passion. He took her hand, and when he opened the door, he looked both ways before stepping out. They walked in silence until they entered the queen's gardens. There was no one there, which suited Kieran's purpose, but he sought a place that was open and light. He wanted to see Maude when he asked, and while he wanted privacy, he didn't want her to wonder if he tried to hide his feelings for her.

"I mean, buttercup, that I want you by my side in everything, day and night. I want you to be the first person I see every morn, and the last person I see every eve. I want to ken I can see you, touch you, hear you, taste you, smell you, everything with you every day for the rest of our lives. I'm asking, will you marry me, Maude?"

"Yes."

Kieran was unprepared for the succinct answer. The certainty in Maude's voice rang in his ears, and her clear gaze confirmed that she'd accepted his proposal. "You mean it?" He still needed the confirmation.

"Aye. I'll marry you, turtledove," Maude beamed. Kieran lifted her off her feet and twirled her around, whooping loudly enough to draw attention from the servants in the courtyard and surrounding buildings. When Kieran put her down, she lifted onto her toes and offered the most tender kiss she would muster, and he returned it tenfold. Even though they'd spoken no words of love, it was in the kiss. Maude prayed that one day Kieran would say them aloud, but accepted that they might never come. It cast a pall on her for a moment before she shook it off, reminding herself that she hadn't the nerve to say them either. When they pulled away, Kieran tucked her head against his chest and kissed her crown. She closed her eyes as she absorbed the steady heartbeat against her cheek.

"May I ask a boon, mo ghràidh?"

"Of course, mo leannan. Anything." Kieran closed his eyes and reveled in the moment of affection after such passion and excitement.

"I realize we might marry here or Stornoway as expected, but I hoped to travel to Dunrobin for the wedding. It would mean a great deal to me to have my mother and brother there."

"If that is what you wish, then we will marry there."

"You don't mind? What aboot your mother and sister? Will they come?"

Kieran's heart sank. Not because he would miss having his mother there, but because he dreaded having to admit that the women wouldn't make the effort. They'd left things on a sour note, and he wasn't sure how they would receive the news, be it an invitation to the wedding or their marriage announcement. He would honor his word to Maude. "I will send them a missive in the morn."

"How soon might they reach Dunrobin?"

"A sennight or less." Kieran shrugged.

"Perfect."

"Lass?"

"I suppose I can survive the delay, knowing it's so your family can join us."

"Delay? It'll take three sennights for the banns to post, and at least that long to be ready for the wedding. I imagine a sennight here for your father to conclude his business and be ready for travel, a sennight on the road to Sutherland, and a sennight for you to prepare for the ceremony and feast." Kieran snapped his mouth shut at the disappointed look on Maude's face. "What is it, buttercup?"

"I don't want to wait that long." Maude fought the tears welling in her eyes and looked away. She couldn't explain why she felt like weeping other than she'd been so excited one moment, and then the notion of another delay crushed her. "I didn't anticipate it would take that long."

"Three sennights? You know we must post the banns."

"Aye, but it doesn't have to be three Sundays, just three Masses. Da's business here was with you, and you both resolved that ages ago. He's only remained to spend time with Blair and me and to monitor our courtship. Your original matters concluded over a moon ago, and things sit well with my father. Blair and I can pack in less than an hour, and I suppose neither you nor Da would take much longer. We'd arrive at Sutherland at the same time as your messenger arrives in Stornoway. We'd still have to wait a sennight for your family to arrive, but I'd rather a fortnight than three sennights."

"One sennight, mo leannan. That's all we need to wait if a priest can read the banns that quickly." Kieran tucked hair behind Maude's ear and sighed. "Lass, I doubt my mother and sister will come. I had a falling out with my mother before I left."

"She wouldn't come to her only son's wedding? I can't believe that." Maude saw the defeat in Kieran's expression and chose not to press. Her heart ached to know there was a rift between mother and son, especially since she suspected she was the cause. She whispered, "Invite her, and we shall go from there."

Kieran tipped her chin up and pressed a kiss beside the corner of her jaw. "You're too good to me, buttercup. I'm a blessed mon to have you as my bride." He kissed her again. "I know you worry this rift is because of you, but it's not. My mother brought this upon herself."

Maude shivered with a sense of dread. It dampened the happiness that had warmed her when Kieran proposed. A sinking sensation that life in Stornoway would be all too familiar took root in her belly.

CHAPTER EIGHTEEN

Kieran observed Maude riding next to her sister. They'd left Stirling the next morning after announcing their betrothal first to Hamish, then to the king and queen. It came as little surprise to anyone, so Maude was relieved when the queen released her from her duties as a lady-in-waiting. The queen's offer to allow Blair as much time away from court as she wanted brought both women to tears. They knew their godmother wouldn't keep Blair from joining her family, but they'd expected a limit to her generosity.

Maude and Kieran's betrothal was announced at evening's meal to many gasps and whispers, but it was an excuse for feasting. Now the sun was sinking low on their first day of travel. The sisters had nattered together for most of the ride. Kieran caught glimpses of how both women must have been before they arrived at court. There was an ease to their banter that his sisters had never shared, and it made him curious about what they would be like when their brother entered the mix. Hamish and his guards led their party while Kieran and his small contingent brought up the rear. Hamish asked if Kieran preferred to ride up front, but he used the excuse that they headed to the Sutherlands' home, so they should lead. The truth was, he didn't want Maude out of his sight. He couldn't stop looking at his bonnie bride, nor was he willing to risk being unprepared to reach her in case of attack. Guards flanked the women while Peat followed behind Trioblaid.

As they moved off the road into a clearing by a brook, Maude dismounted before Kieran could reach her side. She stood on steady legs as she continued to chatter with Blair. Neither woman looked worse for wear after hours in the saddle. She glanced at him and smiled as she took her bow and quiver from her pack. She frowned when he approached, a scowl darkening his face.

"What's the matter?"

"If you insist upon mounting and dismounting without my help, I won't be able to touch you at all on this blasted trip," Kieran whispered. "All I want is to drag you away and make love to you, and now I can't even touch you."

"Would you help me back onto my horse, so you can help me off? Would that make you feel better?" Maude quipped.

"Yes," he grumbled, but her peel of laughter shot straight to his cock. He was grateful to have abandoned his breeks for his breacan feile. The extra layers of wool and his sporran hid what the tight fabric of breeks would not. He covered the hand Maude laid on his chest as she strained to kiss his cheek. He turned his head so their lips met. Her gasp opened her lips enough for him to flicker his tongue inside her mouth before pulling away. He wouldn't shame Maude by being caught kissing her in front of her father and their retinue of men.

"Blair and I are going hunting. Would you like to join us?"

"You two are?" Kieran remembered learning that she liked to ride and hunt, but he'd underestimated her.

"Aye. We're the best shots of the Sutherlands here." Kieran quirked a brow but said nothing. Maude's tone was so matter-of-fact that he realized she believed her own words. He wouldn't argue with her in front of the others. Maude's arms crossed as her lips pursed. "You don't believe me, Kieran MacLeod. You had better catch something for yourself, because neither Blair nor I will share with you if you have so little faith."

Maude stuck her tongue out at him as she slipped away. Blair joined her and grinned over her shoulder at him as if to say he were a fool. An hour and six rabbits and three pheasants later, he felt like one. The sisters brought back their kill and began preparing them for the fire. He lifted the knife from Maude's hand with a kiss on her cheek before taking her place preparing their evening meal.

Maude finished splashing water on her face and neck, enjoying the refreshing sensation after being on Trioblaid's back all day. She wiped a cloth along her arms, but angry voices had her lifting her skirts and running back to camp.

"The bluidy hell ye are," Hamish roared. Maude entered the camp to find Hamish and Kieran standing toe-to-toe, hands on the hilts of their swords as they seethed at one another. "She's ma daughter, nae yer wife."

"Yet," Kieran growled.

"Ever, if ye keep at it," Hamish bellowed. "I'll sever both yer hands and leave ye to the wolves."

"She's my betrothed as of last eve and now mine to protect."

Maude looked around the camp and caught sight of the two men she cared for most standing next two bedrolls laid side-by-side. She recognized one as her own but didn't recognize the other until she spotted the MacLeod plaid. Then she understood. Maude rushed forward to keep the two irate men from beating one another senseless. She slipped between them, a hand on each chest. She looked up to Kieran, pleading with her eyes that he desist. He glanced down at her, then took a step back.

"Da, Kieran's right," she whispered.

"What?" Hamish blustered.

"Da, you've always slept between me and Blair when we travel without Lachlan and Mama. You've also always whittled aboot being able to save us both if we're attacked. You need not worry now. You will protect Blair, and Kieran will protect me."

"He can do that without his bedroll being on top of yours," Hamish lunged forward, and Maude barely pushed her father back before he crushed her between two behemoth chests. Kieran pulled her from between the men and pushed her behind him, even angrier that Hamish trapped Maude between them.

"Would you have a repeat of how your courtship began with Lady Sutherland?" Kieran hissed. "Make a move like that again with Maude nearby, and I won't care whose father you are."

Hamish's eyes widened before looking over Kieran's shoulder at Maude, whose white hands covered her mouth in fear. He looked back at Kieran and nodded.

"Ye'll do as her guard, I suppose." Hamish turned away.

"Were you testing me?" Kieran demanded.

"Nay, but ye passed. Be sure ye wake where ye fall asleep, or I'll skewer ye by the bollocks."

As Hamish walked away, Maude fell against Kieran's chest. He held her as she trembled. He feared she'd be angry that he threatened her father and prepared to explain himself when her slim arms wrapped around his waist.

"I could throttle him," she muttered.

"Buttercup, I'm sorry."

"For what? Defending me the way you thought best? I may not agree with you fighting my father, but I trust you to know when to stop, to know when I'm safe. Besides, I suspect he started it." She attempted to frown, but her smile poked through.

The camp settled to eat the evening meal and then to sleep. Kieran took the first watch as Maude adjusted her bedroll, spreading out a Sutherland plaid across her bedroll and Kieran's before adding his plaid as a second layer. He might not awake alive, but he would fall asleep a happy man if he could slip beneath the blankets next to Maude.

Maude awoke warm and comfortable as the sun peeked through the leaves overhead. She snuggled into the source of heat, thinking her plaid had never been adequate warmth in the past when she traveled. A hand cupped her backside, and she realized the source of her comfort was a very large, very hot, very well-muscled man beneath her. She froze as Kieran stroked her bottom.

"No one else is awake yet, mo leannan. Be still and we can enjoy our time a little longer," Kieran murmured against her ear. Maude relaxed and nuzzled against his broad chest. Her eyes drifted closed as she breathed in Kieran's sandalwood and pine scent. He'd washed while she and Blair hunted, and his fresh scent had greeted her when she slipped under the blankets at the end of his watch. She remembered him pulling her back against his chest as he settled next to her. It was the best night of sleep she could remember.

Alas, her comfort was abruptly ruined when the heavens opened to a downpour. The camp scrambled to pack and saddle the horses. The rain doused the fires, leaving smoldering piles that the men covered with dirt. They were on their horses and back on the road within a quarter of an hour from when the rain started. Maude pushed her sopping hair out of her eyes as she guided Trioblaid into the line of horses.

The rain refused to lighten as the day progressed. Maude's thick hair was soaked, the weight of her bun pulling on her neck. She reached back and pulled the pins from her hair. She covered her hair when she traveled to keep the road dirt from making it filthy, but the rain seeped through the shawl, making the cover useless. Once her hair was down and the strain eased, she twisted her head from side to side before pulling her plaid over her head. They ate the noon meal comprised of bannocks and dried beef in the saddle. Maude looked at Blair, who fared little better than she did. They both looked like drowned kittens huddled under their plaids. They grinned at one another before Maude launched into a bawdy tune that made Kieran choke. Blair picked up the ditty as Hamish whirled around to look at his daughters. The ladies dissolved into laughter, pointing at their father, who looked like a bear woken early from hibernation. He roared at them to cease, which only made the sisters laugh even harder. Kieran's eyes swept back and forth between the Sutherland sisters and their spluttering father. Neither woman feared the man, rather seeming to enjoy nettling him. Maude's smile chased away the chill that made Kieran's bones ache. He looked around and saw all the other men were smiling too, and Kieran leaned forward, certain Hamish settled into humming along in a deep bass. Kieran deduced that Hamish's opposition stemmed from a sense of duty, not an aversion to the song. Maude glanced back and winked, making Kieran realize she'd orchestrated the duet to improve morale for everyone. His estimation of her grew once more. He marveled at the woman who would be his wife, the woman he loved.

As the day dragged on, and the rain persisted, Maude was exhausted and miserable. She huddled into her plaid and tucked her chin against the wind and driving rain. Her weariness made her fear she'd slip from Trioblaid's back, but she refused to complain. She'd seen the pride in Kieran's eyes as she and Blair led rounds of songs until they grew hoarse. She wasn't about to change Kieran's view of her by whining because of a little shower. She looked ahead to where her father arranged Blair behind him as she rode pillory. Her sister fussed, but her horse stumbled one too many times in the mud for Hamish to trust it not to throw Blair. Maude adjusted her plaid once more as it attempted to slip from her head. She rolled her shoulders and hunched into herself, praying the rain would cease or that her father called a halt to the day's ride. She wasn't counting on either; the clouds remained thick and black, and she knew they still had several more hours before they would make camp.

Kieran noticed Maude's attempt to make herself comfortable despite the worsening conditions. She impressed him once again by how she took each challenge in stride without becoming disagreeable. He considered how his sisters and mother would behave in such a situation, and he counted himself lucky they weren't there. Kieran nudged Peat alongside Trioblaid now that they'd tied Blair's horse to a rear guardsman's mount. He leaned forward to catch a peek at Maude's face, but all he could see was the tip of her red nose and her chattering blue lips. He didn't think twice before plucking her from her saddle and settling her before him. He'd pulled the extra length of his plaid over his head and wrapped the loose material over his shoulders. He unwound it now and pulled her shivering body against his before wrapping the wool around them both. She huddled against his larger frame, seeming tiny and fragile to him. He rubbed his hand over her back and arms, trying to get the blood flowing again.

"That's good yet horrible all at the same time," she murmured. "It's good because it's you and because I might be warm again, but the pins and needles burn as the blood starts pumping."

Kieran looked ahead at Hamish, who was looking back at him. A silent communication passed between them as they each looked at the bedraggled women sharing a horse with them. Within the hour, the party rode into the courtyard of a tavern. It wasn't somewhere Hamish or Kieran would have brought the women if there was another choice, but there were no other options before it grew too dark to continue. Kieran eased Maude from his lap before dismounting beside her. She handed Trioblaid's reins—which she'd held onto while she rode with Kieran—to a stable boy before joining her sister. Hamish led the group into the main room, the women huddled in the center of the group. Each man prepared to draw his sword to defend the Sutherland sisters. Kieran scanned the men assembled in various states of inebriation. He slipped his arm around Maude's waist and pulled her close.

"Keep your head down until your father and I can arrange for a chamber for you and Blair." Kieran's gaze followed Hamish as the older man walked to the bar and spoke with the tavern owner. He gestured over his shoulder before nodding and dropping a small sack of coin on the counter. Blair and Maude whispered as they waited for someone to show them to their chamber. Kieran shifted to let a tavern maid past, but she stopped in front of him.

"I ken what ye need, ma laird, to warm a large mon like ye on a chilly spring night like we've tonight," the woman purred. She reached out to touch Kieran's chest, but Maude slid between them and bared her teeth.

"Touch ma mon, and ye will come away less yer fingers." Maude's quiet threat had its intended effect. The woman skittered away as Maude growled. Kieran's chuckle earned him an elbow to the ribs.

"I rather like ye protective of yer mon, lass," he teased, allowing his burr to slip back into his voice, too. He was about to kiss her temple when a drunken voice carried to them.

"Look at the tits on that one. Nay, nae the lady. Her buxom maid. Nay lady is built like a tavern wench. I'd stick ma c--" Kieran's fist plowed into the man's face before the drunkard could finish his vulgar thought. The man flew backward and landed on a table, upturning bowls of pottage and mugs of ale. A serving wench screamed, and several men reached for their swords. The MacLeod and Sutherland men surrounded Maude and Blair with their hands on the hilts of their swords and dirks.

"Dinna! Can ye nay see who it is?" A man near the bar yelled over the crowd. "Tis Laird Sutherland *and* Laird MacLeod. Unless ye wish to die today, dinna pull yer blade."

Maude held her breath as the entire tavern froze in place as men surveyed one another, evaluating their chance for success and survival. None of the tavern goers pursued a fight, but several glared at Kieran, who looked unapologetic.

"Dinna speak of ma bride, and I willna cut out yer tongue," he growled between clenched teeth.

"So much for keeping yer head down, lad," Hamish clapped Kieran on his back before turning to Maude. "Are ye well, lass?"

Maude nodded at her father before looking up at Kieran, whose eyes continued to sweep the crowd while his hand hadn't moved from the hilt of his sword, his other arm anchored around Maude's waist. It wasn't often that Kieran allowed his burr to overcome his control, so it spoke to his anger as he defended Maude.

"I'm sleeping by their door," Kieran muttered to no one and everyone. Maude's insides warmed as she pictured Kieran situated as a roadblock in their doorframe that night. Her father had slept that way more than once when she traveled with Blair and her mother. When she and her sister were younger, Hamish and Lachlan slept on the floor of their chamber when they stayed at an inn. More recently, Lachlan slept at the table closest to the foot of the stairs, if he accompanied them, while their father remained propped in the doorframe. But as tánaiste, he most often remained at Dunrobin when their father ventured away. Kieran leaned close to Maude's ear once again. "I look forward to sharing a chamber with you, lass. And for once, it isn't so I can share your bed. I dislike you being alone in there."

"Alone? Blair will be with me."

"Aye, but my sword and I won't be."

"Will you always be so overprotective?"

"Till my last breath." When Maude looked unconvinced, Kieran sighed. "Before that last breath, I will convince you, you are more precious to me than aught else in this life or the next."

"And what do you mean share? You'll be outside the door."

The innkeeper interrupted their conversation when he ushered them to a table, and a team of tavern wenches brought bowls of pottage and ale. The women were shameless in their ogling of Kieran and Hamish, who despite being old enough to be the ladies' father was a braw man who drew more than one woman's eye. Neither man cast the women a single glance, let alone a second one, so they turned their attention to the guardsmen who accepted the attention until their lairds cut them scathing glances, reminding them that they were to guard Maude and Blair, not tup the whores. The meal and night passed uneventfully once the other patrons realized two snarling lairds and guards armed to the teeth fiercely guarded the two ladies.

The next two nights passed just as the first one had. The rain continued with unremorseful strength, so Hamish insisted they spend the night under a proper roof with hot food for everyone. Only one arrival resulted in Kieran and Hamish throwing punches at men who attempted to touch the ladies. Kieran's knuckles smarted, but it satisfied him that the patrons understood that the Sutherland sisters were off limits.

Maude approached Kieran the morning of their last day on the road. She lifted his hands to her lips and kissed the damaged skin. She slid her gaze to where her father stood with Blair and his captain of the guard, discussing the journey for that day.

"I miss you," she whispered. "I know that's ridiculous since we ride side-by-side every day, but I miss having the chance to talk to you without a score of ears listening to each passing word. I miss your kisses and waking in your arms. That was a cruel tease."

"I know, buttercup. I wake every morning with a raging need to taste you and have your body pressed to mine." Kieran had a moment's guilt for what he was about to suggest, but he knew it was a pointless emotion. "Maude, I would marry you tomorrow evening."

"What aboot your mother and sister? Shouldn't we give them the chance to arrive?"

"They won't come. I told you I had a falling out with my

mother before I left. I don't want you to arrive at Stornoway unsuspecting. She isn't pleased that I'm not marrying someone of her choice after Madeline made Laurel Ross sound appealing to her, and she is angry that you're a Sutherland. She may be one of those who spews that I married you for the alliance and land."

Maude swallowed as she nodded. She adopted her courtly, serene expression, and Kieran wanted to be ill. She was retreating from him before she even arrived on MacLeod land. For the hundredth time, he wondered if he was being selfish, insisting upon marrying Maude when he knew she was sensitive to people assuming her worth came from her dowry and name rather than her person. But he convinced himself that no one would dare speak out against his wife. He was certain she would win them over within a sennight, even his troublesome mother. He assumed Abigail would appreciate having another lady close to her age and would make friends with Maude.

"We shall cross that bridge when we come to it. Perhaps she will surprise you."

Kieran prayed Maude's optimism wouldn't be misplaced. He pulled her into his arms for a quick embrace and heated kiss before taking her hand and leading her to Peat. She didn't ask what he was about before he lifted her into the saddle and mounted behind her.

"You look cold." Kieran offered nothing more, and their mounting signaled the others to ride out of the tavern's court-yard. Kieran made it a priority to announce to Hamish that the wedding would be the next day. He was relieved when Hamish nodded his head without a word. It was a long day in the saddle, but Dunrobin came into view as the sun moved toward the western horizon. Maude squeezed Kieran's arm as a young man and an older woman came into view on the battlements as the bells rang to announce the laird's return home.

"Mama. Lachlan," Maude breathed. "Home."

Kieran prayed that Maude would one day speak with such reverence about Stornoway, but until then, it pleased him to see the rare but genuine wide smile that broke across Maude's face. He grinned at the sight of her crooked teeth and gap. Any chance to see Maude filled with true happiness was worth the days of trudging through rain and muck.

CHAPTER NINETEEN

Maude shifted with eagerness as Kieran brought Peat to a halt and practically pushed him from the saddle in her impatience to dismount. Her feet brushed the ground before she was lifting her skirts and flying into the waiting arms of a woman who resembled Maude more like an older sister than her mother. It surprised Kieran to note that Lady Amelia Sutherland shared a similar build to Maude, and he suspected Lady Amelia had looked much the same now as she did before she had three children.

"Aye, ma lass is the spitting image of her mama when I met ma Amelia. She's as bonnie as the day I bumped into her at court. I kenned the moment I met her that I would make her ma wife. It seems history repeated itself." Hamish didn't wait for a response before pulling his wife in for a kiss that put any Kieran and Maude shared to shame. Despite being married almost a score-and-a-half years, it was clear that passion existed between the older couple, and Kieran prayed he and Maude would share the same once their children grew into adults.

Kieran's imagination jumped to a picture of Maude with a rounded belly, her hand resting over the swell as he slipped his arms around her waist and pulled her back against his chest.

He shook the thought loose as he observed a young man twirl Maude in the air before tossing her and catching her like a young child. Her giggle made him wonder what he could do to elicit such a sound. The young man looked much like Hamish but had a scar that ran along his jaw. It had faded with time, but Kieran could tell it must have been viscous at one time. Lachlan repeated his greeting with Blair, who hooted with laughter. Maude dashed to Kieran's side and grabbed his hand, tugging him with surprising strength.

"Come meet Mama and Lachlan." Maude skipped toward her family as Kieran jogged and humored her excitement.

"Mama, please meet my betrothed, Laird Kieran MacLeod of Lewis." Maude beamed as Lady Sutherland dipped into a curtsy that Kieran returned with a bow.

"It is a pleasure to see you once more, Laird MacLeod. It has been some time, but I would recognize ye as Laird Tieran's son any day of the sennight and twice on Sundays. I thought the Sinclairs bore a striking resemblance between father and son, but ye and yer father were two peas in a pod."

"Tieran and Kieran?" Maude struggled not to laugh. She realized she had never heard Kieran's father's name. She was familiar with the MacLeods of Skye and had heard of Kieran, but she'd been too young when Tieran MacLeod passed away to have any memory of him.

"My father had a sense of humor since I looked like him from the moment of my birth. He detested naming me after himself, said it would be too confusing."

"So Tieran and Kieran was easier?" This time, Maude did laugh. "I rather like it. Can we name our son Tieran, too?" Maude froze as she realized how her words must sound. "I mean any future sons. If the Lord so blesses us with bairns."

Kieran's imagination sprang to life again with the image of Maude carrying his child. He nodded as he glimpsed a lovely blush spread up her neck and into her cheeks. He ran his thumb over her cheekbone before remembering their audience.

"A wedding tomorrow evening sounds perfect," Amelia's voice broke through their not-so-private moment. Maude looked at her mother and pieced together that her father must have already spoken to her mother in the few minutes that she stood in a world comprising only Kieran and herself. Her mother held out her hand, and Maude took it, but not before looking over her shoulder at Kieran. "We have much to plan, and we shall need to choose a gown for you."

"Mama, I'd still like to wear your gown," Hope filled Maude's voice.

"Are you sure, leannan? It's outdated."

"I've wanted to wear it since I was a wean. Please?"

"If that's what you wish. Let's hang it up, so it can air before it's brushed out."

Kieran's gaze followed mother and daughters as they moved toward the stairs as he entered the Great Hall with Hamish and Lachlan.

"I'm afraid you won't see them until the evening meal," Lachlan elbowed Kieran. "Maude may not be one for lace and trim, but my mother and Blair are." Lachlan and Kieran had met several times over the years, and while they were not friends, they were friendly. Kieran hoped he would develop a closer relationship with his soon-to-be brother-by-marriage. He had always longed for a brother, and while Kyle filled that role, Kieran looked forward to a brother who would one day share the same duties and burdens as laird that he did. Hamish and the two younger men took seats on the dais while servants brought out food. Kieran hadn't realized that he was famished until the smell of fresh bread and cheese wafted to him. After they finished their repast, the three men retired to Hamish's solar to draft and sign the betrothal documents.

"The mon is in love with ye, lass." Amelia wasted no time with her proclamation once the three ladies were tucked away in Maude's chamber.

"Mama, please don't say that. He hasn't made any declarations of his feelings. And neither have I," Maude rushed to add. "I wouldn't get my hopes up."

"Hopes up?" Blair chimed in. "Everyone at court was buzzing aboot how quickly the elusive bachelor, Laird Kieran MacLeod, fell in love."

"He's fond of me, but I hesitate to say it's love. Maybe one day," Maude hedged. She didn't want to hear her mother and sister try to convince her of something that might never come true. She didn't doubt her own feelings of love, but she refused to assume Kieran felt the same. The disappointment would crush her to discover he didn't reciprocate her depth of emotion. She was aware he was fond of her and desired her, but she wouldn't believe he loved her. It seemed too farfetched in her mind. While the men in her family might marry for love, it was a rare novelty among her social class. Kieran denied her dowry, including the land that bordered his, mattered, but she would be a fool to believe him. It might not matter to him now, but it would once the newness of their courtship wore off into the daily grind of marriage and being laird to a large and powerful clan.

"Ye are blind, ma lassie." Maude might disagree with her mother, but the sound of her mother's voice, the brogue she never lost despite education and time at court, was a comfort. Maude wondered if she should give up her tight leash on her accent. She had adopted the Lowlanders pattern of speech during her eight months at court to fit in and knew Kieran did the same. She longed to let down her guard and might while they were at Sutherland, but she would decide once she met Lady MacLeod. Maude suspected the woman would look down her nose at Maude if she sounded like a Highlander. She'd learned that her mother-by-marriage-to-be was a

Lowlander. It made her suspect that was why Kieran spoke without a burr with more ease than she did.

"Are you ready for tomorrow eve?" Blair wiggled her eyebrows to Maude's horror as her eyes darted between her sister and mother, but their mother laughed. It was impossible to have parents as in love as Hamish and Amelia, along with live in a large keep such as Dunrobin, without learning much about what happened between a man and woman. Amelia had been honest with her daughters before they left for court, more to warn them of the dangers of how passion could carry them away if they weren't careful. She'd appreciated her mother's warnings even if she had disregarded them with Kieran.

"Aye," Maude admitted.

"And do ye feel prepared?" Amelia stroked her daughter's hair down the length of her back. Maude and Blair both unbound and released their hair to dry the moment they reached Maude's chamber. "Do ye have questions?"

"Nay, Mama. I understand it may hurt at first, but I trust Kieran. He's always been gentle and patient with me. He's, um, generous with his attention." Maude couldn't believe she admitted to her mother that she'd shared intimacies with him, but Blair had left little to doubt with her knowing smile and still waggling eyebrows.

"Ye ken ye're well suited in that area?" Amelia asked with the patience only a mother could offer.

"I suspect as much. So far we are," Maude wanted to sink into the floorboards. She realized she had one question. "Mama, will there be a bedding ceremony?"

The color drained from her mother's face, and she regretted asking. Despite her father's objections and coming to blows with the Earl of Ross for a second time, Maude's mother had suffered through the indignity of the ritual. Amelia's father had his retainers restrain Hamish while women inspected her and shuttled her into bed. Hamish had wrapped his meaty hands around one man's neck until they pulled the covers over Amelia, and the man hadn't been able to speak for a sennight. He'd threatened to murder the Rosses in their sleep if anyone watched the actual deed, and Amelia's father relented when he realized he was on the verge of causing a clan feud as the Sutherlands present in the chamber refused to look at the bed and paired up with Rosses, ready to come to the defense of their new lady. Even the women were prepared to take up arms led by Hamish's younger sister, Kyla Sinclair.

"Yer da would never allow it for any of ye. And I suspect Kieran might murder every mon with eyes if we tried to insist. I dinna get the impression he'll allow any mon to look upon ye."

Maude breathed a sigh of relief, neither wanting anyone else to see her naked nor watch something so intimate. She felt exhaustion wash over her and couldn't stifle her yawn. They were contagious, and soon Blair was yawning too, both women rubbing their eyes. Blair and Amelia left Maude to lie down while Blair did the same in her chamber, and Amelia saw to preparations for the evening meal. Maude didn't realize how deeply she slept until a pounding on her door woke her. She pulled on her robe and trod to the door, which she opened a crack, recognizing only a man would knock so hard.

"I was worrying that you'd fallen unconscious," Kieran teased.

"I think I may very well have. Did you rest?" Maude noticed the shadows under Kieran's eyes were not as dark as they had been when they arrived.

"Aye, but not for as long as you did. It's time for the evening meal. Will you join us, or should I have a tray sent up?"

"I'm coming!" Maude turned away and ran to her armoire. "I'm not missing our betrothal announcement." She assumed Kieran would pull the door closed and either wait in the passageway or belowstairs, so she was unprepared for the muscular arms to slip around her waist. "You can't be in here! My father will butcher you and serve you to the hogs!"

Kieran's laugh vibrated against her back as he nipped at her neck.

"A fine way to go, if ever they was one, buttercup. I shall take my chances for a few moments alone with you." Kieran continued his assault on her senses as his hands roamed over her breasts and belly until his hand cupped her mons. "Your father has moved the wedding forward to the morning. He saw how I chomped on the bit while we completed the documents, and he suspects I might carry you off to the priest before sunset."

"Mmmm," Maude moaned as Kieran's mouth found the sensitive spot beneath her ear. "Even if we wed that early, it's not like we can retire that early."

"I have every intention of doing that very thing. Your mother agreed to a midday feast that can last throughout the night, but I will bring you up here after the first course."

"You told my parents that?" Maude gasped, both from shock from his words and the butterflies that fluttered in her core as his fingers pressed against her entrance through the layers of clothes.

"Mayhap not the last bit, but I doubt it would surprise them. I'm sure that's why they suggested we move the ceremony earlier."

"Do we truly have only one more night until we---" Maude couldn't finish her thought, embarrassment overwhelmed her.

"Until we can make love? Until I can slip inside you and lose myself to the feel of your body and the pleasure we'll share? Until I make you scream my name as I bellow yours? Until I am yours and you are mine forever? Aye, one more night. If I can survive this one."

Lust and need tempted Maude to suggest she would visit Kieran that night, but fear of being caught forced her good sense to return. She turned in Kieran's arms and wrapped hers around his neck. She stood on her toes and kissed him, her tongue flicking across the seam of his lips until he allowed her entry. His hands slid to her backside, pulling her tighter against his cockstand. He enjoyed Maude's control over their kiss as she pressed for more. She was insatiable after days of restraint. Her mewling sounds of impatience spurred him on until he lifted her, and her legs came around his waist.

"I would skip the evening meal and feast upon you," Maude murmured as it was her turn to graze her teeth along his neck before flicking her tongue at the exposed dip between his collarbones.

"Tomorrow, buttercup."

"Now, turtledove."

"Not if you want me to have my cock and cods tomorrow. If we don't appear, your father will skewer me, and it'll be your mother who hands him the sword."

Maude sighed as she eased away from the tempting skin along his jaw. She unfastened her legs and slid down his body before pulling her robe closed over her chemise. Kieran released her but made no move to leave despite Maude's obvious need to dress.

"You have no maid here. Someone must lace you into your gown."

"Ever practical, turtledove?"

"Aught to assist you. Now be quick." He gave her a playful tap on the backside before she pulled a gown from a hook and disappeared behind the screen.

They entered the Great Hall together to cheers from the Sutherlands gathered for the evening meal. Even though the official announcement was yet to be made, many had already heard or deduced that Lady Maude had returned home to marry. By the end of the night, Maude's feet pained her, and she worried she wouldn't be able to walk to her own wedding after spending much of the evening dancing. Kieran had monopolized her time, and it filled her heart to overflowing. She reveled in every moment she spent in his arms, and she enjoyed the opportunity to dance where she wasn't self-conscious. She'd spied a few of the young men who had taunted her when she was younger, but many had already married or turned away when their eyes met. She refused to allow them to ruin her night. She bid Kieran goodnight at the bottom of the stairs as her family observed, and the temptation to promise to sneak to his chamber once more coursed through her, but she tamped it down. They had waited months for their wedding; she could wait another twelve hours.

The morning of Maude's wedding dawned with the first clear sky in over a week. The sun poured into her chamber as she bathed in peace. Maude accepted that her mother and Blair would arrive with maids to help prepare her for the ceremony, but for the moment, she was blessedly alone and able to soak in the steaming water. She'd passed a restless night often running her hand over the space across from her that Kieran would occupy that night. She scrubbed her hair and body before patting herself dry. She rubbed lemon verbena oil into her skin as she imagined Kieran's hands one day completing the task for her. Her body warmed more from her musings than her hands. She'd finished pulling her chemise into place when a knock sounded at her door. She eased her robe on before opening the door to find Lachlan on the other side.

"I wasn't expecting you," she smiled.

"Can't I visit ma wee sister?" Lachlan kissed her on the cheek. "You won't be coming back here often now that you're to be a married woman. I would sneak in a few more minutes with you before you leave us behind once more."

"This will always be my home. I pray Stornoway will come to mean as much to me, but Dunrobin will always hold a piece of my heart since this is where you and Mama and Da will always be. Even Blair's forever connected to Sutherland, even when she returns to court or marries. I'm glad you came."

"I wanted to speak to you for a moment." Lachlan pulled the chair to rest across from the foot of the bed and gestured for Maude to take a seat. "I watched you last night with Kieran. I've never seen you so at ease with anyone, especially not with a mon. Your entire everything shone with beauty and happiness, and it gladdens my heart. I think Kieran has been a gift to us because you seem once again to be the Maude that you've hidden for so long. I have tried to forgive myself for my role in how you changed, but I haven't been able to. It's my greatest regret, and my greatest failure. I will forever be indebted to Kieran for helping you to come out of your shell," Lachlan took Maude's hands. "But if he should ever fail you, should he ever hurt you in any way, you need only tell me, and I will come for you. No questions asked, no hesitation. You'll always have a home here. I ken Da has settled dower lands for you but come here. Come home if you need to. I love you, Maddie." Lachlan reverted to his childhood pet name for her. He hadn't been able to say the "au" in her name when they were young.

"Thank you. You have no idea how much that means to me. It will be strange to move into a new keep and know that it will be my home for the rest of my life. At court, I knew it was temporary. For most of the time I was there, I assumed I would return here one day. At least until you wed and Mama and Da were gone."

"Until? Why would any of those things change whether you remained here?"

"You'll marry, and I doubt your wife would want a spinster sister lurking aboot when she is to be lady of this clan."

"I wouldn't marry the chit if she wouldn't welcome either of my sisters in their home."

Maude smiled and hugged Lachlan rather than argue with him. "I love you, Lach. I always have and always will. You've been a good big brother to me. No, don't disagree with me.

All siblings have their differences, but you have always been there for me, and I love you for it."

They pulled apart, and Lachlan reached into his sporran. Maude watched as he pulled out a beautiful brooch with a large amethyst stone in the center. It was a brooch intended for a laird or his wife.

"Kieran asked that I bring this to you. Mama will bring you a length of the MacLeod laird's plaid, but Kieran requested I give this to you. He wanted you to look at it with no one snatching it from you to 'ooh' and 'ahh'. He said it was his father's, and it would honor him if you'd wear it to the ceremony and accept it as a wedding gift."

Maude looked at the jewel that rested in her palm, running a finger over the filigree and craftsmanship. She nodded and blinked several times before whispering, "Please pass along my thanks. I shall wear it with pride. I love it."

Amelia, Blair, and several maids interrupted them when they entered after a perfunctory knock. Maude closed the brooch in her hand and tucked it into the pocket of her robe. Her finger ran over the stone as Lachlan left, and she took his place in the chair once they moved it before the looking glass. They spent the next two hours braiding her hair and weaving ribbons through the thick plaits before she slipped into her mother's wedding gown. It fit as though someone had stitched it for her. She twisted to look at herself from various angles and felt beautiful without reservation for the first time in her life. She hoped Kieran liked her appearance. She would know soon enough.

CHAPTER TWENTY

Kieran stood impatiently on the steps of the Sutherland kirk as he shifted, trying to glimpse Maude when she exited the keep. He stood taller than most Lowlanders, but his height wasn't exceptional in the sea of Highlanders. He caught sight of a dark head with a crown of early spring flowers, but it wasn't until Maude was nearly to him that the crowd parted wide enough for him to see her face. His breath caught in his chest as he took in his bonnie bride. Her whisky hued eyes sparkled, and the right corner of her lips curled in her shy smile. He took in the brooch on her shoulder and the length of MacLeod plaid that swathed her shoulder. Her trim body looked as though someone had poured her into her gown, and once again, he appreciated his breacan feile and sporran that hid the immediate reaction his body had to her approach. He stepped down to meet her amid gasps and chuckles. He took her hand and wove his fingers through hers, ignoring propriety that dictated he await her on the steps and place her hand on his forearm.

"I have never seen a sight more breathtaking than you, buttercup. I shall remember this moment as I lay in our bed, an auld mon awaiting my chance to enter the Lord's kingdom." Kieran kissed her cheek, once more throwing decorum to the wind. "The sight of you in my plaid makes my world perfect."

Maude's smile widened as her eyes locked on his, and he marveled that the smile was for him alone. His heart thudded to receive a gem rarer than the one in the brooch he'd given her. They stood facing one another as the priest wrapped a ribbon around their wrists and then placed a length of Sutherland plaid over their hands.

"I realize a woman cleaves to her husband, but there is also something so right seeing our hands joined with a Sutherland plaid making us one," Maude whispered. "I would welcome you to my family and clan, just as you welcome me to yours."

The priest cleared his throat as a reminder that it was supposed to be his turn to speak. They exchanged their vows before her family and clan, then entered the kirk for the wedding Mass. Kieran spared little thought for his family, but he understood Maude worried about them as she glanced at her mother and sister. The service progressed at a snail's pace as they awaited the priest's announcement that he'd officially married them. When the time came, Kieran refused to be rushed. He eased Maude to her feet and slid his arm around her waist, stepping close to her. He lifted her chin and peered into her eyes. She searched his steely gray ones, the depth of her feelings for him clear. He recognized it was time to declare himself and regretted not having done so sooner.

"Maude MacLeod, I love you with all that I am and all that I have. I have since the day I met you and will until the day of my passing." Before Maude responded, he swooped in for a kiss that began as a feathering of his lips and breath against hers but soon enveloped her in tenderness and affection before bursting with passion. She returned the emotions without reservation until they were both breathless. "I love you, buttercup."

Maude nodded as she swallowed before finding her voice.

She blinked back tears as she spoke in the strongest voice she could muster. "I love you, turtledove. Now and forever."

They kissed again before Kieran swept her into his arms. Maude rested her head against his shoulder until they emerged from the kirk to more cheers and applause. Kieran scowled at his horse but failed to keep from laughing when Peat knickered at him and nodded his head as if he understood his owner's annoyance that they would have to ride through the bailey and surrounding village before they made their way to the Great Hall. He'd argued vehemently with Hamish and Lachlan when they arrived at the stables and found Trioblaid was also being saddled. He insisted they saddle either one or the other horse, but it would be pointless to ready both since he refused to relinquish Maude to ride apart from him. Father and son acquiesced when Kieran threatened to ride off with Maude if they were each given their own mount.

Kieran lifted Maude into the saddle, and she adjusted her skirts as she sat sideways. He swung up behind her and arranged his plaid and sporran to continue to hide the erection he had sported throughout his wedding. He sighed with relief that God hadn't smote him for such lustiness in His house. Kieran spurred Peat into a cantor and squeezed the horse's flanks once they were through the gate, urging the steed into a gallop.

"I like this detour aboot as much as you do, but we canna gallop through the village. You're bound to run someone over!" Maude chuckled. Kieran slowed Peat but followed Maude's directions for the most expeditious route before they returned to the bailey. Maude's relatives had guided her through the keep at such a brisk pace before the ceremony that she hadn't a moment to appreciate the decorations, but as they entered, she paused to take in the bows of flowers that hung from the second-floor railing and were draped across the dais. A garland encircled the top of her chair, and she wondered how someone collected so many buds and blooms after the weather had been foul for days.

"I gathered them as soon as the weather looked as though it might turn. Your father alerted me that a wedding would take place soon after you arrived, and I wanted you to have fresh flowers for your special day." Amelia explained as she dropped a kiss on her daughter's cheek. Kieran eased her chair back once they reached their places, and once they were settled, his hand found her thigh beneath the table.

"Eat your fill, my wee one, because I don't intend to let you out of that chamber before we pass a sennight. This shall be your last meal that doesn't come on a tray, and I'd have you fortify yourself with some sustenance. You shall need it."

Maude nodded but was too self-conscious to serve herself much with so many eyes upon them. Kieran had no such qualms and heaped food into their trencher. He ceased pushing food onto her side when he caught her look of horror and how Maude's eyes flew from table to table to determine who watched the food accumulate before her. Kieran chided himself for being so short sighted.

"I fear you may need your own trencher, lass. I have left little room for your share," he teased and breathed easier when Maude relaxed.

"Need to keep yer strength up, ma laird," someone called from the tables below.

"Yer bride willna appreciate ye wasting away this eve," another cheered.

Maude ducked her head and picked at her food. The comments and attention were knotting her stomach despite Kieran's soothing caresses under the table.

"I'm sorry, mo chridhe," Kieran murmured. "I didn't mean to draw even more attention. I'm a tad overeager it would seem." Maude nodded, but continued to pick at her food until the clan members lost interest and focused on their own meal. Maude ate more, but not as much as Kieran would have liked. He glanced down at Lady Sutherland and offered a rueful smile, since she had noticed her daughter's discomfort. Lachlan glared at him until he shot his brother-by-marriage an apologetic expression. Since it was the midday meal, they kept their time at the tables short since there was still work for most clan members. They would return in the evening for a cèilidh, but Kieran intended to tuck himself and Maude away in their chamber well before then.

Relief flooded Maude when people trickled out of the Great Hall and Kieran took her hand. He kept his gaze directed at the stairs as he led them away from the dais. A few people caught sight of their intended destination and offered randy suggestions, but Kieran refused to acknowledge them. He tucked Maude against his side until they were halfway up the stairs and noticed even her ears were red. He lifted her into his arms and tucked her head against his chest as he took the remaining stairs two at a time. It only fueled more comments but helped them reach the landing faster. He carried Maude to her chamber door, relieved to see someone had already sent a tray of food and two pitchers of wine. He set her down before locking and barring the door.

Maude waited for Kieran to approach before unpinning her new brooch and plaid. She laid the plaid across the chair near the hearth and placed the brooch with her other jewels. She removed the necklace and earbobs she wore. She looked at the amethyst ring Kieran placed on her third finger during the ceremony. She turned it around her finger twice but left it in place. She sucked in a breath as Kieran pulled the bow loose from her kirtle's laces. The gown slipped loose around her shoulders until she freed her arms. Kieran tugged the ribbons at her shoulders until the chemise slid over her globes and pooled around her waist as the kirtle did. He stepped around her until he could brush the back of his fingers over her nipples, his mouth watering as they hardened into deep raspberry darts. He bent his head to take one into his mouth as his fingers continued to circle the other. He suckled as he flicked his tongue over and over. Maude's head fell back as she mewled. A neediness that surpassed anything Kieran had previously stirred took root deep in her core.

Maude reached for Kieran's belt and loosened it before catching it, his sporran, and his plaid. He laid them over her own MacLeod plaid. With his already hard rod now freed, her hand glided along the smooth skin. Kieran pushed her skirts past her waist as his hands stroked her thighs. He sank to his knees as he inhaled her floral scent. He hummed as he kissed along each inner thigh before flicking his tongue along her seam. Kieran was already looking up at her as his tongue rasped against her heated skin. His tongue once again flicked her, this time tapping her hidden bud. As he worked it from its surrounding petals, Maude grasped the edge of the table behind her. When Kieran's fingers entered her, she could no longer remain upright. She lowered herself onto her elbows as she continued to watch her husband lavish her with attention, but she was growing impatient. She tugged at the material at his shoulder. Kieran obliged and lifted his leine over his head. He led her to the bed and braced her hands on his shoulder while he bent to ease off her slippers and roll down her stockings. He gave her time to examine his body, certain it was the first time she'd seen an undressed and aroused man. Her fingers kneaded the tight muscles in his shoulders before sweeping over his chest and down his arms.

Kieran guided Maude onto the bed and climbed on but laid beside her. His fingers trailed over her belly until they reached her mound. He moved with slow purpose as he readied her body for their joining. They had shared intimacies before but always knowing that it would end before he breached her maidenhead. He didn't want to scare her now that he would make her his. As his finger entered her, he tested her responsiveness. He slipped another finger into her tight sheath and stretched the flesh as he stroked. When her moans grew, and she writhed with need, he struggled to restrain himself.

"Kieran." She arched as she pressed his hand against her mons, the heel of his hand rubbing against her bud. "When?"

Kieran could resist no longer. His need was as frantic as Maude's. He rolled between her legs and stroked damp hair from her temples.

"Now, mo chridhe. Now." He eased the tip of his cock into her and waited for Maude to panic or at least cry out, but a gasp and a moment of tension was her only reaction to his invasion before she rocked her hips again. He'd grazed the barrier as his fingers worked to prepare her, and her maidenhead gave way as he thrust into her with less finesse than he intended. A tightness swelled within his chest as he realized that Maude was truly his wife, and no one could change that, and no other man had the privilege he did.

Once the pain ceased, Maude's eagerness returned. She enjoyed the feel of Kieran's body joined with hers, but she felt restless and unsatisfied despite the joy of knowing they were truly married and the exquisite sensation of him filling her.

"Please tell me there is more. That was divine, and I don't want the feeling to end."

"Yes, little one. This is only the introduction to what I hope to offer you today and every day for the rest of our lives. There is much, much more." To prove his point, he rocked against her, his cock throbbing as Maude's back arched off the bed and her moans filled his ears. He rested his weight on one forearm as the other hand kneaded her breast before his tongue drew circles around her nipple. Maude's breathy gasps encouraged him as her fingers pressed along the ridges of muscle in his back. She stared up at him, mesmerized by how his chest and shoulders rippled with each of his movements. The contained strength Kieran possessed awed her as she watched her warrior husband make love to her with such gentleness. When he suckled her breast, Maude was certain she would explode. The same aching sensation once more thrummed through her sheath as the tightening in her belly bloomed into a powerful climax.

"Kier!" Maude's neck arched along with her back as she called out her release.

Unable to wait any longer, and thankful Maude had found pleasure so soon, Kieran slipped over the edge. His seed jet from him as spots danced before his eyes. His body tautened as his own release seemed endless. He slid his arms beneath her and pulled her body against his as he continued to thrust over and over. Maude clung to him as she wrapped her legs over his, her body reacted once more to him.

"Again," she panted. "Happening again." Maude strained to find the motion that would keep her climax going, but it faded. Kieran feared he would be too heavy upon her spent body, but when he tried to roll off her, Maude tightened her arms and legs.

Kieran looked at his bride and wished he had lasted longer. He'd intended to not to rush and to draw out their first time, but too many moons of repressed longing had made his body demand immediate satisfaction. He was aware she didn't know any better, but he did. His cock remained hard despite the rush of release that had just surged through him. It had been a climax unlike any other, and now a need to cuddle Maude warred with his need to take her again. He prayed his body would cooperate with his mind and be able to make love again sooner rather than later.

"Please. Not yet," she whispered as he shifted, embarrassed by the neediness in her voice.

"I dream of being inside you. I spend most of my day hungering for your touch, and I will have it now." Kieran confessed as his body rocked against hers. "I would stay inside you every minute of every day if I could."

Maude lifted her chin to kiss Kieran with an unleashed passion only a woman who had discovered the power and delight of coupling could possess. It surprised Kieran when his body reacted to the kiss with his own need. He'd never recovered so quickly before, and certainly not from a climax he was certain surpassed any he had ever experienced before. He titled his hips as he tested his cock within her sheath.

"Oh God, Kier. Please. More." Maude's own need drove her kiss as she abandoned any hope of control. Her kiss was demanding and unrelenting, and it drove Kieran far past the brink of control as his body surged back to life.

"I want you," Kieran breathed between thrusts.

"You have me."

"No. You don't understand. What I want isn't gentle nor tender. It isn't what you deserve your first time." Kieran tried to slow down and remember that only minutes ago his bride had been a virgin, but her responses were those of a natural seductress.

"I don't want gentle. I want to know you want me as much as I do you."

Kieran growled as his cock thrust into her over and over.

"Christ's bones, Maude. Demand every damn day and night." Kieran's body slammed into Maude's as she rose to meet him each time. He had never experienced need the way he did with Maude. It overcame all reason and caution, and demanded that he claim her and mark her as his.

Their pants and moans filled the chamber as Maude returned Kieran's passion and aggression with her own. When his arms shook with exhaustion, but he was not ready to be done, he rolled them over so Maude straddled him. He saw her shock at the new position, but her instincts told her what to do. He bucked his hips as she ground her mound into him. Her swaying breasts captivated his attention as his fingers dug into her hips. He was sure they would leave marks, but he couldn't ease his grip. He clung to her as though she might float away.

"Kier, help." Maude leaned forward, bringing her breast closer to his face. "I'm close. But I can't — I don't know— Please."

He pressed her breasts together, alternating suckling and pinching her nipples. When he knew he would not last any longer, he bit down on one, careful not to be too rough, while tweaking the other as hard as he dared. Maude exploded around him, her inner muscles clamping his cock as he once more spilled inside her. He had just done something twice that he had never done before. Not once had he dared to find his release before pulling out. With Maude, he couldn't imagine finishing any way other than being joined with her. Breathless and overwhelmed, Maude stretched across Kieran's broad chest. She wondered if she should move off him and give him his space. She had already begged once, but she refused to be pathetic and beg twice.

"Don't go," Kieran panted. "Not yet. I need it as much as you did."

Maude watched Kieran as his chest heaved and he lay with his eyes closed. He flung one arm out to the side while the other pinned her against his chest. She knew if she tried to move, he would let her, but his desire for them to remain together was the same as hers. She relaxed, and his fingers caressed her back. If his hand hadn't continued its lazy sweeps over her skin, she would have thought he'd fallen asleep.

"I never imagined it could be like that, buttercup."

Maude froze as she laid across him. She was the one who had been a virgin until only moments ago. She had no desire to think of Kieran with any other woman, but his comment made her curious.

"I can't imagine how that was any different from other times," she ventured.

Kieran toppled her off him as he lurched upward. He rolled them onto their side and hooked Maude's leg over his hip, but his depleted body eased free of hers.

"Every single moment of that was different. I have never loved a woman before. I've never made love to a woman before. I didn't understand how different it could be with someone who means the world to me."

"I don't know how to respond to that. Thank you?"

Kieran chuckled as he pushed damp hair from Maude's

neck. He kissed the spot at the end of her jaw.

"I never knew I could love this spot on a woman's body as much as I do on you. A spot that no one else would ever touch. A place I can claim as only mine."

"All of me is only yours," Maude's hand rested over his heart.

"And all of me is only yours. But that is a spot that others wouldn't notice, wouldn't touch. It's a secret I share with only you."

"That is easy for you, since no other mon has ever touched me. What can I claim as my own?" Maude wondered aloud.

"All of me. No woman has touched me the way you have. I've never made love before." Kieran thought for a moment before continuing. "I've shared something with you I never have another woman. The very essence that makes me a mon."

Maude furrowed her brow. She assumed he meant his seed, but surely he'd spilled it every time he'd coupled with a woman. She didn't want to admit her innocence, so she remained quiet.

"Buttercup, I have never climaxed within a woman's sheath. Never. Not even the first time. My father warned me of the dangers of losing my seed without consideration. I've never wanted to sire a bastard and have taken precautions. I've always pulled out well before I found my release. Making love to you is entirely different from the times in the past. The emotions, the sensations, the everything." Kieran kissed her temple, the tip of her nose, and her forehead before tipping her mouth up to his. She returned his kiss, drugged by the passion he stirred within her. She tightened her leg over his hip as he rolled her onto her back. His fingers slid inside of her as he brought her to climax twice more before he pulled the covers over them. He held her as she slipped into slumber. He followed her soon after, but not before he watched his wife fall asleep in his arms, just as he had dreamed since he met her.

CHAPTER TWENTY-ONE

Kieran was true to his word. They remained sequestered in their chamber for a sennight. They received trays three times a day and spent the time not only making love, but talking about their hopes for their life together as both a married couple and as laird and lady. They shared more stories of their childhood, and Maude learned that Kieran had a flare for storytelling, making her laugh and cry as he spun tales of a childhood filled with love from his father and restrained affection from his mother. In turn, she shared more about her upbringing and how she had been a fierce competitor against the boys her age until they became adolescents and male pride turned against her. She told tales of how her cousin Mairghread Sinclair encouraged her to stand up for herself when they were younger, and the boys challenged her as she learned to climb trees and shoot her bow. The four Sinclair brothers had given up trying to discourage Mairghread from joining them. Even Lachlan distanced himself for a while, but the five Sinclairs had always welcomed her. Kieran wished he had such endearing stories from his past, but his family had consisted only of him and his sisters, who preferred to remain in doors to sew and gossip with his mother. He had cousins, but beside Kyle, none were as close to him as Callum, Alexander, Tavish, Magnus, and Mairghread were to Maude. He remembered Father Michael and how Maude had explained that they grew up together. He'd met the priest's parents while he waited at the kirk for his bride.

When seven days passed, the newlyweds admitted that they had hidden as long as they dared. They didn't want to be rude, and the reality that they needed to depart Sutherland also took hold.

"Aught you wish to bring with you, buttercup? What we can't carry on horseback can follow us in the wagon along with your dowry," Kieran watched as Maude moved about the chamber she'd called her own since she was a child. She'd left most of her belongings behind when she departed for court, but now she accepted she would never return to Dunrobin as her home. They might use this chamber when they visited, but it wouldn't be hers any longer. She nodded absentmindedly as she considered what she wished to send to Stornoway. There were several gowns and other pieces of clothing, along with her favorite books that she wanted, but she realized that Kieran and Trioblaid were the only two things she needed. Her mother made the same offer as Kieran the night before, when they emerged from their love nest at last. She shook her head only to pause when she caught herself having nodded and shaken her head in a matter of only moments.

"There is little that I need to have with me. What I wish for I already placed in my satchel. I am ready, turtledove." She looked at Kieran, and a smile played at the corner of her mouth. "While you may call me buttercup around others, I think I should save 'turtledove' for the privacy of our chamber once you are among our people and once more the battle-hewn laird."

Kieran snagged Maude as she walked past and lifted her into his lap where he sat on the end of the bed. It was the first time Maude had referred to the MacLeods as her people. It made him inordinately happy to know she considered herself a MacLeod before they arrived in Stornoway.

"What is it?" she asked.

"Can't a newly married mon want to touch his wife? All the time."

"Aye, and I like it, but I don't understand the look on your face."

"Look?" Kieran leaned far enough to the side that Maude grabbed his shoulders as he attempted to peer into the looking glass. "I enjoy hearing you refer to the MacLeod clan as 'our people'."

"That's what they are, aren't they? I'm a MacLeod now."

"Aye, ye are, lass. Let me see my plaid on you." Kieran eased Maude to her feet and fingered the brooch, but she slapped his hand away with a giggle.

"It's ma plaid now. Ye canna have it back," she teased, and Kieran tickled her ribs as the sound of her burr had its usual effect on him; his cock rose to attention.

"Continue on like that, and it'll be another sennight before I let you go."

"Promise?" Her hand traveled between his thighs, but he grasped her wrist lest they never leave.

"Cheeky wench."

"Only for you---turtledove."

"Aboot that. You may call me that or aught else you wish in front of anyone. I'm not embarrassed. I'm proud to call you wife, to be wed to a woman who loves me nearly as much as I love her." Kieran ceased his tickling when he saw the stricken expression on Maude's face. "What is it?"

"Do you think I don't love you as much you love me? Have I not made it clear how I feel?"

Kieran chuckled. "You've made it clear morning, noon, and night. I believe the entire keep is aware of how much you love me."

"That's not what I mean," Maude blushed as she recalled how Kieran never failed to make her cry out her release. "I mean outside of bed. And before you point out how we've made love on every surface in this chamber, you know what I mean."

"Aye, I do. And I know you love me, lass. I didn't mean to diminish that or have you question whether you've been the most wonderful bride a mon could have. I'd have you know how devoted I am to you."

"I'd say you've made your devotion *loud and* clear."

"Now who is only thinking of our lovemaking?"

"Maude?" Blair's voice called through the door and brought their banter to an end. Maude opened the door to her sister, who hurled herself into Maude's arms, tears streaming down her face. The sisters had shared a good cry the night before as the reality that they'd be separated for the first time in their lives sank in. They clung to one another until they both sniffled and pulled apart. "It's time to leave if you wish to get ahead of the clouds that approach."

They'd had wonderful weather since the wedding, even though Maude and Kieran hadn't ventured out to enjoy it. Mother Nature seemed to understand the mood of the day and chose to match it. Maude nodded and turned back to Kieran, who gave the sisters space but now approached.

"Blair, you need only ask your father or Lachlan to accompany you, and you're welcome at Stornoway without notice. The invitation is standing."

Blair nodded as she once more hugged Maude, who breathed in her sister's matching lemon verbena scent. She held her constant companion and tried not to burst into tears again. She couldn't remember a time before Blair, since she'd been little more than a year old when her younger sister was born. Lachlan, two years her senior, said the same of his sisters. The trio walked belowstairs, with Maude only looking back twice. They joined her family and the MacLeod guards who mingled among the Sutherland guards who would join them. Hamish had insisted, and Kieran had agreed without argument, that they travel with two score of guardsmen even though they would be on Sutherland and then MacLeod land the entire time. Highwaymen cared little for clan land ownership, and neither laird wanted to risk Maude's safety in case of another incident along the border. Amelia and Hamish pulled Maude into a tight embrace as both parents attempted not to cry. Amelia succeeded, but it was Hamish who had suspiciously damp eyelashes. Maude moved into a joint embrace with Blair and Lachlan, who appeared to whisper something that made Maude nod. Kieran suspected Lachlan was reminding her that he would thrash Kieran if he did anything to hurt her and would come for her if she sent word. His brother-by-marriage had reminded him of that pledge several times since he arrived a sennight earlier.

Kieran and Maude mounted with Maude riding in the center as they passed through the gates. She allowed herself to glance back twice before forcing herself to keep her eyes on the road ahead. Once the party settled into a steady cantor with no hazards in sight, Kieran pulled to the side until he could reenter the entourage next to Maude. The Sutherland guards would lead the way until they crossed into Assynt in two days. Kieran rode beside her, plucking her from her saddle when exhaustion threatened to knock her from Trioblaid's back. He set an arduous pace the entire way until they reached the Minch and the birlinns that would ferry them to the Isle of Lewis. Once they were on the island, it was only two more hours' ride until they passed through the gates of Stornoway.

CHAPTER TWENTY-TWO

$\mathbf{M}$aude took a surreptitious look around as they passed through the village. People stepped out to greet their laird while assessing the mystery woman who accompanied him. She wondered if he had informed his people that he would return with a wife. As if reading her mind, he reached over to take her hand.

"It's a small island, and we don't get many visitors, let alone new members to the clan. They're curious, buttercup. They don't mean to be rude."

"I didn't think them rude. I worried that they might think me lacking," she muttered. She tried to keep her eyes straight ahead but failed as more people spilled out to observe them. She focused on the impressive structure that sat along the coast. Lewis was a flat island which made defenses difficult, but the cliffs that wrapped around the northern boundary of the keep limited the means of approach. Maude examined her new home as they passed under the portcullis. The people within the bailey were a little less obvious in their assessment of her, but she felt their eyes nonetheless. She drew in a whistling voice when two elegant women stepped out of the keep. They were mirror images of Madeline, and their clear haughtiness made her stomach sink. She swallowed, took a deep breath, lifted her chin, and set her shoulders back prepared to go into battle as she watched them look down their noses at her. She glanced over at Kieran, who watched her. She offered him one of her half-smiles, and his face took on a pensive expression. Most of the time, she enjoyed when Kieran attempted to decipher what the smile meant, but this time she could tell she worried him.

"All will be well, turtledove," she reassured him, returning the squeeze he'd offered her hand while they were in the village.

"It should be me who reassures you, mo ghaol."

"Riding next to me, holding my hand, reassures me."

Kieran helped Maude from Trioblaid's back and wrapped his arm around her waist before steering her toward the two women awaiting them. Neither made an effort to greet them in the bailey, preferring to wait on the steps leading to the massive double doors. Kieran chose to think they didn't want to risk slipping in the muddy bailey, but he knew that wasn't the case. They refused to dirty themselves on his and Maude's behalf. He escorted Maude up the slippery steps and slid his hand down her arm until he could once more entwine their fingers. He leaned in to kiss on his mother's cheek and embrace Abigail with one arm. He felt apprehensive about releasing Maude's hand, as though she might run for the ferry.

"Can you not do better than that, brother?" Abigail demanded before sending Maude a withering look. Maude made it clear that she let go of Kieran's hand rather than the other way around. She folded her hands before her as Kieran offered his sister a begrudging embrace. They were not off to a good start.

"Mother, Abigail, I would introduce you to Lady MacLeod." Kieran was certain Adeline snarled at the sound of her title being offered to someone else for the first time since she'd married his father. Maude gasped, since no one had addressed her that way yet. "This is Maude, my wife."

"Obviously, she's your wife," Adeline muttered as she

swept her assessing gaze over Maude. Just as she always did, Maude felt as though she came up short. She curtseyed to the older woman.

"It's a pleasure to meet you, Lady Adeline."

"Lady MacLeod," Adeline snapped, and Maude forced herself not to flinch.

"Of course, my lady. I beg your pardon."

"Mother," Kieran warned. "Maude is now Lady MacLeod. Let us be clear on that before any of us enter the keep. You knew this day would come."

"And it should have been Lady Laurel who assumed my title, not a Sutherland."

"Mother!" Kieran was beside himself at his mother's open hostility to Maude. He'd assumed she'd make some snide remarks in passing until she realized how wonderful Maude was, but this was beyond the pale. Maude's hand pinched his fingers together in a vice.

"It'll take me a while to grow accustomed to the title and to become familiar with the duties of chatelaine. I think I'd prefer Lady Maude for the time being." Maude offered a shy smile as she looked at Abigail, but she snapped her gaze back to Adeline before continuing. "I don't want to misplace the chatelaine's keyring this eve, so I will gather it from you tomorrow morning."

Kieran pulled his lips in tight to keep from laughing as Maude's conciliatory offer came with a stipulation. He was proud that she didn't shrivel before his mother's gimlet glare. He watched as she turned a warm smile on Abigail, even though he'd noticed her discomfort when she discovered his younger sister was a carbon copy of Madeline. Even their voices were alike.

"Lady Abigail, it is lovely to make your acquaintance. I'm sure you've been told before, but you bear a striking resemblance to your sister."

"Of course, I've heard it before," Abigail snapped. Her

225

demeanor shifted to match Adeline's. "And I know you're the one responsible for her being imprisoned in a nunnery."

"Abigail!" Kieran wanted the ground to swallow him, or better yet, the women of his family. They hadn't even made it inside, and Maude knew already that she was an unwanted addition to the family. Kieran led his bride into the Great Hall and looked around. They had made only a handful of the improvements that he'd ordered. Agatha and Adam awaited him just inside the door.

"Ma laird, ma lady," Agatha smiled as she dipped into a curtsy for Maude. "Welcome home. The evening meal is aboot to be served. Ye arrived at just the right moment."

"Thank you, Agatha. May I present Lady Maude MacLeod, my wife?" Kieran spoke, so all in the gathering hall could hear. He would make a proper introduction once they were on the dais, and the clan had gathered. He would be sure the priest blessed their marriage along with the food. He guided Maude toward the laird's table but caught himself when he saw his mother had already taken her place in the seat of the lady of the keep. She hadn't sat there in years. He jerked his head, but she responded with an imperious brow raise.

"It's fine, Kier. This isn't the hill to die on. Your people will understand what she's doing, and they can formulate their own opinion. I will look better for being gracious to your mother. Otherwise, some will say that you insisted to protect my dainty feelings, or worse, they will say that I henpecked you into forcing your mother from her seat. I don't need anyone else's help to be made the villain tonight."

Maude eased along the dais until she could sit in the seat to Kieran's right, smiling apologetically to the man she learned was Kyle, Kieran's second-in-command and the person whose seat she took. Abigail sat two seats to her right and leaned past Kyle, Kieran, and Maude to speak to her mother as the meal began. Kieran breathed a sigh of relief when the blessing and announcement went smoothly, but it was short-lived as his sister and mother continued their merciless campaign against Maude.

"Kieran, Madeline tells me that Lady Bevan was most disappointed when you ended your courtship." Kieran's head jerked up before he glared at Abigail. There had been no doubt that he wasn't courting Lady Bevan, but to correct Abigail would mean he had to admit in front of Maude that the widow had been his lover. Maude may have already known, but he was angry that his sister tossed the matter in Maude's face within an hour of arriving at her new home. "Lady Laurel had been so certain you would offer for her. She'd even decided to wait for you to break things off with Lady Bevan, knowing you would realize she was the ideal match for you. From how Madeline describes her, she's stunning. Slender and graceful. Exactly what a laird should want for a wife."

Maude tried not to choke on her food when the conversation on the high table ceased as everyone turned to listen and watch. She felt the heat rise in her neck, so she bowed her head over her trencher to keep anyone from seeing her humiliated blush. She nibbled at the food as her stomach clenched and tears threatened. She was tired, dirty, cold, and now mortified.

"Ladies Bevan and Laurel are not the only ones who awaited Kieran's attention," Adeline chimed in. "Maggie's looking forward to you visiting her croft. I'm sure she will be eager to see you this eve."

When Maude whimpered, Kieran's hand slammed onto the table, making platters and chalices rattle and wobble. He pushed his chair back so hard that it skidded off the back of the raised platform. He thrust his hand out to Maude, who tentatively placed hers into his. He practically yanked her from her seat before glaring at his mother and sister. He moved Maude's seat aside so she could step around it. He looked at the confused faces of his people who had sensed the animosity at the laird's table but hadn't been able to hear the conversation. He looked at Kyle, who sat in stunned silence along with other senior members of his guard who didn't know where to look. He raised Maude's hand to his lips and pressed an obvious kiss to her frigid hand.

"Come, mo chridhe. I'm exhausted, and I imagine you are, too. Besides, we've had too many nights sleeping on the ground. I would show you our chamber." Kieran looked out to the people who watched the spectacle unravelling on the dais. "I am a lucky mon to have a beautiful wife to love. Please excuse us."

Kieran led Maude with such purpose that she feared he might separate her arm from her shoulder. He steered her through the tables until they reached the stairs, where he came close to lifting her off her feet as he rushed them to the second floor. They walked in silence until Kieran locked and barred his chamber door. He turned to find Maude standing before the fire. He doubted she had even looked around the chamber that would now be hers, too. His approach was tentative as this night reminded him of how they met, and from the crushed look on Maude's face, he knew she thought the same.

"Buttercup--"

"Who's Maggie?" Kieran knew the question was coming, but he'd hoped to begin his apology before having to answer.

"She's a woman in the village I visited from time to time."

"She's your leman." Maude's shoulders slumped as her arms wrapped around her waist. She feared the little she ate would make an appearance across the hearth. She yelped, unprepared for the force with which Kieran spun her and pulled her against him. He softened his hold when he feared hurting her.

"No. She is not and never was my leman. I tupped her once in a while when the mood struck, but she was never aught more than that. I haven't been with her since before I met you, so don't even let the notion burrow into your mind that I visited her while I was back here either time. I palmed myself over and over as I pictured you." He turned toward the window and pointed there before pointing to the bed. "I would look out the window as though I might see you all the way in Stirling, or I would lie in bed imagining you were beside me, beneath me, on top of me. I haven't wanted another woman since the moment I saw you on the terrace. I swear to you."

Maude nodded, but Kieran could tell doubt had wriggled its way into Maude's mind and heart in the brief time they'd spent in his family's company. He wanted to rage against her for doubting him, but even the most confident of women would have been only human to feel insecure after the way his mother and sister spoke in front of her. Maude still hadn't looked up, and her arms remained wrapped around her middle. He reached to open her arms when a gentle knock sounded at the door. He stalked across the room and pulled the door open to find Agatha standing there with a dark expression that matched his own. She pushed past him and walked to Maude.

"Lass, dinna fash. I ken it's easier said than done, but the auld biddy, pardon ma language, has always been a jealous shrew." Agatha reached a slow hand toward Maude, who nodded but still didn't raise her head. "I have a bath on its way. Ye'll feel worlds better, I'd say, after a long soak and some attention from yer husband. Dinna punish the lad. He is beside himself," Agatha whispered the last part of her message. Maude looked up at last and glanced at Kieran, who she could see was out of his depth in how to console her. She reached out her hand, and he was back across the chamber in four strides. Rather than take her hand, he encircled her with his brawny arms and guided her toward a chair. He sat and pulled her into his lap as Agatha organized the servants who brought up the tub and steaming buckets of water. She curled against him until they were the only two left. Kieran undressed, then assisted Maude with her clothes before lifting her into the tub and following. They lay in the steaming water together without speaking until Kieran could take the silence no longer.

"Buttercup, I'm so sorry. I never imagined they would behave in such an abominable manner. It will not happen again."

"Yes, it will," she whispered. "Mayhap not in front of you, but it will happen again. You aren't my nursemaid. You can't be at my side at all times, so they'll wait until you aren't around. They'll drop barbs until they believe I'm beaten and defeated. Little do they know that this isn't my first time surviving such taunts. For all they know from Madeline, they seem to have failed to realize I survived her and the other ladies at court. I'm made of sterner stuff than they assume."

"So, you don't want to return to Sutherland?" Kieran wished he hadn't asked as soon as the words leaked from his lips, and the long pause before Maude shook her head made his heart stop. "You'll stay?"

"Where would I go? Run back to my parents and say I couldn't manage having my feelings hurt? Abandon you and our vows because of someone else? There are two of us in this marriage, and I refuse to allow either your mother or sister to join it."

"Maude, I love you even more than I thought possible. I am so proud of you, but I'm so desperately sorry that you're being forced to endure what I would do aught to protect you from." Kieran considered his words. If he would swear to protect her, then he had to do it in truth. "I will find Abigail a husband, and I will send mother to her dower lands if she refuses to cease. I warned her before I left the last time, but she has either conveniently forgotten or thinks to call my bluff."

"No," Maude kept her tone even. "If you send them both away within moments of our arrival, people will resent me. They will think I'm the one who insisted upon it. They'll think I arrived and chased away their clanswomen. Let the dust settle before you decide."

"How did you get so wise, my bonnie wee bride?"

"I survived court after being raised as a laird's daughter. My mother believes diplomacy is a lady's greatest weapon when a dirk doesn't suffice."

"Your mother says that?"

"Aye, and she's the one who trained me and Blair to wield a knife. My father taught her soon after they wed, then supported her when she wished to teach me and my sister."

"And have you had to use your skills?"

Maude nodded and stroked Kieran's legs beneath the water when he went rigid.

"Those are stories for another time."

Kieran lathered soap against a linen square before sliding his hands over Maude's shoulders until he reached her breasts. His cock hardened against her back as he kneaded her bosom. She laid her head back, but her fingers gripped his thighs as she arched and offered her heavy and aching flesh. Once her nipples puckered, he continued his ministrations as he swiped the cloth over each arm before drawing one leg, then the other, out of the water. He passed over muscle and sinew until he reached her feet. He pressed her shoulders until she leaned forward, wrapping her arms around her raised knees as he washed her back. He massaged the knots from her shoulders until she sighed.

"That feels lovely. Mmm," she sighed.

"I will always take care of you, buttercup."

Maude opened her mouth to respond, but he pulled her back against his chest and tilted her chin until he could fuse their lips, and their tongues dueled. He assisted Maude as she turned in the water, straddling him before he eased his rod into her. He cupped her backside as her hands roamed over his shoulders and arms, her breasts caught between their entangled bodies. She couldn't believe the erotic sensations of making love in water, in a tub before the fire. She leaned her head away, offering access to Kieran's questing mouth, her eyes drooping shut as pleasure mounted. Her moans and his grunts filled the chamber with the soft sloshing of water as their accompaniment. The tension built as Kieran's hands guided Maude's hips until they were calling out each other's names.

Maude sank against Kieran's torso as his fingers danced over her back. She never imagined her back could be as sensitive, as responsive, as it was to Kieran's touch. She nuzzled his neck as their breathing slowed, and she watched the flames dance. The afterglow of making love was peaceful and lured her toward sleep, but she enjoyed the closeness with Kieran too much to succumb. They'd slipped away each night they made camp under the guise of Kieran escorting Maude to wash, but the weather, the danger of being too far from camp, and the embarrassment Maude experienced from the men knowing why they disappeared kept their interludes brief and hurried.

"I wish we could stay this way forever, turtledove. It's peaceful and cozy, just the two of us before the hearth. And it's dry and warm at this fireside."

"I wish the same, but I worry you'll grow chilled soon. As much as I don't want to get out, we should finish bathing, so you can dry your hair before bed. I don't want you to catch the ague."

"That's naught but an old wives tale, but I don't want to soak my pillow. You might not appreciate sleeping with a wet chest all night," Maude giggled.

"You shall use me as your pillow, will you?" Kieran tickled her ribs, eliciting another peal of laughter.

"I've never slept so well as I do when I'm sprawled across you. You're warm and soft in all the right places."

"Soft?" Kieran pretended offense. "There is no part of me that is soft when you're nearby."

"Shall we test that theory?"

They hurried to finish their bath. Then Kieran brushed Maude's thick locks as they once more sat with Maude between Kieran's thighs, this time surrounded by pillows on the floor in front of the fire. He spread her hair across her back and shoulders after wringing more water from it. He understood why she preferred to wear her hair up in the stifling heat of the royal castle's Great Hall. Her hair was beautiful, but its weight surprised him. He regretted that the clan would expect her to wear her hair up now that she was married. His fingers massaged her scalp much as they had her shoulders before gliding down to rub the kinks from her neck. He could feel the hard bunches of muscle where she carried her stress. Her body grew heavy as she once more leaned against her bent legs.

"Do you wish to sleep, little one?"

"At some point, but not yet. Your hands are doing wonders for relaxing me, though. Continue and you'll put me to sleep like a bairn."

Kieran helped her to her feet before guiding her to their bed. When they reached the foot of it, Maude paused. She studied the carved posts at the foot of the bed and the forest scene etched into the headboard. She'd seen nothing like it.

"My father and I worked on it when I was four-and-ten. He was a master woodworker, and he enjoyed the hobby as a means to focus his attention on something other than clan business."

"Do you enjoy carving, too?"

"Not as much as he did. He was a mon constantly in motion and needed something to do with his hands. I appreciate being able to read in solitude when I have a few free minutes." When Maude nodded and tucked that piece of information away, Kieran corrected himself. "I used to enjoy escaping to my solar for time alone, but as I think aboot it, I find I'd rather enjoy your company in my free moments."

"We all need time alone now and again. I'm not insulted that you might want to shut the door to the world, and that even includes me. I won't live in your pocket, Kier. I'll find my place here." Maude moved to the chest that sat at the foot of their bed. It was small and contained items Maude knew she couldn't wait for the wagon to bring. They had attached it to one of the pack horses. She knelt before it and lifted her Sutherland plaid out. She unfolded it in her lap and pulled a small wooden carving from the wool she'd used to protect it. "Da is a woodworker, too. He made four of these figurines. One for Mama, one for Lach, one for Blair, and one for me. He gave them to us the eve before Lachlan rode into his first battle."

Maude held up a carving of five people standing arm-in-arm, and Kieran could see it was Maude's family. They stood in a line with their arms around one another, and the detailing was exquisite. Hamish had captured the essence of each person's build and expressions, and Kieran marveled that the man had made one so fine, let alone four. When Maude handed him her treasure, he ran his fingers over the grooves and felt a patch over Hamish and Amelia that had been rubbed smooth, as if Maude's thumb had traveled over the wood countless times. He looked up to catch her observing him.

"I would carry it in my pocket whenever Da and Lachlan rode out, then I often had it with me during my early days at court. Feeling it against my leg was reassuring during uncertain times," she explained. Kieran handed it back to her, and Maude walked to her side of the bed. She knew it was hers because at some point, Kieran's sword had made it to their chamber and rested against the bedside table closer to the door. She placed the figurine on the table facing the bed. For years, it had been one of the last things she saw at night and often it was the first thing she saw in the morning. She knew she would rather Kieran be her first and last sight of the day, but having a small reminder of her family was fortifying, especially after the welcome she received. Kieran stepped behind her and kissed her crown.

"You're a brave lass, Maude. For all the courage people claim men possess, women face far greater tests to their mettle. You're expected to leave everything and everyone you ken when you marry into a new clan. You arrive at a new home, kenning no one. Often not even kenning the groom. In your case, you were taken to court and expected to navigate protocol along with the ugly underbelly of politics. And as though those aren't great enough trials, you must carry and bear bairns. That feat surpasses even the bravest and most heroic on a battlefield. You bring forth new life." Kieran turned Maude toward him and rested his forehead against hers. "I promise never to take for granted all you sacrifice to make a life with me."

"I love you. It makes the challenges and inevitable struggles worth it to ken that at the end of each day, it will always be us, side-by-side."

"I love you, buttercup."

They joined in a tender kiss that communicated their pledges of love and devotion. As the kiss gained momentum and heat, they eased onto the bed where they once more surrendered to one another as Kieran sank into Maude. The rest of the night passed in bouts of lovemaking and sleep.

CHAPTER TWENTY-THREE

M aude looked over her shoulder as she heard Kieran stir. The sun's rays were making their first appearances over the horizon, but Maude was dressed and sat at the small dressing table as she braided her hair. She opted for two thick plaits; one she wrapped around her head, and the other she left to hang down her back.

"Good morning, sleepyhead." She crossed the chamber and climbed onto the bed before dropping a kiss on Kieran's nose. Before she pulled away, Kieran tugged her against his chest for a proper kiss.

"What are you doing awake so early? I assumed I would've exhausted you as much as you did me."

"I confess I am tired, but the keep will wake soon, and I refuse to appear like a slug-a-bed on my first morning."

"And if I don't care to wake with a cold spot beside me?" Kieran grumbled.

"My place hasn't grown cold yet," Maude chided playfully. "But if you're worried aboot that, you shouldn't oversleep." She attempted to scoot away, but Kieran hefted her across his chest.

"And if I had plans for how I wished to awake and start my day? Plans that didn't include finding you dressed." He began picking at the laces to Maude's kirtle, but her hands swatted him away.

"I would like that, too, and I considered it, but Kieran, I want to make a better impression this morning. There will be plenty of other mornings when we can have a lying in."

Kieran scowled, but knew that Maude was probably correct. Making an early appearance would improve people's perception of her, even if they were newlyweds. He climbed from the bed and hurried to prepare for the day before strapping his sword to his back. Maude watched in awe as his muscles bunched and tightened, and his arms and chest flexed, while placing the claymore across his back. He realized that while at court, it was rare that he wore his sword. When he accompanied her to the abbey, he'd already been wearing it. He didn't wear it at Sutherland and only carried it a few times since they were in their chamber most of their time there, and she'd been seeking privacy when he secured it while they traveled.

"Keep looking at me like that, and it'll be another sennight of locking you in a bedchamber and having my way with you."

Maude swallowed and nodded but didn't look away. Kieran walked around the bed and slid his arms around her waist as she melted into his chest. Her kiss was hungry as her arms twined around his neck. He met each swipe of her tongue with one of his own. His hands moved to cup her ample backside, his cock twitching as the soft globes exceeded the breadth of his large hands. He would never tire of the feel of Maude's voluptuous body as his hands kneaded her supple flesh. Maude's hands glided over his chest and the ridges of his abdomen, making him suck in a sharp breath as he anticipated its destination. She pushed his sporran aside before lifting the material of his plaid. Her hand found what it sought, and she wrapped her fingers around his pulsing length. But moments later, Maude slipped from Kieran's arms and looked at the bed before looking at the door. She bit her lower lip, and Kieran was certain he would spend himself just looking at her. She moved toward the bed but paused before looking back at him. He was behind her in an instant, his larger body wrapping around her.

A thought crossed her mind, more a memory of something she had seen several years earlier when she came across a footman and a maid in a passageway. She halted, and Kieran crashed into her. His arm slid around her, but she pressed her hips back against his. She felt his rod harden in an instant. She reached back to grip his backside as she rubbed hers against his cock.

"You don't know what you're asking for," Kieran growled.

"I do. I—I saw a guard and maid once. By accident."

Kieran pulled her tighter against his chest as his hand snaked up to cup a breast while the other turned her chin.

"Maude, I don't know that I can be gentle with you. I've imagined making love to you that way too many times, and I fear my overeagerness."

"And if that's not what I want? Gentleness, that is."

"Perhaps you might listen to someone who has your best interests at heart."

"And if my interest is to couple with my husband again?" She yanked the laces of her kirtle and dropped it and her chemise to the floor in an instant.

"That isn't what I meant, and you know it."

Maude grasped the bedpost they stood near and leaned forward, widening her stance. The image she presented to Kieran with her hips begging for his fingers to grip, her back arched and breasts swinging, and a look of naïve longing on her face as she looked back at him was the image of his dreams. As he admired the view, he caught Maude's expression change into one of doubt and then humiliation. She released the bedpost and stood.

"Wait," he hissed before guiding his cock into her. "I was enjoying the view. It's perfection." He groaned as he slid in to the hilt and pressed his hips forward. "I've fantasized of making love to you this way. You remember how a mon can ease his need when the woman he wants is not available."

Maude gasped and pulled away. She twisted and pushed against his chest.

"How could you bring that up?" She was in tears, and Kieran realized his mother's words about Maggie rang in her ears. "How could you tell me you went whoring?"

Despite guessing her train of thought, her accusation stunned Kieran, but it only took a moment before he understood her logic, and he had to admit he had chosen his words poorly. He grabbed her wrists and brought her back in front of him, but she writhed and tried to break his grip. He spun her around and pulled her hips against his pulsing cock.

"Don't believe what my mother said. Not for a minute. I've already told you several times that I took myself in my hand, Maude." He murmured in her ear from behind her. "I pictured you as I pumped my cock until my eyes crossed. I imagined taking you from behind just like you offered, but what I pictured wasn't gentle lovemaking. I imagined making you moan my name until you screamed. Every time I thought of you, my damn cock ended up hard as a bluidy rock. Even dunks in the frigid loch didn't ease my need while I was away. I would slip down to the loch at night, hoping to cool my ardor that went unspent all day while I missed you. I fisted myself night after night. I showed you last eve that I stood at that window imagining I might see you all the way in Stirling. When I returned to court, it was no different. When I couldn't face the icy water, I called for a bath. Those times I didn't have to rush. I pictured taking you in every position and place I can conceive of. I never went whoring, Maude, nor did I visit anyone from my past. I need you, and only you will satisfy me. So, wife, don't for a moment doubt that I will be faithful to you. If this is what you want, then I shall gladly show you every fantasy I've ever had of you."

When her hips danced against his rather than pulling away, he slammed his cock into her sheath. He maneuvered them so she braced herself against the mattress. Maude realized this time was different. Even when Kieran seemed to lose control in the past, there was still a tenderness in the way they came together. This time, Maude let her body dictate her desires rather than her heart. She was sure Kieran noticed the shift because he growled and increased his pace. His arm snaked around her waist, and his fingers dug into the meaty flesh of her breast, the sensation verging on pain.

"Get on the bed," he demanded, and Maude scrambled onto the mattress, kneeling with her weight on her forearms and her backside in the air. Her moan was pure ecstasy as he thrust into her again and again. Kieran met each of her moans with an answering grunt. He couldn't get enough. The faster and harder he thrust, the stronger the sense grew. He realized it would never be enough. He had claimed his wife's maidenhead, he had brought her pleasure more than once, and he felt more connected to her than he had anyone else in his life, but until there was a way that they could fuse into one being, it would never be enough.

"I don't understand what you're doing to me," Maude whispered. "Why do I still want more? I'm so close, but it's like I want to crawl inside you. What are you doing to me?"

Hearing Maude voice the words he thought consumed him. He climbed onto the bed and pressed her into the mattress. His body covered hers as his hand slipped beneath her. He found her nub and rubbed until she shattered, screaming an incoherent sound. He followed her over the edge as he gave one last thrust. And then reality came clattering back down around Kieran's ears. He jumped away like a scalded cat and backed up until he met the far wall. He looked at his wife's spent body as she labored to breathe. He had a view that only moments ago would have had him thrusting into her glistening sheath but now made him feel revolted at his selfishness.

She asked what I was doing. I was fucking my wife harder than I would any whore. What have I done?

Maude shivered as the air turned cold around her, and she couldn't feel Kieran anywhere near her. She rolled over and sat up, and the sight that greeted her made her heart turn just as cold as her body. Kieran's face was the picture of disgust and loathing, but he wasn't looking at her, or rather, he refused to look at her. Maude looked around the chamber, a sickening dread taking root. She spotted her kirtle and slid from the bed. She grabbed it and said a prayer of thanks that it was one she could get into on her own. She glanced back at her husband and noticed he was watching her with a stricken gaze. It was as though he was hurt by her instead of the other way around. Maude paused and puzzlement showed on her face before she brushed her hands over her skirts. There was something else happening, but she didn't understand her husband's sudden shift in mood.

"I'm sorry," his hoarse whisper barely reached her. "I'm sorry I scared you, and I'm sorry I mistreated you."

"Mistreated me? Scared me?" Maude dropped the gown and inched toward Kieran as though he were an injured and unpredictable wild animal.

"Yes. Just now. The way, I--"

"Made love to me?"

"That wasn't making love," Kieran shuddered.

"I thought it was."

"That's because you don't know any better." Kieran watched Maude bristle and reach for her gown once more. His next words were barely audible. "I meant I fucked you. I fucked my own wife."

Just as she had a moment ago, Maude stood and moved toward him. "You're right; I don't know. And you're not making any sense to me, but you are scaring me now." When she stood before him, she witnessed a hollowness in his eyes that she'd never seen before. "Kieran?"

"That is *nae* how a mon is meant to treat his lady wife. I shouldnae have been so rough with you. I wouldnae even treat--" Kieran snapped his mouth shut before he made it even worse.

"You wouldn't treat a whore like that." Maude supplied for him, and her heart broke when he nodded. The shame in his eyes made her shake her head. "Did aught I said or did make you think I wanted you to stop? I thought I made it clear I wanted it just the way it was."

"You'll feel differently later in the morning when you're in pain because I didn't care for you properly."

"I'd say you did everything properly. I never imagined such pleasure as you've shown me just now. Is it wrong that I enjoy each way we couple? Should I not want to join with you as much as I do? Does that make me a whore?"

"Don't say that," Kieran hissed. "Don't ever say that again. You aren't a whore, and that's precisely why I shouldn't have treated you as one."

"But who says, other than you, that you did? I didn't feel like one until right now."

"Maude." The remorse and pain in his voice was real.

"Does anyone have to know? I mean, will anyone find out I enjoyed coupling with you like that?" Maude's face flamed red at the notion of anyone other than Kieran being aware of how much she enjoyed the sins of the flesh.

"No," Kieran was adamant. "No one will ever see or hear us together. What we do is our business, and no one has a say in it but us."

"Then why are you so miserable? Why do you fear not living up to some husbandly code? Who's going to judge you? It certainly won't be me."

"Maude, I will take more care with you next time."

"Does that mean it can last longer?"

Kieran's mouth twitched. He grumbled as he began to come around, thanks to his wife's practical nature. Passion sparked between them once more, and Maude shifted to join her body with Kieran's again.

Despite the delay, Maude and Kieran entered the Great Hall as people continued to trickle in for the morning meal. Maude looked around, and her stomach sank as varying degrees of suspicion and hostility marked the clan members' faces. She wondered what Adeline and Abigail said after her abrupt departure the night before. She glanced at Kieran, but despite standing next to her, he was already in a deep conversation with Kyle. She refused to appear like she needed her husband's protection in her own home, so she climbed the steps to the dais as Abigail and Adeline descended from the second floor. Maude was relieved she'd arrived before them as she slipped into the lady of the keep's chair. She smiled at Agatha as the older woman approached with a bowl of porridge and a small jug of honey.

"I wasna certain if ye prefer honey or extra cream in yer bowl. I can fetch ye the milk if ye'd rather."

"Nay. Honey is my favorite," Maude offered a tentative smile. She sensed Agatha would be an ally, but it was too early to tell. She'd met more than one lady-in-waiting who appeared interested in being her friend, only to tell tales to the others when Maude turned her back.

"Ma lady, would ye care for a tour after ye break yer fast?"

"I would appreciate that a great deal, Agatha. Thank you." Maude had no chance to say more as Adeline walked behind her chair and flung her ring of keys on the table beside Maude. The rattle made many glance their way. Adeline took a seat at the end of the table too far away for Maude to say thanks, so she offered the warmest smile she could muster only to have Adeline turn her head away from Maude. She turned her attention to Kieran, who took his seat beside her.

"I'll be in the lists this morning, then in my solar after the nooning. I have correspondence to catch up on and grievances to review before I arbitrate them tomorrow morning," Kieran explained as he served himself a rasher of bacon. He watched

Maude from the corner of his eye, pleased to see Maude ate with a healthy appetite. "Would you care to join me in my solar this afternoon? Perhaps to review the accounts or to read."

"I would like that very much. Agatha's taking me for a tour, and now that your mother has relinquished her keys, I'd like to get familiar with the running of the keep."

Kieran winced at the mention of the keys. He hadn't seen his mother drop them beside Maude, but he'd heard them. Everyone near the dais had. His gaze slid to his mother, who glared at him before turning a loathing expression on Maude. He reminded himself that his family and clan would warm to Maude once they grew to know her. They finished their breakfast with small talk about various places around the keep that Maude might want Agatha to show her. He suggested that she meet with Adam after her tour, since he could explain the accounts before she joined Kieran in his solar. Maude watched the clan eat and mingle at the tables below the dais before one after another left to complete the day's work. She prepared to rise and seek Agatha, when Abigail's voice carried to her.

"She inhaled that bowl so fast I'm surprised we didn't hear her scraping the bottom."

"I'd expect two or three wouldn't fill that girth she carries around," Adeline responded, her eyes locking with Maude's.

"I hear her dowry is as fat as she is," Abigail continued. "That must be what Kieran sees in her. I mean, why else would he turn down Laurel? And didn't you say you were considering Mary Mackenzie? I mean, I know she's the laird's cousin, but she is beautiful."

Maude swallowed as she struggled to maintain her composure. She realized Kieran was once more talking to Kyle and suspected he hadn't heard his mother and sister, but the others seated near them did. They looked aghast before passing assessing eyes over her. She feared she was a miserable failure when the women smirked. The men gazed at her bosom, but their smirk meant something entirely different from the women's. She pushed back her chair and made to step around Kieran's, but he grasped her hand and lifted it to his lips. She smiled down at him, but when it didn't reach her eyes, she saw concern register in his. He stood and tucked a lock of hair behind her ear. His gaze darted to his mother and sister before he tilted Maude's chin up.

"Summon me if you need aught at all, buttercup. Never fear interrupting or bothering me."

"I will keep that in mind, but I must go. I don't want to monopolize all of Agatha's morning. She'll have duties beyond showing me around."

Kieran was reluctant to release Maude, but nodded before dropping a kiss to her lips. Her cheeks heated at the public affection, but she wouldn't deny she enjoyed any kiss she shared with Kieran.

"Until the nooning, turtledove," she murmured. She left the dais and joined Agatha, who took her to the kitchens first. The morning passed in a haze of new faces and names as she met the women who staffed the kitchens, the laundresses, the cooper, the distiller, the man who managed the buttery, the blacksmith, and the fletcher. She received greetings of varying warmth. While no one displayed outward rudeness toward her, they were distant and untrusting. Maude wondered if that was their nature, guessing the Hebrideans were just as cautious of new people as Highlanders from the mainland, but she suspected word had already spread about her. She pledged she would work hard to earn their trust and respect.

She was hungry by the time the noon meal arrived, but as she sat next to Kieran, she nibbled at the chunk of bread he passed her, preferring to eat a few pieces of cheese and cold chicken before eating a handful of dried fruit. After her new family's comments that morning, she was self-conscious about eating her fill. She would find an apple before joining Kieran in his solar. She wasn't certain whether Kieran's hold on her hand throughout the meal made things better or worse, since their clasped hands sat on the table as a display to everyone. At first, she assumed Kieran did it as a public statement of support for her, but as his thumb swept over the back of her hand in an absent-minded sporadic pattern, she realized he did it without thought. When the meal ended, Maude promised to meet Kieran in his solar after she collected the ledgers. She found her way to Adam's office and nearly jumped out of her skin when she turned to leave and found Agatha in the doorway with a napkin in her hand.

"Ye didna eat enough to fill a sparrow, lass." Agatha stated as an explanation when she handed the napkin to Maude, who opened it to find three pieces of dried beef and a bannock. "The laird canna keep his hands off ye, so I imagine ye work up an appetite. Dinna let Lady Adeline or Lady Abigail scare ye from eating a proper meal. Neither of them have a braw mon chasing them aboot the bedchamber."

Maude's cheeks heated, but she appreciated Agatha's thoughtfulness and said as much. When the older woman left, Maude inhaled the food before winding her way to Kieran's solar where they passed the afternoon with only two intermissions from their tasks.

CHAPTER TWENTY-FOUR

Maude's days settled into a predictable routine. Kieran grumbled that Maude robbed him of his beauty sleep when she awoke before the sun, but it was the only way she would agree to start the day making love to him and still be in the kitchens as the servants arrived. Neither was willing to cease their nighttime couplings, so both dragged themselves through the day, exhausted but sated.

Maude went to the kitchens each morning and lit the fires, ensuring they were blazing by the time the head cook, and the servants arrived, many still rubbing their eyes. Most mornings, Maude had already kneaded the dough left out the night before to rise and had it in the ovens. She was stirring the cauldron of porridge as the women pulled cured meats and cheeses from the larder and prepared trenchers from the day-old loaves. The first few mornings the women eyed Maude with suspicion, but as they became accustomed to her smile and nod, they accepted her help. None were rude to her, but they also did little to involve her in their conversations. After she broke her fast alongside Kieran, she would make her rounds to ensure everyone who worked inside the bailey had all they needed to contribute to the keep's smooth operation. The laundresses were not as reticent as the kitchen staff. They peppered Maude with questions, but she was never convinced the women took a sincere interest in her so much as they hoped for kernels of information that they might turn into gossip. She was careful what she shared, but kept a practiced naivety to her tone, hoping the women wouldn't realize she recognized their motives. Maude made a conscious effort to blend in as she worked, rather than sweeping in and demanding changes. She made subtle suggestions or led by example as she attempted to assert herself as the lady of the keep.

She overhead more than one comment from the servants that made her heart sink as she tried to earn their respect through hard work. After years of Adeline swanning about and refusing to assist with manual labor, Maude's efforts made her look more like the farm wife Adeline and Abigail called her than the lady of the keep. She attempted to balance her efforts, ensuring other women saw her sewing before the fire as people arrived for the evening meal. She had a loom brought to the ladies' solar and began a tapestry, but it was a chamber Abigail and Adeline favored more and more, so she abandoned the room and asked that someone take the loom to a storeroom where she decided to work. She spent much of her afternoons gathering plants that served as medicinals as the gardens sprouted. She made the error of having only one guard accompany her when she left the keep's walls to forage along the tree line that was within view of the wall walk. It was her first heated argument with Kieran, and to her great misfortune, it took place in the bailey.

"What were you thinking leaving the safety of the keep with only one mon?" Kieran demanded.

"Who would do me harm here? Do you expect a raiding party to come barreling through the trees and steal me away? You're overreacting and making a scene." Maude's look of disbelief only angered Kieran more.

"That is what I fear. This may not be a large island and the MacLeods may control most of it, but we have known the

Morrisons and MacIvers to raid. What better prize than to steal the laird's beautiful bride?" Kieran was bellowing by the time he finished, only possessing a vague awareness that people gathered to watch. It had incensed him to return from the lists to learn Maude had left the walls with only one man. "How could you not imagine it would upset me? We traveled here with two score of guardsmen, and I would have brought the king's army if I could. I insisted upon accompanying you when you had two guards on the way to see Father Michael, and I didn't think that was enough."

"And that was on the roads outside Stirling. Lewis doesn't strike me as a place rife with highwaymen."

"Mayhap nae highwaymen, but ye never ken if there might be lawless men wandering aboot," Kieran's burr slipped back into place as he became more agitated. The thought of someone emerging from the woods and capturing Maude made his chest burn. He rubbed a fist over his sternum, trying to ease the pain. Maude watched Kieran battle the fear that threatened to consume him and realized that, as always, his high-handedness and overprotectiveness came from his deep concern for her. She lowered her basket to the ground and stepped closer to Kieran, resting her hands on his chest. He covered them with one hand while the other cupped her nape. "I love you, Maude, and I will never be careless with your protection. I wish you wouldn't be with your own safety. I'd never forgive myself if aught happened to you when it's preventable by having a few more men escort you. Please."

Maude nodded as Kieran rested his forehead against hers. "I love you, too, and I didn't mean to scare you. It was thoughtless, and I'd even disappoint Da by only taking one guard. He wouldn't have allowed it on Sutherland, and I should've known better here. I'm sorry."

"Then why'd you only request one?"

"I didn't want to inconvenience your men. Which of them would want to watch me pick flowers? That's not a task any of them would wish to perform."

"Inconvenience them? What do you think they're there to do? They're called guardsmen because that's their damn job. To guard. You."

"No. They're there to guard the clan, not one woman traipsing through the grass."

"You're part of the clan now," Kieran reminded her, but it was easy to forget when she knew she was still unwelcome. He pressed a deep kiss against her parted lips, aware now but uncaring of those who watched. He wouldn't spare a minute to ignore his wife's safety, and he wouldn't turn down the opportunity to kiss her.

A week slid into a moon which slid into two, but despite Maude's efforts to fit in, the clan still gave her the cold shoulder. She avoided Adeline whenever possible, but Abigail took any opportunity to question Maude's choices around the keep. She complained when Maude ordered the doors to the keep be opened to air out the Great Hall each day. She whined about the lavender and rosemary mix that Maude added to the rushes. She complained that her nose itched while she refused to leave the Great Hall when Maude had the tapestries taken down and beaten outside, then the hearths scrubbed. Adeline joined the complaints when Maude ordered more tallow candles burned than beeswax. Maude agreed the smell of the tallow was unpleasant, but when she reviewed the accounts, she was astonished to discover how much they spent on candles alone. When her mother-by-marriage's complaints threatened to create a mutiny among the staff, Maude pulled out the candle making supplies along with dried rose petals she found in the spense. She ground the petals into a fine powder before adding it to the wax she melted and poured into the molds. She ignored the women who surrounded her as she worked, many shocked that she knew how to make candles. She grimaced when she ordered the new candles replace the fresh tallows she'd already had put in sconces around the keep and in the large overhead candelabras. She took the barely used scentless tallows to the blacksmith and cooper for them to use in their workshops. She didn't dare comment that the reason for the smell was poor quality. She attempted a peace offering by sending several beeswax candles to Adeline's and Abigail's chambers, but it did little to remedy the growing rift between the women.

As the days passed, Maude retreated further into herself and ate less and less. The constant scrutiny wore on her nerves, but she struggled to determine how to improve her relations with her new clan. Kieran watched as Maude toiled around the keep each day, dark circles forming under her eyes and the skin pulling taut over her ribs. He commented more than once that she worked too hard, but she would offer him her half-smile before changing the subject. He was aware she was unhappy, but he was at a loss to how to remedy the situation. His endeavors to secure a betrothal for Abigail were futile. Word of Madeline's fall from grace had spread, and many clans were leery of accepting a bride said to be similar in disposition to Madeline. He considered sending her to court as Madeline's replacement, but one sister in disgrace was enough for him. When he suggested that he send his mother to her dower lands, Maude became upset and tears filled her eyes. She begged Kieran to give her more time to win over the clan, but he was coming to accept that he'd misplaced his optimism and faith in his people.

"I will order them to cease ignoring you," Kieran growled as they sat together in his solar. He disliked it, but Agatha had become his informant for how his clan treated his bride. The housekeeper had always known all that occurred in the keep and had often shared pieces of information that aided Kieran in the running of the clan. When Maude refused to discuss events that upset her, he turned to Agatha. It shocked him to learn the unkind things said about Maude. He suspected she was aware of the gossip but was thankful that she never heard it, or at least she denied hearing it.

"You can't order them to like me, Kier. They either will, or they won't."

"I can order them to respect you."

"They do, or at least my position within the clan. No one is rude or disrespectful to my face, because I'm your wife."

"But they don't respect the tireless effort you put into improving the clan. The keep has never looked better, our finances are steadily improving thanks to your thriftiness, and their lives are better for it."

"They don't see those small things. To them, I am someone new who has taken over from a woman many of them have known most of their lives."

"A woman who hasn't done a thimbleful of what you've accomplished in two moons."

"Leave be, turtledove. They'll come around. It hasn't been that long."

"It doesn't mean I have to like it," Kieran muttered as he lifted Maude onto his lap from where she perched on the side of his desk. They grew closer each day, relying upon one another's knowledge and experience to run their clan, and their intimacy grew as they learned what brought them to ecstasy. She ceased their conversation as she often did with a searing kiss that wiped Kieran's mind of anything but his need to join with her. He ran his hands over her ribs and breasts as she squirmed to get closer. When she shifted to straddle him, he laid her on his desk. He rested on one forearm while his other hand found the hem of Maude's kirtle. He inched it up until his hand found the thatch of curls between her legs. Maude's head rested on the tabletop as Kieran slid a finger along her seam.

"Kier," she whispered on a moan.

She drew him in for a kiss as his finger entered her. The sensation drove Maude to intensify their kiss as she rocked her hips to meet Kieran's questing finger. He eased a second finger into her as he worked the sensitive flesh. Her soft mewling spurred him to use his thumb to circle her nub. As they kissed, Maude reached between them and tucked his plaid into his belt. Her hand cupped his length before guiding his cock to her entrance.

"I don't want to hurt you. This wood cannot be comfortable," he murmured as he tried to hold in the groan and rein in his need to thrust into her.

"I've ached for you to be inside me ever since you settled me on your lap. Kieran, I need you. The wood won't cool the way my body yearns for you."

Kieran seized her mouth in a brutal kiss that signaled the onslaught of their passion. He plunged into her over and over as she nipped at his lips and clenched her fingers around his backside. He grasped her hip in one hand and raised her arms above her head with the other. Her moans encouraged him to continue when he would have slowed.

"I don't know why I feel like this, Kieran. It wasn't that long ago that I had no idea being with a mon would make me so needy and so brazen, but I can't hold back."

"You don't have to, mo ghaol. I want you, need you, just as much. I don't think I'll ever get enough of you. And you have no idea how hearing your desire makes me feel. I hope that it never goes away."

"You don't think me loose or unladylike for this?" Maude panted as Kieran continued to surge into her.

"God, no. I'm lucky to have a wife who enjoys me and perhaps wants me as much as I want her." They kissed again before Kieran leaned back to surge into her over and over. His hand kneaded her breast, and Maude covered it, guiding him to a firmer hold.

"I didn't know what it meant at the time, but ever since our first kiss, my body seems different." Maude murmured.

"I'm different, too. I've never felt like this before. I still marvel at how it never used to be like this." Kieran realized what he said after the words left his mouth. He expected

Maude to push him away after mentioning his past while he was hilt-deep within her. But she released a purely feminine growl before pulling him down for another kiss. Maude took control of the kiss, and Kieran's body raced to the precipice, but he refused to tumble over the edge into ecstasy without her. "Buttercup, I'm too close. I need to slow down."

"I don't want this to be slow, Kier. Hard," Maude struggled to say each word as Kieran thrust into her, and her thoughts faded. Before he was able to stop himself, his release consumed him. He slammed into Maude over and over until she bit into his shoulder to keep from screaming her own climax. He marveled at how her inner muscles spasmed around him, clinging to him, while her hips still rocked. Despite knowing his body was spent, he continued to thrust. Maude's head thrashed from side to side as her body held her captive. Kieran pulled the sleeve of her kirtle down far enough to free her breast and began suckling her hard. The sounds of Maude's moans were a symphony to him as he suckled, alternating breasts.

"Turtledove, don't stop. So close again."

Kieran had no intention of quitting before he watched Maude come apart in his arms again. He shifted and circled his hips, making Maude bite down on his shoulder, his leine doing little to protect him. Her entire body went rigid before going lax. They lay together on the desk, panting. Maude mindlessly stroked his hair and back as he smattered kisses over her cheek, jaw, and neck. They lay there together until their breathing returned to normal, and Kieran withdrew. Maude's whimper of disappointment matched his own feelings. Their lovemaking abated the heat and need that sparked between them, and they floated back to reality. A sound outside the door drew Kieran's attention. He crossed the room but checked that Maude had covered herself before flinging the door open. Adeline and Abigail stood on the other side, unprepared for Kieran to catch them, so they failed to whisper.

"She sounds like a two-bit whore," Adeline sneered. "He does better between Maggie's thighs than the sausages hiding beneath her skirts."

"Mother!" Kieran roared. He prayed that, while his mother hadn't whispered, her low voice wouldn't carry to Maude, but Maude's sharp intake of breath echoed across the room. He looked back at his wife and saw the color leach from her face. "You go too far. I haven't touched Maggie or any other woman since before I met Maude. How dare you insinuate, nay state, otherwise? When will you accept that I love my wife?"

"Never. You're infatuated with the chit because she lets you rut on her like a bitch in heat."

"Leave!" Kieran's hand gripped the door while the other fisted to keep from throttling his mother. Abigail looked among the three faces with a mean-spirited smile that reveled in Maude's humiliation.

"Mother wouldn't have a point if the entire keep didn't have to listen to you two morning, noon, and night. At least with Maggie, you're discreet and don't do it where everyone can listen."

"Stop speaking as though there is aught still between me and Maggie. There isn't and never will be."

"If you say so, son. Eventually, you'll get your broodmare with child, and then what will you do with that insatiable appetite? You'll get your heir and your spare off her and then come to your senses. At least Maggie has the good graces not to beam and glow after a good tupping."

"It's against my better judgment that I've allowed you and Abigail to remain despite your abominable behavior toward Maude. I never knew you had such a crass tongue. You disgrace yourself and your position as a lady speaking in such a manner. Retire to your chamber and do not let me see your face until morn."

"You're sending me to my chamber like some errant wean? I think not. I'm still your mother."

"And I'm your laird. I warned you that you'd join Madeline at the priory if you tested me. I'll begin the arrangements in the morning."

"You wouldn't dare. The clan will despise her even more if you send me away. Do you think they'll accept you choosing a woman better suited to a tavern wench over both your sister *and* your mother? They'll lose all respect for you. They might even chase her away from Stornoway." Something malicious twinkled in Adeline's eyes that made Kieran pause. He feared she might harm Maude if he reacted out of anger.

"Retire to your chamber as I said. I will consider what I'll do with the both of you after I consult my wife."

Kieran didn't wait for a response before swinging the door closed. He was at Maude's side in a handful of paces. She stood shaken and pale, tremors vibrating against him as he held her. She sobbed as she had the night he met her, and just as he had been then, he was at a loss for what to say, so he cooed nonsensical words as he offered his presence as a balm to her injured spirit. She clung to him as she cried into his chest and remained inconsolable until there were no more tears left to stream from her eyes. She wiped them away but failed to wipe away the pounding headache.

"I think I shall lie down until the evening meal," she rasped.

"I'll join you," Kieran offered, but Maude shook her head. She'd never declined his comfort until that day, and he worried about the vacant look in her eyes.

"I need a little while by myself," she murmured as she pulled away. Kieran walked to the door with her, but she shook her head once more.

"At least let me see you to our chamber and tuck you in," he reasoned.

"No. I'd like to be alone now." Maude didn't look at him before opening the door and slipping into the passageway. Kieran stood watching her walk away and had a paralyzing fear that she might walk away for good one of these days.

CHAPTER TWENTY-FIVE

Maude slipped her gown off and climbed into bed after pulling together the window covers. She allowed the tears to begin once more as her hope for ever reaching a truce with Kieran's family gave way. She mourned the loss of companionship that never took root. She mourned her loneliness as she accepted she would live isolated from everyone but Kieran, Agatha, and Adam. The housekeeper and her son had become her only allies. She had impressed the steward with her head for numbers from the very first time they took inventory. Agatha praised her for her efforts, but despite offering an ear, Maude wasn't ready to trust anyone at Stornoway. She'd even kept her fears and hurt hidden from Kieran, too ashamed to admit to the things she heard or that she failed to overcome how much they hurt. She refused to admit weakness before him, but she feared she wouldn't be able to control her tears. She feared now that they started, they might never end. Temptation to write to her family and beg them to take her home carved a larger place in her mind each day, and as she laid in bed, she forced herself to refrain from pulling out a parchment and penning a missive asking them to rescue her. It was only the painful idea of being apart from Kieran that kept her from doing it. She allowed herself to drift off to sleep, the only escape from the onslaught of doubt, self-recrimination, and hurt.

Hours later, her eyes burned and itched as she pried them open. She reached around in the dark for the flint and candle on her bedside table. As her hand swept the surface, she didn't find the figurine that had taken pride of place on the nightstand. She scrambled off the bed and lit the candle before dropping to her knees to look beside the table and behind it before looking beneath the bed. She slid her hand as far as possible, even slipping partway under the bedframe. She placed the candle on the floor near her head to allow as much light as possible to shine, but the carving wasn't there. She rose and looked around the floor nearby before moving to the table that held her comb, perfume, and hair pins. She looked in her jewelry box and tore through her chests. She looked in Kieran's chest and along his side of the bed. She stirred up the rushes throughout the chamber, but to no avail. The carving her father made was gone.

Maude hurried to dress and rushed belowstairs as people gathered for the evening meal. She looked about, but Adeline was nowhere to be seen; however, Abigail glared at her. Maude searched for Kieran and breathed a sigh when he approached with Kyle. They were in the midst of a heated conversation, and Kieran barely spared her a glance until he stood before her, then his gaze softened before nodding to Kyle. His second-in-command continued on to the dais while Kieran laced his fingers with Maude's.

"How're you fairing, buttercup?" He kept his tone soothing while attempting not to sound patronizing. "Did you rest?" He didn't dare mention she looked as haggard as she had when she escaped his solar.

"I slept, but Kieran, when I woke, I noticed my carving is missing. I searched everywhere, but it's not in our chamber."

Kieran heard the concern in her voice, but Kyle's gestures for him to join his second at the table distracted him. A rider had arrived to inform him that the Morrisons had been riding their border, and rather than be on patrol, they looked to be scouting a few of the neighboring villages. It concerned Kieran that a raid was imminent, and he'd been making plans to ride out when the bell for the evening meal sounded. He needed to continue his conversation with Kyle, but he noted Maude was upset. His gaze shifted back to her as he kissed her forehead.

"I'm sure it'll turn up. I'll help you look when we retire."

"Nay, Kieran. I'm telling you, I looked. I looked beneath the bed, around the bedside table, in my chests, your chests, my jewelry box. I pushed the rushes around, but it wasn't there."

"Perhaps it fell from your pocket," Kieran led them toward the table as he nodded to Kyle. He seated Maude and turned to his chief warrior. Maude opened her mouth to argue that she never took it out of the chamber that day and had seen it when they woke that morning, but Kieran had dismissed her. She blinked several times as the servants moved about, bringing heaping dishes of food to the tables filled with clan members. A serving woman leaned between Kieran and Kyle, flashing Kieran a view of her cleavage, but he leaned away to continue speaking to Kyle. Despite Kieran's clear lack of attention, many of the serving women and maids persisted in flirting with him in Maude's presence. She gritted her teeth to keep from upbraiding the woman for flaunting herself. Kieran sensed Maude's restlessness and looked over at her before following her stare to the woman who continued to linger as she offered him anything he might want. He hadn't dallied with a servant since he was a young man discovering how women fawned over him. His father warned him of the dangers of playing favorites with servants, and it had convinced him to look elsewhere. The young woman annoyed him, so he waved her away in time to see another batting her eyelashes at him as she approached the dais with a platter of blood sausage just beneath her loosely tied blouse. A crack underfoot made the woman pause, and he saw Maude lean forward. Just as it had earlier that afternoon, the color leached from Maude's face as the serving woman put down the platter and reached for what she'd stepped upon. Maude's hands gripped the sides of the table as the woman lifted two small pieces of wood that had once been the family figurine Maude cherished. Kieran feared she might collapse as she swayed beside him. He reached to ease her into her chair, but she pushed his hands away. She reached across the table for the woman to put the remnants of her most prized possession into her hand. She turned the two pieces over; the wood splintered.

"Ma lady, I am vera sorry. I didna ken it was there," the young woman croaked.

"I'm certain you didn't, but someone did." Maude's eyes hardened as she looked at the others at the dais before casting her stare at the diners. She'd reached her limit for patience and forgiveness. If they cared so little for her that no one but the servant before her looked shocked or even dismayed, then she was finished trying to win them over. Her hand curled around the wood as she pushed back her chair and left the dais without a word. Kieran watched her in stunned silence. Her eyes were dry and her back ramrod straight as she walked with dignity to the stairs. He watched her climb them and then disappear on the landing. Once she was out of sight, rage consumed him to a degree that paralleled his emotions on the battlefield.

"Who?" he bellowed. "Who did this? Who stole from my wife and purposely hurt her?" No one moved. He didn't expect anyone to admit to their guilt, but he hoped someone had seen something. "I will punish the culprit. I dinna care if it be a mon or a woman. I will take the lash to them. My wife has done naught to any of you since she arrived but be kind and generous. She has worked as hard as any other member of this clan, hoping to earn your respect, but naught she does is good enough for you. You've judged her based on the opinions of a bitter and spoiled woman and a temperamental and equally spoiled chit."

Kieran suspected his mother or sister, perhaps both of them, were behind this, but he also was certain they found someone to do their dirty work. Someone they would lay the blame on when he confronted them. He turned toward Abigail and leaned over the table as far as his tall body could reach.

"You had something to do with this," he hissed. "You and mother are behind this. You have crossed a line from which there is no return. Leave this table before I beat you."

Kieran had never in his life threatened a woman and been so close to following through. Red dots danced before his eyes as he drew a deep breath through his nostrils. He was grateful for the several chairs and people between him and Abigail. She dashed from the dais, not needing a second warning. He once again looked out at the crowd who watched him with guarded expressions, but he saw the fear on more than one person's face. In the past, he would have regretted causing alarm among his people. He had never wanted them to cower before him, but the lack of healthy fear for his authority led to the conspiracy and actions that wounded Maude. His lip curled in disgust as he looked from person to person.

"I've never been ashamed to be laird of this clan. At least not until today. I've tried to convince myself over and over that you'd come around and see beyond Maude's appearance to the woman beneath. But you're shallow and spiteful to judge her because she's not frail and dainty like my mother and sisters. You'd rather admire their selfishness and laziness rather than appreciate a woman who has done naught but serve you since the morning after she arrived. Who bakes the bread you eat? Who ensures you have meat at each of your meals? Who hunts for that meat? Who brought medicinals, working alongside our healer and visiting our sick when the ague swept through a few sennights ago? Who has borne the embarrassment of hearing your snide comments with grace and an open heart? My wife, your lady. You are a disgrace. Those who have spoken ill toward my wife are without honor, but those who did naught to stop the others are just as bad, if not worse. You're the ones who turned a blind eye to a wrong. I do not jest when I say I will take the lash to whoever played a part in this. I will learn who it was."

Kieran spun on his heel and marched to the stairs, which he took three at a time, leaving a stunned crowd to their own devices. He turned toward his chamber but paused when Abigail called out to him.

"They'll hate you for that, just as Mother warned. She doesn't belong here, Kieran. She'll never be one of us."

"Why do you hate her so much? You don't even know her."

"She's the reason you locked Madeline away. She ruined our sister's life."

"She did no such thing. She argued against my decision and is the only voice that has kept you and Mother from joining Madeline. She's been protecting you since before she met you. Madeline sank her own ship with her words and actions. She disgraced herself and embarrassed our clan, threatened to weaken us before the court with her unguarded tongue. It was her comments and actions that kept her from remaining at court or even marrying. She could've just as easily spewed her bile at another lady-in-waiting and caused even more damage. We're all lucky that Maude and the Sutherlands forgave the slight. Other clans might not have. But you know Maude now. You've seen how hard she works and how hard she's trying. What do you still have against her?"

"You mean how she's trying to ingratiate herself? How she's trying to pretend she belongs when her clan killed our people only a few moons ago? What aboot how she spreads her legs for you like a whore? Everyone knows you can't keep your prick to yourself. She looks like a tavern slut and acts like one. She's not even pretty. She's fat and plain with tits that belong on a jersey cow."

Kieran's ears rang as he listened to the venom his little sister spewed. He wasn't sure if it was their mother's influence or if all the women in his family had a propensity to cruelty and jealousy. He shook his head as he looked at the young woman Abigail had grown into.

"What if you marry a mon whose sisters don't meet your standard of beauty? Would you disparage them? Shun them? Who are you to decide whether Maude is considered beautiful? I love my wife and believe she's the bonniest and most desirable woman I've ever met." Kieran realized he spoke the truth. He had been aware from the start that he desired Maude above all others, but he hadn't been struck dumb by her beauty. He'd even thought her face was pretty but unremarkable in the beginning. Now, as he pictured her, he couldn't think of anyone more lovely. Her rich chestnut hair as it curled over them as they made love. Her smoldering eyes that twinkled when she teased him. The long, thick lashes that hid her eyes when she was shy or guarded. Her crooked, gap-toothed smile that she rarely shared but warmed him to his toes when he was on the receiving end. Her curves that made him drool. Her button nose and soft chin that jutted forward at just the right angle when she was determined. Everything about her appearance appealed to him without considering who she was beneath the superficial. "Your vanity and haughtiness make you ugly, Abigail. You shall always come up lacking compared to other women. You may have an appealing face and frame, but your soul is ugly. I wish there was a way to change that, but I don't think there is."

Kieran walked away and didn't look back despite leaving his sister with her mouth agape. His heart hurt for his family, but it broke for Maude. She'd endured more than her share of pain in her short life. She'd proven stronger than the adversity she met, but it had taken its toll on her. He eased into their chamber before locking the door. He looked around and found her curled into a ball on the window embrasure. He approached with caution, not wanting to startle her or intrude if she wished that he not touch her. She turned haunted eyes toward him, and he noticed she clutched the broken wood in her hand. She looked back at the dark night sky without a word or sound. She was folded into such a small form that there was room for him to share the window seat. He was at a loss. He remained unsure how to comfort her when she was so closed off to him. Nothing about her body language said she wished for him to touch her, so he sat in silence across from her. He would wait until she was prepared to speak, but as time drew out, her silence became deafening. He feared she would tell him she would leave him, that she would ask her family to retrieve her. He would fight her until his last breath, plead with her to stay, but guilt gnawed at him for bringing her to a home he suspected all along would be unwelcoming, all because of his mother and sister. He fidgeted until Maude looked at him and sighed.

"I'm not leaving you, if that's what has you in a dither. You're my husband, and I'm the lady of this clan, for better or for worse."

"Buttercup, I am so sorry for all of it. I'm sorry I brought you here. I'm sorry I didn't protect you despite my promises. I'm sorry they've been cruel and unfair to you. I'm sorry they've hurt you. I'm just so very, very sorry. I was selfish and insisted upon getting what I wanted, and I should have thought of you instead. Really thought of you rather than assuming, in my own vanity, that I could control everything."

"Are you sorry you married me?" Maude whispered.

"No." Kieran's response was instantaneous and vehement. "I'll never regret marrying you, even if I regret how our marriage has affected you. I love you and would walk away from this all if I could."

"I would never let you do that."

"I know. You alone are why I couldn't."

"Kieran, I can't continue on as I have. I'm too tired to continue pretending that their words and actions don't hurt

266

me. I'm too worn to the bone to keep working harder than most just to please people who may never like me. I'm done guarding everything I say and do in case I give offense. And I'm bluidy well tired of being hungry all the time. I've felt ill for ages, and I'm certain it's because I'm too scared to eat too much in front of people."

"Maude, your lack of appetite has worried me, but I was nervous aboot mentioning it. I didn't want to upset you further by bringing attention to it, but I'm glad to hear you'll eat more. You've scared me more than once, looking like you might collapse."

"I'm aware. I've given myself a good scare more than once. I'm hungry so often that I'm nauseous much of the day now."

"Between working too long and eating too little, I feared you'd succumb to the ague just as so many others did. Promise me, buttercup, that you will take better care of yourself. Agatha will send a tray up any time you'd like if you're still not comfortable eating in front of others."

"So the women can gossip aboot how three meals aren't enough for me and that I need extra sent to me so I can eat in hiding? I think not."

"Fine, but will you continue to accept the food Agatha saves for you?"

"You found out aboot that?" Maude gasped.

"I've seen her a few times, but she's confessed to it. She worries aboot you and needles me to take better care of you every day." Kieran stood and stepped beside Maude. He pulled the pins from her hair, letting them drop by his feet until her hair unraveled and he could massage her scalp and neck. Maude purred with contentment as the tension fell away. When she untucked her legs and leaned against him, Kieran eased her into his arms before carrying her to their bed where he set her down and undressed her. When they were both bare, he pulled down the covers and slid into bed beside her. His palm cupped her scalp as she pressed their bodies together. "I'm going to show you how devoted I am to you, wife. I love you to distraction, and while I can't control what others think of you, I'll leave you without a doubt that I adore you and am hopelessly devoted to you."

Maude sat up, serious, as she looked at Kieran. "There were times when I first arrived that I worried you might tire of me, that you would find it easier to leave me alone than live with the snide comments, but you've proven time and again how you feel. You don't have to keep proving it. I didn't believe Adeline's comments aboot Maggie. I know you love me. I know your honor would never allow you to stray. And I know you haven't had the time to sneak away. If you're not in the lists, then you're with me. How could you be with anyone else?"

"You may know that, but it doesn't mean I'll ever stop showing you."

When Maude purred and grasped his rod, Kieran growled as he lowered to them to the bed. He pulled her leg over his hip and slipped into her before groaning and rolling them, so Maude's back pressed against the bed. He nipped at her ear before suckling her neck and shoulder. Maude clutched the sheets as he kneeled between her legs. He lifted her hips, his fingers biting into the skin hard enough to guarantee he would leave bruises. He surged into her over and over, rocking and circling his hips as the sounds of their bodies and their moans filled the chamber. When he arrived in their chamber, he'd intended to be gentle with her all night, but her need spurred him on. He'd be tender the next time, and every other time that night. Right now he would show her that no matter what anyone said, he desired her beyond reason.

"More," Maude panted.

"Might hurt," Kieran grunted.

"More," Maude demanded as she reached up to graze her teeth along his neck. Kieran leaned over her on his forearms. She raised her arms over her head to entwine her fingers with his. She met him thrust for thrust as she ground her mound against him. Their mouths found one another as their need coalesced into an inferno of desire as they both raced toward their climax. Maude ripped her mouth away.

"Kier!" She screamed. "Yes!"

"Fuck," Kieran gritted out before bellowing, "Maude!"

Maude was certain she could feel the jets of his seed, and he continued to rock against her as she shattered once more. She held Kieran as their chests heaved, and she couldn't imagine leaving the man she loved. While the physical pleasure he brought her was immeasurable, it was the moments after, the tenderness they shared, that made her realize he was as devoted to her as she was to him. She didn't believe he could fake the way his eyes lingered on hers, the soft kisses he pressed to her temples, his murmurs of love. She felt wholly accepted by Kieran, and she understood that even if she were to return to Sutherland, she would never find another person who made her feel complete.

CHAPTER TWENTY-SIX

M aude snuggled under the covers as Kieran slumbered
pressed against her back. She was warm and secure as
she floated into the land of the living, but all too suddenly the
memory of the night before came flooding back. She felt
anger and sadness warring within as she looked at the broken
figurine she'd left on the window embrasure. She gritted her
teeth as she felt her entire demeanor shift. It hardened into
determination and a disinterest in kowtowing any longer to
the MacLeod women. The men could think what they
wanted, since the only male opinion that mattered to her was
Kieran's. She feared her plan would lead to an argument, but
she didn't care. She would run the keep as she saw fit, with no
further delay. There were still several challenges to her authority, and the first would begin in the kitchen with Fiona.

Maude slipped from the bed but didn't step away before a
brawny arm pulled her back against a muscular chest.

"You weren't planning to run away, were you, buttercup?"
Kieran's groggy, deep voice rumbled through her back and
shot tingles into her core.

"I have a few tasks I would like to complete before the
women fill the kitchens."

"Oh?"

"Kieran, I'll forewarn you that I'll make several people angry today, but I don't care in the slightest. You can expect to hear complaints aboot me, but if this is truly my home and I'm truly the lady of the keep, there are several more things that need changing. The most pressing is Fiona's cooking. It's atrocious. I don't understand how she's lasted so long, but everyone deserves food with more flavor and variety. If I eat one more turnip, I will turn into one. There is meat that will soon putrefy if we don't cook it this sennight, but despite my suggestions, she refuses to heed me. It's as though she intends to defy me."

"It wouldn't surprise me. She's set in her ways. My mother hates spending time in the kitchens, so she allows Fiona to do as she pleases, which has caused several furors with Agatha. If you can improve the fare that comes from the kitchens, I'll sing your praises from the rooftops."

"I also intend to remove the beeswax candles from your mother's and sister's chambers and save them for Beltane. It approaches in a few weeks, and we don't have enough of the finer candles. I also want the entire Great Hall floor swept and scrubbed before the women lay fresh rushes. Had the floor been tidy, no one would have been able to hide my figurine, nor would anyone have missed it and stepped on it. Agatha is a fine housekeeper, but the maids can be as defiant to her as they are to me. I suspect that's also your mother's doing. I get the sense she and Agatha don't rub along well."

"You're right aboot that. Agatha has been the housekeeper since my father was a bairn. She raised him and me, so neither of us was ever willing to entertain replacing her, but my mother hasn't made Agatha's life easy ever since Agatha made the mistake of thinking my mother would run the keep as you do. Agatha welcomed Mother as a young bride and deferred to her in the beginning, but Mother turned her nose up at the work. My grandmother raised Mother to be a competent chatelaine, but my mother refused the responsibility. She's naught like my grandmother was, but my sisters follow in her footsteps."

"I'll be unpopular with your men, too, because I'm going to insist the women scour the kitchen fireplaces as well. That's half the problem with the food. But if the women dawdle or give me any argy-bargy, it'll be a cold supper for everyone."

"I'll give my men notice, and I'll suggest the married ones check with their wives during the nooning to ensure the women's cooperation, or it'll be their fault their husbands get bread and cheese."

"So, you'll support me in this? Even if it's a showdown?"

"Of course, I will. I trust you implicitly, and even if you haven't solved all the problems here, the keep runs better than it ever has in my memory."

"Even if I tell rather than ask?"

"Why should you continue to ask? You've tried to blend in and not upset the apple cart, but they've chosen to be difficult. Bring them to heel and to understand you won't be chased away."

Maude saw no patronizing look in Kieran's eyes, nor did she sense he was placating her. The opposite seemed true: he was cheering her on to take a stand. She gave him a loud, smacking kiss before he rolled them so she straddled his hips. The sun hadn't risen when they left their bed, but a few of the women were already in the kitchens when Maude arrived.

Maude took a deep breath and squared her shoulders before turning to face Fiona. Their battle was about to commence, and she had a room full of witnesses.

"The morning meal has ended, so I want at least ten buckets of water boiled before you douse the fires. You'll need to shovel the embers out before you scrub the grates and hearth along with the chimney." Maude announced as her gaze swept across the women gathered before her. She'd alerted Agatha to her plans, since some work she expected done would encroach upon the other woman's domain. The older woman had been all too happy to support Maude and thanked her for showing some gumption at last. She was also done with her prim court accent.

"Nay," Fiona refused. "There's nay time for that. I have a pottage to prepare."

"I dinna believe I asked a question, so 'nay' is nae an acceptable response. Ye will do as I say. I am fed up to my eyeteeth with the abysmal food ye serve. I've tasted better when eating two-day-old stew in a dirty tavern. I've ignored the issue for long enough. I've made diplomatic suggestions aboot seasoning and cooking that ye ignored, but I refuse to continue to ask for any of ye to do what I have always expected. If ye want a hot meal served tonight, ye'd do well to move sharpish. And if I taste pottage again this moon, I will replace ye, Fiona. If we relight the stoves in time, we will have the cured beef that's aboot to turn putrid if we dinna use it within the next few days. We'll add it to lamb and bone marrow with fresh vegetables from the garden that needs weeding. There's barley that needs using before we find weevils. It will be hotchpotch for the evening meal. I'll send some lads out to fish for haddock this morning, and we can smoke their catches all day. Even if hotchpotch isnae possible because the women dinna work fast enough, we can at least serve Arboath smokies as something hot."

"Nay," Fiona declared as she banged a wooden bowl onto the workstation where she was preparing to chop turnips. "Ye dinna run this kitchen. I do. I will take this up with the laird. He willna stand for this. Ye'll see."

"And this is where ye are wrong. Where ye are all wrong. I run this keep. I am chatelaine, and I make the decisions, including setting the menu. We've met every sennight, and yet ye insist upon preparing dishes that we didna agree upon. I warn ye now, Fiona. Challenge me again, and ye'll be out on yer arse. There isnae a servant in this keep who I canna replace. Ye'd all do well to remember that. I've tried to blend in, and ye've been a disrespectful and ungrateful lot. I dinna give a bluidy damn if ye like me. Nae anymore. Ye'll follow ma instructions without complaint or defiance. Ye've erred in assuming I'm a pushover. What ye see now is what ye've reaped from the rotten seeds ye sowed when I arrived." Maude looked around the kitchen at the varying looks of shock and anger. She crossed her arms and tapped her foot. "Get to work or leave. But if ye go, dinna come back. Dinna come back to work. Dinna come back to eat. Dinna come back to wag yer chins. And if ye wish to tittle-tattle to the laird, he's in the lists. But ye should be aware that I discussed this with him and have his full support. I believe he asked why I hadnae taken the lot of ye in hand sooner. Now work!"

Maude glided to the stack of buckets beside the door and began handing them out before leading the women to the well. She carried two buckets back and set them to boil. Once they bubbled with steam rising, she poured them onto one of the fires. When the fires were extinguished, she chose four women to sweep out the grates while she tied a cheesecloth over her hair.

"While we clean these fireplaces, some of you can heat more buckets of water in the Great Hall. I expect the older women to sweep away the rushes and the younger ones to scrub the floor. When that is complete, a team of you will go to the gardens and begin weeding. It's impossible to tell the weeds from the vegetables. I'll be along to pick herbs that we'll dry. There will be flavor to our food from now on. If you don't care for it, you can have bannocks for all three meals or cook in your own homes."

Maude turned back to the hearth she stood beside and sank to her knees. She dipped a scrub brush into the mixture of lye and water before proceeding to scrub the stones surrounding the fireplaces. It took a moment before the women organized themselves, and two slender women climbed into the chimneys and began knocking the soot loose with flue brushes. When they finished, Maude dismissed them to wash and change their clothing. She scooted over and began scrubbing the walls behind where the flames usually roared. She called over a woman who'd been willing to help her in the past and asked her to join her in scrubbing. Fiona stood, watching as Maude turned her kitchen upside-down as women scurried about to follow Maude's orders. The older woman seethed, but she realized there was little she could do. Even if Maude hadn't spoken to Kieran about her plans, Fiona understood he'd support Maude before taking anyone else's side.

The work went faster than Maude expected, and it pleased her that by the time they served the noon meal, the kitchen's fireplaces sparkled. She beamed at Kieran and nodded as he met her at the doors of the kitchen. He peeked inside and whistled as he saw that not only had they cleaned the fireplaces, but they'd cleaned every surface and door in the kitchens. He caught sight of Fiona scowling at Maude's back, and he feared what the woman might do to retaliate. He bid Maude wait for him before he stepped into the kitchen. Several of the women were still preparing platters when he entered. He stepped in front of Fiona and crossed his arms.

"I can imagine what's caused your snit, Fiona, but you can cease immediately. Lady MacLeod will run this keep as she sees fit, and I support her choices and edicts. I hadn't realized the state of disrepair this kitchen existed in until now, when I can see how it should be. I'm certain my wife has warned you that you're to fall in line, or she'll replace you. If she hasn't, then let me make that clear to you." He swept his gaze over the women. "To all of you. My feelings from last night haven't wavered. I'm ashamed of this clan, and I expect changes to be made immediately, and that includes obeying and fulfilling Lady MacLeod's instructions. My mother has spoiled not only my sisters, but those employed in this keep. Fiona, you've been given far too much freedom, and we have suffered for it. You'll cook as my wife wishes, or it'll be my wrath you face."

Kieran didn't wait for any responses before turning on his heel and pushing through the doorway. Maude remained where she'd been when he left her. She gave him a rueful smile and shook her head.

"Thank you for your support, but the women must recognize that it's my wrath they should worry aboot. I must be the final authority on what happens within these walls, or they'll also think they can run and complain to you."

"I didn't mean to undermine your authority."

"I know you didn't, and that's why I'm not upset. But I'd have it be clear between us."

"I defer to you, buttercup. This is your domain, and I won't intervene unless you ask." Kieran wrapped his arms around her and burrowed his nose into the lemon verbena scent of her hair after he pulled the cheesecloth from it. "I threatened to find you a kertch before we married. Do you find this to be an improvement?"

"No," Maude chuckled. "But it was what was available when I decided I must continue to lead by example. If I am going to make demands no one's prepared for, then I must share in the work. They're already going to call me a bitch for ordering them aboot. I don't need to add prim and lazy to the list of my faults."

"You are hardly any of those things, mo chridhe."

"You may believe that, but I doubt many others would agree."

They took their seats at the dais, and Kieran filled Maude in on his morning and the tasks he had to accomplish that afternoon. It disappointed him that she wouldn't be able to accompany him when he rode out to inspect the fields. Halfway through the meal, he changed his mind and decided the visit to the fields could wait until the next day. He finished the last bite of his meal when a loud slamming of a door abovestairs rang through the hall. Kieran stifled a groan as he waited to see if it was Adeline or Abigail coming to complain. After what Maude shared of her plans, he assumed whichever woman it was had discovered the change in candles. According to Agatha, his mother and sister hid in the ladies' solar all morning. Abigail stormed down the stairs and onto the dais, shaking tallow candles as she marched. She tossed them in front of Maude before putting her hands on her hips.

"What's the meaning of these foul things? Where are my candles?" she demanded. When Kieran made a move to admonish Abigail for her tone, Maude laid a hand on his arm.

"I had the finer candles removed and stored for Beltane. You'll make do with the same candles as everyone else, including your brother, *the laird*. If you don't care for the scent, I suggest you gather some flowers for your chamber." When Abigail's mouth pursed and a conniving glint entered her eyes, Maude laughed. "You won't be able to get to them. They're locked away, and only two people have the key. I won't give them to you, and neither will Agatha. By the by, I also collected the spare keys your mother had hidden. You will learn to live with this, or you may ask to live elsewhere. I'm certain you'll find Queen Elizabeth as accommodating as I am, or better yet, a withered and fat widower looking for sons might be tolerant of your tantrums. But I am not."

Abigail huffed before bursting into tears. "You're hideous. An ogre who's cruel to me and doesn't care aboot anyone but herself. You're selfish believing you know more aboot this clan than my mother, who's been a true lady since before you were hatched, you old crow."

Before Maude could respond, Kieran was out of his seat and storming around the table. He hoisted his sister over his shoulder and carried her abovestairs where he dumped her inside her chamber.

"Pack, Abigail. I heard from the priory this morning, and there is a cell next door to Madeline's that awaits your arrival. We depart in the morning."

"You can't be serious, Kier. No. I don't want to become a nun. I deserve a keep of my own and children with a husband who adores me."

"You deserve naught but a sound thrashing. I won't ruin an alliance before it begins by off-loading you onto another clan. And as for a keep of your own, you haven't a clue how to run one. If you did, Maude wouldn't have so much work to do. The only selfish one at that table was you. Have your tantrum here where I don't have to see you." Kieran slammed the door behind him, tempted to call Agatha to lock the door but refusing to hold his sister prisoner. He drew the line there despite the temptation. By the time he returned to the Great Hall, Maude was directing men to take down the tapestries and lower the massive candelabras on their metal link chains. He shook his head as she turned toward his approach, dropping a smacking kiss before playfully swatting her backside on his way to his solar.

The remainder of the day passed in a blur of activity for Maude. It came as a pleasant surprise to find how willing the women were to fall in line once she asserted herself. The respect she'd hoped for seemed to arrive in spades when she put her foot down. The evening meal went off without a hitch, despite another argument with Fiona about seasoning the food. Maude relieved the cook of her evening meal duties, allowing her only to oversee the morning and noon meals. The improved fare pleased Maude, and she saw the looks of appreciation as people savored the food. She fell into bed next to Kieran, exhausted but lighter. Kieran was relieved to see Maude's improved spirits and tended to her every wish that night.

Pounding on the door had Kieran bolting from their bed, grabbing his sword but not bothering about clothes. He yanked the door open, expecting to learn they were under attack. Kyle stood on the other side of the doorway, studiously avoiding looking at Maude as she pulled a robe on in the dark and joined Kieran at the door.

"There's been a raid on a village bordering the Morrisons. A lad arrived on a lathered horse saying it happened after sundown. His father sent him on horseback when the attack began, so he has no idea if anyone survived or the extent of the damage. Nearly broke his neck and the horse's galloping through the dark." Kyle rushed to explain.

"We leave at daybreak. Ready the men and meet me in the bailey. We'll gather supplies and ride out." Kieran barked as he ran a hand over the back of his neck. He had a sickening feeling that things would get far worse before they got better.

"I'll take care of the supplies," Maude said, wobbling on one foot and then the other as she shoved slippers onto her feet. She darted between the men and was already running toward the stairs before he could stop her. He made to follow her, fearful she would fall down the stairs in the dark, but Kyle pushed against his chest and pointed to his waist. Kieran realized he was naked. He hurried to dress and made his way belowstairs and into the bailey as Maude slipped out the side door, with several guardsmen following with satchels of food and blankets. She disappeared before he could say anything. He bellowed orders and checked Peat's saddle. He was about to dash back into the keep to find Maude when she bounded down the stairs. He couldn't believe his eyes. She was dressed in a tunic and leggings much like those he'd been forced to wear at court. Neither did much to hide her curves, and he growled as he heard several appreciative sounds from his men. She'd braided her thick hair with a leather thong wrapped around it. She had her bow and quiver strapped across her back. She signaled someone behind him, but he couldn't take his eyes off her to look. He was just as stunned at how quickly she'd changed as he was by what she wore.

"Where do you think you're going?" he snapped. Possessiveness and wariness warred within him as a sense of urgency pressed a suffocating weight upon his shoulders. He didn't intend to be short with her, but he wasn't about to take her with them. He was unsure what they faced, and he wouldn't put her life at risk.

"We can have this out now and be done with it. Does the village have a healer? Can you be sure he or she is alive? There may be people who survived and need care. Are you and your men skilled enough to do that? You can refuse to take me and discover I've followed you with or without a guard, or you can allow me to come and know I'm well protected by you and your men. Make your choice, Kieran, but one way or another, I'm going."

"No. I won't allow it. I'll have you locked in our chamber before I have you ride into a possible battle."

"Do you think I came dressed like this because I've never done this before? Look at me. This isn't the first time I've ridden out after a raid. My mother and father took me and Blair plenty of times. Your duty might be to fight and defend our clan, but my duty is to tend to any and every member in need. I do not jest, turtledove. I'll follow you if you leave me behind. You know you're taking your best horses now, and you know what Trioblaid can do. Once I set off, none of the horses you leave behind will overtake me."

Kieran wasn't certain that he liked this newly independent and fierce Maude when he was on the receiving end of her iron will, but he'd known it lurked beneath the surface since he met her. He looked over her garb once more before pulling a plaid from his saddle.

"You'll freeze," he barked, but Maude's grin told him she knew he wasn't worried about the temperature so much as he loathed the men looking at her. She snatched the plaid from him and strode over to Trioblaid, who had been brought out of the stables. Kieran realized she must have signaled to a stable boy. She vaulted into the saddle, once more surprising him. He knew she could mount on her own, but he hadn't been aware of her ability to leap and pull herself up without using a stirrup. He recalled what she'd told him of her childhood. She'd raced and played with the boys of her clan until they became adolescents. He had supposed her strength had faded, but she was wheeling Trioblaid around and staring at him as the horse pranced and whinnied. He pulled himself into his own saddle as she threw the plaid around her shoulders. It was one of his own plaids, and had several extra yards of wool to accommodate his height and muscular thighs. It drowned her, and he was relieved to see the only thing visible to his men was her head.

They galloped onto the road with Maude nestled into the center of the party. She leaned low over Trioblaid's withers and kept apace.

The men and Maude rode for an hour as the sun broke over the horizon, but the sky was still dark enough for them to spot the trails of smoke from several miles away. Kieran slowed them and sent scouts ahead to determine whether the enemy lurked nearby. Maude checked her satchel once more for the medicinals she packed, praying she had enough and that there would be people alive to need them.

"They razed the village. We didna enter, but we didna see anyone moving aboot either. Dyland and Peter rode the periphery and spotted no one," Kieran's scout reported. They nudged their horses forward until they rode into the smoldering village. Maude took in the devastation and swallowed against the acrid smell of smoke and burning flesh. They dismounted, but Kieran ordered her to hang back until he was certain no one would charge them. She swept her gaze across the charred remains of crofts, taking in the bodies that littered the ground. She would never understand why one clan raided another, intent upon murdering villagers. Maude wondered what the Morrisons, or whoever the guilty party was, hoped to gain. They could have stolen anything they wanted without the farmers being able to stop them. The deaths were needless.

Kieran and his men moved further from the horses and spread out. As their voices no longer monopolized her attention, she thought she heard someone calling out. She edged away from the horses and sneaked a look at Kieran, who had his back to her. She lifted her bow from her shoulder but didn't draw an arrow. She moved toward a ridge that she could tell dropped into a chasm. As she crept closer, the voice became clearer.

"Mama! Da! Help us!"

Maude's heart somersaulted as she realized there were children still alive but likely trapped on a ledge over the side of the drop off.

"*Kieran! Kieran!*" She called as she sprinted toward the gap. "*KIERAN!*"

Maude heard the unmistakable hiss and snarl of a Highland tiger or wildcat. They weren't large animals, but they were known to maul people when they felt threatened. She drew an arrow from her quiver as she looked over the edge, relieved to see the drop was insignificant. It wasn't a chasm so much as a deep trough.

"*KIERAN!*" She screamed once more as she spotted two young children, a little girl and a toddler boy, huddled together with a large wildcat prowling toward them. As the cat lunged toward the children, she leaped forward, putting herself between the animal and the children as she released her arrow. It embedded in the animal's chest, but its forward momentum carried the cat. It swiped its claw over her shoulder down her ribs and hip to her thigh. The wildcat landed dead at her feet, but she had little time to consider the pain that blazed through her side. Another wildcat lurked less than ten feet from where she landed. She fired off another arrow, this one landing in the animal's neck. Maude dropped her bow and turned to the children. Despite blood pouring from her wounds, Maude squatted on her haunches as she peered at the two terrified children.

"I'm Maude, and I've come with Laird MacLeod to help ye. Will ye let me lift ye up?" The little girl, who couldn't have been more than five or six, nodded while her tiny brother cowered. Maude kept her voice smooth and soft as she slowly reached for them. "I ken it looks bad and mayhap I looked fierce, but I wouldnae hurt ye. Only something that might want to harm ye."

When neither child screamed nor shied away, she lifted the pair and bit her tongue to keep from yelping. She spotted Kieran and his men running toward them. She wondered what took him so long, but she suspected only a few moments had passed since she took off at a run to discover who called out.

CHAPTER TWENTY-SEVEN

Kieran was certain his heart would beat out of his chest. Maude's scream had turned the blood in his veins to ice until he saw her running toward the ridge. He knew the drop wasn't significant, but he feared she would hurt herself. When she pulled an arrow from her quiver as she jumped forward, his stomach lurched, and he broke into a sprint. He was sure he'd never run so fast in his life as he did to reach his wife, who had time to release another arrow before her head disappeared for an instant. When she stood, she had two children in her arms. He skidded to a halt when he reached them. Maude had already placed the children on the ground above her and prepared to climb, but her arm gave way, and she pitched forward. Kieran fell to his knees and scooped Maude under her arms. He touched the blood before he saw it. As he cradled her against his chest, his hands skimmed over her, searching for the wound. She cried out, then whimpered as his hand touched her side and the sticky liquid coated his hand. Kieran twisted to look at Maude's left side and saw something had shredded the material of her tunic and leggings. He looked past her shoulder, spying the two dead wildcats, and wanted to be ill. The animals could have killed her with a bite to her neck; they killed larger prey by crushing their windpipes. He'd seen the aftermath of more than one fawn taken down by a Highland tiger. Maude was saying something as his attention shifted back to her, but he failed to make out her words over the pounding of his heart.

"The weans, Kieran. They need tending. They must have been down there all night. Let go." Maude struggled to stand, but Kieran shook his head and refused to release her. He didn't trust his voice as he cast a long look at her before peering at the children. They watched him and Maude with eyes as wide as saucers; the little boy sucked his thumb. Maude pushed against his chest until he loosened his grip enough for them to stand.

"Are ye hungry, little ones?" Maude once more squatted in front of them. They nodded but said nothing. She took each of their hands, careful not to rub blood on the little girl who walked on her wounded side. When they reached the horses, Maude pulled out blankets for the children and wrapped one around each before spreading one on the ground. She pointed for them to sit and moved to another satchel that contained food. Kieran intercepted her and guided her toward the blanket and eased her onto it. He fetched the satchel and pulled cheese, bannocks, apples, and a jug of ale from it. He whispered to the children as he handed them the food, but he never took his eyes off Maude, who rested with her own eyes closed. She yelped with surprise when he lifted her and carried her behind a wall that still stood. The sun was higher in the sky, and he was able to see saw her injuries. He lowered her to her feet and removed the stopper from a jug of whisky. Maude took it from him without a word and placed the opening to her lips, taking a long draw before sucking in a deep breath. The alcohol burned, but she'd had it often enough that she did not splutter. She handed the jug back to Kieran and looked at her arm.

"Don't take that far away," she muttered.

"I'm not leaving your side. What happened? One moment

you were by the horses and the next I see you running toward the unknown."

"I heard them crying out for help. I spotted them at the same time I saw the first wildcat. It attacked just as I reached them. I jumped in front of it and shot it, but before it dropped to the ground, it sank its claws into me." Maude grabbed the rent sleeve and ripped it from the shoulder seam. She dropped the dirty fabric to the ground and twisted to see her ribs. The animal had shredded the tunic there too, so she tore along the side seam to open it. Maude looked in every direction before unlacing the leggings and dropping them to her ankles. Kieran sucked in a breath and uttered several oaths as he turned her toward the sun and examined the damage. She took the jug back and consumed several more gulps before taking a fortifying breath and pouring a steady stream of whisky over her wounds. She grunted from the pain but refused to cry out. She flushed the wounds as best she could until she emptied the jug.

"Waste of bluidy fine whisky," she grumbled. "Can you fetch some bandages? And there's a fresh tunic in my bag. Oh, and the plaid. Please."

She was panting by the time she finished speaking. Despite his hesitation about leaving her, Kieran jogged over to the horses. Maude leaned heavily against the wall and prayed it didn't collapse beneath her. She gritted her teeth and pulled her tunic over her head before bending to unlace her boots. When the pain had her seeing stars, she decided she would wait for Kieran to assist her. He returned and began unpacking the satchels he brought with him. Maude began winding the bandages he handed her around her thigh and hips. She took another roll and bound her ribs before moving on to her arm and shoulder. She recalled the Egyptian mummies she'd read about when her tutor taught her geography. She swayed on her feet, and Kieran shot up to steady her.

"Can you loosen my boots? I can't reach them." Kieran nodded and untied them as she braced her hands on his shoulders. Once they were off, she kicked the leggings loose. "Is there any rope? I didn't think to ask before you walked away."

"Aye. We brought plenty. What do you need it for?"

"A belt. I have to wrap the plaid around me, and need to tie something around my middle."

While Kieran went to retrieve the rope, Maude struggled into the spare tunic and groaned as she kneeled on the ground. She laid out the plaid and pleated it. When Kieran returned, he had the lack of grace to laugh as he realized she intended to wear the breacan feile like he did rather than as an arisaid.

"I suppose it won't cover your legs otherwise." He kneeled beside her and slid the rope beneath the material. He helped her to lie down before wrapping one side over the next. The plaid was far too long; rather than end at her knees, it finished at the sole of her feet. He was careful not to rub the material over her hip or thigh. He knew that, despite the bandages, the wool would irritate her skin. He tied a loose knot around her waist before cutting the extra length of rope with his dirk. He moved with slow purpose as Maude took his hand and stood. He draped the extra fabric over her good shoulder and wrapped his arm across her upper back before leading her back to the others. She leaned most of her weight against him, but he noticed she fought not to limp. He guessed Maude worried he would chastise her if she showed weakness. Recrimination was the last thing on his mind; he was too filled with pride and fear.

"You're the bravest lass I ken. I can't think of too many men who would've done what you did. I'm so very proud of you, buttercup. You saved those weans' lives."

Maude rested her head on Kieran's shoulder as she let him guide her back to the horses. "You're not angry with me? You don't regret bringing me?"

"Am I pleased you've been injured? Nay. Was I scared witless? Am I still scared? Aye. But I told you, I'm proud of you, Maude. You risked your life for those weans without a moment's hesitation. I'm not angry. I just thank God you're alive. I'd ask you not to terrify me like that again, but I know it's not in your nature to put yourself first. You'll race into danger if you believe it'll save someone."

"You'd do the same. And don't tell it's not the same thing because you're a warrior. I heard those voices and knew they were defenseless. I couldn't ignore children who needed protecting."

The men surrounded them and applauded, cutting their conversation short. Maude wanted them to cease since her head ached, but she smiled and offered her thanks. She felt accepted by Kieran's guards; she just wished the women of their clan would see her worth as easily as the men had.

"Ma lady, is there aught we can do?" A young guard stepped forward.

"Aye. Two things. Carry the weans back with us. And someone give me more whisky. This burns like the bluidy devil."

Several men turned toward the horses, and moments later jugs and flasks appeared from all sides. Maude reached for a smaller flask and unstopped it. She down the contents of the full container in a few gulps. She wiped the back of her hand across her lips before nodding her head.

"The laird will give ye more," she rasped. She'd allowed her burr to slip into her voice on purpose when she spoke to the children. She wanted to put them at ease and not sound too posh, but now it remained because she hadn't the strength to regulate it. She didn't move from her spot as Kieran and his men continued investigating the remnants of the village. The children she'd rescued had fallen asleep once they'd eaten. Maude watched them and longing crept over her. She wondered if she and Kieran would have children. She prayed it would be soon even though she enjoyed the time alone with him each day, and she knew she had more than enough challenges awaiting her upon her return to the keep. But the notion of creating a new life with Kieran made her ache to carry and bear a child. She chalked her sentimental longing up to an excess of alcohol. She rested for another hour before Kieran called an end to the search for any survivors or evidence to why the attack occurred. He helped her onto Trioblaid despite his protestations, but Maude feared having her side jostled against Kieran even if he tried to be careful.

As the horses galloped back toward Stornoway, Maude swallowed the bile that rose in her throat. The two bannocks she'd eaten on the ride to the village threatened to revisit her, and the whisky sloshed about her stomach. She refused to be ill while she rode, and she would not ask Kieran to stop. She wondered if she would have been better riding in Kieran's arms after all; he could have held her in place instead of every jarring hoofbeat sending excruciating pain through her side as she rode. It wasn't long before she broke into a sweat as she tried to control her body. She pushed the extra plaid from her head and shoulder, grasping it and wrapping it loosely around her waist. The crisp morning air helped at first, but it wasn't long before perspiration was dripping between her breasts and trickling down her spine. She attempted a surreptitious wipe of her brow, but Kieran's head whipped toward her as soon as she shifted again. He'd observed her rearrange the plaid and now cocked an eyebrow at her, but she forced a smile. When she recognized her surroundings, Maude drew a relieved breath. Her sight had tunneled, and she gripped the reins to keep from tumbling from the saddle. She blinked several times to clear her vision as they barreled down the final hill, but despite her best efforts, everything turned black.

Kieran swerved to catch Maude as she lurched to her far side. He squeezed Peat with his thighs and caught Maude as she fell away from him. His hands cinched around her sides as he plucked her from Trioblaid's back. When she didn't make a sound of pain or protest, his pounding heart surely stopped.

She was burning with fever as he cradled her and called the riders to a halt. What he assumed were cheeks pinkened by the wind was actually a flush caused by fever. He absorbed the heat radiating from her and forced himself not to panic. She was a veritable inferno. He'd never touched someone so hot, and while her cheeks were darker, the color had leached from her chapped lips.

"Buttercup," he whispered as fear choked him, but he glanced about for his best rider and called out, "Fetch Eara and bring her to the keep. Tell her Lady MacLeod is ill, and she should bring everything she has that can bring a fever down and fight an infected wound." The clan's healer was the oldest person in the village, and Kieran had often wondered as a child if she'd walked with Jesus, she'd seemed so old even then. But so many years as a healer lent her a talent and skill that kept most clan members alive when something ailed them. He prayed the same would be true for Maude.

Kieran pushed Peat to take the last few furlongs until they entered the bailey. He called for Kyle as they passed under the portcullis and handed Maude to him as he dismounted Peat, then scooped her back into his arms and ran toward the keep. Two guards barely managed to open the doors before Kieran hurtled through, yelling for Agatha to get a cool bath to his chambers. He took the stairs two and three at a time until he reached the landing. He spied his mother and sister peeking out from the ladies' solar, but he had no interest in acknowledging them. He slammed open the door to his chamber and took Maude to the bed, where he began stripping her. He only paused long enough to draw the bed-curtains closed as servants filed in. He saw the blood that seeped through the bandages and watched Maude's chest rise and fall with ragged, shallow breaths. When the servants left, he unraveled the bandages and had to turn away lest he retch. Maude's injuries were far worse than he'd believed. The whisky had flushed them of the embedded fabric from when the claws shredded her clothes, and it washed away dust, but it hadn't done enough. The cuts were deep, and angry, red lines already flaring out from their edges. Infection had taken hold within two hours.

"What happened to the lass?" Agatha asked as she approached the bed.

"She saved those two weans we brought with us when two wildcats attacked. She killed them and protected the weans, but one of them sank its claws into her first. Agatha, she said she was fine. God, what if she isn't? What if I lose her?" Kieran choked out the last words as tears threatened. Agatha laid her hand on his back and patted him as she had done so many times when he'd been an upset child.

"Get her into the tub, and I'll clean her wounds, lad."

Kieran lifted Maude and carried her to the tub, but he insisted that he bathe his wife. He refused the linen square, afraid it would be too abrasive, but Agatha asserted that while Maude was unconscious, the wounds needed a good scrubbing to remove whatever lingered and caused the infection. They worked together and were efficient, so Kieran was holding Maude in his lap before the fire as Agatha combed her hair when Eara, the healer, arrived. Her walking stick clacked on the floor as she moved to the bed and began laying out her tools and remedies. Kieran returned Maude to the bed but lingered beside her.

"Lad, I canna reach her if ye dinna move." Eara was the second person to call him a lad in the space of one half hour. She and Agatha were the only two who would dare, but it was calming and soothing. He abandoned his efforts to hide his burr when he was with these two women, who had known him as long as his parents had. Both had attended his birth. He trusted these two women above all others to tend to his wife. "Wildcat maul her?"

"Aye. She was protecting two weans from the village that was attacked. She jumped between them and the wildcat. It clawed her as it lunged. She killed it, but nae before it landed on her."

"They carry something in their claws that causes a fever to people they scratch. Ye did well to get her in a cool bath. The wounds look clean. Does she feel cooler?"

Kieran stepped forward and ran the back of his hand over her forehead and cheeks before nodding and giving Eara his spot beside Maude.

"There isnae much I can do besides pack the wounds and give her willow bark tea to bring down the fever. If the infection worsens, then I must cut away the putrid flesh, but I dinna fear it'll come to that. Did the lass flush them with whisky before bandaging them?"

"Aye, doused them. Used an entire jug. I dinna ken how she didna faint. It must have burned like the flames of hell, but she barely made a sound." Kieran couldn't tear his eyes from how small and helpless Maude looked lying alone in their enormous bed. He'd been so proud of her bravery and stoicism earlier, but now fear threatened to consume him as he blamed himself for her condition.

"Kieran," Agatha's hushed tones broke through his haze of guilt. "Ye ken she spoke true. Even if ye hadnae let her ride out with ye, she would have followed. Eara couldnae have made the ride with ye, and it was the right thing to do to take a healer." The healer grunted her agreement as she crushed yarrow leaves with a pestle and mortar. She added wormwood and chamomile, but paused when she reached for the angelica.

Eara returned to Maude's side and ran her hands over her belly, poking and pressing as she moved. She shook her head and looked back at Kieran. "I canna use the angelica to help with the fever. It'll get into her womb, and she might lose the bairn."

"Bairn?" Kieran gasped. Tremors coursed through him as he stared at Maude.

"Didna ye ken? She's nearing three moons, I'd say." Eara gave him a reproachful glare. "A lad yer age and with yer experience didna question why his wife hasnae bled?"

Kieran shook his head. He hadn't given it much consideration since he'd ridden out for weeklong patrols at least once a moon since they returned to Stornoway. He'd dreaded leaving Maude behind knowing things were a struggle, but as laird, he'd had little choice but to take his turn. She'd never discussed her cycle with him, but he supposed he assumed it had come during one of those sennights.

"I didna think aboot it. I was away for a sennight at a time more than once. I suppose her courses might have come and gone while I was away, but she was never indisposed while I was home." He chided himself for being so unobservant, but a realization flashed through his mind. "That's why she's been nauseous so often. She believed it was from being anxious, but now I dinna think that's the case. She's had nay appetite, but she's struggled for years with what she eats. The vicious things ma mother and sister said to her aboot what she eats reminded her of cruel things she heard when she was growing up and from other ladies-in-waiting. It might have been from the strain she's been under, but it could also be symptoms of carrying a bairn. But I dinna believe she kens. She wouldnae have kept that from me, and I saw how she looked at the lad and lass this morning. She wants bairns of her own. It was longing, not anticipation. I'd even thought to speak to her, reassure her that they would come when the Lord is ready and that I'd love her even if we never had any. I ken she'd fear I would set her aside for a woman who could give me an heir."

Kieran knew he was rambling, but he found speaking kept his mind from dwelling on the image of the wildcat attacking her. He climbed onto his side of the bed before sliding across to lay beside her. He lifted the hand on her uninjured side and cradled it between his much larger ones. Everything about her seemed frail as he brushed the hair from her forehead. He was aware that Agatha and Eara spoke to one another, and he even noticed a servant who brought in boiling water and hooked the pot into the fireplace, but he wasn't interested in anything but Maude.

"Prop her up so I can spoon the willow bark into her. I dinna want her choking." Eara ordered, and Kieran was quick to obey. The old woman followed the tea with spoonfuls of plain water before ordering Kieran to let Maude rest. Kieran noticed that Eara had packed and dressed the wounds at some point, but the sight of Maude's sunken, flushed cheeks and the sweat that continued to roll along her temples monopolized his attention. He pressed the cool compress that Agatha handed him against her brow and wiped it along her temples. And so began the routine that carried them through the rest of the day and into the night. Eara offered Maude medicinals every few hours and sat by the fire sewing and humming while Kieran lay on his side observing Maude for any slight change or movement.

As the night grew late, Maude's fever spiked, and she moaned until Kieran spoke to her. He murmured reassurances of how much he loved her and that she would be well. He promised they would go for long rides alone once she was well. He promised to take her to the loch when the weather warmed and teased her about making love in the water, since she loved coupling in the bath. He teased that they would have an enormous tub all to themselves. He offered to take her back to Sutherland to visit her family as soon as she was well enough to travel. He swore to do a better job protecting her and their bairn. He asked whether she had any hint if the bairn was a lad or lass and whether she'd ever considered names. He shared ones he wondered if she might like. He whispered to her until his voice grew hoarse, but he was convinced she heard him even if she didn't respond. He remembered being ill from more than one injury, and he'd heard voices through the fog of fever.

CHAPTER TWENTY-EIGHT

By the third day of Maude's fever, Kieran was beside himself with fear that she wouldn't recover. He'd sent off a missive to Hamish and Amelia, asking that they come as soon as possible. He wasn't sure if he believed their presence would improve Maude's condition or if he wanted to offer them the chance to say their goodbyes. Eara warned him that if the fever continued much longer, even as the wounds healed, Maude might lose the bairn or it might be born with ailments that would never be set right. Kieran sobbed as he listened to Eara's warning. Unabashed tears poured down his cheeks as he clung to Maude's hand. His sobs became so wrenching that Agatha insisted he get off the bed because they were shaking Maude too much. Agatha barely came to his chest, but she held him as he wept. He hadn't cried so hard and for so long since his father passed away. Dread and doubt niggled at him day and night, denying him sleep and an appetite.

Kieran turned away food and refused to close his eyes except for when his body overcame his will. He bathed and changed his clothes, but didn't bother shaving. His beard grew in, and he wondered if Maude would recognize him if she awoke. He thought in "ifs" rather than "whens" as the hours turned into days. He slept alongside her, but he spent his days in a chair beside the bed. He turned away everyone but Agatha and Eara, allowing Kyle to visit once a day to report on the clan and their land. The Morrisons had taken responsibility for the raid, but it was a similar situation to what happened in Assynt. The laird hadn't sanctioned the attack, and sent two calves and five lambs along with a purse of coins as restitution. It did little to ease the grief of losing an entire village, but it was a peace offering. The Morrisons were a strong clan but not as prosperous and powerful as the MacLeods. They offered what they had to spare, but Kieran recognized they hadn't resolved the matter; however, it would wait until Maude recovered.

Kieran sat in the chair with his head bowed in prayer for the umpteenth time since he laid Maude on their bed. He clung to her hand and brushed his thumb over the back of hers and around to the underside of her wrist, calmed by the beat of her steady pulse. He heard the door creak open, but assumed it was Eara or Agatha who entered. As the vigil stretched out, the two women left Kieran in peace for hours, only returning when Maude needed medicinals, the sweat-drenched sheets needed changing, or the servants brought in a bath. He didn't glance up until a hand squeezed his shoulder. He started when he saw his mother and sister standing beside him. He glared at them and curled his lip in disgust. He didn't want either of them anywhere near his wife.

"Get out," he growled.

"Kieran, you need to rest," Concern filled Adeline's voice as she gazed at her haggard son. She'd never seen him in such a state, and she feared he would fall ill. "You won't be able to care for her if you succumb to exhaustion and hunger."

"Get out," he repeated.

"Kier, we may not have liked her," Abigail interceded. "But we never wished her dead. We heard what she did. We heard how she argued with you to allow her to go. She did it to serve people she'd never met before because they're part of our—her—clan. She risked her life for someone else's children, and from what the men shared, she did it without hesitation. Kieran, Mother and I have been so incredibly wrong aboot Maude."

"Now you see it? When she might die? How convenient. Get out before I have you thrown out. I don't want you anywhere near my wife. You've both done more than enough." Kieran's temper rose, and he released Maude's hand in favor of gripping the arms of the chair to keep from lashing out.

"You're right," Adeline agreed. "We've been horrid to her because I didn't get what I wanted, which was to choose your bride. I wanted a woman like me, someone I'd have as company once Abigail left to marry. I wanted someone to be a companion to Abigail while she was still here. I refused to accept that Madeline brought aboot her own fate, and it was easier to blame Maude than Madeline, or you. She wasn't the beauty I believed you deserved, and I detested her on sight. She never stood a chance of me liking her, through no fault of her own. Your sister and I have made her miserable and been happy for it, but Abigail speaks the truth. Neither of us want her to die. Whether we want to admit it or not, she makes you happy. She's done wonders for the keep, and our clan is better for it. It's been painful to accept, but her selflessness has forced your sister and me to examine our vanity and greed."

"Mother is right that you need rest, Kieran," Abigail added. "You don't appear well. Let us help. We'll keep watch while you sleep."

Kieran stared at his mother and sister. He knew they were right about how he looked and how he felt, but he didn't trust them. He shook his head and looked back at Maude, dismissing the women.

"Kieran," Adeline adopted a tone he hadn't heard since

he was a child. "*You* may be laird, but *I'm* still your mother." She turned around his words from months ago and used them against him. "I tended you, your sisters, and your father when you ailed. It wasn't just Agatha and Eara. I may have failed in many ways as the lady of the keep, and I may not have seemed a loving mother, but I care aboot you. It's obvious to anyone to see how you're suffering. I won't pretend that I cared aboot Maude before now, but I've always cared aboot you. You need to eat, and you need to sleep. You will do as I say, Kieran. Not because I demand it, but because you won't last much longer if you don't. What will Maude do if she awakes to you ill? You and I both know she'll try to get out of bed and tend to you well before she should dream of moving. Is that what you want? You poorly wife to have to take care of you?"

Kieran shook his head as a new wave of guilt assailed him. He knew his mother had guessed correctly. She'd described what Maude would do if she was worried about his health. He looked back at his mother with bleary eyes and nodded. Eara and Agatha had other duties beyond just Maude; that was why he'd sent them away and insisted he would summon them if needed. But he'd feared shutting his eyes for too long in case Maude needed something and he missed it. His mother went to the door and spoke to someone in the passageway; shortly after, a knock came. Kieran grumbled, but his mother met the person at the door. She and Abigail each carried in a chair, and Kieran understood his mother knew he wouldn't allow anyone else in the chamber. She was being mindful and considerate. Abigail left but returned with a sewing basket over each arm and a large tray of food. Adeline pulled the table beside him, and Abigail placed the tray upon it. Fiona had fixed his favorite foods and a large bowl of steaming bone broth was there for Maude. The cook had been on her best behavior since learning of Maude's injuries. She'd sent food up for Maude without being asked, and when Kieran tasted the bone broth the first day, it had surprised him that the normally bland food actually tasted good. He picked at what Fiona sent to him, but the need for sleep nipped at his heels. He watched his mother and sister sit in silence by the fire as they sewed. He discovered he appreciated the companionable silence. Eara and Agatha had kept up steady but quiet conversations when all Kieran wanted was peace. He rubbed his eyes and tried to stifle a yawn. He had to trust his mother and sister enough to lie down next to Maude and close his eyes. Sleep claimed him within moments of his head hitting the pillow.

The next two days came with their own routine. Adeline and Abigail helped Kieran bathe Maude twice a day. They took turns reading to her in hushed tones when Kieran slept. They stepped out when he bathed but returned to help change the bedding and her bandages. Kieran spooned broth and tea into her throughout the day, and he even began eating proper meals. His mother was wiping a cool compress over Maude's face and neck while Abigail was reading when Maude's voice drifted to him for the first time in a sennight.

"Hungry," she croaked. Kieran's eyes flew open to find pools of whisky brown staring at him. She offered him a half-smile while her fingers twitched more than squeezed within his hand. She turned to peer at who ministered to her and the expression of shock when she recognized Adeline had Kieran cooing soothing words.

"They've been helping for the past two days, while insisting I sleep. Mother has been gentle and a great help."

"Nae throttled me?" Maude rasped.

"Nay, buttercup."

"Nay poison," she grinned but her chapped lips made her wince.

"Nay." Kieran's gaze jumped to his mother, fearing she would take offense, but the relief in her smile made him relax.

"Nay, lass. We didn't try to kill you. You gave us all a good scare, and it seems just what Abigail and I needed to get our heads out of our arses." Adeline smiled, but grew somber moments later. "My son loves you more than I've ever seen a mon love any woman. I don't think he'd be long for this world if aught happened to you. I love my son, and I will do any and everything to keep him hale. It was no great struggle to realize aiding in your recovery would keep Kieran well. Your illness gave me pause to acknowledge how selfish I've been and what spoiled daughters I've raised. It's also made everyone in the keep recognize how much responsibility and work you've shouldered in the short time you've been here. To maintain the keep as you've made it, the servants had to admit how much work you do once they divided those duties among themselves. I realize these are but words, Lady MacLeod, but I am deeply sorry for how I have wronged you."

Maude shifted her gaze between Adeline and Kieran, who looked as shocked as she felt. She hurt all over and was nauseous, so she didn't feel gracious about receiving the apology. She nodded her head and offered a tight smile as Abigail stepped closer. She held something in her closed hand, and Maude's eyes watered when her sister-by-marriage opened it.

"I don't know who did this. Honestly, I don't. It wasn't me or Mother, but that doesn't matter. Whoever wanted to hurt you believed they could because of the example Mother and I set. I'm sorry for what I did, and I'm sorry for being responsible for you being so badly hurt by this being broken."

Abigail handed the carved figurine to Maude. What had been fractured into two pieces was now one. She turned it over in her hand and discovered a thin piece of metal connected the broken parts on the back and the bottom.

"Who mended this?" Maude whispered.

"I spotted it on your table by your comb. I took it to the blacksmith and asked him to show me how to fix it."

"Show you? You did this?"

Abigail shrugged, but nodded. "It was the least I could do. Mother has been taking care of you while Kieran rested, Agatha has been running the household for you, Eara has been bringing you healing tinctures, and Kieran hasn't left this chamber since he returned home with you. I wanted to do something for you too."

Maude's eyes leaked tears from the corners as she ran her thumb over the smooth patch where her parents were carved side-by-side.

"Thank you." Maude struggled to sit up, and Kieran assisted her, tucking pillows behind her back and head. "This means more to me than you'll ever know. This is, besides my wedding ring, my greatest worldly treasure."

"I know. I didn't want to admit my regret or guilt at the time because I was too mired in my dislike to show you any kindness. Seeing you like this, how wrong it felt to watch you not be able to shrug this off as you seem to do with aught that challenges you. It scared me."

Maude tried to absorb what Adeline and Abigail told her. It was the antithesis of everything that had passed between them thus far, but the women's expressions were contrite and worried. The best she could offer Abigail was the same nod and half-smile she gave Adeline. She turned to gaze at Kieran, who'd been watching her. It shocked her to see how disheveled and browbeaten he looked. She reached out a hand to touch his beard, but she found she was too weak to raise her arm that high. As it dropped, Kieran grasped it and brought it to his face. His eyes closed as her fingers stroked the hair that grew along his jaw.

"Kiss," she murmured, and Kieran was only too happy to oblige. The kiss was soft and tender, Kieran fearful of over-doing it while Maude was still so weak. When they pulled away, Maude scrunched up her nose. "You're just as hand-some with it, but it's scratchy and tickles my nose. I don't think I like it."

Kieran grinned as he kissed her again, this time with a little more pressure. She opened to him but shrank back a moment later, covering her mouth with her hand.

"I don't care," Kieran growled before licking the seam of her lips until she parted them. He swept a languid tongue against hers and did nothing to stifle the groan that escaped as Maude kissed him back. Adeline and Abigail slipped from the chamber as Maude rolled toward Kieran, and he held her in his embrace. When the kiss ended, he tucked her head against his chest as she fell back to sleep. They remained that way through the night and into the next morning when the door burst open.

CHAPTER TWENTY-NINE

K ieran jerked awake to the sound of someone storming into his chamber. He grabbed his sword, ready to spring from the bed, but Maude's words made him focus on who entered unannounced.

"Mama! Da!"

Kieran recognized his parents-by-marriage as Amelia entered first, followed by Hamish close on her heels. Amelia stumbled as Hamish pushed past her and cupped Maude's face before pressing a kiss to her forehead. Amelia ducked under Hamish's arms to embrace Maude with great care. Kieran watched tears slip down both parents' cheeks. He felt like an intruder in his own chamber and moved to leave, but Maude's hand grasped his forearm, her fingers biting into his skin. She shot him a look that warned him not to consider leaving. She turned back to her parents and greeted them with one of her wide, toothy grins. Kieran hadn't seen one since she awoke, and his heart calmed. While a selfish part of him wished he'd been the first recipient of such a warm greeting, he recalled the kisses they'd shared since she roused from unconsciousness. While they hadn't shifted their position through the night, they'd woken more than once, both needing the assurance the other was still there. They'd kissed and held hands before drifting back to sleep.

"Ah, ma wee one," Hamish choked. "We didna ken how we might find ye. It does ma soul good to see ye awake. I feared the worst when we received Kieran's missive."

"Kieran wrote to you? How's it possible that you got here so fast?"

"We left as soon as we read it, and we rode through most of the nights," Amelia explained. They all turned when the door eased open and Blair and Lachlan peered in. The siblings ran to Maude's side when they realized she was alive and looking far better than they expected.

"You all came?" Maude wondered aloud.

"Of course," Lachlan answered.

Maude turned to Kieran, looking defeated for the first time since her injuries. "You worried I would die." Kieran couldn't speak around the lump in his throat, so he nodded. "Oh, turtledove, I'm not ready to leave you yet. I have too many more years to spend with you before I'm ready for us to part."

Blair stepped closer to the bed as Amelia and Hamish made room for their children to see their sister.

"Are you really improving?" Blair whispered.

"Aye. I feel better this morning than I did when I awoke yesterday. I suspect I'm over the worst of it. A few days of fever wasn't enough to do me in."

"A few days?" Hamish repeated. "Lass, the bluidy beast injured ye over a sennight ago."

Before she had the chance to respond, Amelia shifted her attention to Kieran. "Does she ken?"

Kieran shook his head before taking Maude's hand. He pressed a kiss to her temple to ease her panicked reaction. He nudged her chin, so she locked eyes with him. He couldn't resist dropping a kiss on her lips before he explained.

"Buttercup, we're going to have a bairn."

Maude blinked several times, but still looked confused. "A what?"

"A bairn. Eara examined you and discovered you're carrying. She figures you're close to three moons already."

"A bairn. I can't believe it. I didn't consider it. Before, when I was younger and didn't eat enough, my courses were unpredictable. I assumed that's all that was happening."

"And I never gave it any consideration either. I guess I figured they came while I was on patrol. I never thought to ask."

"Turtledove, we'll really have our own bairn?"

"Aye, lass. Our own bairn."

Maude fell silent as she attempted to pull forth a memory. It was cloudy, but she was certain she remembered something from when she was unconscious. "Did you ask me aboot names and what I would want to call our lad or lass?"

"I did. I talked to you aboot it several times. I hoped you'd hear me, and it would make you fight to come back to me."

"I think it did. I remember being on fire and my side itched, but I also recall voices, yours in particular."

"Aye. I talked to you a great deal, and Abigail spent hours reading to you."

"I think it helped. It was as though I kept trying to run toward the voices, even though I never seemed to get anywhere. It gave me purpose." Maude looked back at her family and smiled once more before yawning. "I'm so glad you're here, but I'm sorry for giving you such a fright."

"There's naught to apologize for," Amelia reassured her. "Kieran explained how you were injured, and we're so proud of you."

"What happened to the weans?" Maude asked in a rush.

"Turns out they have an aunt and uncle who live in the village. It was their older brother who rode to inform us. Their kin took them in, and they're doing well now that they're safe. Their father sent them to hide as soon as the first riders approached. It was too dark for them to see aught, so they have no memories of their parents being killed or the fate of the others. They were too frightened to go near the fires, so they'd remained hidden."

Maude relaxed as she sighed. A sense of calm settled over her once she knew someone was taking good care of the children. She yawned again, and Amelia shooed her family from the chamber, promising to return the next time Maude woke. Maude nestled against Kieran and fisted his leine, the only thing he wore.

"Thank you, turtledove. I love you beyond measure." She drifted back to sleep before Kieran responded, but he kissed the crown of her head and whispered his pledge of love.

The next moon passed in a blur for Maude as her health improved each day. Within three days of her family's arrival, she was well enough to make her way to the Great Hall for meals. She still felt weak as a bairn, so she capitulated to Kieran's pestering and took naps twice a day, but she soon walked about the bailey and gardens without perspiring. Kieran and her family took turns accompanying her during her morning constitutional. She returned to her duties in the kitchen to find the servants jumped to assist her without being asked or told. Fiona was like a new woman, asking for Maude's advice and deferring to Maude's requests with respect. But the greatest turnaround was Adeline and Abigail. Both women assisted in the kitchens and gardens. While Maude was still too ill to make her rounds to the cooper, the spenser, the distiller, and the laundresses, mother and daughter divided the responsibilities. Abigail continued to read to Maude when she grew tired and rested before the fire in the Great Hall. Adeline created a beautiful kirtle for Maude, with embroidery across the bodice and hems. She used material she'd ordered but tossed aside as too frivolous to consider the expense to the clan. She made the gown based on one of Maude's but added extra fabric to the skirts to accommodate Maude's soon-to-be swelling belly. It had surprised and moved Maude too much for her to speak when Adeline presented it to her. The women exchanged a hug that expressed genuine affection. Maude found she was willing to forgive more each day as Abigail and Adeline continued their efforts. She'd feared they would be fair-weather helpers, and once the novelty or scrutiny passed, they would revert to their old selves, but both women continued their efforts.

Maude's family spoiled her. When she became too restless to remain within the keep, Lachlan took her to the targets near the lists to practice with their bows. Blair shared the latest *en dite* from court and brought special notes of well wishes from Arabella and her godparents. Amelia ensured the kitchens served fortifying meals that included Maude's favorite foods. Hamish took her for longer and longer walks beyond the keep's walls. She enjoyed having the chance to visit with her loved ones, but it was the time spent with Kieran that she most savored.

Kieran took her for rides on Peat, often stopping at the loch to paddle or fish. Eventually, Maude had the strength to ride Trioblaid as long as they walked or trotted. They went on picnics in the nearby meadow or on the banks of the loch. They talked about clan business, the ongoing difficulty with the Morrisons, and prospects for Abigail's marriage. They eased back into their physical relationship, enjoying rediscovering one another's bodies, and as Maude displayed signs of her pregnancy, Kieran marveled at the wonder that she grew another life within her. He doted on her and was rarely beyond reach except for when he trained in the lists. When his rotation for patrols arrived, Lachlan took his place, so he wouldn't have to leave Maude's side. On days when they didn't venture from the keep, Maude returned to sharing Kieran's solar as she worked on the accounts or read while he managed the clan's affairs. Their bond grew stronger with each passing day, neither taking for granted their time together. They visited the orphaned village children who found a loving home with their relatives near the keep.

The one event that threatened to darken her happiness occurred when she met Maggie by accident during a visit to the village. She and Kieran had been walking hand-in-hand when Kieran suddenly attempted to change directions to avoid a stall in the market. When Maude asked why, Kieran avoided looking at her and suggested a vendor she might like. She peered into the crowd and spotted a beautiful woman who glanced in her direction but returned her attention to the man she haggled with. In an instant, Maude knew who the woman was. She looked at Kieran with doubt and suspicion. Why would he avoid Maggie if he had nothing to hide? Had he become tired of waiting for Maude to heal and resumed his relationship with Maggie? Kieran saw the fear and hurt, understanding immediately that his attempt to spare her embarrassment made her question herself. He continued in the direction they had intended, passing by Maggie who spared them but a glance. She bobbed a polite curtsy and offered Maude a smile but showed little interest in Kieran. When they moved into a shady spot, Maude burst into tears, her emotions already running at odds and ends from being pregnant. Kieran embraced her and stroked her back until she calmed.

"I feel as though your lack of faith in me should hurt, but I understand your feelings. I suppose I'd be the same in your position," Kieran confessed. "I want naught more than for you to believe me when I say that I'll never stray from you. There's no woman more beautiful to me than you. There's no woman who'd ever be worth risking what I have with you. I love you fully and completely, Maude, and I will till I draw my last breath."

Maude nodded as she sniffled. "I know you do. It's ridiculous for me to get so upset, but I don't seem to be able to stop the tears. I'm positive you haven't strayed. You haven't had time to since you've been attached to my side for sennights. I

310

know you wouldn't abandon your time training to stray, and every other hour of the day, you're with me. But she's beautiful. I had an overwhelming sense of failure, as though I'll never measure up, especially as I gain weight with the bairn."

"You're carrying the bairn we made together. I'll never care aboot your weight, Maude. I'd fear for you and the bairn if you didn't gain weight. I look forward to seeing your belly swell, knowing we created this life together because we love each other." Kieran kissed the corner of her jaw before whispering, "Besides, your breasts have always been divine, but now that they have filled out even more, I find myself drooling with want to suckle you."

Maude shivered as Kieran's words stirred an ache within her core. She stroked her hand over his back down to his buttocks, which she squeezed. Kieran growled and pulled her further into the shadows before capturing her lips in a kiss so filled with passion, he grew lightheaded. Maude slid her hand under his plaid, reaching for his lengthening rod. Kieran groaned and pulled away, looking around. He led her to the postern gate and a side door to the keep. They raced up the stairs to their chamber. It was only moments later that they were stripped bare and clinging to one another. Their sounds of relief as their bodies fused together filled the chamber, neither caring if everyone in the keep knew what husband and wife were doing.

"How does it keep getting better every time?" Maude wondered. "I pray this never changes."

"Shh, my love. I feel the same. I never want to stop, never let you go," Kieran soothed.

At the end of their sixth sennight at Stornoway, Maude's family accepted that they had to depart. Maude arranged a feast for their send-off, and it was the first time she had enough energy by the evening to dance. She twirled and laughed as she moved from one partner to another, including her father and brother. She prayed her family would arrive in time for the birth of her bairn or soon after, but she was due in winter, and travel in the Highlands was unpredictable. Kieran claimed most of her dances, but he beamed as he watched her enjoying herself. He looked around the Great Hall, noting all that was right in his life. His wife was healthy and happy, and his family-by-marriage hadn't murdered him for Maude's injuries, nor when they learned of her cold reception. His mother and sister were like new women, and he had a bairn on the way. His life had never been so full of blessings, and he intended to appreciate every moment.

As the music ended, Maude squeezed her way through the crowd until she reached Kieran, who leaned against the far wall. She flashed him the wide smile she reserved for him as he opened his arms to her. As he enveloped her in his embrace, she snuggled closer.

"This is the best day of my life, with the exception of our wedding. Thank you for allowing my family to remain for so long."

"Allowing? It's thrilled me to have them here. They've made you so happy, and I'm sure it helped speed along your recovery. And it let me leave your side without fretting."

"Without fretting?" Maude giggled. "You fret more than an auld woman. But I confess: I like it when you fret over me. I do the same when you ride out on patrol. I don't think I'm controlling, but I don't care for you being out of sight and out of reach."

"You may fret aboot me anytime you'd like. I know it means you love me."

"Just a little," Maude giggled again and dissolved into peals of laughter as he tickled her healed ribs and the crook of her neck.

"Keep pressing against me like that, and I'll take you to bed before you bid your family goodnight."

"Then I'd better hurry because I have every intention of you taking me to bed right now."

Kieran swept her into his arms and carried to her the dais. "Maude wishes to say goodnight," he announced.

"Goodnight," she chirped before Kieran raced to the stairs and took them two at a time.

The night slipped into early morning before they fell asleep, exhausted but sated.

Morning came too soon, and Maude found herself in the bailey saying goodbye to her parents, brother, and sister. After her emotional ups and downs of the past sennights, she expected she'd fall apart, but she found peace as her family prepared to depart. She'd enjoyed their time there. She'd been proud to have her parents see what she'd accomplished, and she enjoyed her time gossiping and laughing with Blair. She'd shared several lengthy conversations with Lachlan as he confessed his fears of one day inheriting the lairdship. Maude suggested tactics Kieran used to lead their clan, and she reassured him that he'd grown into a man anyone would follow without hesitation. She admitted her own worries about what life would be like once the Sutherlands left and she was once more left to manage the keep. She appreciated his council as much as he did hers.

As her family rode out of the bailey, she felt a contentment that hadn't existed before they arrived. She wished it hadn't been under such inauspicious circumstances, but it did wonders for her. Kieran wrapped his arm around her and watched as she waved once more to her relatives. She reached into her pocket and retrieved a small pouch her father had given her that morning with strict instructions not to open it until after they departed but to be sure she did it with Kieran.

"Da gave this to me this morning. I have no idea what it is, but he said I was to open it with you once they left." Maude drew the strings open and dumped the contents into her hand

and gasped. Hamish had carved another figurine for her. This one had a man with one arm wrapped around the woman and the other helping to support the babe the woman held. It didn't take any imagination to see the couple was Kieran and Maude. The etching was clear and intricate, capturing their likeness.

"It's remarkable," Kieran's voice held reverence as he ran his finger over the notches and grooves. "Your father possesses a gift, and this is a rare treasure."

"It is. This is us," Maude murmured as the tears welled in her eyes, but she blinked them away. She pressed the carving to her lips, then her heart. "This is our future. Yours, mine, our family's."

Kieran placed his hand over Maude's belly. "I never imagined when I caught you eavesdropping that I'd meet the most remarkable woman who would steal my heart. Discovering you on the terrace was the greatest gift God ever gave me. I found my other half; the half that makes me a better mon. I love you, buttercup."

"And I love you, turtledove, just as much."

Kieran and Maude stood together in the bailey, embracing and kissing as clan members passed by, now accustomed to seeing their laird and lady share their deep and abiding devotion.

EPILOGUE

Maude looked across the solar to where Kieran sat, pulling his hair until it stood on end as he attempted to write a missive while jiggling a three-year-old lad on his knee. She would have laughed if her breath hadn't escaped in a puff when their five-year-old daughter leaped into her lap, waving a leaf she'd gathered earlier that day. Maude glanced down at their six-year-old twins—a son and a daughter—as they played with wooden soldiers Hamish had carved before the birth of his first grandchildren. Maude inhaled deeply before releasing a slow sigh. She had more than she'd ever dreamed of when she arrived at court all those years ago. She shared a wonderful life with a doting husband and adorable children. Maude smiled as she watched Kieran adjust their son as a small hand kept attempting to capture the quill that danced before him. When the little boy succeeded, Kieran gave up and carried a squealing toddler to the chair beside Maude's. The four children returned to playing together as Kieran took Maude's hand. They watched in silence as the children marched the soldiers across the floor, the fire crackling and popping in the background. Dissatisfied with the distance between them, Kieran lifted Maude into his lap and nuzzled the corner of her jaw as she stroked his chest and shoulder.

"Do you think Da will have time to carve another set of toys if I give him six moons' notice?" Maude mused.

Kieran froze and leaned to look at her. Maude's enigmatic smile made his heart race for more than one reason. It still aroused him in an instant, but as her words registered, his mouth broke into a wide grin.

"Another bairn?"

"Aye. I don't understand how you haven't figured it out this time."

"I suppose it was like with the twins. I assumed your courses came when I was on patrol."

"Would that it were always that convenient. Nay, Eara says I'm four moons along. She fears it might be twins again from how my waist has already expanded."

Kieran placed his hand over Maude's belly. After four children, it wasn't as taut as it had been when they married, but he still desired his wife with a fire that threatened to send him up in flames. He hadn't noticed any changes in her middle, though he'd wondered about the fullness of her breasts, but they, too, had grown even more luscious after nursing four bairns.

"You've already blessed me with four wonderful weans. I'm more fortunate than any one mon should ever be."

"You blessed me just as much as I did you. We've created a happy home for our family and a life together that continues to bring more joy by the day." Maude cupped Kieran's jaw as she offered a tender kiss imbued with the love and devotion they shared. "I love you, turtledove."

"And I love you, mo chridhe. Wilder than the Highland hills and more beautiful than all the lochs and mountains. I thank God every day that my wallflower bloomed into my bright buttercup."

They melded together, kissing and embracing as their children played at their feet, the sound of young laughter filling the chamber.

THANK YOU FOR READING A WALLFLOWER AT THE HIGHLAND COURT

Celeste Barclay, a nom de plume, lives near the Southern California coast with her husband and sons. Growing up in the Midwest, Celeste enjoyed spending as much time in and on the water as she could. Now she lives near the beach. She's an avid swimmer, a hopeful future surfer, and a former rower. When she's not writing, she's working or being a mom.

Visit Celeste's website, www.celestebarclay.com, for regular updates on works in progress, new releases, and her blog where she features posts about her experiences as an author and recommendations of her favorite reads.

Are you an author who would like to guest blog or be featured in her recommendations? Visit her website for an opportunity to share your insights and experiences.

Have you read *Their Highland Beginning, The Clan Sinclair*

Prequel? Learn how the saga begins! This FREE novella is available to all new subscribers to Celeste's monthly newsletter. Subscribe on her website.

www.celestebarclay.com

Join the fun and get exclusive insider giveaways, sneak peeks, and new release announcements in

Celeste Barclay's Facebook Ladies of Yore Group

THE HIGHLAND LADIES

A Spinster at the Highland Court **BOOK 1 SNEAK PEEK**

Elizabeth Fraser looked around the royal chapel within Stirling Castle. The ornate candlestick holders on the altar glistened and reflected the light from the ones in the wall sconces as the priest intoned the holy prayers of the Advent season. Elizabeth kept her head bowed as though in prayer, but her green eyes swept the congregation. She watched the other ladies-in-waiting, many of whom were doing the same thing. She caught the eye of Allyson Elliott. Elizabeth raised one eyebrow as Allyson's lips twitched. Both women had been there enough times to accept they'd be kneeling for at least the next hour as the Latin service carried on. Elizabeth understood the Mass thanks to her cousin Deirdre Fraser, or rather now Deirdre Sinclair. Elizabeth's mind flashed to the recent struggle her cousin faced as she reunited with her husband Magnus after a seven-year separation. Her aunt and uncle's choice to keep Deirdre hidden from her husband simply because they didn't think the Sinclairs were an advantageous enough match, and the resulting scandal, still humiliated the other Fraser clan members at court. She admired Deirdre's husband Magnus's pledge to remain faithful despite not knowing if he'd ever see Deirdre again.

Elizabeth suddenly snapped her attention; while everyone else intoned the twelfth—or was it thirteenth—amen of the Mass, the hairs on the back of her neck stood up. She had the strongest feeling that someone was watching her. Her eyes scanned to her right, where her parents sat further down the pew. Her mother and father had their heads bowed and eyes closed. While she was convinced her mother was in devout prayer, she wondered if her father had fallen asleep during the Mass. Again. With nothing seeming out of the ordinary and no one visibly paying attention to her, her eyes swung to the left. She took in the king and queen as they kneeled together at their prie-dieu. The queen's lips moved as she recited the liturgy in silence. The king was as still as a statue. Years of leading warriors showed, both in his stature and his ability to control his body into absolute stillness. Elizabeth peered past the royal couple and found herself looking into the astute hazel eyes of Edward Bruce, Lord of Badenoch and Lochaber. His gaze gave her the sense that he peered into her thoughts, as though he were assessing her. She tried to keep her face neutral as heat surged up her neck. She prayed her face didn't redden as much as her neck must have, but at a twenty-one, she still hadn't mastered how to control her blushing. Her nape burned like it was on fire. She canted her head slightly before looking up at the crucifix hanging over the altar. She closed her eyes and tried to invoke the image of the Lord that usually centered her when her mind wandered during Mass.

A Spy at the Highland Court **BOOK 1.5 SNEAK PEEK**

A Companion to the Series

Dedric Hage watched as the English king continued his royal rage as courtiers and advisors eased away from their irate sovereign. His Majesty's face was mottled with red splotches that only accentuated his fair complexion, and spittle formed at the corners of his mouth as his rant amplified. King Edward stalked about the chamber on the long legs that earned him the moniker "Longshanks."

"I don't give a bloody damn who oversaw the attack. It failed!" He railed against the last advisor who tried to reassure him that the recent loss was not the end of his campaign against the Scots. "Failure is failure. That usurper believes he's gotten the upper hand, and he will continue worming his way further into England now that he thinks he has outsmarted me. I should have killed him when I had the chance."

King Edward muttered his final comments as he sank back into the engraved and carved chair that sat on a dais. His bile spewed the king retreated into his own thoughts as the rest of the chamber was left wondering what to do next.

Dedric had seen this pattern countless times over the course of his life. He was all too familiar with the king's mercurial temper and unpredictable outbursts, but he also knew Edward was one of the best strategists and logisticians to have every lived. While he might not like the man, he respected him. At times. Ric watched as the king scanned the crowd, assessing each knight present until his eyes settled on rich, who wished he could melt into the curtains and watch the people in the gardens below.

"Sir Dedric, approach."

A Wallflower at the Highland Court **BOOK 2 SNEAK PEEK**

The din of music and loud conversation–along with the pervasive odor of too many unwashed or over-perfumed bodies crowded into Stirling Castle's Great Hall–gave Maude Sutherland a pounding headache. As she observed the dancers from her position at the side of the chamber, part of her envied the other ladies-in-waiting who twirled with ease and confidence, but mostly she wished for nothing more than the blessed silence of her chamber. While Maude propped up the wall, she spied her younger sister, Blair, who moved through the country reel with what must have been her seventh partner that evening. Though she was only an observer, sweat trickled down Maude's back and between her breasts. A warm snap —unseasonable for spring in the Highlands— had the doors to the terraces wide open. This should have been enough to ease Maude's discomfort, but the breeze did little to offset how her thick brown hair trapped the heat on her head and neck. Unlike most maidens, Maude wore her hair up almost every waking moment. She possessed a massive amount of thick, coarse, mousey brown hair that was unruly even on the best of days. By evening the weight of the hair, regardless of whether it was up or down, pulled on her neck and contributed to her headache. She would have loved nothing more than to cut it all off and wear it short like her father, Laird Hamish Sutherland, or her brother, Lachlan. She envied them the freedom to wear their hair however they wanted.

A crimson gown floated in Maude's periphery, so she turned to watch her closest friend, Arabella Johnstone. She and Arabella were as different as chalk and cheese but had somehow struck up a close friendship. Where Arabella's hair glowed in the candlelight, Maude accepted her hair was dull. Where Arabella's face looked like an artist's masterpiece, Maude was aware she was plain. Where Arabella was petite and lean through her hips and legs, Maude considered herself far too broad across the beam. As she grew into womanhood, her frame filled out, and while she had a bust most women would envy, her hips and legs were proportionate. Whenever Arabella or Blair glided across the dance floor, she recalled the many adjectives her brother and his friends had come up with for her when they were younger. "Sodgy," "bamsey," "bowzy," "jostly," "podg," and "flobbed up" were the ones that always came to mind. Her brother had since repented for the unkind and merciless teasing. Lachlan noticed that the more he and his friends teased Maude, the less she ate. On the day she collapsed and nearly fell down the stairs leading to the family chambers, he was the one to catch her and carry her to her chamber. In her hazy state, she confessed to have only eaten dried fruit and bannocks the previous three days in hopes of slimming. Lachlan never said an unkind word to his sister again and thereafter became fiercely protective of her, fighting more than one friend when they failed to cease teasing her.

A Rogue at the Highland Court **BOOK 3 SNEAK PEEK**

The crunch of frost echoed in Stirling Castle's royal gardens as Allyson Elliot trudged along with the other ladies-in-waiting, enduring another one of the queen's morning strolls through the struggling blossoms. It was mid-March, and spring had arrived for their neighbors to the south, but Mother Nature seemed to have forgotten that Stirling wasn't truly in the Highlands. Sitting on the border between the Highlands and Lowlands, the weather in Stirling was fickle, playing both sides of the fence. Allyson puffed out a cloud of condensation as the ice crackled beneath her booted feet. She didn't mind the distance of the morning constitutional, but having been raised in the Lowlands, Allyson was still unaccustomed to the frigid temperatures of the north.

"I still can't believe he married her." Allyson caught the waspish voice of Cairstine Grant as her attention returned to the young women around her. Allyson realized Cairstine spoke of Maude Sutherland without hearing the former lady-in-waiting's name. Maude had been a shy lass from the northern Highlands, and several of the other ladies-in-waiting—Cairstine Grant included—had teased her without mercy. It had come as a shock when Kieran MacLeod arrived at court and immediately took an interest in Maude, who the other ladies considered overweight and plain. He'd been one of the most eligible lairds, and more than one nose was out of joint when he chose a woman so many believed was beneath him.

Allyson struggled to smother her giggle as she considered just how Maude was beneath Kieran these days. Allyson arrived at court four years ago as an impressionable girl overwhelmed by the attention her fair hair and robin-egg blue eyes garnered. She soon realized she enjoyed the attention after being the youngest of her parents' six children. A few batted eyelashes and a coy smile earned her the appreciation of the young courtiers who flocked to court hoping to gain attention and favor from King Robert the Bruce. While Allyson wasn't as daring as some of her peers, she had stolen a few kisses from these men, hoping to find one who would make her his wife and take her away from both the royal court and her family. Her attempts hadn't garnered a husband, but it had resulted in a reputation as a flirt.

"Allyson. Allyson, are you listening to me?"

A Rake at the Highland Court **BOOK 4 SNEAK PEEK**

Eoin Gordon raised his chalice once more to toast his twin brother, Ewan, and his new sister-by-marriage, Allyson. As he did, he had a sense that someone was watching him. As the hairs on the back of his neck rose, Eoin passed a quick glance over the diners seated below the dais, but no one seemed to be paying attention to him. He raised his chalice again but didn't take a sip; instead, he continued to scan the crowd. He looked for anyone doing the same: studying him while attempting to ensure no one else noticed.

"What's amiss?" Ewan, the elder twin by five minutes and the heir to Clan Gordon, leaned toward him. The brothers had been inseparable since the day of their birth. They possessed an uncanny intuition for one another and seemed to share the same thoughts more often than not. Until Ewan fell in love with Allyson, neither trusted anyone more than they did each other. As he heard Allyson laugh, Eoin's memory flashed to her courtship with Ewan. Their relationship started poorly when Allyson ran away rather than consider a marriage to Ewan. More than once during that time, Eoin had wanted to shake Ewan, whose views on marriage and fidelity had changed all too slowly. Eoin was grateful for Allyson's influence; he was certain his brother was a better man for it.

"Naught. I just have a sense that someone is watching me," Eoin explained. "It's making me want to squirm."

"I haven't a clue why women find you so attractive, but it's probably some bored wife or lonely widow," Ewan grinned. His reputation as a rogue was entrenched in many women's minds, but his obvious devotion to Allyson no longer caused Eoin concern that his brother intended to stray from his marriage vows. "You do have a reputation as a rake. One of them is hoping they'll warm your bed tonight."

"Only one?" Eoin cocked an eyebrow and grinned. "My charm must be slipping."

"You assume you had any to begin with. Perhaps it was my charm that lured the women, and they figured two is better than one," Ewan teased. The twins were mirror images in every way except for their battle scars. Ewan had a scar that split the left corner of his lip, and Eoin had a less noticeable scar above his left eyebrow. While their scares weren't in the same place, they were still on the same side. There was little to distinguish them apart, and they'd relied upon that throughout their lives, often trading places.

"That very charm had me running for the hills," Allyson elbowed her husband as she leaned around Ewan to speak to her brother-by-marriage. "It's Cairstine Grant. I don't have a clue why she keeps looking at you, but she can't seem to distract herself."

"Cairstine? Why would she be staring?" Eoin wondered aloud.

An Enemy at the Highland Court **BOOK 5 SNEAK PEEK**

A crack of thunder followed only moments later by a blaze of lightning made several ladies-in-waiting jump within the queen's solar. The early autumn storm seemed to rattle one's bones as much as it did the window embrasures. Cairren Kennedy glanced around Queen Elizabeth's private salon and stifled her chuckle as the newest ladies-in-waiting trembled. Mostly Lowlanders, these young ladies were not yet accustomed to the raging storms the Highlands flung upon Stirling from the north. Cairren arrived at Robert the Bruce's court three years earlier as a wide-eyed and quiet girl. But in the time she'd spent there, she'd developed a thick skin and a significant cynicism. As she watched the newer arrivals, she wished she could return to her days before becoming a lady-in-waiting to Elizabeth de Burgh. It had been just over a year since her best friend, Allyson Elliot, married Ewan Gordon and moved to the Highlands. During that year, Cairren awaited the announcement of her own betrothal, and with each passing month, she found her mood increasingly matched the weather outside.

Cairren received a hint from her father around the time of Allyson's wedding that he was in the midst of arranging a betrothal to a Highlander, but he'd volunteered no specifics. Cairren suspected that news came several prospective suitors ago. Growing up near the border, with constant strife between the Scots and the English, made life among the contentious Highlanders seem peaceful. While her clan's land sat along the coast, their allies were the Dunbars and Armstrongs, which meant the two border clans often called upon the Kennedys to lend warriors to the cause. She understood her father wanted her away from the ever-shifting political dynamics that were a daily part of life in the south. However, moving to the Highlands sight unseen terrified her. She was blessed with a doting father who always had her best interests at heart, but she couldn't help but wonder how he thought the Highlands were a better option. She'd rather move to her mother's people in southern France. At least there, she would blend in.

"Lady Cairren," Queen Elizabeth's voice drew Cairren out of her pensiveness, forcing her to abandon her thoughts. "Please pick up where you left off yesterday."

Cairren retrieved the vellum copy of *Summa contra Gentiles* from the table upon which she'd laid it the day before. With a slight French lilt to her voice, Cairren was among the queen's favorites to read aloud. She was also one of the few women who read fluently. She accepted that the queen had committed her to an hour of droning prose on providence and the soul. While she was as devout as the next person, Cairren swallowed her sigh as she prepared to read the divine insights of Thomas Aquinas. As she settled onto a stool, a page entered the solar and whispered to the Mistress of the Bedchamber who, in turn, cast an eye at Cairren.

"Your Majesty, I beg your pardon, but Lady Cairren has been summoned to see her father and mother, who are newly arrived," the Mistress of the Bedchamber announced, all eyes swinging to Cairren.

A Saint at the Highland Court BOOK 6 SNEAK PEEK

"Sister," Lachlan Sutherland approached Blair with Arabella Johnstone on his arm. Arabella had been Maude's only other close friend while she was at court. The women had been roommates, and Arabella took Maude—and by extension Blair—under her wing when she arrived. "Every mon in this gathering hall keeps looking at you, and yet you seem to be in a world of your own, uninterested in them. Well done. I approve."

Lachlan grinned at his youngest sibling as Arabella released his arm. He swiped three mugs of ale from a passing servant, handing one to each lady. The three Sutherland siblings were very close, and Blair was ecstatic any time Lachlan appeared at court. The only family she knew that shared this kind of closeness were the Sutherlands' cousins, the Sinclairs. Lachlan wrapped his arm around Blair's shoulders and dropped a kiss on the crown of her head. They hadn't seen one another since Lachlan's unexpected arrival in late autumn, when he accompanied Cairren and Padraig to Stirling, but he had returned to settle the annual taxes their clan owed the crown. The brother and sister enjoyed a fortnight of each other's company. With Maude no longer beside her, Blair was starved for time with her family. Lachlan never shied away from showing his affection for his sisters, and Blair welcomed it.

"Shall I take you for a lap around the floor?" Lachlan inquired as he grinned at Blair. "Or will you prop up this wall a little longer? I may be your brother, but I shall be the envy of every mon with a heartbeat."

A Beauty at the Highland Court **BOOK 7 SNEAK PEEK**

"I just need a few moments more," Blair looked over her shoulder at Arabella.

"You needn't rush. We still have time," Arabella reassured as she dabbed rose water behind her ears and into her cleavage. She knew the Great Hall would be sweltering, and the fresh scent was as much for her as it was for anyone else. It would offer her a reprieve from the stench of too many unwashed and overheated bodies.

As Arabella watched Blair, she wondered when her friend would find her match. She suspected that it would happen soon, since Blair and Hardwin Cameron were inseparable. It wouldn't surprise Arabella if Blair and Hardi (as she called him) handfasted before a priest could read the banns. Thoughts of Maude and Blair inevitably turned her mind toward their older brother, Lachlan. Arabella stifled her sigh as she thought about the handsome, dark-haired man who appeared at court every few months. She didn't envy him his lengthy rides south from Dunrobin. The keep was along the northeastern coast of Scotland, almost as far north as that of the Sinclairs, and marriage linked the two clans. Arabella had long admired Lachlan's easygoing nature and protectiveness of his sisters. The three siblings were extremely close, and both Maude and Blair had looked forward to his visits. Arabella knew Lachlan looked for excuses to see them. She couldn't help the sadness she felt when she realized Lachlan would rarely make the long trip to court once Blair left.

"I'm almost done," Blair said as she bent to pull up her stockings and slip on her shoes. She disliked wearing stockings, so she put them on last.

Arabella thought about her other friends who had left over the past three years. Nearly all her original friends were gone, one after another marrying and leaving court.

THE CLAN SINCLAIR

His Highland Lass **BOOK 1 SNEAK PEEK**

She entered the great hall like a strong spring storm in the northern most Highlands. Tristan Mackay felt like he had been blown hither and yon. As the storm settled, she left him with the sweet scents of heather and lavender wafting towards him as she approached. She was not a classic beauty, tall and willowy like the women at court. Her face and form were not what legends were made of. But she held a unique appeal unlike any he had seen before. He could not take his eyes off of her long chestnut hair that had strands of fire and burnt copper running through them. Unlike the waves or curls he was used to, her hair was unusually straight and fine. It looked like a waterfall cascading down her back. While she was not tall, neither was she short. She had a figure that was meant for a man to grasp and hold onto, whether from the front or from behind. She had an aura of confidence and charm, but not arrogance or conceit like many good looking women he had met. She did not seem to know her own appeal. He could tell that she was many things, but one thing she was not was his.

His Bonnie Highland Temptation **BOOK 2 SNEAK PEEK**

The pounding in Callum's head as he awoke made him wonder if he had been mistaken for the blacksmith's anvil. Slowly, he opened his eyes and looked over at the curvaceous blonde sleeping next to him. The previous night began to drift through his memory. His father, Liam Sinclair the chief of Clan Sinclair, had announced less than a sennight night ago that not only had he arranged a betrothal for Callum, his heir and tánaiste, but that the woman would be arriving before the sennight was over. She was expected some time late this day, so last night he had celebrated his upcoming nuptials by drowning his sorrows in more drams of whisky than he could remember and taking his current lover to bed for a night of entertainment and pleasure. He had been very sure to tell Elizabeth that this was his last night of freedom and that their short, albeit passionate, liaison was coming to an end. While Callum Sinclair may have enjoyed more than a few women's attention and considered himself a well experienced lover, he was also a man committed to fidelity to his wife. Whomever she might be.

His Highland Prize **BOOK 3 SNEAK PEEK**

I just need to make it to the light. Heavenly Father, please let there be a light over this hill. I canna go much farther. I must go farther. Will there never be a village or a keep nearby? I dinna think I will last much longer. Please, in the name of the Father and all the heavenly saints, just let me find someone who can help me.

Brighde Kerr pushed her sopping wet hair from her eyes as she stumbled onward. She had lost her shoes days ago after they had fallen apart while on the run from her pursuers. Her kirtle, which had once been a daffodil yellow was now a murky shade of beige with a ripped sleeve, frayed hem, and at least two holes that she had noticed in the skirts. Brighde ached all over. Her feet were raw from walking and running for nearly two weeks. Her legs protested taking even one more step, and her chest burned from trying to breathe through her efforts and the torrential downpour in which she once again found herself.

Light! I'm sure of it. I can finally see it coming from a keep. Dear God above, please allow me in. I just need---

His Highland Pledge **BOOK 4 SNEAK PEEK**

Magnus Sinclair detested being at the royal court. There was nothing redeemable in his eyes, and his face ensured everyone knew the Highland giant was not there to exchange pleasantries. Standing at six and a half feet tall, he towered over almost every man in the king's household and all the men who sought the monarch's attention. Only a few visiting Highlanders mirrored him in height and physique. As though sticking out like a sore thumb from his height and his insistence upon wearing his plaid was not enough, he felt naked without his claymore. Locked away in his chamber, his two-handed broadsword was as much a part of him as either hand. For the safety of the king and his family, they allowed no one to wear or carry a sword into the main gathering hall. Magnus's sword forged to accommodate his size, and even though custom designed, the enormous sword looked like little more than a young lad's wooden practice sword when Magnus held it. Needless to say, it was not a welcome sight strapped to his back. When he arrived the day before, he resigned himself to just carrying his dirks, of which he had at least eight on various parts of his body.

Arriving early the previous morning, Magnus spent all of the day and much of the evening in a passageway, standing, awaiting an audience with the king. This day came and went, just as the previous one had, with no indicator of when the king would meet with him. This only aggravated Magnus more as a representative from the Sinclair clan summoned rather than volunteered to attend court.

His Highland Surprise **BOOK 5 SNEAK PEEK**

Tavish Sinclair stood frozen in the Great Hall of his clan's keep as he listened to his father.

"Ye canna be serious!" He realized his voice was quiet as he spoke to Laird Liam Sinclair, but in his head, it was a roar. "I dinna need a wife. I dinna want a wife."

Tavish's body was so still he looked like a statue carved from marble, his expression like a death mask.

He canna mean it. I simply flirted one too many times with the elder man's daughter, Isabella. I will stay away and then this nonsense will pass.

"It isnae aboot Isabella or any of the local lasses ye ken so well. The king has decreed that I must make a match between our clans. Ye are the older of ma two unmarried sons. The duty falls to ye."

"But Magnus is already at court."

He recognized he sounded petulant, but Tavish Sinclair was a confirmed bachelor. He never intended to settle down with one woman. The Sinclair men, once their oath made, never were unfaithful to their wives. He refused to make that traditional vow, so instead he avoided marriage like it were a fire sweeping through hay.

"Aye, Magnus is at court. And taking far longer than expected. I worry something befell him. The king's message was rather cryptic on that front. I would have ye go to court and see that yer brother fares well, and while there, ye can meet the lass. Ye ken I will force none of ye into an unhappy marriage. I ask only that ye meet her. See if ye suit."

PIRATES OF THE ISLES

The Blond Devil of the Sea **BOOK 1 SNEAK PEEK**

Caragh lifted her torch into the air as she made her way down the precarious Cornish cliffside. She made out the hulking shape of a ship, but the dead of night made it impossible to see who was there. She and the fishermen of Bedruthan Steps weren't expecting any shipments that night. But her younger brother Eddie, who stood watch at the entrance to their hiding place, had spotted the ship and signaled up to the village watchman, who alerted Caragh.

As her boot slid along the dirt and sand, she cursed having to carry the torch and wished she could have sunlight to guide her. She knew these cliffs well, and it was for that reason it was better that she moved slowly than stop moving once and for all. Caragh feared the light from her torch would carry out to the boat. Despite her efforts to keep the flame small, the solitary light would be a beacon.

When Caragh came to the final twist in the path before the sand, she snuffed out her torch and started to run to the cave where the main source of the village's income lay in hiding. She heard movement along the trail above her head and knew the local fishermen would soon join her on the beach. These men, both young and old, were strong from days spent pulling in the full trawling nets and hoisting the larger catches onto their boats. However, these men weren't well-trained swordsmen, and the fear of pirate raids was ever-present. Caragh feared that was who the villagers would face that night.

The Dark Heart of the Sea **BOOK 2 SNEAK PEEK**

Ruairí MacNeil opened the door to the Three Merry Lads and tried not to curl his nose in disgust. The overpowering odor of too many bodies, stale beers, and burned food created a cloud of stench inside the tavern. Ruairí scanned the crowd as he stepped inside and immediately noticed that many members of his crew were already settled, a pint in one hand and a woman in the other. His ship, the *Lady Charity*, had docked an hour earlier. With their most recent bounty already stored in the nearby cave, Ruairí had granted them shore leave. He nodded his head once to his first mate, Kyle, who was the only sober one in the lot. Ruairí made another visual sweep of the room, checking whether there were any other sailors who might be less enthused to see him come ashore. When he was satisfied none of his rivals were waiting to stab him, he attempted to make his way to the bar. As he pushed through the standing-room-only main room, he noticed a tavern wench attempting to carry a tray of empty mugs to the bar. She was a sturdy sort, but short when compared to the mountainous Highlanders and Hebrideans who made up the patrons of the Lads. Ruairí couldn't help but smile as she tried to twist and shoulder her way past men who blocked her on purpose to give themselves more time to ogle her body.

It was rare that Ruairí felt mercy, sympathy, or compassion for anyone, let alone a woman, but there was an odd twinge in his heart as he watched her try to maintain her smile as she became more frustrated. The woman swatted away a hand that dared come too close to her modest neckline. That observation caused Ruairí to quirk a brow and inspect the woman. She had on a clean white blouse—a rarity in this tavern—and it fit loosely over her entire bust. It left much to the imagination, and Ruairí found his was alive and well. Her skirts reached her ankles instead of hiked up on either side like the other women who worked in the tavern. From what Ruairí could tell, she looked more like a farmer's wife than a tavern wench. She didn't fit in.

Ruairí's sense of compassion grew alongside his annoyance at not being able to make his way to the bar. He began to elbow men around him, and the crowd parted. Between his size and reputation, Ruairí MacNeil was a hard man to ignore. He grasped the top of the woman's hips and propelled her forward. She attempted to look over her shoulder, but she couldn't make out the man who was either her captor or her protector. When they made it to the bar, the woman set her tray down and spun around.

VIKING GLORY

Leif BOOK 1 SNEAK PEEK

Leif looked around his chambers within his father's longhouse and breathed a sigh of relief. He noticed the large fur rugs spread throughout the chamber. His two favorites placed strategically before the fire and the bedside he preferred. He looked at his shield that hung on the wall near the door in a symbolic position but waiting at the ready. The chests that held his clothes and some of his finer acquisitions from voyages near and far sat beside his bed and along the far wall. And in the center was his most favorite possession. His oversized bed was one of the few that could accommodate his long and broad frame. He shook his head at his longing to climb under the pile of furs and on the stuffed mattress that beckoned him. He took in the chair placed before the fire where he longed to sit now with a cup of warm mead. It had been two months since he slept in his own bed, and he looked forward to nothing more than pulling the furs over his head and sleeping until he could no longer ignore his hunger. Alas, he would not be crawling into his bed again for several more hours. A feast awaited him to celebrate his and his crew's return from their latest expedition to explore the isle of Britannia. He bathed and wore fresh clothes, so he had no excuse for lingering other than a bone weariness that set in during the last storm at sea. He was eager to spend time at home no matter how much he loved sailing. Their last expedition had been profitable with several raids of monasteries that yielded jewels and both silver and gold, but he was ready for respite.

Leif left his chambers and knocked on the door next to his. He heard movement on the other side, but it was only moments before his sister, Freya, opened her door. She, too, looked tired but clean. A few pieces of jewelry she confiscated from the holy houses that allegedly swore to a life of poverty and deprivation adorned her trim frame.

"That armband suits you well. It compliments your muscles," Leif smirked and dodged a strike from one of those muscular arms.

Only a year younger than he, his sister was a well-known and feared shield maiden. Her lithe form was strong and agile making her a ferocious and competent opponent to any man. Freya's beauty was stunning, but Leif had taken every opportunity since they were children to tease her about her unusual strength even among the female warriors.

"At least one of us inherited our father's prowess. Such a shame it wasn't you."

Freya **BOOK 2 SNEAK PEEK**

"Does he have nothing better to do than stare?" Freya huffed as she and Tyra left the training field.

Freya Ivarsdóttir was a renowned and much feared shieldmaiden and the daughter of a jarl. At twenty-four years old, she had already spent half of her life training and raiding with her Norse tribe.

Tyra looked back over her shoulder and scanned the field of battling Norsemen as they trained. As Freya's best friend, Tyra was used to Freya's sometimes brittle disposition, and she knew when her friend was hiding something. Nothing seemed out of the ordinary. The ongoing skirmishes against their neighbors and the general way of life in the northern Trondelag meant the men and women tasked with defending their tribes trained daily. Tyra watched as they swung axes, swords thrust, and spears hurled. She looked around at the many longhouses that created the perimeter of the homestead. Women stood outside doing laundry, one woman swept dust out her front door, and several people stood around engaged in easy conversation.

"I don't see anyone. Well, maybe a ghost from your past, but he's watched you for years."

"What? No. Wait, what do you mean he's watched me for years?"

"Ever since the two of you a few summers ago--- Well, you know. Skellig's had his eye on you, and I think you broke his heart. I believe he's hoping for more than just a reunion under the furs."

"Never."

"Then who could you have meant?" Tyra smirked before adding in a sing-song voice, "Erik?"

Tyra & Bjorn BOOK 3 SNEAK PEEK

10 years ago

Tyra extended her arm to Bjorn and jerked him from the ground where she had just knocked him onto his backside. She slid her foot under the hilt of his sword and kicked it until her hand wrapped around the handle. She handed it back to Bjorn with a smirk.

"Maybe one day you'll be able to keep up. Today isn't that day," Tyra goaded.

They had been sparing once more, and the result was typical. Tyra Vigosdóttir knocked Bjorn Jansson onto his arse time and again despite being two years younger, only coming to the middle of his chest, and being a woman. They had been sparring since they were children, and at seventeen, Bjorn resented Tyra, who was only fifteen, still being able to best him. He was a renowned warrior in his own right, but somehow Tyra read him better than he knew himself. She was always one, but usually three, moves ahead of him.

Before Bjorn could say thank you, she spun on her heels and marched away, her honey blonde braid swinging down her back. Bjorn grimaced as he recalled the loathing he had seen in her eyes as they fought. For the longest time, there had been a teasing glint as she bested him, but for the last three moons, it had been anger and disgust. He accepted that he deserved it, but it still stung.

He moved to the side of the training ring and stepped into the shadows as he took a long draw from the water skin. He watched as Tyra stood speaking to their friend Strian. Bjorn wanted to grimace at the sight of Strian and Tyra together, but he knew it was not his friend's fault. Bjorn's mind wandered to when they friendship ended three moons ago. Bjorn remembered as though the events were happening before his eyes. The early spring weather was unseasonably warm, and after training, Bjorn looked for Tyra as he usually did. He did not make a habit of talking to her or standing near her but having been in love with her since he was seven, he was used to being drawn to her. When he was unable to find her but spotted his cousins Leif and Freya, he wondered where Tyra disappeared to. She and Freya were best friends and rarely apart, so he made his way to his cousins as he looked around.

"You seem to be missing your other half," he grinned at Freya.

"Tyra was hot and wanted time to soak, so she went to the fjord."

"Alone?" Bjorn's heart began to race. Tyra was a force to be reckoned with when she was armed, but she would be vulnerable undressed and alone. "Why didn't you go with her?"

"She said she wanted some time to herself," Freya shrugged. "We aren't one person. We do things apart."

Bjorn grunted as he walked to the tree line then ran until he spotted the fjord to his left. He slowed his pace, cautious not to make his presence known in case someone did lurk within the trees watching Tyra. He drew his sword as he approached the shore. He scanned the area but could not hear nor see anyone else. His chest was tight with alternating pangs of fear and anger for Tyra's foolishness. He sheathed his sword and waded into the water. He had seen Tyra's blonde head sitting at the surface as the rest of her soaked. She stood and spun around a knife pointing at him when she heard his splashes.

Tyra's eyes opened wide as she took in Bjorn standing knee deep with a look of fury on his face. She had seen him angry countless times, usually directed at her for beating him, but this was far more intense than she had seen before.

Bjorn's mind screamed that his chest and cock would detonate simultaneously as both throbbed. He had been with more than one woman, and he had seen different body types over the years, but he had seen nothing as beautiful as the water nymph who stood before him. She was exquisite with long legs and slender hips. She had broad shoulders and muscles from years of training. Her breasts were not as large as usually drew him, but they would easily fill his hands. He forced his eyes from the thatch of dark hair that protected the place he most wanted to be at that moment.

"Bjorn?" her hushed tones barely carried to him.

Strian **VIKING GLORY BOOK 4**

Strian looked over his shoulder at the woman rowing just two benches behind him. Other Norsemen surrounded her, but she appeared out of place and alone. Despite trying to remain focused on navigating his ship towards the fjord just beyond his home, Strian Eindrideson failed to overcome the temptation to look back at Gressa time and again.

Gressa Jorgensdóttir refused to lift her gaze from the shoulder blades of the people seated in front of her. She followed the rhythm of the other rowers as her oar dipped and slid first through the water then in the air before returning to the water. She could feel Strian's eyes on her even though she had not looked up in hours. She refused. She refused to acknowledge him, and she refused to acknowledge her own feelings, or rather the ones he stirred in her. She forced her mind to focus on the motions needed to keep her oar synchronized with the other rowers. She would not allow herself to think about how her hands, blistered and raw, ached from rowing for hours after not having touched an oar in years. She would not think about how her stomach rumbled from refusing anything but the most meager amounts of food; one of the few rebellious acts available to her. She would not think about how once again fate forced an abrupt sacrifice of the life she had. She would not think about Strian. There was far more for her not to think about than what she was willing to entertain, but her attempts to force her mind away from the painful topics only made them linger in the forefront of her mind even more. Gressa caught herself before she shook her head.

Strian gave up all attempts at ignoring Gressa the second day aboard his ship. It was an exercise in futility to pretend she did not exist. He had never been able to ignore her, and ten years of separation had not changed that. Gressa stood out from the rest with her heart-shaped face, dark brown hair, and deep blue eyes with their almond shape, giving proof to her Sami heritage. None of her clothes resembled the ones he remembered. Gone were the conical rolled toes on her boots or the beading at the hems of her wrists and collar that she wore at home. The more subdued forest colors of a Welsh bowman replaced her Sami clothing. Her clothes had always made her stand out, first as a Sami and now as a Welshwoman. But Strian knew the clothes did not matter. His memories clutched to the images of Gressa when she was undressed. He snapped his eyes back to the water and slammed the door shut on those memories. They had haunted him ever since he last saw Gressa, and now they caused a painful knot to squeeze his heart.

"Captain, Tyra's given the signal that we are only five knots from the entrance to the fjord. We will be home soon." Strian nodded once to his first mate and followed the man to the stern where he took the rudder from one of his oarsmen.

Now that Strian was behind Gressa, it was easier for him to watch her. It was not so obvious when she was in his line of sight as he navigated the ice and sandbars. He had been sailing in and out of his homestead's natural harbor since he was a child. He could spare some of his attention and continue to watch Gressa. The linen shirt she wore stuck to her sweaty body, and he could see the muscles ripple through her back and shoulders as she continued to row. He watched her head twist slightly to the side as though she might look back at him. He knew she was aware he watched her, but he had caught her staring at him just as many times.

Strian guided his longboat into the harbor and docked beside Bjorn's and Tyra's boats. He avoided Freya because their falling out just before they left Scotland remained unresolved. Strian knew Freya felt guilty for their argument, and he did not enjoy being at odds with one of his oldest friends, but he would not overlook her high handedness as their leader or her unwillingness to hear why he wanted to remain in Scotland. Strian approached Gressa and waited until she noticed him. It was only a matter of a heartbeat before she looked up at him.

"Stay next to me," Strian whispered. When Gressa looked ready to object, Strian raised an eyebrow in warning. "It's been ten years."

Ivar's eyes swept across the battlefield as the hair on the back of his neck caused his sweat-covered skin to prickle. He took in the overcast skies—skies that did not match the scorching sun the Norse warriors had experienced during these last weeks in the Mediterranean. The darkened skies matched his current mood as he panted, trying to slow the adrenaline coursing through him after his last engagement with their Arab enemies. He had just slayed an enormous dark-skinned man whose guttural Arab language was still foreign to Ivar Sorenson's Norse ears. As Ivar looked into the dead man's vacant eyes, he watched a crow's reflection fly overhead. Odin's messengers Hunnin and Munnin brought a cheer from Ivar's fellow Norse warriors, who celebrated their victory with praise to their gods. But Ivar could not be less interested in prayer as he once again scanned the fallen bodies and those still on their feet, looking for a particular blonde head with a face that possessed the deepest cobalt-blue eyes he had ever seen. Ivar's stomach clenched as he searched for Lena Tormudsdóttir.

"Lena? Lena!" Ivar called out as his heart began to pound with fear unlike any he had experienced in the battle only moments earlier. "Lena!"

"Ivar?"

Ivar ran in the direction of the voice that he feared he would never hear again; it had never sounded sweeter. He wove through members of his clan and leaped over the bodies of fallen Arabs and Norsemen, pushing past a group of women to where Lena stood. Disregarding those around him, Ivar pulled Lena into his arms. After a brief glance to reassure himself that she was uninjured, he stroked her cheek and dove in for a searing kiss that brought conversations around them to an abrupt end.

Lena's toes curled within her boots. The feel of Ivar's body pressed against hers reminded her of their time spent coupling the night before. Her hands roamed over his back and shoulders as the tension eased with each of her caresses. The intensity of his kiss deepened as he groaned within her mouth, his tongue swirling and mating with hers, mimicking what they both longed to do with their bodies.

When they broke apart at last, their foreheads pressed together, Ivar smattered kisses on the tip of her nose as he cupped her jaw.

"You scared me," Ivar's hushed voice brushed warm air across Lena's face.

"You're scared of nothing, or so you told me," Lena brushed her lips against Ivar's.

"There is a first for everything. I couldn't find you."

"But you did. You're holding me now," Lena pressed another soft kiss to Ivar's mouth.

Ivar pulled back and swept Lena into his arms. He did not look back to see who snickered or tossed randy comments at his back, nor did he care that his father's commander, Magnus, was calling to him. Ivar carried Lena across the low grassy field to a copse of olive trees, cursing that their spindly branches would not give him the privacy that the fir trees in the Trondelag would offer. When they were a safe distance from the others, he placed Lena on her feet again and pulled her against him.

"Now I am holding you," Ivar's voice rumbled within his broad chest. "And I intend to hold you all through the night as I make love to you over and over until I am convinced you are safe and within my reach."

Made in the USA
Coppell, TX
26 August 2021

61281371R00193